"The day before the ex-president got himself snatched in Havana, the Coast Guard and the DEA trailed a C-47 out of Colombia that supposedly contained either a missile or stuff with which to make a WMD. As usual, the plane disappeared into Cuban airspace and was picked up again on the way out. That's where things begin to get fouled up. To make a long story short, the plane that came *out* of Cuba wasn't the same one our bubbas saw go *into* Cuba. The one we got was full of cocaine. Either that was incredibly bad luck for the dope runners, or—"

"—it was used as a decoy."

"Exactly. Anyway, Act One, Scene Two: we've seized a C-47 forced to land in Georgia with engine problems. I think it's the original article we were trying to catch to begin with. Whatever it was hauling was already gone—but detectors picked up the recent presence of radioactive materials."

The General went silent for a minute, as though mentally connecting the dots. "You think the plutonium from Mindanao has found its way through Colombia and Cuba to Georgia?"

"Something is about to happen, General. And we ain't gonna like it when it does."

Also by Charles W. Sasser

DETACHMENT DELTA: PUNITIVE STRIKE
DETACHMENT DELTA: OPERATION IRON WEED

DETACHMENT
DELTA

OPERATION DEEP STEEL

CHARLES W. SASSER

AVON BOOKS
An Imprint of HarperCollinsPublishers

This is a work of fiction. Names, characters, places, and incidents are products of the author's imagination or are used fictitiously and are not to be construed as real. Any resemblance to actual events, locales, organizations, or persons, living or dead, is entirely coincidental.

AVON BOOKS
An Imprint of HarperCollins*Publishers*
10 East 53rd Street
New York, New York 10022-5299

Copyright © 2004 by Bill Fawcett & Associates
ISBN: 0-380-82060-9
www.avonbooks.com

First Avon Books paperback printing: January 2004

Avon Trademark Reg. U.S. Pat. Off. and in Other Countries, Marca Registrada, Hecho en U.S.A.
HarperCollins® is a registered trademark of HarperCollins Publishers Inc.

Printed in the U.S.A.

10 9 8 7 6 5 4 3 2 1

This novel is dedicated to my old friend,
Scott Anderson

AUTHOR'S NOTE

While this novel is a work of fiction with no intentional references to real people either dead or alive other than the obvious ones, discerning readers will make obvious connections between recent history and events in this book. For example, I have used the tragic terrorist attacks of 9/11, the War on Terror, and subsequent global events of the war as a setting for the adventures described.

This is the third book in the Detachment Delta series dealing with the U.S. Army's elite Delta Force and counterterrorism. The first book, *Detachment Delta: Punitive Strike,* centered upon events prior to September 11, 2001. The second, *Detachment Delta: Operation Iron Weed,* placed Delta clandestinely into the war in Afghanistan. This third continues the epic of the Kragle military dynasty. This time, the War on Terror has expanded and the Kragles find themselves battling terrorists in Korea, the Philippines, on the high seas, and within the boundaries of the United States.

For thirteen years I was a member of the U.S. Army Special Forces (the Green Berets), and therefore have some understanding of covert and SpecOps missions. I hope to continue this merging of fact and fiction to create stories that may very well reflect the *real* stories behind counterterrorist operations by the United States.

Finally, I want to make clear that my rendering of certain high profile characters, such as former-President John Stanton and Senate Majority Leader Jake Thierry, are largely creations of my own imagination and are interpretations necessary to the plot.

DETACHMENT DELTA

OPERATION DEEP STEEL

CHAPTER 1

Pyongyang, North Korea

Dusk and the latest power cuts by the Democratic Peoples Republic shrouded the North Korean capital in gloom. The circular bar on the forty-fourth floor of the Koryo Hotel in Pyongyang buzzed as it filled with nationalities from all over the Third Underworld. Furtive conversations were held in groups gathered in capsule chairs pulled close to low-slung plastic-topped tables opposite the dimly lighted bar. Such was the ambience that any of the exotic characters from *Star Wars* might have sauntered in and rated little more than a glance. If the "Axis of Evil"—as the President of the United States had dubbed Iraq, Iran, and North Korea—had a watering hole for international dealers in arms, it was the Koryo Hotel Bar.

"Let us say that the North Koreans have been known to go around with glossy brochures about their ballistic missiles," commented MacArthur Thornbrew, director of the U.S. National Homeland Security Agency. "They are stocking a lot of the world right now."

Three muscled Koreans wearing Western sports shirts and tinted glasses paused at the door like a trio of Hollywood Asian gangsters in an old Bruce Lee movie. They gave things the once-over, obviously looking for someone. Spotting him, they threaded through the crowd and stopped at a table dominated by a man hard to overlook in any bar. He was a squat fellow built like a sumo wrestler, only more compact and harder. He looked Filipino or Indonesian, from somewhere out there on the Rim. His collar, though unbuttoned, was too tight. It seemed to cause his eyes to bulge beneath his shaved brown head. A ropy scar started above his eyebrow and tugged his left eye down on his cheek, making his huge head appear lopsided.

Sitting at the table with him was his Korean interpreter, a skinny man with a flat face and a rosy-yellow complexion.

The Koreans smiled and bowed slightly, observing the formalities. Scarface looked at them. He shook out a Russian cigarette and lit it. He did not offer the pack.

"Cimatu?" the Korean-in-charge asked.

"Like with this face I could be someone else?"

Each side had an interpreter. Both translated the exchange. In such negotiations there must be no misunderstandings.

"You may call me Li Shiek," the Korean said. He was a man in his mid-forties with an expensive haircut and a gold-and-diamond ring on his left pinkie finger. "My associates are—"

Cimatu cut him off. "I don't care who they are. Sit down."

The three sat. At least one of them was armed, the big man. Cimatu recognized the bulge of the weapon through his loose shirt. Fair enough. Cimatu was also armed.

Li Shiek blushed with a flash of anger, but hid it behind a slightly contemptuous smile. He ordered a Japanese beer and waited until it came. He leaned back in his chair.

"Do you have the merchandise?" Cimatu demanded impatiently.

"It is prepared to be loaded as soon as funds are transferred."

"The arrangement was half in advance, the remainder upon delivery. If you will check your bank account in *South Korea*—" No one trusted banks in the North—"you will find everything in order when the freighter sails."

The two interpreters sounded like an echo of each other.

"Why would your nation require only three when they are most effective in larger batteries?" Li Shiek mused.

Cimatu's eye in the middle of his cheek narrowed. "You are being paid. That's all you need to know."

"So we are." Li Shiek smiled, fighting to suppress his disdain. "That you would use them against the United States is not our concern. In fact, my government will applaud it, as we applauded the strikes upon the capitalists' World Trade Center and their Pentagon."

Cimatu said nothing.

"I might suggest," sneered the Korean, "that perhaps a longer-range missile would serve your needs . . . more adequately."

It was Cimatu's turn to sneer. "Such as your Taedong 11?"

The Taedong had veered unpredictably off-course during its last test and splashed down in the Sea of Japan, barely missing Tokyo.

Li Shiek shrugged, refusing to let the Scarface get the better of him. "Weapons such as these are very expensive," he noted. "The Pakistani president said the Americans killed Osama bin Laden. Are these all you can afford now that your benefactor has gone on to Allah to claim his virgins?"

Cimatu's connections, whatever they might be, were none of the Korean's business. Cimatu glared. "Mullah bin Laden is alive and well in Pakistan," he snapped.

"Perhaps he will become a new industry," Li Shiek said slyly, entertaining himself. "The world's most feared and sought-after terrorist leader, wanted dead or alive, will provide sightings around the world. He will be seen having dinner in Manila at Casa de Marcos. Munching on a hot beef pie in London. Praying at Al-Aksa in Jerusalem. Who knows, he might even be spotted in Memphis in the United States having a Big Mac with Elvis."

He chuckled drolly.

Cimatu was not amused. He leaned his bulk menacingly across the table. "Two things I need from you: Which ship and when will it sail?"

Li Shiek sobered. It was his experience that revolutionaries and terrorists of whatever nationality or bent possessed remarkably little levity. Yasser Arafat was the most humorless man he had ever met.

Thirty more minutes and all arrangements were made. The "freight" would leave Nampo on Friday two weeks from today aboard the Saudi freighter *Ibn Haldoon* and arrive in the Philippines four days later. The ship would offload wherever Cimatu designated before it proceeded to Manila to take on a cargo of sugar bound for Europe.

Deal finished, the two groups parted coolly in the marble-walled lobby of the hotel. A taxi waited for Cimatu and his interpreter. Li Shiek and his escort climbed into a black limousine reserved for government use.

CHAPTER 2

Mindanao, Philippines

Colonel Buck Thompson, commander of U.S. Army 1st Special Forces Operational Detachment-Delta, otherwise known as the army's counterterrorist Delta Force, stood outside on the little porch of his headquarters at Wally World, which is what most soldiers at Fort Bragg, North Carolina, called the walled-off Delta compound, and watched Major Brandon Kragle making his way across from his Troop One command. The major was as tall and lean as Thompson himself, even taller in fact. He walked in a brisk, no-nonsense manner, his keen gray eyes focused straight ahead. His dark high-and-tight haircut supported a patrol cap on which he wore a major's gold leaf. It was almost eerie how much the son of General Darren E. Kragle, commander of United States Special Operations Command (USSOCOM), looked like his old man did twenty-five years ago when he and Colonel Charlie Beckwith created Delta Force to fight terrorism worldwide. Mustache, build, attitude and all—they were alike.

Colonel Thompson had summoned Major Kragle. He returned to his office. Command Sergeant Major Adcock showed the major in.

"At ease, Major Kragle," the colonel said. "Sit down, son. Brandon, do you think you can drag yourself away from that pretty little girl you brought back from Afghanistan?" His eyes twinkled behind the glasses he had recently started wearing.

Brandon's romance with Summer Marie Rhodeman was the talk of Wally World. Brandon had taken two weeks leave in order that they could be together following their return from Afghanistan and Operation Iron Weed.

"She's received another assignment," Brandon evaded.

Colonel Thompson nodded, serious again. "I know it's a bit soon after Iron Weed, but I also have an assignment for you. I'm sending Dare Russell to Qatar to evaluate how Delta may assist in the military buildup against Iraq."

Dare Russell was commander of Troop Two.

"That leaves you as my most experienced commander."

"Yes, sir. We're ready to go."

"It's not an operation as such," Colonel Thompson said. "I want you to take one other man from Troop One and TDY to Manila. First, and officially, you're to evaluate the situation and make a report for USSOCOM and the National Command Authority. Islamic guerrillas in the Philippines continue to grow in power and may threaten the democratic government."

Brandon looked interested.

"Elements from the 7th and 5th Special Forces Groups have been in the Philippines for the past three months training, equipping, and advising local forces fighting the guerrillas," he went on. "We also have about three hundred Navy Seabees building roads, bridges, waterworks, and other infrastructure projects on Basilan Island. Outside of Afghanistan, the Philippines is the largest military deployment in the War on Terror."

In 1993, USSOCOM deployed an average of 2,036 SpecOps soldiers away from home station each week. That number rose to 5,141 in 1999. SpecOps troops deployed after the 9/11 attacks exceeded 10,000 weekly.

Filipino Islamics were a particularly ruthless band of thugs and radical fundamentalists who received funding from Osama bin Laden's financial network, Colonel Buck explained. Organized into two main groups—Abu Sayyaf and the Moro Islamic Liberation Front—many of them had trained with Hamas in Palestine and at terrorist camps set up by al-Qaeda in Somalia, Iran, Libya, Iraq, and other rogue nations who supported terrorism against the West. A large number were so-called Afghans who fought in the Russian war with the Afghan mujahideen.

Of the two organizations, Abu Sayyaf was the most murderous. Its leader, Aldam Sabaya, was killed in an action the previous winter. His place was taken by a little-known terrorist named Albaneh Mosed. Rumor placed Mosed in Kabul when Americans began bombing Taliban and al-Qaeda forces. He had reportedly gone there to obtain plans and materials for constructing a WMD—weapon of mass destruction. He escaped into Pakistan and returned to the Philippines by way of Saudi Arabia and North Korea.

During Operation Iron Weed, Major Brandon Kragle's Delta detachment had pursued Osama bin Laden to his Tora Bora redoubts in the White Mountains of Afghanistan. Brandon assumed bin Laden was killed when the detachment, working with the CIA and local mujahideen guerrillas, blew up the terrorist kingpin's cave command complex. It made little difference, however, whether bin Laden lived or died. The networks the wealthy radical Islamic built and funded with his billions stretched tentacles into more than forty countries around the world, including the United States. There was never a shortage of fanatics and crazies eager to carry on the Holy Jihad of suicide bombings, sabotage, and attacks against Israel and the "Great Satan" America. It was also assumed bin Laden might have had nuclear materials to pass on to his associates.

Brandon waited patiently for Colonel Thompson to finish with background and get down to details. He knew all this, having kept up with classified intelligence reports filtering down to Delta from the CIA, the FBI, the National Security Administration, and the National Homeland Security Agency.

"We're to evaluate the situation, sir, officially," Brandon summarized. He lifted a brow. "Can I assume there's another part of the mission?"

The colonel drew in a deep breath and flipped a photo across his desk. Brandon picked it up. A middle-aged man bald on top and a frightened plain-looking woman stared glassily into the camera. Both were bound and sitting on the dirt floor of what appeared to be a native bamboo hut. They looked haunted, gaunt, almost starved.

"Martin Hoffman and his wife," Colonel Thompson said. "Bringing salvation to the world."

Not quite a month ago, Abu Sayyaf kidnapped eleven people from a beach resort. Three were American missionaries—Martin Hoffman, his wife Grace, and William Sobero. Some of the captives, including Sobero, were beheaded. Others escaped or were released until only the Hoffmans and their Filipino nurse, Edi Macapagal, remained in terrorist hands. Albaneh Mosed repeatedly threatened to also machete off their heads unless the world met his demands, one of which was to grant the southern Philippines independence as an Islamic state molded after the recently toppled Taliban government of Afghanistan. He also wanted an independent Palestinian state, and money. Send money. American money.

"Remember the *Wall Street Journal* reporter—Daniel Pearl, I believe—who was kidnapped in Pakistan last January?" Colonel Thompson said. He stood up and looked across his cluttered desk.

"Tangos videotaped him being beheaded," Brandon said. "Some kind of bizarre statement to the world."

"Major, the Hoffmans are Americans. I'm surprised they've lasted this long, our official policy being not to negotiate with terrorists. Filipino Scout Rangers are putting the squeeze on Mosed. They may be getting close. It's the missionaries' last chance of being rescued. If we don't get them back this time, we may as well count them dead."

"We'll arrange to link up with the Scout Rangers, sir. I'll take Sergeant Gloomy Davis with me."

"Major, officially we're advisors and evaluators."

"I understand, sir. Officially, we don't shoot at them. Officially, I suppose, they don't shoot back."

The captives were first transported by boat across the Sulu Sea to Basilan Island, where hundreds of Filipino troops were dispatched to hunt for them. Hard pressed, the guerrillas fled Basilan. U.S. Special Forces surveillance teams detected unusual boat traffic between Basilan and Mindanao. Philippine marine reconnaissance units and Army Scout

Rangers sealed off Zamboango del Norte province on Mindanao. For the past five days, Major Brandon Kragle and Master Sergeant Gloomy Davis had tramped the highland jungles with a platoon of Rangers commanded by Captain Jessie Dellosa.

It began raining on the third day and had continued raining steadily since then, obliterating sign and making it almost impossible for trackers to do any kind of a job. Captain Dellosa was about to call it quits when a plantano farmer provided a tip about an abandoned cabin in the mountains. Early that morning, a recon patrol located the cabin and spotted a large force of armed terrorists resting among the trees under makeshift rain shelters.

It was risky business, approaching an enemy unit of such strength with a platoon of fewer than twenty men. Dellosa radioed Colonel Sua, who promised to truck in a reinforcement company to nearby Sirawai town. A platoon guide would meet the company and lead it in to the terrorist camp. In the meantime, Dellosa's outfit was to move up and establish blocks to prevent the guerrillas from escaping. Mosed was both cagey and jumpy.

"We surround him and hold him in place until B Company arrives," Dellosa explained. "We do not fight unless we have to. Major Kragle, I have chased Albaneh Mosed for five days. We are too close. I will not lose him this time."

Like most military in the Philippines, he spoke good and rather formal English.

Rain drummed hard on the upper canopy of the rain forest with an urgent torrential downpour that echoed on the jungle trail below. Lightning flashed, momentarily turning the midday twilight world to black and white. The drencher lost much of its fury by the time it filtered down through the foliage. On the trail, the jungle merely wept. Wept copiously, but wept nonetheless. Leaves torn off by the upper storm showered down. Now and then a rotted jungle giant toppled with a muted thud. Rain on Major Kragle's patrol cap sounded like drumming fingers.

"There will be typhoons this year," Captain Dellosa predicted.

In this gray veil of rain and fog, the platoon might well walk up on the terrorists and step on them. But if the Rangers couldn't see the guerrillas, it would be equally difficult for the guerrillas to see the Rangers. The element moved cautiously, proceeding up a creek in a deep, vine-clogged ravine, then out and back up into thick forest where Captain Dellosa called a halt while he sent out a patrol. The hut wasn't much farther ahead.

Gloomy Davis's brimmed bush hat expelled water in a curtain in front of his face. He resembled a stray terrier with his drooping mustache and somber blue eyes. Hungry, lean, and wiry peering through a waterfall. Brandon shot him a grin. Gloomy dropped to his knees to readjust the straps of the case that contained his .300 Winchester, Mr. Blunderbuss, which he carried attached to his backpack. The sniper was one tough little Okie.

"Boss," he drawled. The roar of the falling rain masked voices. "I'm beginning to think I liked all that snow in Afghanistan better than this stuff. It reminds me of the flood we had back in Hooker, Oklahoma, the year Arachna Phoebe jumped off the Beaver River Bridge . . ."

Gloomy Davis was loaded with stories about Hooker, the Hooker Hogette cheerleaders, and his old girlfriend Arachna Phoebe. "Gloomy's so full of shit his eyes oughta be brown instead of blue," Mad Dog Carson always said.

Brandon was more interested in the returning scouts than in one of Gloomy's stories. The three scouts came down out of the gray wet mist, materializing like ghosts, coming fast and excited. They had seen the guerrilla camp.

"Did they see the hostages?" Brandon asked.

Dellosa sadly shook his head. Prisoners would only slow down the guerrillas when they were being chased.

"Many of the *terroristas* are inside the hut—fifteen or so perhaps," Dellosa said. "Others are scattered outside in the surrounding forest in poncho-covered hammocks."

Dellosa divided his men into fireteams and committed them to creeping through the noisy rain jungle to surround the enemy camp. Major Kragle and Gloomy stayed with the command element as it maneuvered uphill to obtain a clear field of fire for its machine gun. If the Hoffmans were still alive and still with the guerrillas, their only hope of salvation lay in surprise—fierce, swift, and deadly.

Gloomy unsheathed his Winchester, a beautiful piece of walnut and blue steel machinery that under his expert handling became a lethal extension of his eye. If he could see a target, he could hit it. He levered in a cartridge and quickly tested the Redfield scope to make sure it was fog-free and had not been knocked out of adjustment. He scrambled up a long slippery slope behind the major and Captain Dellosa. Both officers carried M-16 rifles. Old A-1s left over from the Vietnam War. Up ahead, the two-man machine gun crew and a soldier carrying a 60mm knee mortar followed the point, who now proceeded slowly and carefully, stopping every few paces to look and listen. The radioman with the short whip antenna trailed Captain Dellosa's every step.

At a signal from point, the machine gunners plopped onto their bellies and looked back. The command group went to ground and crawled up to them. Runoff water rivuleted down from the top of the hill in little gurgling streams, cutting trenches in the soaked humus of the jungle floor. The officers and Gloomy crept through a stand of head-high ferns that slapped wetly at their faces. They came upon the point man crouching behind a rotted, moss-congealed log. He gestured toward the front with his head.

Ahead appeared a small clearing in the forest. Rain in undulating sheets blew across it, skeining and skittering and turning it into an ankle-deep pond. On the far side sat a two-story native hut, its outline blurred gray by the deluge. The bottom floor was open on two sides, apparently as a shelter for livestock and farm implements.

Brandon ran a hand across his eyes to clear them of water. He pulled the brim of his patrol cap low to ward off the slashing rain. He and Gloomy studied the hut and surrounding forest carefully for a long minute, beginning to think it abandoned until he spotted movement on the open bottom floor. The guerrillas were all curled up underneath their ponchos like a bunch of puppies. Obviously they weren't expecting pursuit in that kind of weather.

Gloomy nudged his commander and nodded toward where several poncho hooches had been erected under nearby trees. Gloomy readied Mr. Blunderbuss for action. Captain Dellosa brought the machine gun and the mortar up on line at the log. Now they waited until the fireteams moved into position and B Company arrived.

The waiting ended abruptly five minutes later, more quickly than anyone expected or wanted. One of the Ranger fireteams moving around the edge of the clearing, but deeper in the jungle, stumbled upon a guerrilla who had ventured out to answer an urgent call of nature. Squatting with his pants down and his bare butt up against a tree for shelter, he saw the patrol before it spotted him. His shouts of alarm and surprise alerted the camp.

A Scout M-16 rattled on full auto and dropped the man before he could get his pants up. Armed men piled out of the hut and unassed their hammocks, looking confused as they sought the source and direction of the attack.

Oh, shit!, Brandon thought. *If the missionaries aren't already dead, they are now.*

CHAPTER 3

Cammie-clad terrorists pouring out the door of the hut like stick-poked wasps made a run for the cover of the jungle, darting and dodging. Captain Dellosa sprang to his feet.

"Fire! Fire!"

The machine gunner opened up with his M60. Tracers sizzled through the rain, chewing into the dilapidated farm hut and exploding tufts of bamboo and mud from its thin walls. Brandon grabbed the gunner and pulled him off the trigger.

"Not the house!" he barked. "Don't shoot the house!"

The gunner understood. The hostages might be inside. He shifted fire, the flaming muzzle rat-a-tatting at indistinct targets flitting across the clearing, splashing water in the pond with their flying feet, desperately yelling at each other in surprise and fear. M-16s from Scout positions in the forest began popping angrily, echoed in the deeper, throatier responses of AK-47s and other weapons of the former East Bloc nations.

Two guerrillas tumbled in the clearing. One lay still like a wet bundle of old rags. The other, winged badly, thrashed about in the shallow water of the little meadow, screaming in pain. The rest merged into the gloom of the forest. The battle disintegrated into individual duels unseen and only heard in the jungle at several different points. Deprived of targets, the machine gun fell silent. Brandon shed his pack behind the log. He had his eyes on the hut.

"Gloomy, cover me."

He dashed into the open like a sprinter from the starting line. Combat zigzagging toward the shack where he hoped to find the Hoffmans. He made it halfway across the clearing before movement caught the corner of his eye. Two rifle shots. Muzzle flashes blossomed from jungle shadow to his right.

He thought the shots were directed at him until he veered to confront them. He spotted a poncho hooch just inside the treeline. A man in the shadows next to the hooch, a mere outline in the rain, was shooting point-blank into human forms crumpled on the ground at his feet.

An anguished cry tore from Brandon's throat. *"No!"*

The terrorist was executing the captives.

Brandon cut toward the executioner at a dead run, squeezing off waist shots from the M-16 he carried, firing semiauto. His CQB—close quarter battle skills—were excellent, honed by frequent exercises at the firearms training facility called the "House of Horrors" at Wally World.

The tango jerked back as the first round stitched into his gut. He staggered. Brandon kept firing, charging straight at him, squeezing off shots, each of which found its mark. The guerrilla toppled backward into a thick bush of tropical blooms.

A second terrorist opened up. Brandon heard the crack and felt the sonic passage of the round singe past his head. He tilted the barrel of his rifle to follow the direction of his eyes. He fixated on the muzzle of an AK, like looking down a tunnel out of which he expected death to instantaneously explode. Rain reduced the shooter behind the rifle to a ghostly blur. But Brandon clearly saw the dark, blazing eyes of hate reaching out through the deluge to snatch him by the heart.

He was running too hard to switch targets in time. The guy was going to get off a second shot. He wouldn't miss this one, not at such close range.

So this was what it was like to die in combat?

A single rifle shot from the rear! The report possessed a greater force of presence than the loose rattling of the M-16s and AK-47s that continued to spar in scattered pockets. The 173-grain dovetail projectile shrieked past Brandon at more than 2,500 feet per second. It struck the enemy rifleman with solid impact, not like the little piss-me-off 5.56mm ammo the M-16s fired. The bullet actually flipped the guy out of his tracks. It entered the left side of his chest and exploded his heart and lungs out the fist-sized hole it made in his back. He was dead before he hit the soggy ground.

Gloomy! It wasn't the first time the wiry sniper from Oklahoma had saved his officer's ass.

Brandon slowed and entered the trees at the ready. Both tangos were dead, their bodies twisted and grotesque in the rain. They weren't the only corpses, however. The poncho shelter had been stretched about waist high between two trees. Partially underneath it rested a thin Filipino woman with the top of her head blown off and her brains spilling out in the mud. Body heat rose from the opened skull in a thin steam. This, Brandon thought, must be the nurse, Edi Macapagal. Her bare feet were bound tightly, but her hands were free.

The man Brandon shot lay in bushes next to an emaciated, balding Caucasian with a short, tangled beard almost white around the edges. He was without a shirt. Air still hissed and burbled from two angry-looking gunshot wounds to the chest. His eyes were slitted half-open, unseeing. He was bound hand and foot. Martin Hoffman.

Grace Hoffman lay in a fetal position, one hand reaching out to grasp the trousers of her dead husband. Only her feet were tied. She looked filthy and wasted in a long *Balintawak*-type dress so thin and worn that her bones showed through the wet fabric.

All were dead, slaughtered at point-blank range at the last

moment. Obviously, their guards had been instructed to shoot the hostages first if anything happened. Helpless rage ran like bile in Brandon's throat. He almost wished the dead guards would come back alive so he could shoot them again.

Grace Hoffman shivered, her entire body suddenly wracked with chills of terror and shock and exposure. She was still alive! Brandon dropped to his knees. Her dress from the waist down was soaked with blood which, diluted with water, made a pink pool around her. Brandon pulled up her hem and found that a round had caught her in the thigh, missing the artery but shattering her femur. It seemed Brandon must have thrown off the executioner's aim when he opened up. He was astonished that she was still alive. She moaned, in serious condition.

Gloomy ran up from behind. "Boss?"

"I'm all right."

"Oh, Jesus the Christ!" Gloomy exclaimed when he saw the carnage.

"Mrs. Hoffman is still alive," Brandon said. "See if you can round up a medic. Have Dellosa call in a medevac chopper if he can get one in the rain. Otherwise, we'll have to carry her out fast."

"Hoo-ya!" Gloomy took another look at the missionaries, shook his head, and trotted off in the rain to find Captain Dellosa and the radioman.

Mrs. Hoffman lifted her head weakly in returning awareness and stared directly into Brandon's face, blinking her eyelashes against pain and the dampness.

"You're going to be okay," he said. "I'm just putting on a pressure bandage."

"You . . . You're an American," she managed, her voice cracking. "Martin? *Martin . . . !*"

One fist still clutched her husband's trousers. She began jerking on him.

"Martin. Oh, God. Martin—"

She broke into sobs that left her even further weakened. "Don't . . . don't . . ." she stammered. "Please don't leave us behind."

"We won't leave anyone behind," Brandon promised.

Shooting in the surrounding jungle died down to an occasional rifle pop here and there. Captain Dellosa and his men secured the hut. Disappointed Rangers straggled back in from the forest. Four Scouts had received flesh wounds in the brief skirmish. Two soldiers dragged in a dead guerrilla by his heels. A Ranger walked over to the wounded enemy in the meadow, pulled out his pistol and shot him in the forehead before Brandon could intercede. Guerrilla war was especially brutal.

There was no use giving chase under these conditions. The trap had been sprung inadvertently before reinforcements arrived and before fireteams could block off escape routes. Mosed and most of his bloody jihad junkies had escaped once again.

"Boss, you might want to take a look at this stuff," Gloomy called out from the hut.

The platoon medic and some men had placed the missionary's wife in the shelter of the poncho hooch. Helicopters weren't flying, but a truck was on its way from Sirawai. Captain Dellosa had soldiers chopping saplings for a stretcher while everyone else sought relief from the rain.

Gloomy and Dellosa inside the hut's lower livestock floor were going through backpacks full of manuals and other papers wrapped in plastic trash sacks against the weather. The fleeing rebels left them behind in their haste to flee. Much of the material was in English, although some of it was in Arabic, Tagalog-Filipino, and German.

Extracts from training manuals showed diagrams of weapons. Brandon found various formulas and designs for nuclear weapons, bombs, and missiles. There were tech manuals for rockets. One manual excerpt explained how the detonation of TNT compresses plutonium into a critical mass, sparking a chain reaction that ultimately leads to a thermonuclear reaction. One booklet offered advice on how to survive a nuclear explosion. Another appeared to be a training or operating manual, written in Korean, for an SS-1 SCUD short-range ballistic missile system.

Scary stuff. It had long been known, even before the attacks against the U.S. mainland, that Osama bin Laden and other terrorists were attempting to obtain nuclear or other weapons of mass destruction. It appeared from all this that their efforts might be nearer success than originally thought.

One of the packs was exceptionally heavy. It contained an empty canvas satchel-like case lined in lead. Gloomy retrieved his and his commander's rucks from the jungle where they were dropped when the fight started. From his, Brandon extracted a pocket-sized radiation detector that all Deltas now carried with them in the field. When he passed it over the outside of the closed leaden satchel, the instrument's hands quivered slightly. When he opened the case, the detector's hand pegged to the DANGER side of the dial and hung there, vibrating.

"Hot as Arachna Phoebe on a Saturday night in July," Gloomy noted. "But where is the—?"

The two Americans looked at each other. Whatever radioactive materials the case once contained had either already been delivered somewhere, or Mosed and his jihad guerrillas had escaped with it. Brandon guessed it had been delivered. Whichever, its ultimate intended destination was undoubtedly the United States of America.

CHAPTER 4

NUCLEAR TERRORISM CONCERNS U.S.

Washington (CPI)—Materials recovered in the Philippines, plus materials left behind in a compound in Afghanistan used by Osama bin Laden's al-Qaeda network, suggest terrorist groups are attempting to develop or to acquire nuclear weapons. Homeland Security Director MacArthur Thornbrew warned that "we have to be prepared for all eventualities, including a nuclear threat."

Philippine Army Scout Rangers raided a secret camp on the island of Mindanao and freed the wife of American missionary Martin Hoffman. Grace Hoffman, 46, is being treated for gunshot wounds to the thigh at a military hospital in Manila. Her husband and Filipino nurse Edi Macapagal were both executed as Rangers closed in on the camp of Islamic guerrilla leader Albaneh Mosed. Mosed and at least twenty men of the Abu Sayyaf organization, an al-Qaeda affiliate, escaped and disappeared into the maze of unnamed islands in the southern Philippines. Mosed demands a separate Islamic state.

Seized in the raid were a large amount of materials about the construction and utilization of nuclear devices and missiles. A lead-lined case, empty when found, was said to have once contained radioactive material.

Before a chain reaction (explosion) can take place, fissionable material must be present in a critical mass. A sphere about the size of a golf ball, one pound, is subcritical, or too small. In producing an atomic explosion, scientists start with subcritical amounts of fissionable materials, which are then brought together using TNT to a critical mass the size of a softball or larger to release a large amount of energy.

"What this means," said Thornbrew, "is that enough plutonium to set off a bomb or missile equivalent to 20,000 tons of TNT can be carried inside a briefcase."

Even a crude device, he said, could create an explosive force enough to demolish an area of about three square miles. If such a device had been used instead of hijacked airplanes on 9-11, not only the World Trade Center but also all of Wall Street and the financial district up to Gramercy Park would have disappeared.

Since the breakup of the Soviet Union in 1991, newly-independent Central Asian states have dealt with a legacy of abandoned nuclear materials that remain scattered and often poorly controlled in the region, increasing availability to potential terrorists. It is an uncomfortable reality that the monopoly of nuclear weapons by a handful of countries has now ended.

The United States is poorly prepared to deal with attacks from such weapons of mass destruction, as it was poorly prepared to deal with the terrorist attacks of 9-11 and the follow-up anthrax bio-terrorism.

All Customs inspectors are now equipped with pocket-sized radiation detectors. Hundreds of sophisticated sensors have been deployed to U.S. borders, overseas buildings, and sites around Washington. However, Director Thornbrew admitted that there is no assurance that increased security will stop terrorists from smuggling in a nuclear weapon. The borders of a free society remain simply too porous.

The U.S. Department of Health and Human Services recently bought nearly two million doses of potassium iodide and plans to purchase six million more. Potassium iodide protects against thyroid cancer, a product of radioactive fallout. U.S. Health and Human Services is also considering resuming smallpox vaccinations against a possible future bio-terrorism attack.

"We don't know if al-Qaeda or related terrorist organizations have a nuclear device," avowed Senior Agent Claude Thornton, director of the FBI's National Domestic Preparedness Office, which also oversees the FBI's Joint Terrorist Task Force. "What we do know is that for at least the past three years or more they have attempted to get radiological materials to build a nuclear device. We must seriously contemplate that they are capable of planning a nuclear attack on America . . ."

CHAPTER 5

Washington, D.C.

The meeting on the "Korean problem" started early and ended late in the bickering and posturing that General Darren E. Kragle, USSOCOM's commander, associated with politics. He rubbed huge hands through his salt-and-pepper crewcut, a mannerism of his whenever he felt tense or edgy. The lean face beneath hair as stiff as nails hammered into his skull looked permanently weathered. The well-kept mustache was almost white. Hard gray eyes surveyed the politicians and high administration officials gathered around two huge polished oaken tables in the largest conference room at the Old Executive Office Building. To the General, politics was work only for the mad, the naïve, and the venal, an illusion of service that cloaked lies, deceptions, self-interest, and self-aggrandizement in search of power in that corrupt city on the Potomac.

It was an opinion shared by senior FBI agent Claude Thornton, whom the President had had the good sense to appoint head of the FBI's National Domestic Preparedness Office. Thornton, in his late forties with a head as black and as smooth as a bowling ball, stood some five inches shorter than the General, although he was also a big man. Old friends from the days of Operation Punitive Strike, when Thornton was senior resident agent in Cairo, the two men arrived together for the meeting. They were ushered to the second table occupied by CIA deputy director Thomas Hinds, Central Command's (CENTCOM) General Paul Etheridge, and various other second-drawer assistants to those at the first table.

"Back of the bus again," Thornton quipped.

His irreverence toward sensitive racial issues and his utter disdain of political correctness had firmly sealed bonds of friendship between himself and the equally outspoken commander of USSOCOM. Thornton and CENTCOM were two of the few men present in the conference room whom General Kragle trusted unequivocally.

The topic of discussion was deemed so vital to U.S. interests that the President of the United States chaired the meeting from the first table. He was a slim Texan of hardheaded common sense who, in spite of an occasional malapropism—"If we don't succeed, we run the risk of failure"—had become the most popular chief executive in modern history, a condition his opponents and enemies schemed to make short-lived before the next elections. It was he who declared the War on Terror, Operation Enduring Freedom, following the 9/11 attacks on the World Trade Center and the Pentagon.

Gathered at the first table with the President, as befitted their station, were the vice president; the secretaries of state and defense; representatives of the National Security Council; MacArthur Thornbrew, director of Homeland Security; General Abraham Morrison, chairman of the Joint Chiefs of Staff; and majority and minority leaders of the Senate and the House.

Thornton leaned toward the General and nodded at the first table and Senator Jake Thierry, Senate Majority Leader, who was busily going through his notes.

"Thierry the douche bag sharpening his rhetoric of 'peace in our time,' " he said. "Wonder if he knows what happened to the last two pols who got in bed with John Stanton?"

"If you're a whore, it doesn't matter who the John is you get in bed with as long as he has the money," the General said, intending the play on names.

In the General's opinion, Thierry had to be an idiot to get mixed up with former-president John Stanton, considering how Stanton's associates and protégés so often ended up dead, in jail, or disgraced, falling on their swords to save the man's worthless hide. Twice, General Kragle had defied and thwarted Stanton. Once was when the man was President and didn't have the balls to send a mission into Afghanistan to recover American Navy hostages seized by Osama bin Laden and al-Qaeda. General Kragle formed the clandestine mission himself, Operation Punitive Strike. Although he couldn't prove it, he knew beyond doubt that no SAM had shot down the Delta detachment's C-141 over Afghanistan; Stanton had ordered it downed by carrier fighters to save his "peace initiative." Had an *American* aircraft shot out of the sky! Stanton's National Security advisor had taken the fall for that scandal, enabling Stanton to complete his term in the White House.

The General batted heads with Stanton again at the start of the war with the Taliban and al-Qaeda in Afghanistan. Stanton, by then a former President but still titular head and power broker of his party, schemed to place his own man, Senator Eric Tayloe, in the White House by disgracing the popular current President, at the expense of Delta Force operatives working behind enemy lines in Operation Iron Weed. The fortunate "suicide" of Senator Tayloe saved Stanton from exposure.

It was well known around Washington, D.C., that you associated with Stanton at your own risk. Nonetheless, such were the passions and ambitions in the capital that there was never a shortage of those willing to sign a pact with the devil in order to take a chance at power and historical fame. Lately, the press began linking Thierry's name with Stanton's. Stanton, the power broker grooming another possible presidential candidate. Thierry wanted to be President in the worst possible way.

Feeling himself scrutinized, and not favorably, Thierry looked up. His eyes narrowed as they met General Kragle's hard gaze. He was a thin-faced man with a round flaccid body and skinny arms that looked unprepared to lift anything other than a PAC campaign contribution. The corners of his mouth twitched as he attempted to stare down the General; he looked away first, quickly, nervously covering his eyes with a pale hand.

"The man is proof that electors *can* be fooled 100 percent of the time, know what I mean?" Thornton said.

The debate over what action should be taken concerning North Korea quickly broke into two camps. Secretary of Defense Donald Keating adjusted the glasses on his craggy face and read a lengthy paper, after which he looked up and concluded with, "The CIA, as we see, has uncovered irrefutable evidence that North Korea is supplying arms, including ballistic missiles, to rogue regimes and terrorist organizations. That, plus confirmation from the Philippines that al-Qaeda and its affiliates have—not *may have*—nuclear materials make it imperative that we act promptly to halt weapons shipments."

Vocal and critical, Senator Thierry led the opposition from those who would do *nothing* overt. He leaped to his feet. "You are suggesting that we stop and board the ships of other nations on the high seas?" he cried, outraged. "A very dangerous message is being sent when the pillars of international sovereignty are attacked. The entire edifice could crumble. Attacking shipping at sea is tantamount to an act of war."

That set the tone. The wrangling went back and forth most of the day. The President's supporters insisted that America had the legal right under international law to proactive self-defense by stopping arms runners. Those influenced by Senator Thierry demanded appeasement of those nations listed by the State Department as the "Axis of Evil" in order not to trigger a third world war.

"Not *appeasement*," Thierry protested. "What I'm insisting on is that we negotiate first, not go off half-cocked like Marshal Dillon in Dodge City. We don't need more gun smoke. When President Stanton returns from his goodwill tour of Cuba, I propose we name him as a special envoy to North Korea. His peace initiative between Israel and Palestine was working until—"

He paused to glance at the President, who coolly sipped from a glass of water and then folded his hands in front of him on the table.

"Well . . ." he amended, "it *was* working until this happened on 9/11." His tone insinuated he and his colleagues in the Senate held the President personally responsible for the terrorist assault. "For eight years in the White House," he said, as though lecturing a class of rather dim-witted fresh-men, "President Stanton presided over a nation at peace and blessed with prosperity. We're asking that his initiatives be continued. Give peace a chance first. North Korea will not stand by while we board ships that use her ports of call. This is the surest way I can imagine to start World War III."

General Kragle lowered his head and slowly shook it. Thierry was spinning the truth like a spider spins its web, dancing the "D.C. Tango" around the issues. What Thierry didn't understand was that World War III started when organized global terrorists attacked America on her home soil—and the policies, short-sighted self-interest and corruption of the Stanton administration were largely to blame.

From the General's harsh and admittedly biased view-point, Stanton belonged behind bars in Leavenworth instead of cavorting around Cuba and North Korea looking for socialist ass to sniff. General Kragle considered him the most immoral and destructive leader in the nation's 225-year history. While President of the United States, he had been impeached but not convicted. He *had* been convicted, however, of perjury and other crimes and accused, sometimes with cause, of everything from murder and bribery to violations of campaign law and selling nuclear secrets to the Chinese.

He had kept the peace all right—by kowtowing to and kissing the ass of every two-bit ragtag despot or would-be guerrilla terrorist in the world. It was he, in the General's opinion, who personally elevated Yasser Arafat from an aging cold-blooded terrorist to the status of a world leader. The arrogance gained by Arafat from Stanton's support, the General believed, directly led to the reopened outbreak of violence between Israel and Palestine.

Stanton's limp-wristed responses to Osama bin Laden's terrorist attacks against U.S. embassies in Africa and America's military barracks in Saudi Arabia, to the first bombing of the World Trade Center in 1993, and to the bombing of the destroyer USS *Randolph* in 2000 encouraged bin Laden's al-Qaeda network to become even bolder, culminating in the 9/11 surprise attack.

It baffled the General how, considering all this, Stanton was reelected President, completed two terms, and still remained as ex-President the darling of his party pulling strings of power. Claude Thornton sometimes referred to him as "the Don."

The meeting ended late with Senator Thierry and his supporters still demanding a Neville Chamberlain–peace in our time. No conclusions were drawn, or at least not announced, on whether or not the U.S. Navy and Special Operations forces should stop, board, and search vessels suspected of transporting weapons to terrorists. The President stood up at last and looked around the conference room.

"May I remind you all," he said, "that everything that went on here today is classified. Whatever the decision concerning North Korea and shipping, it does not become public. I have made good judgments in the past. I have made good judgments in the future."

After the meeting broke up, General Abraham Morrison, chairman of JCS, took General Kragle aside.

"Darren, are you on your way back to Tampa?"

"I have a flight booked at 2200 hours."

"Expect a phone call at your residence tomorrow morning before you leave for the office," he said. "I suspect the President has made a decision. We already have a situation with North Korea involving the sale and transport of missiles. That's what prompted this meeting, although it wasn't specifically brought up. CENTCOM will likewise receive a call. I think the President will find in favor of a Special Operations mission to be launched immediately."

CHAPTER 6

Tampa, Florida

It was early, the sun not yet risen above the city to shine on Tampa Bay. General Kragle had already donned full-uniform Class A greens and stood at the wide window of his second-story home study, gazing speculatively out over the dawn-dusky city where lights were still on and the bay farther out lay in inky blackness. Waiting for the call from Washington.

Although only in his late fifties, he seemed to have aged under the pressure of the past few days. He stood six-six and weighed a well-conditioned two-thirty, physical dimensions passed on through genes to his three sons, but his shoulders appeared somewhat stooped and there were new lines around his eyes. The War on Terror took a toll. Especially from the commander of the United States Special Operations Command whose duty it was to send young men into harm's way. Especially when that commander had three sons all attached to USSOCOM. Major Brandon Kragle, Captain Cameron Kragle, and Sergeant Cassidy Kragle represented a new generation of a military line passed down through the Irish Kragles from fathers to sons since at least the French and Indian Wars. The General, although he rarely expressed it in keeping with his taciturn nature, was exceptionally proud of his sons.

Gray eyes snapped toward the telephone on his desk, as

though daring it not to ring. It remained mockingly silent. Two TVs, both turned on, provided background noise.

Even though it was late the previous night when he got back from Washington, he alerted JSOC, Joint Special Operations Command, and gave Colonel Buck Thompson at Delta Force a call. Something big was likely coming down the pipe, he told them. Start preparing.

Gloria quietly entered the study in her faded long robe and the rabbit-ear slippers Cassidy gave her. She balanced a tray containing a pot of coffee and two cups. She set it on the corner of the General's desk and poured both cups. The General looked at the fat black woman with controlled affection as she handed him one cup and sipped from the other.

She wore a red bandanna tied over hair dyed almost as red as the kerchief, a personal fashion that made her look like Aunt Jemima. Aunt Jemima with a beautiful round dark-brown face. Gloria was more than housekeeper; Gloria was *family.* She literally raised the three Kragle sons after their mother Rita died during childbirth with Cassidy. "Brown Sugar Doll," or "Brown Sugar Mama," as the family called her, was almost the only mother the Kragle boys had ever known.

"I'm going to miss you, Brown Sugar," the General said in a soft voice. That simple statement, coming from him, contained great emotion beneath the surface. Kragles always controlled their feelings.

Gloria didn't, couldn't contain hers. The men in the family might be self-contained and emotionally suppressed, but Gloria wore her feelings honestly on her dark face. Tears spontaneously flooded her big eyes and rolled down her cheeks. You always knew where you stood with her.

"Lawdy, Lawdy, Darren. Just 'cause I getting married don't mean I ain't never gonna see ya'all no more. Ol' Gloria is gonna be near until ol' Gloria ain't nowhere no more."

"The boys are looking forward to the wedding, Sugar.

Cameron has been up at the Farm making sure things are all spruced up for the ceremony."

"Darren, I am gonna warn you now: Don't you send them boys off nowhere. They better be there too. They still ain't too big for this old colored lady to take across her lap. Lawdy, my old bones. I always 'spected I'd be 'tending their weddings, not them mine. 'Course, I did go to Cassidy's when he married Kathryn, but then . . . Lawdy, Lawdy. It was the saddest day of my life when that pretty girl die."

"Yes."

The General turned away to stare out the window, his eyes narrowing to icy gray slivers at the too-recent memories of deaths in the family, all due to terrorism. First there was Gypsy in Afghanistan, who would likely have married Cameron by now. Little Nana, the General's mother and the Kragle matriarch, died in one of the planes that crashed into the World Trade Center. The General always wondered if the old woman, suffering from Alzheimer's, was aware of what was happening before she died. Finally, the anthrax attack in the wake of 9/11 claimed Kathryn.

"Raymond had better treat you right, Brown Sugar," the General said to change the subject, "or he'll have Delta Force to answer to."

"Oh, he treat me just like I a queen." She chuckled. "He be scared to death of you."

She regarded the back turned toward her. When the General was quiet and meditative like this, it often meant some or all of the Kragles were about to go into harm's way. Brandon had just survived some kind of hush-hush trip to the Philippines. Surely he wouldn't be going out again so soon. Why couldn't he and his brothers get regular jobs and stay home safe instead of being so much like their father and Grandfather Jordan? Only Cameron, as a chaplain, held any kind of decent job. But even he was assigned to Delta Force.

"Darren, why is it I be having some bad feelings that something be about to happen?"

The General stared silently out the window, not answering her. She took a deep sigh.

"Drink your coffee while it be hot, Darren. I'll go and bring breakfast. I'll have breakfast with you if it be okay?"

"Of course."

She lowered the volume on one of the two TVs on her way out. General Kragle turned to his desk with another accusing glance at the telephone. He sat down to sip coffee and wait on breakfast.

One of the TVs was tuned to CNN, the other to FOX News. The General called it balancing the press. The world, as Gloria often put it, was going to hell in a handbasket. Jesus was coming back and, boy, was He mad. Cameron had a different way of putting it. He called the chaos "cultural madness." If an individual could go insane, he said, why couldn't an entire culture go mad?

FOX panned onto anticapitalist protestors around the world. Self-described anarchists whooped and screamed as they set cars on fire and hurled rocks and bottles at police in Germany; in London, about seven thousand people marched on Trafalgar Square shouting slogans and carrying banners against everything from global warming to right-wing extremism; protestors in Greece proclaimed solidarity with the Palestinians in their bloody struggle with Israel; police in Zurich used tear gas, rubber bullets, and water cannon to disperse leftist protestors; Philippine socialists protested the government and the U.S. military presence while a grenade explosion killed three people and wounded thirteen others in the southern city of Cotabato; activists in Washington, D.C., marched to highlight the plight of civilians killed in Afghanistan.

CNN focused on former-president John Stanton, spotlighting his recent appearance at the World AIDS conference in Barcelona.

"We cannot lose our war against AIDS and win our battle against poverty, promote stability, advance democracy, and increase peace and prosperity," he lectured. "I will do all I can in the United States to get more money, more action."

The camera then switched to real time in Havana where Cuban dictator Fidel Castro—the commentator referred to him as *president*—stood next to John Stanton and, with no sense of irony, proclaimed Cuba to be the world's most democratic country.

The camera zoomed in on Stanton as he began to speak, his handsome face hanging out there bald, scolding America from the soil of a ruthless dictatorship that provided succor to international terrorism.

"We believe that people of conscience must take responsibility for what their governments do," he rambled on. "We oppose injustice wherever we find it in the world. It is our duty, our obligation, to resist war and oppression, and we must repudiate any inference that such wars are being waged in our name and for our welfare. We peace-loving Americans extend a hand of friendship to peace-loving countries such as Cuba and others around the world who may be suffering from unwise policies. We choose to make common cause with the people of the world . . ."

"Asshole," General Kragle muttered.

Gloria returned with eggs and grits, toast and butter and slices of cantaloupe. She started to set the tray on the desk, but jumped back, startled, when the phone rang. The General picked it up before the second ring.

"General Kragle. This is a secure line."

"Darren. General Morrison here. It's a go. The designation is Operation Deep Steel."

CHAPTER 7

Nampo, North Korea

The red-and-white freighter *Ibn Haldoon* flying the green flag of Saudi Arabia lay moored to the long wooden-and-concrete docks at the port city of Nampo while it took on cargo overnight. Its master intended it to sail at first light. However, the piers were poorly lighted due to another partial power outage in the Peoples Republic. Frequent delays in the work occurred whenever the lights went out and plunged the port into darkness. Armed Komar patrol boats lying off the ship's stern turned on their bow floods, but they provided insufficient light to keep the work going.

The captain of the *Ibn Haldoon*, a bow-legged Arab with a thick trunk and an even-thicker head, paced both the ship's deck and the adjoining pier, raging at everyone within range, punctuating his invective with the probing beam of a flashlight he carried like a weapon. His name was Captain Khalid, but the common seaman operating the crane arm machinery that lowered cargo into the freighter's hold thought of him as Darth Vader from the *Star Wars* movies. Khalid's full black beard seemed attached to the ancient WWI British combat helmet he wore constantly, assigning to him Darth Vader's masked air of sinister mystery.

From an elevated position at the controls of the crane, the

common seaman called Ismael commanded a perfect vantage point from which to observe onloading cargo. Little
missed his scrutiny. He was a perfect illustration for the old
maxim that looks could be deceiving.

He was small, almost tiny, with short-cropped black hair
covered by a too-large red baseball cap. His skin was olive-
dark, as from a full suntan, while the mouth was wide and the
nose small. His most remarkable feature were his eyes. They
were a brilliant emerald, a trait not that uncommon in the
Arab world. As both conqueror and conquered, Arabs and
Muslims had marched back and forth over the globe for cen-
turies, mixing with the rest of the world. He was dressed in
loose linen trousers of the type worn in Saudi Arabia and a
long robelike shirt held at the waist by a blue sash.

Thing was, Ismael was a *woman*. A woman disguised as a
man because women in the Muslim world were not allowed
to serve aboard ships. Women in the Muslim world, for that
matter, were not allowed to do many things. They could wear
burqas that covered their entire bodies and faces—and they
could breed in the darkness.

Ismael swung the long steel arm of his crane out over the
pier. Dock laborers attached slings and cables to crates
hauled onto the piers by trucks. The seaman lifted the freight,
swung it out over the freighter's deck in the flickering light
and lowered it deep into the bowels of the hold where other
workers detached it and released the cable in order that the
maneuver could be repeated.

Cargo so far consisted of machinery manufactured in Pyongyang, packed in boxes uniformly six-by-eight feet or so
and stamped for delivery to Manila. None of the boxes was
large enough to contain items against which Ismael had been
alerted. Loading was almost complete. She considered mark-
ing that night off as a dry hole when three flatbed trucks
growled onto the pier bringing the last of the shipment.
Aboard each of the three trucks was one enormous wooden

crate about forty feet long and some six feet in diameter.
They immediately attracted her attention.

She swung the crane arm out over the first trailer truck.
Workers attached the crate to the crane arm. She lifted it. She
noted, significantly, that these goods were being loaded last
in order that they could be offloaded first. She lowered the
crate into the hold and it was released. She was in the process
of bringing aboard the second crate when three strangers appeared on the docks. Each carried some kind of duffel bag
and stood underneath one of the lights while they spoke to
Darth Vader, allowing an observer to get a good look.

The man who appeared to be in charge would have attracted attention anywhere in the world because of his bulk,
shaved head, and the ugly scar that disfigured one side of his
face and made his head look lopsided. He was neither Korean nor Arab. Possibly he was Filipino or Indonesian, as was
the second man. He was bulky as well, but had a full head of
straight black hair and no scars. Maybe the WWF or WWE,
whatever it called itself these days, was holding a wrestling
convention. These two looked perfectly capable of compet-
ing.

The third man was a skinny Asian, either Japanese or Chinese. He resembled a ninja, his face expressionless and so
hard and cruel he seemed to be looking for someone to murder. These guys were people you didn't want to run into in a
dark alley.

After a brief conversation, Darth Vader pointed to the
gangplank that connected the *Ibn Haldoon* to the pier. All
three newcomers picked up their gear and started toward the
ship. Scarface looked back at Captain Khalid's WWI helmet
and grinned with sarcasm.

They were barely on deck before the pier lights flickered,
came back on momentarily, then dropped the port into darkness. The ship likewise blacked out because it had hooked
into the pier's power source in order to conserve its own bat-

teries and generators. Flashlights came on in isolated cones. Komars swept the deck with their floods. Darth Vader began shouting and blackguarding.

Ismael looked quickly about. The blackout could be expected to last up to a half-hour if previous ones were any indication. Plenty of time for her to hurry below, check the crate already loaded to confirm what it contained, then return topside without anyone being the wiser.

She spotted a passing seaman because of his flashlight and hailed him.

"Nature is calling," she said in Arabic. "Will you take over the crane in case the lights come back on?"

"Piss over the side," he suggested.

"I have to do more than that."

"Hurry then. I have my own job to do."

"We all have jobs, nature included," she said, climbing down. The second big crate remained suspended in midair from the crane cable.

Stars and a low quarter-moon provided enough ambient light to guide Ismael until she went through a watertight door on the 02 deck and began descending. She turned on her flashlight. The *Ibn Haldoon* was an ancient, rusted tub that had not been well maintained. Ismael stifled a sneeze from mildew and mold growing in the dank below-decks environment.

The cargo hold, nearly the length of a football field, opened just below the main deck and extended down through four others. Ismael knew exactly where she was going since she did the loading. She secured a hammer and pry bar from a tool locker and proceeded down ladders to the floor of the hold, lighting her way with the flashlight. The door to the hold led into a vast space whose blackness was relieved only by oil lanterns on the far side that attracted crew like moths to flame.

She didn't bother switching off her light. The others would

think she was a ship's officer inspecting freight. She would have found out what she needed to know and be gone by the time they grew curious enough to leave the vicinity of the coffee and tea pots placed at the far bulkhead for their convenience.

The little seaman padded on rubber-soled shoes along a thoroughfare lined in stacked wooden crates. The hold, far from full, held only what the crew onloaded that night along with a section of freight picked up two days earlier in Hokkaido. The beam of her flashlight picked out the forty-footer she had lowered into the ship only a few minutes before. Stevedores using forklifts had arranged it for easy access, leaving nearby spaces for the other two pieces of the shipment.

After making sure none of the crew had selected this particular site for a little nap while the lights were out, she quickly pried loose one of the boards on the side of the long carton and was clearing away interior packing to take a look at the contents when the furtive sounds of quick footfalls arrested her.

Alarmed, she doused her light. Listening intently, she heard nothing but bilge pumps humming from their own battery-power sources and the voices of the workers on the far side, echoing as sound does in large and near-empty chambers. Satisfied that it was nothing except her imagination, she resumed her efforts on the crate until she came through the packing to a metal object. She knew exactly what she was looking for, having been previously cued and having undergone a crash course in the types and nomenclature of the various weapons she might encounter. Another minute of inspection confirmed her suspicions.

It was definitely a missile—an SS-1 SCUD short-range ballistic missile of the type that first appeared in the old Soviet arsenal in 1957 and had gone through a number of modifications since then. Although SCUDs were relatively inaccurate, they were true enough for large-area targets such as cities. In recent years, they had proliferated in the Third World countries of Southwest and Southeast Asia primarily because of their ready availability through China and North Korea. They received wide attention during the 1991 Gulf War when Iraq fired a number of them at Israeli cities, although Israel was not even involved in the Allied effort to drive Saddam Hussein out of Kuwait.

Each missile was 37.4 feet long, 2.75 feet in diameter, and weighed 9,700 pounds. Mounted on a self-propelled transporter-erector-launcher (TEL) based on a MAZ 543 8X8 truck, it could be stored horizontally for travel and erected vertically off the rear of the vehicle for firing. It had a range of up to 112 miles with a conventional or a 40-100 kiloton nuclear payload.

Truck bases were obviously not included with the missiles. Not that they were necessary. The missiles could be transported on any heavy-duty civilian or military truck and either fired from the bed or from a ground mount.

Ismael felt smugly pleased with herself for having identified the weapon and remembering all the details. The wrestler with the scar, his WWF buddy, and the ninja were undoubtedly associated with the missiles and had come aboard to escort them to their destination. The weapons were likely destined for rebel, guerrilla, or terrorist groups with big bucks to spend and an agenda to promote in violence. No legitimate transaction with another nation would have required only three of them delivered under such secrecy.

She had to make her report, having smuggled aboard in her duffel a hand-sized SATCOM radio and a SAT cell phone, high-tech equipment capable of sending a signal around the globe. A word from her, she knew, started the action. This ship was going to be taken down by U.S. SpecOps forces—SEALs or Delta—somewhere in international waters.

What a relief it would be to get off this bucket of rust and resume her identity as a woman. She didn't like being a man, although she had masqueraded as Ismael at other times in Israel and Afghanistan. This time she had been under cover for nearly three weeks, since the CIA targeted the *Ibn Haldoon* as a smuggler vessel and arranged for her to go aboard in Jidda disguised as a seaman named Ismael. Maintaining cover under such close quarters over time required concentration and constant vigilance. It wore on the nerve endings.

Replacing the padding and boards she had ripped from the crate, she started toward the gangway ladder that returned her to the main deck, hurrying but not to the extent that it might attract attention. Her light beam reflected from side to side against the walls of freight.

A noise like a muffled sob or a gasp stopped her cold. She crouched. Fight-or-flight instincts kicked in. Nervous sweat made her head itch underneath the ball cap. Her shaft of light darted, probing among the stacked crates. She flinched and jumped backward when it unexpectedly illuminated three small wretches cowering in a dead-end space among the boxes. A gaunt teenage boy and two much younger children, Koreans by the looks of them, huddled in each other's arms, looking like starved kittens cornered by a vicious dog.

Ismael took an uncertain step toward them. They stared unblinking into the light, the teen holding the children tighter as if he feared they would be wrenched from his arms. The little girl whimpered in fear. She looked to be about eight or nine. The little boy was even younger, surely no older than six.

Ismael realized with a sinking feeling of dismay what she had come upon. Stowaways from communist or despotic nations always posed a problem for shipping. These three must have sneaked aboard during one of the lights out. She searched her mind for some way to avoid confronting the situation. She had to be practical. She couldn't be bothered

with these little vagrants when there was so much else at
stake. Thousands of people, *hundreds of thousands,* might
perish if these missiles weren't intercepted. She couldn't let
three half-starved kids compromise her mission.

Her frustration grew as she stared at the children. She lowered the flashlight beam out of their eyes and bounced it off
the deck so it illuminated her as well as them. She held out an
open palm to show she meant no harm. The little girl's dark
eyes, huge, as in an old Keane painting, looked into Ismael's
and reached all the way to her heart. Ismael knelt in front of
them. She spoke little Korean and they undoubtedly spoke
even less Arabic. She tried English.

"Do you speak English?" Ismael whispered.

The Koreans clung to each other and stared with big,
frightened eyes. After a moment, the teenager gave an almost
imperceptible nod.

"You speak English?" Ismael repeated more hopefully.

Again the nod, unmistakable this time.

"Good. You can't stay here. You'll be found."

They stared at her. So they couldn't stay here. What was
she going to do with them?

Why should she have to do anything with them? They
weren't her responsibility.

Lights in the hold flickered dimly. They caught for a moment and held, filling the gigantic spaces with shadows and
edges. The Koreans seemed to shrink as though willing
themselves to disappear into their surroundings. It only made
them appear more vulnerable.

The lights went out again to reestablish Ismael's flashlight
beam and the plight of these stowaways cringing in it. Power
would return within the next few minutes. These kids
couldn't hide out here much longer. They were bound to be
discovered.

She cursed herself for a sentimental fool, sentimentality
being something she thought she had lost long ago as the Ice

Maiden. But what kind of a brute would she be to leave these pathetic little vagabonds to be cast back ashore? She had heard too many tales of horror about what happened to citizens attempting to flee the benevolent Peoples Republic. She made up her mind.

"Follow me," she said. "I'm going to hide you in a rope locker where you'll be safe for the time being. Do you understand? Be quiet, keep low, and hurry."

They dutifully got up and followed. It was going to be her neck if they got caught. Worse still, the mission would be put at risk.

CHAPTER 8

Fort Bragg, North Carolina

Sergeant Cassidy Kragle pressed his back against the wall in the darkened outer hallway. His face, painted black, merged into the black watch cap and sweater he wore above camouflage BDU (battle dress uniform) bottoms and combat jump boots. He adjusted his NVGs, night vision goggles. Through their liquid-green vision, he watched Staff Sergeant Theodore "Ice Man" Thompson for the signal.

Sergeant Thompson was considered the best weapons man and combat shooter in U.S. Army's 1st Special Forces Operation Detachment—Delta. Even at rifle distance shooting—sniping—only his teammate on Major Brandon Kragle's Troop One, Master Sergeant Gloomy Davis, bested him. Ice Man, or simply Ice, was an average-looking laconic man in his early thirties. His background, however, was anything but average. In addition to his expertise with weapons—he could disassemble, reassemble, and fire virtually any weapon in any arsenal, in the dark—he had also won the North Carolina middleweight kickboxing championship three years in a row and had recently developed a passion for gourmet cooking. His main flaw of character, if it even existed, was that he seldom spoke and when he did only in the fewest words possible. It was said that Ice Man used words the way a traveler in the desert rationed his last canteen of water.

On stand down in garrison, Ice Man often instructed the CQB course. Sergeant Cassidy now waited in the hallway outside the section of the course known as the "House of Horrors," a live-fire exercise conducted in total darkness, using NVGs, inside rooms whose walls were constructed to absorb bullets and prevent ricochets. Other sections of the course trained Delta troops to clear skyscrapers or airliner cabins of armed, hostage-taking terrorists—"Tangos" in the Delta vernacular.

Ice Man nodded the signal.

Cassidy vaulted into action, swift and violent. With the Walther PPK 9mm semiauto pistol thrust out ahead in both hands, he launched himself against the door and burst through into darkened rooms turned into an eerie liquid-green world by the NVGs. He merged against an interior wall to avoid silhouetting himself in the lighter frame of the doorway. A tango target cutout armed with a machine pistol popped into the opposite doorway. Cassidy fired one shot, the bark of the Walther sharp and explosive in the confines. Muzzle flash lit up the room, but the NVGs muted it so it didn't blind the firer. The target dropped instantly.

Cassidy continued swiftly through the course from room to room, jinking and twisting, dropping to one knee or to his belly to get off a shot and avoid becoming a target himself.

Running, kicking in doors, firing quick deadly shots as man-targets appeared unexpectedly from all quarters.

Given the opportunity, the targets shot back with laser beams, buzzing the trainee's belt if they scored a hit. Cassidy's belt remained mute.

A tango cutout target using a woman as a shield backed across the room. Only the terrorist's head and his gunhand at the woman's throat were visible. The young trooper drilled him between the eyes and kept moving.

A hostage cutout, a teenager, escaped his captors and jumped out of a closet screaming in horror. Cassidy properly held his fire.

The last mannequin had a submachine gun and scooted from right to left. Cassidy's pistol was empty and he had insufficient time to reload. He whipped out the SOG SK 2000 combat knife he carried in a sheath at his belt. The knife whistled as he threw it. It thunked as it buried its seven-inch blade in the mannequin-target's chest.

Cassidy strode triumphantly from the course. He was a tall, slender man of twenty-four with the dark looks of his father, USSOCOM's General Darren Kragle, and of his older brother, Major Brandon Kragle, commander of Delta's Troop One. His eyes were a striking blue. His mother, who died giving life to him, had eyes that blue. She had golden hair though. Only the middle Kragle brother, Cameron, Delta Force's chaplain, had inherited their mother's blondness. Brandon and Cassidy were like their father with hair only a few shades lighter than black. All three sons, however, were in the six-four range, slightly shorter than their towering, broad-shouldered old man.

"Smart ass," Ice Man said, acknowledging in the flippant comment that he understood Cassidy was showing off with the knife, a display of theatrics no Delta trooper would dare during regular training. Cassidy, however, had completed the

Delta course three days earlier and was just killing time waiting around for an assignment to a squadron and troop.

Cassidy realized how close he came to blowing any chance
he had for being accepted by Delta. Two years before, when
he was serving in the U.S. Navy, he, Kathryn Burguiere, and
another sailor were taken hostage by al-Qaeda terrorists who
blew up the destroyer USS *Randolph* in Aden Harbor,
Yemen. Kathryn and he were secreted out of Yemen into
Afghanistan while the third sailor was executed. Terrorists
raped Kathryn in captivity.

"When we get out of here," he promised her, "I'll never let
anything harm you again."

His brothers Brandon and Cameron, leading a Delta detachment, parachuted to their rescue in Operation Punitive
Strike. Nothing official was ever written about the fury
within him that led to his killing Kathryn's abuser, but he
knew his father and Brandon always wondered if he might
not be too hot-headed for Special Forces and Delta.

Nonetheless, Cassidy got out of the navy and enlisted in
the army where the Green Berets accepted his application.
His ultimate goal was to join Delta Force. He was still in the
SF "Q" Course when terrorists struck New York and Washington. The new President of the United States declared a
War on Terror. Brandon led a clandestine Delta detachment
into war-torn Afghanistan on a top secret mission, Operation
Iron Weed, to assassinate al-Qaeda's ruthless leader, Osama
bin Laden. While Cassidy felt he should have been a part of
the mission, if for no other reason than to seek revenge for
the torment al-Qaeda heaped upon Kathyrn and him, he had
no choice but to sit it out and complete his training.

It was not to be that simple. The war came home in a personal and terrible way through anthrax contamination spread
by "sleeper" terrorists. Cassidy found himself unable to keep
his promise to always protect Kathryn. Pregnant with their

child, she died in his arms, poisoned by an Islamic who had
enlisted in the army as a cover.

Cassidy lost it when she died. Consumed by hate and a lust
for revenge, he sought only one thing—to annihilate the man
responsible for killing his wife. He owed Cameron and he
owed FBI senior agent Claude Thornton for stopping his
hand when he went after Rasem Jameel. If he had murdered
Jameel that morning in the Boston subway system as he intended, he would never have made it anywhere in the army
except to the federal prison at Leavenworth.

He couldn't blame Colonel Buck Thompson and his own
father, the General, for being leery of his fitness for Delta after that. He might blame his father for not being a *real* father
when the sons were kids and needed him, but he couldn't
fault him for being cautious in selecting counterterrorist candidates. The last thing a CT outfit needed in the middle of a
mission was a psycho or some would-be Rambo.

"Son, after what happened with . . . your wife's death and
all," the General explained, "we have to be sure you've recovered, that you're going into Delta for the right reasons."

"Sir." Even the General's sons called him *General* or *sir*.
"Sir, I don't want to go out and start murdering terrorists, if
that's what you mean. Look, sir, I can handle it now. But I do
want to be in on the action. I wanted that even before Kathryn
died."

"I know. But you cannot receive preferential treatment just
because you're my son."

"I wouldn't expect it, sir."

The objective of the entire grueling selection process for
Delta was to look at the volunteer's values and how he handled himself under pressure. Individuals had to be capable of
both working with a team and of operating independently
without orders. Fewer than 10 percent of all applicants ever
actually made it into Delta.

The final and most critical part of the Delta selection process was *the interview.* A board of Delta veterans, including Colonel Buck himself, grilled the surviving candidates to determine who continued on into training. The General insisted a psychologist sit in on Cassidy's interview.

Cassidy stood before the board and answered questions while the psychologist took notes and kept adjusting his glasses.

"So, Sergeant Kragle," the questions went, "you're infiltrating an unfriendly area to take down a terrorist hideout. You come across two little girls about six years old. You can't leave them to spread the alarm. Do you take them along, tie them up, or do you cut their throats . . . ?"

"So, Sergeant Kragle, tell us a little about Machiavellian principles . . ."

"Well, Sergeant Kragle, you've given an outstanding performance so far. Now, tell us what it is you tend to blow up over . . ."

"So, Sergeant Kragle. Why should we take you on? So what if you're a good soldier and Honor Grad of the 'Q' Course? We're full of good soldiers. What can you offer Delta?"

Apparently, the shrink couldn't find anything in Cassidy's answers to keep him out of Delta. He was accepted on one condition—he would be placed on a probation period even more strict and lengthy than the other trainees.

"What it means," Colonel Thompson bluntly stated, "is that if you fuck up in any small way due to poor judgment or inability to maintain self-control, you're out of Delta and out of Special Forces. You'll find yourself rigging parachutes for the 82nd Airborne. Clear enough?"

"Clear enough, sir."

For the previous five months, Cassidy had undergone extensive training in counterterrorism at the SOT (Special Operations Training) facility located behind a high Cyclone fence within the rough horseshoe formed by Gruber, Lambert, and Manchester Roads at Fort Bragg, North Carolina. Training covered a wide range of subjects: marksmanship and CQB skills; tactics; climbing and abseiling; radio communications; surveillance; combat medicine; driving both wheeled and tracked vehicles; navigation; hostage rescue and protection; the conduct of airborne, airmobile, and maritime operations . . . He had already trained in and won his MOS designator as an engineer/demolitions specialist in Special Forces.

Sergeant Cassidy was ready to join his brothers.

"Kragle, Colonel Thompson wants to see you," Ice Man said as Cassidy left the House of Horrors.

"I'll head that way."

Sergeant Foster, who had gone through the shooting course first, was waiting for him. She fell into step. "I'll walk over with you," she offered.

Like the other Kragles, Cassidy found it hard to swallow the idea of females associated with combat outfits. Women couldn't belong to Delta, but there were four or five of them in the intel detachment the Delta males called Funny Platoon. They served as intelligence operatives to infiltrate countries to recon targets for the assault forces.

So many of the women in the military attempted to copy the macho walk and talk of the men with whom they associated. That wasn't so of Margo Foster. She was good at shooting, good at her job, but she remained thoroughly feminine from the round, firm little ass that worked against her BDU cammies to the honey-colored ponytail kept tucked underneath her uniform "ball cap."

She grinned flashing white teeth up at Cassidy. "So, Kragle?"

"So, Foster?" he said.

"Got your assignment yet? I saw the raging Arapahoe, Bobby Goose Pony, and he says you're trying to go to Troop Two with him. Major Russell's bunch of reprobates."

"That may be why the colonel wants to see me now."

"Rumor has it that there are several missions coming down."

"We're at war, Sergeant Foster."

"So, Kragle. I've been intending to ask you. Do you always dazzle a girl with your brilliant and erudite conversation?"

"I'm a man of few words."

"The strong, silent type like Sergeant Ice Man—or just big and dumb?"

He grinned down at her in spite of himself. He liked her. She was pretty, witty, and filled with self-assurance. It was just that he wasn't ready yet. Kathryn hadn't been gone all that long. It wasn't fair to Margo or any other woman to pretend otherwise.

"We're here," he said, stopping in front of Delta HQ. "Thanks for the walk and the erudite conversation."

"Anytime, Kragle." She hesitated and took a deep breath, looking up at him with a mischievous lift of eyebrows. "How about the NCO Club over on Smoke Bomb tonight? It's only a beer, Kragle. I'm not trying to jump your bones."

He looked at her for a long moment. "Deal," he said finally.

"Great. Eight o'clock? I promise not to wear anything enticing."

He shook his head, grinning at her forwardness. She waited outside while he walked into HQ.

Cassidy made his way to the second floor where Command Sergeant Major Gene Adcock admitted him to Colonel Buck's inner office. He snapped to attention precisely six inches in front of the colonel's desk and saluted. Colonel Buck returned it with an informal one of his own. He was a tall, serious man in his late forties who had recently started wearing glasses when he read. He removed his glasses.

"At ease, Sergeant Kragle."

"Yes, sir."

"I wanted to personally congratulate you on completing training."

"Thank you, sir."

There had to be more than that.

"I understand you really tore up the shooting range and that you're a pretty decent engineer and demolitions man."

"I do my best, Colonel."

"I can say that for the Kragles—you always do your best." He picked up several official-looking papers stapled together and handed them across the desk. He smiled. "Sergeant, I'm assigning you to Troop One."

Cassidy swallowed, astonished. "That's my brother's troop, sir."

"I'm aware of that, Sergeant."

"His troop already has two good demo men, sir. Sergeant Thumbs Jones is the best there is. Sir, may I ask a question?"

"Shoot."

"Is this my father's idea? So Brandon—Major Kragle— can keep an eye on me?"

"I make assignments in Delta, Sergeant, according to the needs of the service."

"I wasn't questioning you, sir. It's just that—"

Colonel Buck stood up. He rubbed his eyes with his thumbs as he walked around the desk to place a fatherly hand on Cassidy's shoulder.

"Look, son," he said. "I've known you since you were playing Little League baseball and Gloria would cheer so loud if you even *tipped* the ball that the home plate ump placed cotton in his ears. You've always been an independent little cuss. All three of you boys were—*are*. You don't belong in Delta if somebody has to keep an eye on you. It so happens that Troop One is my most combat-experienced and most available since Dare Russell is off playing in Qatar. Delta is being tasked with a very important mission—*tomorrow.* Troop One is on deck. You've had combat experience in Afghanistan with Operation Punitive Strike, even if you *were* the object of the operation, and the troop requires another good engineer. So, want it or not, you've been assigned. Those are your orders."

"Yes, sir."

"Sergeant, don't discuss this with anyone. Understand? Be prepared to receive the alert and move out at zero dark thirty in the morning."

CHAPTER 9

STANTON CRITICIZES U.S. POLICY ON CUBA

Havana (CPI)—Following his tour of Cuba's Center for Genetic Engineering and Biotechnology with Fidel Castro, former U.S. President John Stanton took issue with U.S. Government claims that the island nation allows terrorists to use Cuba as a base for terrorism against the United States.

"I asked President Castro specifically on more than one occasion if Cuba was involved in aiding any other country on Earth with terrorist activities," Stanton said. "The answer was an unequivocal 'no.'"

The U.S. Government, however, stands by its assertions.

Stanton is being shown Cuban revolutionary "triumphs" in the midst of communism's remaining ruins. He visited an agricultural cooperative, tossed out the first pitch of a Cuban all-star baseball game, toured a medical school and the Los Cocos AIDS sanatorium, where Cubans with AIDS are "quarantined" for life.

Speaking from University of Havana's elegant Aula Magna, Stanton delivered a speech that amounted to a carefully balanced appeal for Washington to drop its embargo against the island nation. Reminding his audience of how hard he worked to normalize relations between Israel and Palestine when he was President, he said the United States should lift the 43-year-old embargo on travel to and trade with Cuba.

Stanton, who traveled with official permission from the U.S. Government, which licenses all American travel to Cuba, is the most prominent American political figure to visit Cuba since Castro's successful 1959 revolution. The U.S. State Department warns all Americans, including political and cultural figures, that they travel to Cuba at their own risk, as the U.S. cannot protect them while they are in the country . . .

CHAPTER 10

Fayetteville, North Carolina

Major Brandon Kragle came instantly awake in that animal-like way of men conditioned by combat. He was sweating. Another of those nightmares he kept having since returning from the Philippines. Terrorists were shooting the missionaries, and, dream-frozen, he could do nothing about it. They just kept shooting and shooting and shooting while he watched.

He rolled away from the sleeping girl in bed with him to avoid soaking her with his sweat. He had already soaked the sheet underneath. Not that they hadn't sweated on each other plenty last night. Her panties hung on the bedside lampshade. How had they gotten there? It was the tiniest silk bikini with a red-white-and-blue motif. At least she was a patriot. He swung his legs over his side of the bed and ran hands through his dark, short-cropped hair. He glanced back at the sleeping girl.

What was her name? One of those cutesy ones girls often assigned to themselves. Candi? Brandi?

Brandi.

"Brandon and Brandi," she had giggled last night, high on three "martoonies." She did a little strip dance with her American flag bikini, twirled it around her little finger and flung it. That must be how it ended up on the lamp shade. She struck a naked attitude in front of him, hip thrust to one side, displaying everything. She was a natural blonde, he saw that, and her breasts were full and only slightly drooping with the nipples aroused and hard as raspberries.

"Brandon and Brandi," she tittered thickly. "Lets do it for Old Glory."

She grabbed the back of his head where he sat on the side of the bed and forced his face toward her triangle. "Have you got your muff-diving badge?" she asked lewdly, more than a little drunk.

He disliked the way she grabbed the back of his head, as if she were in charge. What was it with women these days that they thought they had to be in control? He removed her fingers from his head, pinned her hands to her bare sides and gently but forcefully placed her on the bed. He spread her legs around his waist. He grasped the cheeks of her fine, firm little ass and . . .

They did it for Old Glory or for recreational sex or because it seemed the thing to do.

Things always looked different the morning after. Brandi lay face down, the sheet thrown back and her bare bottom exposed. She had one leg bent toward him so that he saw the tangled tuft of yellow hair between her legs. He wasn't aroused. He felt like getting out of bed and going home, except he was already home. If you called home a bachelor's pad outside the north gate of Fort Bragg, headquarters of U.S. Army Special Forces, the 82nd Airborne, and 1st Special Forces Operational Detachment—Delta.

Her makeup had rubbed off on the pillow. She was still pretty, but plainer than last night. He thought he remembered her telling him she was a dancer at the Pirate's Den, a joint out on Hays Street.

"What do you do when you're not dancing?" he asked her.

"Depends?"

"Depends on what?"

"On who the guy is."

So he bedded the girl. Why should he feel guilty? Because he had been in love with Gypsy Iryani and had let her get killed in Afghanistan? She would likely have married Cameron anyhow. The Kragles were lucky in war, unlucky in women. Brandon and Cameron lost Gypsy. What a triangle that was. Anthrax took Cassidy's wife. The General lost their mother in childbirth with Cassidy. The General never remarried.

Brandon got up, slipped on a pair of faded jeans and, shirtless, started to the kitchen to make coffee. He looked back at Brandi from the door. She slept in the place Summer had occupied until the CIA beckoned after so brief a time together and she disappeared. Maybe he would never see her again.

What he should do, he admonished himself, was stick to ordinary women like Brandi. What was there about him that made him fall for warrior women? Everything in him revolted against the idea of sending females into combat. That was especially true after Gypsy's death. Yet, he parachuted his detachment back into Afghanistan to take out Osama bin Laden in Operation Iron Weed and there met his CIA contact already in-country with a band of anti-Taliban mujahideen. "Call me Ismael." Right. Ismael the Afghan *boy* turned out to be Summer Marie Rhodeman, the Jewish *girl*. Her courage and athletic beauty, those emerald eyes that reminded him so much of Gypsy's, attracted him in ways he had never thought possible again.

"Just because we made love, or had sex, or whatever you want to call it," Summer had said, "doesn't mean we have an investment in each other. We can't afford to make investments like that in our line of work. Agreed?"

They had no investment in each other, so why should he feel guilty about Brandi? A man needed a woman in his bed, at least occasionally. He didn't even know where Summer was.

He went into the kitchen, ran water into a battered coffee pot and put it on the stove to boil. The old-fashioned way. He dropped four scoops of coffee grounds directly into the water. Ranger coffee.

"Hot and black, the way I like my women," Troop One's black demo man, Thumbs Jones, would have said.

To which the commo specialist, Mad Dog Carson, would have responded, "And *ugly*. Hot, black, and *ugly*."

The phone rang. Brandon answered it quickly to avoid it waking Brandi. He didn't relish breakfast conversation before he could graciously get her out the front door. It was Cameron; they had successfully repaired the rift that existed between them over Gypsy.

"You awake, Brandon?"

"It's six in the morning. This is Brandon's butler."

"You sound like you've had a hard night. Maybe I should see you in church Sunday for confessions."

"Padre, you couldn't stand it. What do you want?"

Cameron was in Tennessee on the Farm outside Collierville, getting it ready for Gloria's wedding to Raymond. The Farm had been in the Kragle family for nearly three hundred years, since an ancestor first settled it during the French and Indian Wars. The Blake family lived there as caretakers; the Kragles used it only as an occasional retreat and for traditional weddings, family reunions, and for burials in the family plot behind the main house and the original log cabin. In recent times, the cemetery had received the most use. Cassidy's wife Kathryn and Little Nana were buried there, both victims of terrorists.

"Raymond's folks live in Durham," Cameron said. "Sugar Doll wants to know if Raymond's already in Durham, could he come up and ride with you to the wedding?"

"Whatever Brown Sugar wants is what Brown Sugar gets. That old gal deserves everything good in the world after having put up with us. But that's not what you really called about. You wanted to remind me to put my dress blues in the cleaners."

"Did you?"

"Does a chipmunk have ears?"

"How did you know that was the reason I phoned?"

"Elementary, my dear Watson. You're a worrier."

Cameron chuckled. "You're always right, Major. Just think, Brown Sugar Doll will be *Mrs.* Brown Sugar Doll in two weeks. I worry about how the General will make out after having had her around all these years."

"The General is adaptable."

It was, in fact, almost as if their mother was moving out of the house to marry someone else. For all practical purposes, Gloria *had* been their mother. It was she who accepted the role of surrogate mother and reared the General's three sons while he was away most of the time making war. He might not have been much of a father, but he was one hell of a soldier. It took a hell of a soldier to win the Congressional Medal of Honor.

Cameron said, "God bless and keep you, brother. See you Sunday in church?"

"I'll see you at the wedding."

The coffee boiled, sifting into the air that eye-opening aroma Brandon relished the morning after the night before. He poured a cup, blew on it, sipped, and made a face. You almost needed someone to hold a gun on you so you could drink it.

Still thinking of Summer, he took coffee with him to the inside entranceway of the apartment, an area Cameron wryly referred to as "the Shrine." Everything else in the apartment was stock bachelor, minimalist, barely functional, no pictures on the walls, empty beer cans on the counter and pizza boxes in the trash. Only the Shrine personalized the quarters. It was the Shrine that rooted him, anchored him to his military legacy and his place in it. He did his best thinking there.

The Kragle sons through their father grew up on the folklore of Delta Force, on how Charlie Beckwith had a vision of creating an elite counterterrorism force composed of super soldiers who arrived by sea, air, or land anywhere in the world, on a moment's notice, to do literally any damned thing required of them. General Kragle, then a major, teamed up with Colonel Beckwith to make it happen. The CT unit they formed, molded partly after the British SAS, grew into the finest, toughest weapon in the battle against terrorism that the world had ever known. Circumstances following the terrorist attacks of 9/11 and the subsequently declared War on Terror placed Delta Force on the point of the spear aimed at the heart of international terrorism.

Brandon's alcove told the story of Special Operations and

Delta Force in mementos, awards, and photographs. Shelves and walls on either side of the front door were crammed with history: the Alamo Scout patch Grandfather Jordan wore when he made the raid at Cabanatuan to free the Bataan Death March survivors; the General's old paratrooper helmet and a pair of worn combat boots from Vietnam; a copy of the citation for the General's Congressional Medal of Honor; early Delta shoulder patches; commendations; photos of Brandon and Cameron being awarded their green berets; a Mark 3 SEAL knife; a blown-up photo showing a much-younger version of his father standing between Colonel Beckwith and actor John Wayne from when the movie *The Green Berets* was filmed; an autographed portrait of Colonel Arthur "Bull" Simons and the Son Tay raiders; another of Dick Meadows in Teheran before the failed Iranian rescue mission, Delta's first operation; copies of two books Uncle Mike Kragle, a journalist for Consolidated Press International (CPI), had published—*The 100th Kill,* about Vietnam, and *Medals and Body Bags,* about Delta and the Iranian hostage crisis . . .

Summer had contributed to the Shrine before she left. The eight-by-ten color snapshot showed Delta's Iron Weed detachment and Bek's guerrillas of the Northern Alliance in the White Mountains of Afghanistan before all the trouble. Summer as Ismael, looking tiny and dark and *Arab* in her mujahideen garb, stood next to an armed, bearded Brandon dressed in similar clothing. She looked into the camera wearing a somber expression.

Brandon reached out and touched the image of her face with his fingertips.

"Hey, sweetie . . ."

He stiffened. He slowly turned, forcing himself to smile. You couldn't screw a girl in the night and then turn her out the next morning without at least a smile and a cup of coffee.

She stood in the bedroom doorway wearing one of his

green Class B uniform shirts, hip up thrust in an assumed dance pose. Her blond hair looked tousled, her lips red and swollen from last night's sex. Her uplifted arm braced above her head against the doorjamb tugged up the tail of the shirt to expose long slim legs and a few tangled puffs of pubic hair.

Why couldn't she just put on her clothes and go on home, like a man would have under similar circumstances?

Brandon had never wanted Summer to leave in the morning.

The phone rang. Saved by the bell.

"Don't answer it, sweetie," Brandi chirped, batting her blue eyes. He hated being called sweetie. "Come back to bed with me."

"I have to answer. I'm on call."

It was Colonel Buck Thompson. "Major, this is a Raging Bull."

Raging Bull was code for a mission call-up.

"Yes, sir. The entire troop?"

"One eight-man detachment. It is now 0615 hours. You'll be moving to a brief isolation phase at Langley. Transportation will be available at Pope Air Force Base at 0900 hours."

"How long will we be gone, sir?"

He was thinking of Gloria's wedding.

"Indefinite," Colonel Buck said. "Is that a problem, soldier?"

"We'll be at Pope at 0900 hours, sir."

He hung up and looked at Brandi. "You'll have to get your own coffee," he said.

CHAPTER 11

Camp Peary, Virginia

Newly designated Delta Detachment 2-Bravo—eight fit-looking young men in starched BDU cammies and green berets—filed off the lowered tail ramp of the MH-47E helicopter shortly before noon. The detachment would not be returning to Fort Bragg before skying-up for mission, which meant the men were burdened with rucks, weapons, radios, and various other items of combat equipment.

Camp Peary, a secure twenty-five-square-mile facility used by the CIA for training in covert and unconventional warfare, had the look of government all over it—landscaped grounds, neutral-colored buildings well kept and looking interchangeable, unmarked sedans and pickup trucks so alike they may as well have been stamped U.S. GOVERNMENT. The Agency referred to it as "the Farm," a nomenclature Deltas also applied to their compound at Fort Bragg for more obvious reasons. Operatives at Bragg often went around wearing cowboy boots and chewing tobacco. These CIA guys, Thumbs Jones noted, wore buttoned-down shirts, Dockers, slacks, and pinched-asshole faces.

"Beware of spooks bearing gifts," murmured Gloomy Davis, looking around.

Lieutenant Colonel Doug "No Sleep" Callahan, Delta's

deputy commander under Colonel Buck Thompson, met the detachment at the helipad. He was a slender man of medium height, in his late thirties, with red burr-cut hair and freckles. Brandon saluted. The light-colonel returned the salute, grinned, and shook hands all around. He paused when he came to Sergeant Cassidy Kragle.

"You're General Kragle's youngest boy?" he said.

"Yes, sir."

"You'll be a fine operator if you're half as good as your old man or your brother."

Cassidy flinched, but said, "Yes, sir."

"Men, welcome once more into the Valley of the Shadow of Death," No Sleep said, his way of letting the detachment know this was "real world" and not another full mission profile training exercise.

"Goody, goody," Mad Dog rumbled sarcastically, hoisting an AN/PSC-5 "Shadowfire" radio onto one shoulder and readjusting his Colt carbine and full ruck on the other. "We get to go to war again."

"You are such an animal, Sergeant Dog," admonished Master Sergeant Winfield Brown.

"Winnie" Brown was wiry with lanky brown hair and a stilted manner of speaking acquired, he claimed, from a semester he spent at Harvard University during his wasted youth. A former troop intelligence specialist, he moved up to operations sergeant, a troop's top NCO, after Roger "Mother" Norman failed to make it back from Iron Weed.

Mad Dog, the troop's communications specialist, was thickly built and gloweringly dark with lots of hair growing on his broad shoulders and abnormally long arms. He had once lifted the front of a Humvee and placed it on a block so Thumbs Jones could change a flat tire.

"Fu-uck, Winnie Pooh," the Dog said. "You eat this shit up."

Colonel Callahan led the detachment walking briskly

along trimmed sidewalks winding among red-barked pines. "Parts of them are edible, you know," Mad Dog ribbed Ice Man's newly discovered penchant for gourmet cooking.

Special Forces men were rough, direct-action men with few pretenses. Good men to go with if you had to dive into hell to capture the devil. Major Brandon had carefully selected the members of Det 2-B because they were exceptional men at their jobs in an outfit full of exceptional soldiers. Limited to seven men, not including himself, he chose: Master Sergeant Winnie Brown, ops and intel specialist and new operations sergeant for Troop One; Master Sergeant Gloomy Davis, sniper; and Sergeant First Class John "Mad Dog" Carson, communications.

He selected "Doc TB" Blackburn as medic. He was a huge bear of a young Catholic with an after-five perpetual shadow on his jaws. Doc TB honor-graduated last year from the SF med course and distinguished himself after being wounded in Operation Iron Weed.

Sergeant First Class Theodore "Ice Man" Thompson, no kin to Colonel Buck, was an obvious choice as weapons specialist. He wore a scar from a bullet that crushed his left cheekbone during Operation Punitive Strike and another one in the torso from Iron Weed. He had only spoken ten words, as counted by Mad Dog, about both incidents since they occurred.

Sergeant First Class Calvin "Thumbs" Jones took the engineer and demolitions slot. He was a light-complexioned black man from Mississippi who purported to be a descendant of both slaves and slave owners. He blew off his left thumb a few years previously in an explosion while experimenting with nitro, thus the source of his nickname. His life's philosophy was simple and straightforward: "There are few of life's problems that can't be solved by a good stick of TNT."

The only choice of personnel denied Brandon had been

Cassidy, his little brother. That choice had been made for him. The General had telephoned Brandon immediately after Colonel Buck called Raging Bull.

"Major, I know the selection of men for a mission is your decision," he said. "I would consider it a personal favor, however, if you included Cassidy on the detachment. I talked to Buck about it yesterday. He has no objection. He assigned Cassidy to your troop."

"Cass will make a squared-away Delta soldier, sir, whether he's with my troop or not."

"I realize that, son, but . . . Well, I'd like you to ramrod him on his first official mission."

It wasn't always a good idea to have brothers in the same combat outfit. Brandon knew he could reject Cassidy and the General would accept his reasoning without questioning it. He also knew why their father made this request. Something changed in the younger Kragle following Kathryn's death. It was as if his soul hungered for revenge. That had to be controlled in him by external means until he could control it himself. The General wanted Brandon to look out for his little brother.

"Consider it done, sir."

He added Cassidy to the roster as the eighth man and extra demolitions specialist. He harbored few reservations about it. After all, Cassidy had fought with Punitive Strike halfway across Afghanistan to the Turkmenistan border following his and Kathryn's rescue from al-Qaeda nearly two years ago, and fought coolly and well.

"One other thing, Major," the General said. "I don't want him to know I had anything to do with this. The boy can be obstinate if he thinks I'm interfering."

"Obstinacy runs in the family, sir."

The General chuckled.

* * *

Colonel Callahan halted in front of Operations, a square, flat-roofed building with beige metal siding.

"Major Kragle, have you been informed about the SEALs?" he asked.

"Furry creatures that live in the sea and eat fish?"

"SEALs as in DevGroup, Major. Due to the nature of the operation, you'll have four DevGroup SEALs attached to 2-Bravo."

"No problem, sir."

The Naval Special Warfare Development Group (Dev-Group) was the navy's answer to army's Delta Force in counterterrorism. It began back in 1980 when Lieutenant Commander Richard Marcinko created SEAL Team Six to combat increasing incidents of international terrorism. Scandals within Team Six involving alleged bribery and misuse of government funds led to Marcinko's being relieved and eventually convicted and sent to federal prison. The 1992 publication of his autobiography, *Rogue Warrior,* prompted the navy to avoid further notoriety by changing the name of SEAL Team Six to Naval Special Warfare Development Group and hiding it administratively within the navy's chain of command. DevGroup, however, continued with essentially the same CT missions and responsibilities as Six.

Six, and later DevGroup, had been involved in a number of CT operations, both overt and covert. These included the *Achille Lauro* hijacking; rescue of Governor Paul Scoon from Grenada during Operation Urgent Fury; and the search for Panamanian strongman Manuel Antonio Noriega during Operation Just Cause.

A large room inside Operations was equipped for a mission briefing. Up front, drop cloths covered maps and charts, pencil boards, globes and other aids arranged around a podium. A long table with chairs faced the front. At each of twelve placings on the table lay a thick blue folder marked OPERA-TION DEEP STEEL and SECRET. Next to the folders were, curi-ously enough, bags of snack food.

"Deep Steel," Gloomy Davis dryly commented. "Reminds me of an ole girlfriend back in Hooker, Oklahoma . . ."

Thumbs Jones rolled his eyes in a long-suffering expres-sion. Mad Dog rumbled, "Fu-uck, Gloomy. *Everything* re-minds you of an ole girlfriend."

Brandon had the detachment stack its gear at the back. The men were just finishing when four other young men filed into the room. They also wore tiger-stripe cammies. One of them barked like a sea lion.

"Good morning, cunts!" the leader of the group sang out. "I see the domestic help has finally arrived."

He wore the bars of a naval lieutenant on his cap. He was young and fit, a few inches shorter than Brandon, with coal-black hair cropped short and eyebrows so dark and sinister-looking they appeared to be stage-painted on his face for a role in a play about Satan.

"Lucifer!" Brandon said, scowling. The other Deltas bris-tled visually.

"Fucking-A ditty bag. Your Mark One Mod Zero basic SEAL fucking weapon," Lucifer replied, grinning a truly evil grin. Only Lucifer could insert more "fucks" in a single ut-terance than Mad Dog Carson.

Two of the other SEALs seal-barked while the third, a chief petty officer in his early thirties with a blond mustache and blue eyes, looked embarrassed.

"Toss 'em a herring," Mad Dog suggested.

"I see you commanders have met," Lieutenant Colonel Callahan observed, looking both amused and a little aston-ished at the encounter between the two bands.

Brandon had worked with Lieutenant Sean L. "Lucifer" Shape in Bosnia before the War on Terror began. An Annapolis grad, a ring knocker, Lucifer was an arrogant, pushy son-ofabitch who was almost as good an operator as he thought he was.

Brandon was wrong. There was going to be a problem after all.

CHAPTER 12

The priority being placed upon Operation Deep Steel became apparent by the number and ranking of brass who showed up for mission briefing. It seemed the entire top crust of Special Warfare and the War on Terror hierarchy was present, starting with MacArthur Thornbrew, director of the National Homeland Security agency. General Darren Kragle, USSOCOM, arrived with Delta's commander, Colonel Buck Thompson, and General Carl Spencer, who headed the Joint Special Operations Command (JSOC). CENTCOM's General Paul Etheridge escorted in Admiral Sheldon Nimitz, NAVSPECWARCOM from Coronado's Navy Special Warfare Center.

Along with the top commanders came an assortment of operations, intelligence, communications, and logistics officers carrying briefcases. The only man in civvies was introduced as Thomas Hinds, deputy director of the Central Intelligence Agency. He was built like a college halfback starting to turn a little to pot in his middle age. He parted his dark hair straight down the middle.

"Who's manning the store while they're all here?" Gloomy Davis wondered aloud, awed by the turnout.

"Fu-uck," Mad Dog carped, pronouncing the expletive in two distinct syllables, which served to magnify its obscenity. "One good fart would catch them all in a stink storm."

There was a chill between Major Kragle and Lieutenant Lucifer that transmitted itself to the Deltas and went beyond healthy interservice rivalry. The three enlisted SEALs seemed all right, even though filled with themselves.

Chief Petty Officer Kenny Gorrell, in his thirties with a square jaw, blue eyes and blond mustache, was the quiet SEAL who felt no apparent necessity to bark like a sea lion every few minutes, a major plus for him.

The barkers were Ordnanceman Second Class Claudius "T-Bone" Jones, a shortish concrete block of a man with dark hair and a nervous habit of cracking his knuckles that was even more annoying than his barking; and Boatswain's Third Class J.D. McHenry, a dark Indian-looking kid, whip-thin and built for speed. He was from Oklahoma.

"No shit, an Okie?" Gloomy said. "From where at?"

"Fort Supply. Where do you come from?"

"Hooker."

"Hooker! You mean the Hooker Hogettes and Arachna Phoebe?"

The other Deltas stared in astonishment. Gloomy cracked a rare grin. "Everybody out there knows Arachna Phoebe," he explained to his teammates, feeling validated.

"Take seats!" a staff weenie major ordered.

The single table compelled Deltas and SEALs to mingle. Mad Dog pulled up a chair, absently opened the munchies package next to his target folder and began snacking. None of them had had lunch yet. It was a minute or two before he or any of the others noticed what was on the packages—a picture of Yasser Arafat superimposed on a Palestinian suicide bomber wearing an explosives belt. The writing was all in Arabic.

"Look at this shit," Mad Dog invited.

General Kragle noticed the interest, as he intended, and stepped to the podium. His was an impressive figure in dress greens with ribbons decorating both sides of his breast.

"It's a new food group," he said. "They're called The Hero cheese puffs. 'Terror snacks' manufactured in Egypt. Three percent of all profits go to the families of suicide bombers like those who hijacked our airplanes and crashed them into the World Trade Center. It's another illustration of the fanaticism we're up against in the War on Terror."

Disgusted, Mad Dog spat chewed food back into the package and deliberately crumpled it in one huge hand. Chief Gorrell got a trash basket and collected packages from everyone. He spat in it, put the can outside the door, and returned to his seat next to Lieutenant Lucifer.

General Kragle waited until the room settled down and the brass took seats in a semicircle behind him.

"I'll deliver the 'Situation' portion of the operations order for Deep Steel," he announced. "Leave your folders closed for the time being."

He paused, then resumed. "On June 22 and 23, the Center for Strategic and International Studies under federal supervision conducted a Dark Winter exercise to test the nation's capacity to deal with a hypothetical bioterror attack unleashed simultaneously with weapons of mass destruction against several U.S. cities. Gentlemen, our nation may be facing a crisis."

He let that sink in. He had his audience's attention.

"From a Dark Winter command bunker at Andrews Air Force Base, the participants established that thirteen days from the time of the attack America would come apart at the seams. The U.S. would be thrown into chaos by acute vaccine shortages and the overwhelming of medical facilities and emergency responders. Fleeing, panicked citizens would, in this scenario, quickly spread the plague zones outward to twenty-five states and fifteen countries. Radioactive fallout from a 'dirty' detonation would contaminate large portions of the states in which the explosions occurred, resulting in even more panic and the slow deaths of more thousands of people. If WMDs and smallpox struck as few as five of our largest cities simultaneously, civilization would damned near be destroyed in this country."

Lieutenant Lucifer expelled a pent-up breath. Brandon had never seen his father so bleak.

"We know three things with certainty," the General went on. "First, we know that terrorists possess bioweapons, as we discovered last year during the anthrax attack. Second, they either have or are on the verge of attaining nuclear devices, which they are acquiring from rogue nations like Iraq and North Korea. Third, they are making concerted efforts to smuggle these devices, along with the means of deploying them, into the United States. There has been speculation bolstered by some evidence that missiles may already have been delivered across our borders.

"A week ago, Delta Force soldiers present in this room recovered evidence of radioactive plutonium from an Abu Sayyaf camp they raided with Filipino Rangers on the island of Mindanao. Abu Sayyaf and its current leader, Albaneh Mosed, who calls himself *commander,* are affiliated with Osama bin Laden's al-Qaeda and as a result can tap into rich financial and international transportation networks. You may open your folders now."

The SpecOps warriors needed no further invitation. They dived into the blue folders with burning curiosity.

"That brings us to Operation Deep Steel and Combined Detachment 2-Bravo," the General resumed. "Gentlemen, Army Delta Force and Navy SEALs—"

T-Bone Jones barked.

"—will work together because your combined skills and talents are required. Major Brandon Kragle is ranking officer. He has recently been in the Philippines and butted heads with Albaneh Mosed. He has more front-action CT experience than any other front-line operator in SpecOps. He will receive the full cooperation of every man on the detachment. Any interservice rivalry and competition between the services will cease as of this moment. You are all members of the Special Operations community. Is that clear?"

The barking SEALs barked. Thumbs Jones grunted, "Hoo-ya!" Lucifer cast a glance at Brandon. General Kragle looked up and down the table. He nodded.

"General Carl Spencer from JSOC will present the 'Mission' portion of the briefing. General Spencer."

The JSOC took General Kragle's place at the podium. He was a no-nonsense man of about fifty with an iron-gray crew-cut and an angular build.

"Your mission folder," he began, "contains area studies, target data, communications CEOIs, weather—which is expected to get progressively worse—and other essential elements of information. Let me preface all this with background.

"The United States has seemingly open borders that are an invitation to terrorists hell bent on our destruction. We have 361 river and seaports through which some 95 percent of foreign trade passes. The danger lies in the millions of cargo containers being brought in and transited around the country, the hundreds of ships moving in and out of these ports daily, and literally hundreds of private airfields along the borders and seacoasts. The fact is that our Coast Guard, Immigration, and Customs personnel are not sufficiently equipped or numerous enough to guard our ports or the thousands of miles of shoreline. We cannot prevent—I repeat, we *cannot prevent*—entry of weapons into our country with any more success than we've stopped drug trafficking. Therefore, we must not sit at home and wait while terrorists arm themselves and prepare to strike. We must find and destroy threats to our national security wherever in the world they surface."

Cassidy Kragle listened, engrossed. He had hardly moved since the briefing began. This was his first experience with the procedure.

"The *Reader's Digest* version of the scenario," General Spencer continued, "is that we have long suspected certain rogue nations—I say *rogue,* not *nations of concern* as in the previous PC administration—of providing weapons to terrorists. The President has referred to them as the 'Axis of Evil.' The CIA has successfully infiltrated a number of agents into shipping believed to be transporting arms. The enterprise has largely been unsuccessful. We have too few qualified personnel to cover the demand. However—Mr. Hinds, would you like to cover this topic?"

The college halfback in civvies stood up. The CIA deputy director had a graveled smoker's voice.

"Those few qualified personnel we *do* have," he said, "are exceptional people. Night before last, one of our undercovers aboard the Saudi-registered freighter *Ibn Haldoon* reported that three SS-1 SCUD missiles were loaded aboard the ship in the North Korean port of Nampo. We have not been able to reestablish contact so far. At this point, we don't know if our undercover was compromised.

"The *Ibn Haldoon* departed Nampo at 0530 yesterday morning. Its destination is listed as Manila. It is being tracked by satellite and appears to be in the correct sea lane for the Philippines."

One of the lower-ranking officers on the briefing staff, a rather portly captain with a puckered mouth, got up and lifted a drop cloth to reveal a large blow-up photograph of the ship.

"We suspect the freighter is going to offload the SCUDs at a prearranged rendezvous point with Abu Sayyaf somewhere in the southern Philippines," the CIA deputy concluded. He looked to General Spencer and sat down.

General Spencer resumed the briefing. "SCUDs are perfectly capable of nuclear or bio delivery at short range," he said. "We expect the Philippines are only a way station for the missiles en route to sleeper terrorist cells in the United States."

He paused and looked out on the silent room where even a sigh echoed.

"The President called an emergency meeting in Washington, D.C., yesterday, out of which came an executive finding to deploy Special Operations forces. Deep Steel's mission is to take out those missiles and destroy the ship without the action being attributed to the United States."

Mad Dog Carson translated underneath his breath: "The U.S. will disavow all knowledge if we are captured or killed."

"It must be implicit, if not explicit," General Spencer continued, "that anyone who delivers weapons to our enemies will pay a price. The concept of the mission is explained in detail in your folders. Summarily, the action will proceed in this manner:

"Detachment 2-Bravo will rendezvous with Polaris-class submarine USS *Sam Houston*, which is following the *Ibn Haldoon* even as we speak. To avoid possible compromise, and to avoid pulling *Sam Houston* away from the *Ibn Haldoon,* you will be choppered out of Manila and inserted by helo-casting. The sub is equipped with a dry deck shelter for an Advanced SEAL Delivery Vehicle, an underwater minisubmarine, which I understand your contingent of SEALs are experts at."

"When is the insertion, sir?" Major Brandon asked, eager to cut to the chase.

"You must be introduced into the AO (area of operations) as quickly as possible. A storm is brewing to the west of the Philippines. The *Ibn Haldoon* may be counting on it to conceal its movement from satellite and aircraft surveillance. You have twenty-four hours to memorize your folders and get prepared."

The team members exchanged looks of surprise.

"We'll be ready, sir," Brandon said.

"Good. Mr. Hinds of the CIA, as well as operations, intelligence, and logistics personnel from USSOCOM, CENTCOM, JSOC and NAVSPECWARCOM will remain with you to assist readiness until you depart Camp Peary. Now, as your folder explains, you will first extract our agent from aboard the *Ibn Haldoon*. You will then wait and watch until the freighter makes its rendezvous with the terrorists before you destroy the ship and any other terrorist vessel it contacts. Postmission recovery, as explained in detail in your folders, will be accomplished by the USS *Sam Houston* working with the aircraft carrier *Abe Lincoln*. The *Abe* is being dispatched immediately to those waters in support."

Lieutenant Lucifer raised his hand. "Sir, why not simply get the agent off the freighter and let aircraft from the *Abe* take care of things?"

"The *Ibn Haldoon* flies a Saudi flag," General Spencer explained. "Saudi Arabia is ostensibly an ally, although a questionable one at times. The freighter is also transporting cargo from North Korea. Both the Saudis and the Koreans would consider it an act of war if we attacked overtly. But if the ship is covertly destroyed, the message will still get across without our throwing down the gauntlet. Plausible deniability will prevent international confrontation and soothe the President's peacenik critics on Capitol Hill. Needless to say, you will go in sterile, without identification or markings that may tie you to the United States."

Winnie Brown leaned toward Mad Dog Carson and whispered, "If I catch one this time out with my name on it and check out, I've left three thousand dollars in a bank account for Troop One to celebrate the good times in my name."

"I assume Ice Man, our gourmet chef, will prepare the

meal," Mad Dog said, then added sourly, "What's the matter with you, Winnie? Talking this shit."

"It's for good luck," Winnie said. "I've always had an account for this purpose—and I've always come through. It's like a lucky rabbit's foot."

"And look what happened to the lucky fucking rabbit."

"Hold down the grabass," General Spencer admonished. "All other questions as to details will be answered either in your folders or during the 'Execution,' 'Service Support,' and 'Command and Signal' portions of the briefing. Men, good luck out there, and God go with you one and all."

CHAPTER 13

ABU SAYYAF THREATENS TO KIDNAP AMERICANS

Washington (CPI)—MacArthur Thornbrew, Director of the President's National Homeland Security Agency, warns Americans traveling abroad that Abu Sayyaf terrorists have threatened to kidnap or execute prominent Americans around the world. The threat comes on the eve of the deaths of two American missionaries in the Philippines and the wounding of the wife of one of them.

Abu Sayyaf guerrillas, reportedly affiliated with Osama bin Laden's al-Qaeda network, demand a separate Islamic state. Under the leadership of a man named Albaneh Mosed, they have terrorized the southern Philippines with a string of kidnappings and brutal executions. The U.S. has dispatched more than 1,500 Special Operations troops to the Philippines this year to help solve the terrorist problem.

Materials were recently captured indicating terrorists in the Philippines and elsewhere may be developing or obtaining nuclear weapons capable of being used within the borders of the United States. Increased security has been initiated by the U.S. Coast Guard and the Homeland Security Agency in an attempt to prevent devices of mass destruction from being smuggled in . . .

CHAPTER 14

Florida Straits

After two days at sea, senior FBI agent Claude Thornton still felt a bit stomach-queasy. Sleeping in the Coast Guard cutter's bow compartment where his stomach turned at every swell and wave had bolstered his opinion that his son attending the Naval Academy at Annapolis must be a glutton for punishment. Perhaps a career in the U.S. Navy was okay for Junior, but for a Mississippi boy grown up on a sharecropper's farm Claude had preferred to keep solid land underfoot. He was even beginning to regret at the moment being a hands-on administrator who used every excuse to participate in and see for himself how the domestic side of Operation Enduring Freedom, the War on Terror, was being conducted. Old habits were hard to break. The miracle of satellites and modern communications furnished him the means to go into the field while he continued to keep in touch with Quantico and the FBI's National Domestic Preparedness Office.

By all accounts, the deal would come down sometime that night and the wait would be over.

Restless, Thornton climbed to the flying bridge of the USCG *Padre* to get a little fresh salt air while he scanned the blue horizon in the direction of Cuba, not really expecting to see anything yet. Just watching and trying not to think of his stomach. He wore a blue uniform PADRE ball cap to protect his shaved head from the tropical sun. Even men as black as he were susceptible to sunburn.

The sun, a bloody red, slid into the Caribbean, leaving the ocean darker and the sky a thin, pale blue streaked with color. On the foredeck below, Coasties removed the protective cover from a mounted .50-caliber machine gun. The boat's armorer, a chief petty officer, came out on deck carrying a .45 Thompson submachine gun. Two other petty officers accompanied him, one armed with a pump shotgun, the other with an M-16.

It wouldn't be long now. An hour earlier, the targeted aircraft, an ancient C-47 two-propper, made a landing approach to Jamaica and disappeared from the radar of the Coast Guard Falcon Interceptor flying its trail. If it followed usual smuggler procedure, it would circle the island at wave-top level and fade into Cuban protected airspace. Castro's Cuba had long served as a "safe house" for smugglers running South American cocaine to the noses of Yankee gringos.

Caribbean Snow, however, had not brought out the director of the Domestic Preparedness Office, nor had it been the purpose for assembling an armada of CG Falcon Interceptors, Dolphin helicopters, cutters, forty-one-foot patrollers, and other small boats from CG Key West and CG OPBAT (Operations, Bahamas, Turks and Caicos). Everything went into place early that morning when the word finally came down. Since noon, *Padre* had been patrolling slow circles in open seas north of the Cay Sal Bank seventy miles southeast of the Florida Keys.

The C-47 that had at that point disappeared somewhere within Cuban airspace ran something far more lethal than cocaine. Although intel failed to specify precisely what it contained, it presumably cargoed nuclear materials, "dirty bombs," perhaps a missile. Another terrorist attack was being planned. CIA intel generated in Bogotá and Panama indicated terrorists would attempt to funnel WMDs into the Southern states using cocaine routes that had proved so successful for dope smugglers over the preceding thirty years. Even though the President's meeting in Washington, which Thornton attended with General Kragle, resulted in the President's authorizing SpecOps to intercept suspect shipping in international waters under Operation Deep Steel, thereby attempting to stop missiles and nukes near their source, it wasn't enough. In the high-level intelligence briefing presented after Deep Steel was authorized, Director Thornbrew warned that the Korean connection was only one of several attempts terrorists were making to smuggle WMDs and missiles into the United States. It would take a coordinated effort by all the elements of the military and Homeland Security to stop them.

Of the Coast Guard's ten districts protecting U.S. shores, the 7th District was one of the largest and by far the busiest. It stood guard over 1.8 million square miles of Atlantic, Caribbean, and Gulf of Mexico waters. Its AOR (area of responsibility) touched twenty-four foreign countries and included Puerto Rico, the U.S. Virgin Islands, and most of the Caribbean from the Yucatan Straits to the coasts of Colombia. Its U.S. continental area alone had 1,600 miles of coastline that included the states of Florida, Georgia, and South Carolina. During the most recent ten-year period, 7th District Coasties and the DEA (Drug Enforcement Administration) interdicted in excess of $200 *billion* of contraband drugs.

Thornton couldn't help reflecting, however, that only one load of dope out of every twenty inbound for the U.S. was ever discovered and confiscated. Those who estimated such things said the total value of cocaine and marijuana that actually reached the U.S. would pay off the entire national debt within two years.

By the law of averages, Thornton ruminated, take something even as big as twenty intercontinental ballistic missiles, disperse them on boats, ships, and airplanes across the Caribbean, head them for the United States, and nineteen of the twenty would successfully make it to the woodlands and hills of Florida, Georgia, or Mississippi.

Thornton's eyes narrowed. Those weren't odds in favor of the good guys.

The ocean gradually turned black. First stars appeared, hard and bright. The FBI agent removed his cap to let the balmy night breeze cool his shaved head. The ship rocked gently on the sea, maintaining only enough speed to keep it slowly circling in its holding pattern.

He turned at the sound of footsteps climbing the steel ladder to the flying bridge. Captain Roscoe Monroe was a salty redhead in his late thirties. He wore blue utilities, a PADRE ball cap and had buckled on a sidearm.

"The plane left Cuba," he announced. "Our interceptor picked up the target on FLIR and is now tailing it on a heading of one zero degrees. It's coming."

Thornton nodded. If the C-47 followed protocol, it would maneuver on either of two options, depending on its cargo. If its freight were lightweight, such as the nuclear materials with which guerrillas escaped in the Philippines, it would clip waves to some predesignated spot somewhere in the isolated Cay Sal Bank where it would make a night drop to a shrimper or "cigarette boat." Sometimes smugglers used flotillas of fast boats that scattered to confuse any possible surveillance or pursuit.

If the cargo were heavier, such as a missile, the plane would ride the waves off the coast in international waters until it suddenly zipped in to land at some small isolated airfield.

Coast Guard aircraft had earlier located and placed under surveillance suspected receiver watercraft. Pursuit vessels, such as the *Padre,* waited out of sight over the horizons, ready to block escape routes. Military aircraft and radar installations were alerted along the coastlines in the event the aircraft attempted to penetrate U.S. airspace without authorization.

It appeared at this point that the C-47 intended to make a night drop.

Captain Monroe picked up the handset and had the XO pass control of the cutter to the open flying bridge. He took the wheel and opened throttles briefly to test torque after hours of slow cruising. The ship rocked as its wake caught up with it. Red and green running lights lit up port and starboard.

"How long?" Thornton asked.

"Less than an hour. Funny," he mused after a few minutes, starting a conversation to fill the time, "how half the population in the world is trying to get to America to live while the other half wants to destroy us. Sometimes it's hard to figure why the Islamics hate us so much."

There was little else to do but talk while they waited. Agent Thornton was almost as outspoken and opinionated as his friend, General Kragle. Especially when it came to terrorism and threats against the nation, the protection of which he had dedicated his life. To him, there were no African-Americans, Japanese-Americans, Hispanic-Americans, and all the other hyphenated American rot that divided people for political purposes. There were only *Americans*—and anyone or any nation that threatened *Americans* became his sworn enemy.

"I've lived and worked in Arabia for many years," Thornton said, hesitatingly at first but warming to it as Captain Monroe expressed a keen interest. "Listen to them and they'll tell you why they hate us. They say it's because we give arms to Israel—but at the same time we provide F-15s to Saudi Arabia and funnel hundreds of millions of dollars into Egypt and other Muslim countries. They hate us because of Iraq—but we're the only power that prevents Saddam from pulling a holocaust against Kurds and fellow Muslims. We protected Muslims in Kosovo and brought food to starving people in Somalia. Where were the Arabs and Muslim nations when all this was happening? They were providing hideouts and refuges for Osama bin Laden and his mad ilk. The World Trade Center was our reward."

Bitterness edged his voice. Captain Monroe encouraged him to continue. "It's a religious war then?"

"You bet your sweet bippy, know what I'm saying? I made many friends in Egypt and the Middle East and met Muslims I respect. But the moderates have all been intimidated into silence. There are millions of Muslims, even in America, who support the Islamic fanatics and would like to see us pounded into dust. Political correctness would have us call it something else, but if you want my opinion—"

"That's why I asked."

Thornton gazed out across the black gentle sea and the bright stars reflected in it.

"It's my opinion that Islamics want to control the world and convert it through mass global terrorism. They hate us mostly because we're nonbelievers, infidels, and because their mullahs tell them to hate us. Let's not automatically mark them off as a bunch of nuts either. Europeans are too wimpy to put up much of a fight and the rest of the world is disorganized and chaotic. That leaves America. Even many of our own wacky leaders will consider surrender to these thugs as the easiest path to 'peace.'"

"The President won't cave in."

"This war will extend beyond his presidency," Thornton said grimly. "If we're not careful, what we end up with is Neville Chamberlain appeasing the Nazis all over again. Peace in our time will turn into hell in our time. You asked for it, and that's this poor black man's opinion."

The C-47 flew so low that had the sea been choppy instead of as smooth as a sheet of black steel, it would have been picking off the tops of waves. The pilot, whoever he was, was skillful and knew his business; he had made these runs before. The CG Falcon that shadowed it flew at five thousand feet. A CIA observer behind the pilots' cockpit followed the target's progress on the FLIR (forward looking infrared radar) screen. There were a lot of boats down there. Some of them might even be legitimate. The others were dope smugglers, pirates, Cuban refugee runners, black marketers, revolutionaries of various sorts and other schemers. There were always a lot of boats between Florida and the Bahamas, fewer between Florida and Cuba.

The Coast Guard pilot alerted the elements of the seizure team when it appeared a drop was going to be made. Without reducing power—it *couldn't* reduce power at such a low altitude—the C-47 kicked out its bundles as it zoomed past a phony shrimper. Chemical lights blurred across the FLIR screen as large flotation containers tumbled briefly through the night sky and splashed down. Immediately, the shrimper kicked in power and began hooking the shipment out of the drink. The C-47 made a U-turn and set a course back to Cuba, climbing to a more normal altitude as soon as it was "clean."

"Go-fasts"—thirty-foot cigarette boats with powerful inboard V-8s—were waiting at predesignated spots to make recovery from the shrimper. They converged on it, running lights extinguished, and began transferring bundles from the fishing boat to their own.

The CG operations commander passed the signal for all elements to move in. Captain Monroe shoved in throttles. *Padre* roared and vibrated throughout her hull before picking up speed, rising up on her step, and racing toward the rendezvous site. Thornton followed the action on the radio that came alive once radio silence was lifted. Briny spray blew against his face in the night wind. He liked the exhilarating feel of it. Finally there was some action.

One of the go-fasts headed toward Florida with its bundles, on a track that would lead it across the *Padre*'s intended course.

"That bastard is *ours*!" Captain Monroe exclaimed, sounding as excited as a patrol cop on U.S. 1 pursuing burglars down through the Florida Keys.

A CG Dolphin helicopter started the chase when it blasted down out of the darkness, surprising the smugglers with huge floodlights and sky speakers: *"This is the United States Coast Guard. Heave to and stand by to be boarded."*

Instead of stopping, the cigarette boat took off soaring across the Florida Straits toward the distant Keys, cutting back and forth in a desperate attempt to elude the chopper's floodlights. The Dolphin air-skidded and chandelled as it maneuvered to stick with the fast boat. *Padre* vectored toward the action, angling to cut off the go-fast. From Thornton's place on the flying bridge, the chase appeared as a bright cone of light jerking erratically against the black horizon.

In the meantime, coasties from USCG *Bear* boarded the shrimper and seized unclaimed bundles from it and from the sea. Group Key West and OPBAT had enough cutters, helicopters and small boats in the area that most of the go-fasts were smartly captured, freeing assets to join the pursuit of the one bound for the Florida Keys. Choppers attached to cones of light filled the sky while forty-one-footers and RBIs (rubber boats, inflatable) hurried to arrange a reception in the shallow waters off the Keys.

Thornton got on the radio and attempted to determine the contents of the bundles seized by *Bear*. There was so much confusion around the chase, however, and undoubtedly the same kind of confusion and excitement at the scene of the shrimper, that the only information he succeeded in obtaining was that the contraband so far consisted of three pieces. That didn't include what some of the other cigarette boats might have picked up, or what the fleeing boat ahead of the *Padre* possessed.   .

To the experienced agent, that seemed a hell of a load for an airplane purportedly transporting nuclear materials. No terrorist band could *afford* that much nuke, even if it were available. Most *nations* didn't have that quantity available. Thornton had a bad feeling about that.

He raised on the air the Falcon that had tailed the C-47 from Cuba.

"*We're still with the target,*" the pilot reported. "*It's just now reentering Cuban airspace.*"

"Are you certain there weren't *two* airplanes?" Thornton demanded.

The pilot sounded galled, as though the director were questioning his competence and judgment. "*One airplane entered Cuba,*" he responded crisply, "*and one airplane exited.*"

He *expected* to see one airplane, Thornton thought, so that was exactly what he saw.

The pursuit lasted for more than two hours. The cutters, including *Padre,* pulled off just before encountering shallow water. Helicopters, RBIs, and forty-one-footers continued the chase. Surprisingly enough, the smugglers hadn't jetti-

soned their illicit cargo. Either they were afraid of consequences threatened by their superiors if they lost the merchandise, or they still harbored some hope of escape.

The go-fast crashed into mangroves on Islamorada. The
three frantic boatmen abandoned the craft and scrambled for
land, only to find themselves tackled by heavily armed RBI
crews, DEA agents, Duval County deputies, and FBI agents
from Thornton's Joint Terrorism Task Force. By the time
Thornton caught a small boat ashore, flashing blue lights
from cop cars lit up a section of Highway 1 like a carnival.
Lawmen and Coasties surrounded the three perps who,
soaked in seawater, lay handcuffed face-down on the pavement.

One of the DEA agents was ecstatic. He lugged into the
headlights a bundle recovered from the smugglers' boat and
slit it open with a knife. He reached in and extracted a small
plastic bag full of white powder.

"So far," he said, "we've found about seven hundred
pounds of nose candy worth nearly two hundred *million* dollars on the streets. This is one hell of a haul."

Agent Thornton looked at it, disappointment evident in the
slump of his shoulders.

"Was there anything else?" he asked.

The DEA man blinked. "My God, man. Isn't this
enough?"

Thornton walked off alone and stood in the darkness outside the lights and excitement of those unaware that the real
objective of the operation had been something far more vital
to the security of the nation than a load of cocaine. He gazed
south toward Cuba. There *were* two airplanes, he thought.
The law of averages dictated that one of them had succeeded
in entering the United States.

CHAPTER 15

Quantico, Virginia

Director Claude Thornton leaned back in his chair and regarded his caller from across the desk. He rubbed his eyes wearily. He had just returned from the Florida Keys and had not slept.

"Maybe I'm only a Mississippi nigger sharecropper's son," he said, "but I'm sharp enough to know when we've been had."

Deputy CIA director Thomas Hinds looked frustrated. "The intel we had was good," he insisted. "The airplane we followed *into* Cuba had nuclear materials aboard. The one we picked up on the way *out* of Cuba were dope smugglers with the most incredible bad luck to be somewhere at the wrong time."

"I don't think it had *anything* to do with luck," Thornton responded. "The dopers were a deliberate decoy. It's a shrewd plan. The dope smugglers get caught if there's been surveillance while the actual cargo gets delivered by a second plane, know what I'm saying?"

Hinds took a deep, speculative breath, considering it. He took a sip from his coffee. "That's good java."

"Black is beautiful."

The CIA deputy director looked around for an ash tray. He was a chain smoker, the effects of which had hoarsened his voice. "Mind if I smoke?" he asked while he thought over the situation.

"Mind if I fart?"

"Damn, Claude. The only thing worse than a reformed drunk is a reformed smoker. I remember when you smoked three packs of unfiltereds a day."

He put his cigarette pack away and regarded his old friend with a troubled look.

"Okay, Claude," the spook conceded, "let's grant the terrorists threw us off and succeeded in getting a nuclear device through. Now what?"

"It may not be the first," Thornton said. "I have a feeling there's something big about to go down. If the tangos have nuclear materials and the technological capability of building a warhead, all they lack is the means to deliver it. We know the *Ibn Haldoon* is attempting to turn over SCUD missiles to Abu Sayyaf in the Philippines."

"Terrorists don't need missiles. All they need is a crazy to carry a suitcase nuke into the Mall of America and blow himself up for Allah and the jihad. Besides, the *Ibn Haldoon* missiles will soon be on their way to the bottom of the Pacific."

"Can we be sure that other missiles haven't already been smuggled into the U.S.?" Thornton pointed out. "The terrorists wouldn't put all their eggs under the same hen. All your intel said about the Cuban misadventure was that nuclear materials were aboard the plane. Could there have been a missile? Could there be a number of such planes sneaking into the United States?"

"Well, unfortunately, the answer is yes to both questions. But they don't *need* a missile . . ."

"It's not a matter of need. I think they want missiles to prove something politically. A suicide bomber is one thing, but imagine the demoralizing effect on the American public if two or three missiles bearing nukes or bios were fired simultaneously. Then, having proved their ability to do so, terrorists announced they were poised to fire two or three more—"

"We'd have a panic."

"John Stanton and Senator Thierry and their cronies," Thornton said with distaste, "would scream for a truce, for appeasement, for anything to 'stop the violence'—and people and politicians would listen to them and demand we surrender. It would create a crisis in government we haven't experienced since the Civil War. And for all we know, Thomas, missiles could be concealed right now in old barns or buildings near Chicago or Oklahoma City or Denver."

Hinds looked as tired as Thornton felt. "Claude, I can't speak for what may already be *inside* the country. The American people won't stand for CIA snooping at home, so that ties our hands and makes us merely spectators here. I'm not passing the buck, but the FBI and Homeland Security have jurisdiction in-country . . ."

"The buck's in our corner," Thornton acknowledged. "I have the JTTF spread out from Florida to Texas trying to come up with something on the terrorist base. I'm flying to Georgia tomorrow morning. Fred Whiteman's team picked up some ragheads at a municipal airport in St. Marys. That's right on the coast. They were flying a C-47."

"Cargo?"

"None. There's evidence they might already have dropped it off."

The CIA deputy stood up slowly. "Claude, if those terrorists have brought something in, we have to find it before they have a chance to use it."

They shook hands solemnly. There was nothing else to say.

"If you need me," Hinds said, "I'll be no more than five minutes from contact with my secretary until this thing in the

Philippines is over. We also have a little flame in Haiti to stomp out. Something about VIP hostage-taking."

"Maybe I'll start smoking again," Thornton said.

"Maybe I'll start farting."

CHAPTER 16

East China Sea

CIA deputy director Thomas Hinds had had reservations about sending a female agent into such a dangerous under-cover assignment, but in the final analysis had had to make use of available assets. There were simply not enough males—not enough of *anybody*—in the Agency proficient in Arabic, Mid-Eastern, and Far Eastern dialects to cover the territory. Summer Marie Rhodeman, the tiny half-Jewish young woman whose father was a former Israeli army officer and her mother a Texas belle, was literally a genius when it came to Middle Eastern and Arab dialects.

A suicide bomber blew up her two younger sisters in Israel when Summer was sixteen years old. Her parents brought Summer back to the U.S. where she would be safe. The CIA recruited her out of Yale University and promptly sent her back to work in the Middle East. She had successfully passed as Ismael, a boy, in Afghanistan during Operation Iron Weed, fooling both Northern Alliance mujahideen and the Delta de-tachment infiltrated into the mountains on assignment. She felt she could do it again.

"You're too valuable an asset to sacrifice," Hinds had instructed her. "If anything happens, just transmit the emergency signal and we'll get you off that boat."

"It's a ship, a freighter. Boats are what you paddle around in on the duck ponds in Central Park."

"You really *are* a wiseass, Summer."

"*Ismael* is the wiseass."

It amused Summer to think how Brandon first knew her as Ismael the wiseass in Afghanistan. He would be horrified if he knew she was back at it again. He could be so old-fashioned when it came to women. Still, they had no investment in each other. They both agreed to it.

The crew of the *Ibn Haldoon*, including its captain Darth Vader, accepted Ismael's cover as a Saudi brat whose wealthy parents apprenticed him out to sea to "make a man out of him." The CIA had somehow arranged it; Summer had no need to know the details. It had been an easy passage to Hokkaido, where the freighter took on a small amount of cargo. A diversion, Summer suspected, to camouflage the ship's true business, which was expected to take place when the *Ibn Haldoon* ported in North Korea.

She managed to get a message through on SATCOM about the illicit cargo and had received an acknowledgment. She knew nothing of the plan to stop it and extract her. Again, she had no need to know. The less one knew while undercover, the less one revealed if caught. She had to trust in the CIA and in her country.

The sumo wrestler with the scarred face who boarded in Nampo with his WWF buddy and the ninja posed an immediate threat. Cimatu immediately singled out Ismael upon whom to lavish his attention. He was either a little light in the boots and liked boys or, worse yet, suspected that the small seaman with the remarkable emerald eyes wasn't a sea*man*. His greedy eyes seemed to burn right through her disguise.

He attempted to cop a feel in the galley during mealtime when he "accidentally" bumped into her, either for the thrill of it or to check her out. He didn't get much. Loose pantaloons with underwear stuffed and padded in front and a thick tight wrap around her breasts underneath her loose chambray shirt foiled his clumsy effort.

"You are pleasing like a girl," he leered in broken Arabic. Summer suspected he must be Filipino.

"You are pleasing like a pig," she shot back.

For a moment she thought she might have gone too far. Cimatu scowled, drawing his left eye down onto his cheek. Just what she needed—a fight with a brute the size of Hulk Hogan. Then he threw back his great shaved head and roared with mocking laughter.

Just what she needed—a would-be suitor who didn't care if she was a boy or a girl. She would have to make an extra effort to stay out of his way until she extracted and U.S. forces boarded the freighter to seize and destroy the missiles.

It also wasn't enough that she must avoid a nutty pervert bigger than a Volkswagen. Foolishness and sympathy made her take on responsibility for three kids fleeing the Bamboo Curtain. What was the matter with her? Wasn't she the notorious Ice Maiden, cold-hearted, with ice water for blood, a mission-comes-first bitch without feelings? If Darth Vader discovered the kids, he likely uncovered her identity as well.

Brandon said it best: You could always depend on Murphy's Law—anything that could go wrong *would*.

Cimatu, his buddies, and some of the sailors were clearing out a tool storage locker next to the Koreans' hiding place in the rope locker when Summer attempted to deliver breakfast to her little charges. Cimatu's men had already removed the inner wheel-lock on the hatch so it couldn't be opened from the inside. It almost appeared they were clearing out the locker and making it secure in order to use it as a cell. Why couldn't they have selected some other compartment on the freighter's port side instead of this one in this particular passageway? Murphy's Law. It puzzled her, but she didn't stick around to ask questions. She pretended to be on some other mission. The Korean children had to go hungry.

The evil grin on Cimatu's hideous face suggested he thought Ismael the pretty sailor man actually came belowdecks looking for him because he was so irresistible. The disgusting bastard. Summer had killed men before when it was necessary and mission and survival required it. It was something she never relished. However, she thought it wouldn't bother her a moment to personally pop a cap on this man.

She tried again at noon meal when everyone came to the galley to eat. She stuffed rice and dates, bread and roast lamb into the front of her loose trousers while she ate quickly, adroitly avoided Cimatu, and hurried belowdecks. No one occupied the dimly lighted passageway. The watertight hatch next to the Koreans' rope locker stood slightly ajar. Summer looked inside out of curiosity and found that everything had been removed except for an empty five-gallon paint bucket. It seemed the ship was anticipating prisoners. But who? And why?

The ship wallowed in a trough and banged the open steel hatch against the back of her legs. The seas had grown rougher and the winds stronger as the *Ibn Haldoon* departed the more-protected Yellow Sea and sailed onto the edges of the East China Sea on a course for the Philippines. Summer felt secure in the knowledge that military satellites were tracking its progress.

She thought about moving the children to another hiding place, but decided that might be riskier than leaving them where they were. She supposed the Koreans and she were lucky the rope locker hadn't been selected for remodeling.

With a final look around, she wheeled open the hatch to the rope locker, stepped inside, and secured the hatch behind her. She was off-watch and wouldn't be missed for awhile.

The compartment lay against the outer hull of the ship. A small porthole dispelled some of the gloom with pale gray light. The children were nowhere in sight, having followed her instructions to hide whenever they heard footsteps or saw the wheel on the hatch turning.

"Jang?" Summer called out softly. "Jang, it's me."

The locker was a storage area for not only rope but all manner of other seafaring stocks and tackle—chains, cargo nets, machinery, crates of various rusted tools . . . It smelled of soured seawater, rotted wood, and stale air. After a moment, three heads popped up from behind piles of junk against the far bulkhead. The teenager, thirteen years old at most, and two tiny waifs with big eyes and coal-black hair smiled at her.

She sat near them on a thick coil of hawser, gave them a bottle of water, and removed food wrapped in oriental newspapers from her trousers. The little girl, Lee Soon, and her younger brother, Gil Su, stared hungrily at it but politely refrained from touching it until Jang gave permission. Then they dived into the dates and rice as though they hadn't eaten in days, which they probably hadn't. Jang refused to eat anything until he was sure his siblings would have enough. He looked gaunt, starved, his face hollow around protruding cheek bones that made his eyes look enormous.

"Eat, Jang," Summer encouraged. "I'll bring more after the evening meal."

They ate their fill rather quickly, their stomachs having shrunk. Jang saved leftovers in case they had to eat later. All three children kept their eyes on their benefactor as though they didn't quite trust her.

Summer hadn't decided how she was going to get them off the freighter when the time came that the Americans launched their raid. Were she alone as expected, she simply would go overboard when things started and wait to be picked up at sea by submarine or fast boat. She couldn't do that with the kids. Nor could she leave them behind to certain death. She kept postponing reporting the situation to her control station, afraid of what her orders might be. Again and again, she had heard it stressed that emotions and sentimentality must not interfere with a job. Missiles capable of deploying nuclear strikes against U.S. citizens could slaughter hundreds of thousands; by comparison, the lives of three Korean waifs meant nothing. Neither did the life of an American agent, for that matter, even if she were a valuable asset.

The two younger children spoke only Korean, a language in which Summer lacked proficiency. However, no language was needed to express what happened after Lee Soon finished eating. The little girl decided she trusted Ismael after all and crawled up on the hawser next to Summer and lay her head against her protector's arm. After a moment's hesitation, Summer encircled the child with her arm and drew the tot close. Lee Soon immediately fell asleep. Jang smiled sadly.

"Where is your mother?" Summer asked him.

The smile vanished. "My mother is passed," he said in his fair English.

Summer inhaled deeply. "How about your father?"

Jang's eyes clouded and he dropped his chin to his chest. He seemed unable to speak. Rather, he got up and produced a sketch pad from a small worn valise that constituted the travelers' entire luggage. He sat down on the other side of Summer while Gil Su edged over and rested his head on Summer's knee. Jang opened the pad to display one-by-one a series of crude but heartbreaking sketches done in colored pencils.

"A teacher gave to me pencils and this paper and ask me to

put on it what we see in our home," Jang explained. "He say I must show it to the free world if ever my brother and sister and I are free too."

The first sketch depicted a North Korean soldier shooting in the head a prisoner tied to a stake.

"This is our father," Jang said in a hoarse whisper. "They shoot him because he go under the wire nets at an orchard to get grapes for us. We are hungry and everyone is starving."

Another sketch showed a Korean woman sitting on a bridge overlooking a stream where a little boy and girl seemed to be pleading with her. Jang translated the caption written beneath the drawing.

"Mother is saying, 'I am unable to satisfy your little bellies. It is not worth living.' Sister is saying, 'Mommy, I promise not to ask for more food. Please do not kill yourself.' "

Summer's eyes clouded. She looked at Lee Soon sleeping in her lap. The little girl gripped her clothing with both hands, as though afraid to let go.

"Is that how your mother . . . passed?" Summer asked past the knot in her throat.

"It was not yet her time."

Another rendering showed a woman on her knees while a soldier stood with one foot on her infant. A silent tear eased onto Jang's hollow cheek.

"This is my mother and our baby sister," he said. "After Father passed, we escape to China with some neighbors, but the Chinese send us back. Our little sister came into this evil world while we are in prison. A doctor and a guard come to our cell. The guard step on the baby's neck until it stop breathing. The doctor push some scissors into the baby's brain to make sure she is dead. My mother become ill after that and she die of a broken heart. It was my mother who teach me English because she say one day we will go to America and an American must speak English."

The story told in such simple, stark terms touched Summer's heart. She blinked back tears; she hadn't cried in . . . She couldn't remember the last time she cried. Jang's drawings reminded her that terror was more than fanatics running around blowing up people and buildings. There were still places in the world where states and their leaders officially sanctioned terror against the weakest and most humble of their own people.

She didn't want to see more. Jang turned the page.

"They are Kochebis," he said, indicating children hiding in a cave. "They are without parents. Gil Su and Lee Soon sleep inside the cave with the other little ones while we older are staying toward the entrance to protect them."

The last drawing showed a red-and-white ship, the *Ibn Haldoon*. In it were Jang and his brother and sister and a young Arabic-looking man whom Jang identified as Ismael. Jang apparently drew it that very day while they languished in hiding. The Ismael figure had a yellow halo over his head.

"We are going to America," Jang said. "America will not send us back."

"Yes. You are—" Summer's throat caught.

Whatever it took, Summer vowed, she was going to get these little stowaways safely to the United States. They deserved it after all they had been through.

She explained that she had to get back before she was missed. She warned them once again to stay hidden and not to leave the locker for any reason unless she gave them permission. Jang had already located a bucket to use as a toilet.

"Keep it covered to keep down the odor," Summer warned.

She looked back at them from the hatch and gave them a smile of encouragement. She listened a moment for movement in the passageway outside, then spun the wheel and cracked the heavy door. She looked out just in time to see Cimatu swaggering down the passageway toward her. She closed the hatch immediately, frantically motioning for Jang and the little ones to hide. They darted for piles of debris against the darkened far bulkhead and disappeared like mice in a city dump.

She heard Cimatu stop outside the hatchway. He had seen her after all. She checked around for any scraps of food or other items that might betray the children. Her mind sought an explanation for what she was doing down here.

The wheel on the hatch turned. The door started to open.

Her eyes settled on a large spanner wrench. Thinking quickly, she picked it up and pushed the hatch door the rest of the way open. She pretended to be surprised when she saw the scarface.

"I needed a tool," she said in Arabic, casually brandishing the spanner and stepping into the passageway past the smirking mountain. She started to close and seal the hatch.

Cimatu blocked it. Curious, he stuck his head through into the locker and looked around. Summer pretended not to care what he did.

"Secure the hatch when you finish," she said in an offhand way and made to walk off. Her heart pounded as he started inside.

He stepped back out quickly to keep her from escaping. He moved in front of her with his evil grin.

"Come inside with me," he offered. "I have a tool for you."

She brandished the spanner. "I have a tool for you, pervert," she shot back.

"Ohhh . . . I *like* little boys with fire."

"Be careful I don't burn your ass," she said with as much bravado as she could muster.

He laughed and let her go. She heard the hatch clang shut and the wheel turn but dared not look back to see if he had gone in or stayed out. A wave of relief swept over her when Cimatu's lust-throaty voice called after her. He had accepted her explanation. The children were safe.

"Ismael," he taunted, "we have time."

CHAPTER 17

Fort Bragg, North Carolina

A dozen years ago, *Desert Storm*'s one hundred-hour ground war began in the dark along a 250-mile line stretching westward from the seacoast. The U.S. Marine Expeditionary Force led the push. The XVIII Airborne Corps brought up the left flank. The U.S. Army VII Corps came next, with its two armored divisions and its platoons of M1A1 Abrams main battle tanks. Then-corporal Cameron Kragle, only nineteen, rode an Abrams at the trigger of its 120mm tank killer gun. His head had started hammering as soon as word came to start moving. The faster the tank moved, the nearer it drew to the enemy, the harder his heart thumped against his ribs. He was going into battle for the first time. Inside the lining of his helmet he had inscribed a verse from Psalms: *A thousand shall fall at your side and ten thousand at your right hand, but it shall not come near you.*

The tanks raced across the salt flats. They grunted and chuffed up a kind of broken wadi. Cameron stared into the therma-imager. He saw ghostly, glowing, boxy shapes swimming in a kind of green mist. The TC's voice blasted through his helmet. "BMPs! Kragle, what the fuck's going on? Get on your fuckin' gun, boy."

BMP—a Russian-made infantry fighting vehicle with a

.74 smooth-bore and a Sagger antitank missile launcher.
Cameron froze at his gun.

"Sagger!" the tank commander was yelling. "Get that
fuckin' Sagger!"

He must not dishonor the General . . . He must not dishonor the General . . .

He went through the firing sequence automatically, just as
he had been trained. The Abrams lurched with the recoil. The
BMP exploded. Little man-figures appeared in the hatch,
scrambling out of the inferno. Machine-gun fire ran them back
inside the burning vehicle. It burst into full flame, white phos-
phorus sparking as the machine blackened and settled into the
ground with its load of infantry. Cameron imagined how they
must have been screaming as they died trapped in hell.

"Oh, my God!" What had he *done*?

Minutes later, a Sagger rocket slammed into Cameron's
Abrams. Cameron never recollected how he got out through
the hatch past the TC and out of the tank. He remembered the
TC yelling out, cussing at him, trying to tell him they were
still in action. Damaged but still in the fight. They were trying to stop him, and he was screaming in such terror that he
wet and defecated his pants.

Nothing, not even Satan himself, could have stopped
Cameron from getting out of that steel coffin. He ran blindly
back in the direction from which they came. Wild-eyed and
terror-stricken at what he had done to others and what others
were doing to him.

Combat MPs policed him up wandering alone in the desert
the next day. He would have been court-martialled for cowardice in the face of the enemy except for the General's inter-
vention. The General couldn't have it said that one of *his*
sons was a craven coward.

Cameron's faith had been weak. His faith in God had not
sustained him.

So what right had he as an army chaplain these years later to preach about faith and courage and moral duty in the face of the enemy when he himself had *run*? Never mind that he had redeemed himself—*redeem* was his father's word—during Operation Punitive Strike and been awarded the Silver Star for valor. He had had much more to fight for then. It was personal. Gypsy was killed anyhow.

Cameron's Sunday services on the previous day asked the questions: *Should the Christian fight for his country? Did God's Commandment* Thou shalt not kill *apply literally to soldiers in war, and, if so, how did God expect free Christians to deal with enemies set on destroying them? Did God really mean for Christians to turn their other cheeks all the time?*

The tall chaplain, wearing a dress green uniform and his green beret, was still pondering the questions the next morning when he parked his black Chrysler on the predawn street in front of the little white wooden church on Smoke Bomb Hill at Fort Bragg. He strode inside and turned on the main lights. He always left the door unlocked. Although he was officially assigned to Delta Force as its chaplain, he requested and received a church accessible to the entire Special Operations community, including the 82nd Airborne. Still, even a good Sunday rarely swelled his congregation to more than one hundred. Tough, gung-ho SpecOps soldiers thought they didn't need God—or at least they thought so until bullets started flying.

He paused inside the door, seeking tranquility and spirituality from the simple building. Up front on a little raised stage stood the pulpit, backdropped by a royal purple curtain displaying a large golden cross and the motto GOD IS GOD IN ALL LANGUAGES. The General might speak of redemption on the field of battle, but it was in the house of God that Cameron sought true redemption. His ordination as a minister of God and his commissioning as a chaplain in the U.S.

Army symbolized his deliverance from the world of sin and the flesh.

"Lawdy, Lawdy, honey-chile, I be so proud every time I done see you walking with Our Savior Lord Jesus," Gloria had said the last time he saw her, her pride in him always evident. "My Raymond also be a good God-fearing man, else I never marry him. These am the end times, honey. Jesus is coming. I wants to be ready. You the preacher, so it be up to you to get the rest of the fambly ready for the Coming. You got a job cut out for you too when it come to your daddy and your brothers."

In spite of himself and his moral convictions, Chaplain Cameron occasionally envied his brothers. He sometimes thought of himself as the *outside brother*. Not only was he blond and blue-eyed like their dead mother, whereas Brandon and Cassidy were dark like their father, he also lacked the Kragle direct-action black-and-white mentality. Living in a world they saw as clearly divided between right and wrong, they depended upon themselves, their skills, their inner resources, and each other. All they had to do was discern the right path and go for it.

Cameron on the other hand depended upon his faith in God and love of the Redeemer who shed His blood on the cross. Even so, he often felt inadequate in his faith. His faith had not sustained him in crisis during Desert Storm. One day, he realized, his faith would be tested again. It was necessary that his beliefs be strong and clear.

It was his fate as a man and as a minister to forever wrestle with his theology. Constant vigilance was the price he must pay to retain and sustain it.

Christian soldiers shipped to Afghanistan and elsewhere to fight the War on Terror confronted the same issues about God with which Cameron continued to struggle.

"It is moral to defend your nation from brutal people who wish to kill and enslave," he advised his Sunday morning worshippers. "A better expression for a 'righteous war' is a 'moral war.' The Sixth Commandment exhorting 'Thou shalt not kill' seems to be clear. But the Hebrew word for 'kill' in this commandment refers to 'murder.' 'Thou shalt not *murder.*' The Bible tells us that there is 'a time to kill and a time to heal . . . a time of war and a time of peace.'

"You should know that God may be a God of war when you are called upon to defend your homeland. He said He would teach your hands to make war. Jesus Himself is known by titles of war, such as 'Lord of Hosts.' Jesus is the leader of the armies of angels in heaven. He has never lost a battle yet . . .'"

The chaplain glanced at his watch. It was time to be getting on his way. Department of Army had assigned him to represent the military Christian community at the Hands of God Conference in New Orleans. The week-long congress had been organized in a stated effort to foster better understanding and communications in the United States between Christians, Muslims, and Jews. Cameron remained uncertain as to what good it might accomplish. He doubted the radical sects of the Muslim community would show up, the ones who wanted to destroy the infidels, who argued that they were like Joshua in the Old Testament when God told him to destroy the Canaanites by killing men, women, and children, along with their cattle, goats, camels, and dogs. Leave no remembrances of them behind.

Cameron elected to motor down. He liked long drives. Sitting behind the wheel provided him opportunity for sustained thought. Besides, he felt uncomfortable traveling commercial air since 9/11.

He walked briskly to his small office to the right of the steps and gathered notes and references he would need to write the following Sunday's sermon. He also retrieved the family Bible given to him by Little Nana before she contracted Alzheimer's. He knelt at the altar with it and opened it to Hebrews, Chapter 11, which seemed to apply to the issues of war and warriors.

. . . For the time fails me to tell of Gideon, and of Barak, and of Samson, and of Jephtha; of David also, and Samuel, and of the prophets; Who through faith subdued kingdoms, wrought righteousness; obtained promises, stopped the mouths of lions; quenched the violence of fire, escaped the edge of the sword, out of weakness were made strong, waxed valiant in fight, turned to flight the armies of the aliens . . .

He thought of his two Delta brothers who had suddenly been called to conduct a top secret mission somewhere in the world. The Hebrews passage seemed to have been written specifically with them in mind. They went out to "wax valiant in fight, turn to flight the armies of the aliens" while the chaplain remained behind to go to a conference and pray for peace. After all, a man of God should be above the fray, shouldn't he?

The chaplain prayed for his brothers, he prayed for American soldiers everywhere in their battles against terrorists and terrorist regimes.

"Thy will be done. Amen."

He rose, went out, got in the Chrysler, and drove out the front gate toward New Orleans.

CHAPTER 18

MacDill Air Force Base, Tampa, Florida

The idea of war being directed from a distance was not new. Count Alfred von Schlieffen, head of the German general staff from 1892 to 1906, predicted that modern communications would allow generals to direct battles from maps at substantial distances from the battlefield. Napoleon in the dust of Waterloo, MacArthur fighting off the Japanese in the Philippines, even General Norman Schwarzkopf directing Desert Storm from the sands of Saudi Arabia were melodramatic anachronisms from a past age. Wars were going high tech into a new space age where military commanders and strategists got the "feel" of battle from directing it thousands of miles away instead of actually on the battlefield. General Darren Kragle called it "video-game warfare," as impersonal and sanitary as kids shooting *Star Wars* baddies in a video arcade.

In Central Command (CENTCOM) headquarters at MacDill Air Force Base, enough brass gathered around satellite-fed TV screens to draw lightning. CENTCOM's General Paul Etheridge, a decorated combat veteran who nonetheless resembled a soap company CEO more than he did a commander of armies, played host to USSOCOM's General Kragle, Delta's Colonel Buck Thompson, NAVSPECWARCOM's Admiral Sheldon Nimitz, and General Carl Spencer from JSOC, Joint Special Operations Command.

CENTCOM provided all the command and control necessary in a combat theater. From there, aircraft, ships, ground troops could all be viewed by satellite feed. Sophisticated commo and video allowed commanders to make decisions and to have a sense of a situation in real time. There was an immediate transmitting of orders to the field and instantaneous communications back and forth that Schwarzkopf would have envied during the Gulf War.

After 9/11, discussions ensued among the Joint Chiefs of Staff and the Washington high command over whether or not the major command post of the War on Terror should be moved to bases in Saudi Arabia or elsewhere near potential war zones. General Etheridge argued that CENTCOM should remain at MacDill since it already oversaw interests in the twenty-five nations in the Afghanistan region and since the War on Terror would likely change locales from time to time, and rather quickly at that. General Kragle thought he ought to be on the ground near his troops. In the end, however, he had to agree with Etheridge. Operation Deep Steel was a case in point. The situation was fluid and moving hour by hour, from ports in North Korea toward unknown destinations in the Philippines.

The danger of video warfare came in treating real people out there as mere computer code, abstract figures in an elaborate game. General Kragle thought he would never succumb to that temptation. He had been on the battlefield, smelled the gunpowder and blood, understood fear and courage and duty. Plus, there was also the matter of his two sons. Both were at this moment on a helicopter flying out of Subic Bay en route on a mission to intercept missiles intended for terrorist hands.

General Kragle rubbed soreness around his eyes acquired from staring too long at TV and computer screens. One of the satellite screens showed the Saudi freighter *Ibn Haldoon* in rough seas steaming south. It had become clear by late afternoon, Philippine time, that the freighter would not port at Manila as manifested.

A major who ran one of the ops shops popped into the large operations center. "Sirs? We have a weather update. It doesn't look good."

"How bad?" General Etheridge asked. Weather had been a factor to consider since Deep Steel was initiated.

"Predictions call for deteriorating weather throughout the evening and night. More weather is forecast for the rest of the week. There's a low pressure south and west of the Philippines brewing up a typhoon. We may lose our satellite feed."

As though to emphasize that possibility, the screen showing the *Ibn Haldoon* plunging through white caps flickered, blackened, then picked up again.

"What's the difference between a typhoon and a hurricane?" General Spencer asked.

"They're hurricanes if they form in the West Indies, typhoons if they form in the Pacific Ocean," the major said.

General Kragle continued to stare at the screen. "How much time before it hits?"

"It's forecast for two days, maybe three," the major replied, "but has started to pick up speed since this morning. There's weather there already."

On the wall a huge backlighted map on glass showed the Philippine Islands. Three movements were depicted on it— the Saudi freighter; a U.S. submarine; and an MH-47E helicopter, all bearing to converge in a region south and west of the island of Luzon. A fourth movement considerably north and east depicted the nuclear aircraft carrier USS *Abraham Lincoln,* dispatched with its aircraft to support Operation Deep Steel were it required. The carrier had changed course at noon to skirt the budding typhoon.

"There's still time to pull the detachment back to Subic," Admiral Nimitz noted.

"The team should be all right if it can link up with *Sam Houston* before nightfall," General Etheridge responded. He watched the televised freighter. "I suggest we give things another hour to see what shakes loose. If the *Ibn Haldoon* changes course and runs for port, we'll know it's not going to meet the terrorists yet. We can call in Deep Steel then. Otherwise—"

He glanced at General Kragle.

"Otherwise, we can't afford to lose it in all those islands and take a chance on terrorists getting the missiles. I recom-

mend the mission remain a go as long as the missiles are a
go. Agreed?"

General Kragle knew he shouldn't think of his sons. Mission always came first. You had to take chances in war. Operation Deep Steel and the destruction of the *Ibn Haldoon*'s
cargo were vital to the national interest. Lose those missiles
now and the next place they surfaced, along with nuclear
warheads, was Philadelphia or Washington, D.C.

"Agreed," the General said.

In one hour, if the situation remained as is, Delta Det 2-B
would helo-cast into the sea to rendezvous with the submarine *Sam Houston*. The General was glad he let Gloria think
the boys were still at Fort Bragg.

All anyone at CENTCOM could do now was wait and
watch the screens while the communications center coordinated traffic. General Kragle leaned forward in his chair before the screens and sipped from a coffee cup, not
relinquishing his vigil except to make a quick run to the la-
trine. General Etheridge chain-smoked cigarettes and Admiral Nimitz chewed on a sandwich. It smelled like tuna fish.

God, this new kind of war was hell.

"The freighter's continuing," General Kragle observed at
last. "It knows where it's going and is confident it can reach
safe harbor somewhere in the islands before the storm breaks."

"The Nightstalker helicopter is reporting it has reached its
destination," General Etheridge reported. "We're making the
drop. The insertion is a go."

General Kragle tensed but said nothing. Almost no words
were exchanged for the next quarter-hour as the Center
awaited confirmation of the detachment's link-up with the
submarine. Marrying the Delta detachment with the submarine at sea was risky business. But it had to be done—first for
speed, second because the sub couldn't be called off the
freighter's trail. It and the Deltas it was taking aboard had to

be ready to strike immediately when the time came.

The satellite screens continued to flicker. They blanked out abruptly. Colonel Elton Rogers rushed into the war room.

"General Etheridge, sir," he exclaimed. "We just received a message from *Sam Houston*. It's experiencing reactor problems and will be delayed. He said he was unable to get through until now because his commo was also acting up."

General Kragle shot to his feet. "Delayed? How long?"

"He said two hours, maybe three."

How could this be happening? All that technology brought to its knees by a little weather!

"Pull the drop if there's time," General Kragle snapped.

General Etheridge was already moving. "Get Deep Steel on the horn immediately," he ordered the commo chief. "Use my code and order the link-up aborted. Understood? Abort immediately."

"Yes, sir."

Colonel Rogers darted off, followed by most of the brass in the war room. He took the handset personally in the commo center. After a hurried exchange, he looked up, his face draining of blood.

"Too late, sir," he said. "The detachment has already been dropped. The helicopter can't retrieve them in these seas in the dark. They're going to have to wait for the submarine."

CHAPTER 19

South China Sea

Joint Exercise Balikatan involving U.S. and Philippine forces battling terrorist guerrillas in the islands had reopened the old U.S. Navy base at Subic Bay to a limited number of U.S. military personnel. Mostly SpecOps types. Detachment 2-Bravo counted on a single helicopter leaving the base attracting little notice from terrorist spies. Last-minute preparations were under way. The twelve men of the team, all clad in tiger-stripe camouflage devoid of insignia or markings of any kind, sterile as to country of origin, repacked rucks and rechecked weapons. Weapons, mostly for close-range combat, consisted of 5.56-caliber carbines, a stubby MP-5 submachine gun, Brandon's personal choice, Gloomy's .300 Winchester, and Mad Dog Carson's shotgun.

Because of the compressed-time nature of the mission and lack of time for logistical coordination, the detachment had to jump into the drink with virtually all the gear it might require for a vessel take-down on high seas—Draeger SCUBA gear, navigation boards, explosives, weapons, ammunition, communications gear, flotation, grenades, medical supplies . . . Even Mad Dog Carson grunted when he finished waterproofing and packing his PRC-137 radio into his ruck and hefted the full pack to test its weight.

"I'm going straight to the bottom with all this shit," he complained.

Each ruck with attached, tied-down weapon container was filled with flotation so it wouldn't sink. A ten-foot nylon line would be D-ringed to each ruck and snapped into its owner's combat harness to prevent their being separated once the detachment hit the drink. No one should be in the water anyhow more than a quarter-hour, a half-hour at most, before the submarine surfaced and took the detachment aboard.

Cassidy Kragle and the two Joneses—Thumbs from Delta and SEAL T-Bone—worked on packing explosives, electrical and mechanical blasting caps, det cord, and other materials. Young Doc TB inventoried his medical supplies. Everyone worked cheerfully, on a high as always at the start of a mission, eager to get into the operation. Mad Dog teased Ice Man about his gourmet cooking while Ice Man dismantled a Glock pistol and repaired its firing pin. Master Sergeant Winnie Brown oversaw preparations. He was turning into a good team sergeant.

"Winnie Pooh took 'mommy' lessons from Mother Norman," Mad Dog teased. "Say, Winnie, you wanna come over here and wipe my ass and blow my nose for me?"

"Not unless we have a HazMat team on standby," the senior NCO shot back.

SEALs T-Bone Jones and J.D. McHenry barked in chorus.

"Squids," Mad Dog said.

Gloomy sidled up to J.D. "Looky here, Injun," he said, "did you ever attend the big mountain oyster-eating contest back in Hooker? You had to eat 'em raw, right off the vine, so to speak. Well, Arachna Phoebe decided she'd enter—"

"Arachna had experience at that sort of thing, along with salami-swallowing," J.D. put in.

"Arachna was a *lady,* J.D."

"A lady that can swallow a salami is *my* kind of slut," J.D. shot back with a lewd grin.

Lieutenant Lucifer went by and cast them a look. "You ass-wipes wouldn't know a lady from a fucking rubber blow-up doll," he said.

"Fu-uck," Mad Dog said under his breath and walked off. Banter and rough, good-natured insults among men of equal or near-equal enlisted rank was good for morale and esprit de corps. For an officer to attempt to join it before he was accepted and invited violated the code and was tantamount to insult. Lucifer should have known better. Brandon turned away, trying to hide the disgust in his expression.

"What's between you and Lieutenant Lucifer?" Cassidy wanted to know.

"It goes a long way back," Brandon said and left it at that. It was bad for morale when commanders had bad blood between them.

The sun was still shining when the MH-47E SpecOps helicopter took off from Subic, gained altitude and passed over the Walled City and the Pasig River and on out over the sea. Soon, however, banks of clouds were blotting out the low western sun, leaving an ugly gray light. Lightning crackled against the glowering horizon. A wind blew up out of nowhere, battering the wave tops into froth. The modified Chinook scooted along above white mare's-tails wind-whipped into the crests of waves. The popping of its red-and-green running lights lent it an impression of urgency.

Plans called for the detachment to be aboard the submarine *Sam Houston* before nightfall. But night was coming early because of cloud cover. A half-hour before scheduled insertion, Brandon checked with the pilots to see if they had received confirmation from USSOCOM or commo from the sub. A negative on both counts.

"Get ready!" he called out above the noise as he returned from the cockpit, thrusting out both palms in the visual signal.

Because of unexpectedly heavy seas, 2-Bravo would fast-rope out of the chopper instead of helo-casting. The helicopter lowered its tail ramp as the time approached, opening up a panorama of wind-whipped seas and distant lightning. Brandon balanced himself at the edge of the ramp, holding on with one hand against the jolting ride while with the other checking the thick rope of woven wool to make sure it was securely fastened to the aircraft. They flew so low that he tasted salt spray and felt the cold whip of seawater against his face.

Lieutenant Lucifer checked the second rope on the other side of the ramp. The ends of the ropes lay coiled at their feet. Brandon consulted his watch, then looked back into the red-lighted interior where Winnie Brown had already formed the detachment into two sticks of five men each, a stick lining up behind each rope. The aircraft was too noisy for conversation; there was no need for conversation at that point anyhow. The men put on gloves and held onto the walls of the bucking aircraft for balance and waited for the signal to unass it. They wore inflatable black personal flotation devices that, along with rucks attached to their combat harnesses in front, made them look fat and misshapen in the dim light provided by red night-vision lights.

Brandon cast an eye down at the white-capped seas passing underneath. Less than optimum conditions for what should otherwise have been a routine maneuver. Lucifer seemed unconcerned; SEALs were half-fish anyhow. Brandon gave another consult to his dive watch, turned toward the men and thrust out one hand, fingers splayed. *"Five minutes!"*

He grabbed the aircraft crew chief and had him ask the pilots over his helmet intercom if there had been any last-minute word from USSOCOM. There hadn't been. How about from the submarine? Nothing from it either. Was there supposed to be? It was employing radio silence to avoid giving itself away to possible enemy RDF tracking capabilities.

Okay. Launch time. Red paratrooper signal lights on either side of the open tail ramp blinked twice. The helicopter pulled speed to a precarious hover. The red signal lights turned green. The bird bucked and yawed against the rising wind. Brandon, followed by Lucifer, tossed his coil of rope at the white caps. He lost his footing and nearly went out with it. He recovered and saw the tops of waves snatching at the thick rope, popping it like a whip. Blowing brine stung his face.

Good thing, he thought, they were being inserted instead of extracted. Any team in *this* stuff depending on the chopper to pull it out might be in the water for a very long time. Especially with night falling.

The officers thrust their palms toward the sticks, then crisply pointed to the ropes. "*Stand in the door!*"

Winnie Brown led Lucifer's stick. Ice Man led Brandon's. Brandon snapped a point at Ice Man. "*Go!*"

Ice Man went out immediately, followed hard by Mad Dog, Thumbs, Cassidy, and T-Bone Jones. On Lucifer's side, Winnie released his grip on the chopper and reached for the rope with gloved hands. The helicopter bounced out from underneath his feet. He lurched sideways, made a last desperate grab for the rope before he plunged head first out the awful yaw of the open ramp to disappear into the sea.

There wasn't time to see to him. He should be all right, having merely made a rather impromptu and unintended helo-cast, albeit head down and face first.

"*Go! Go! Go!*"

"That fucking sub better be there!" J.D. McHenry screamed as he went out, barking.

The detachment vacated the bird in less than five seconds. Brandon and Lucifer went out last. Wave action at the bottom of the rope caught Brandon and jerked him off. The sea felt almost warm after the wind against his wet skin. The helicopter lifted immediately, taking blade wash with it, and vanished into the blackening sky.

"Bring up the head count, Winnie!" Brandon called out. It would be too easy in the rough sea and darkening sky for the team to get separated. No reply came from the ops sergeant, but the detachment was already assembling, calling out to each other as the men alternately bounced high on swells and rolled into the deep following troughs, bobbing in their life vests like fishing corks. As they found each other, they roped themselves together to prevent scatter.

Brandon activated his CSEL, Combat Survivor Evader Locater System, a combined GPS receiver/transmitter and remote tracking beacon that signaled the submarine to surface and pick them up. Lucifer carried a backup. The submarine should rise within minutes.

Winnie Brown still hadn't been found. Finally, Cassidy spotted him bobbing when a wave lifted him into view. Cassidy and Chief Gorrell left their floating rucks with teammates, swam out and brought him back to the group. The top sergeant was unconscious, his breathing ragged. Doc TB made his way over, coughing and sputtering, and examined the comatose soldier as best he could under the circumstances for broken bones and other obvious injuries.

"The only thing I see is a mark here on his throat," he finally concluded. "I think his larynx is crushed. He must have struck something in the water when he fell out. He probably also has a concussion or a skull fracture. Major, he's in bad condition."

A freak accident. Murphy's Law again.

"Can you do anything for him, Doc?" Brandon asked.

A swell lifted the medic and deposited him on its other side, separating him from the others. He splashed back to them, coughing from swallowing more salt water.

"Foolish question," Brandon acknowledged. The rest of the detachment gathered in a protective circle around the injured man.

"Major, he's breathing, so he has a patent airway," Doc TB said. "What I'm concerned about is shock. It won't take long in this cold water. We have to get him somewhere warm and dry, quick."

The sub should have picked up the signal and surfaced by now.

"All right, lets not get separated," the major said. "Cass, link in to Winnie and Doc. I'll tie us into the SEALs."

It got darker, quickly. There was little talking. What could you say? In addition to having snapped themselves together, the men grasped each other's battle harness and formed a tight knot. Their rucks floated on attached lines outside the perimeter. Winnie's breathing hoarsened and there were long seconds when it seemed he would not catch another breath.

"Where the hell is that fucking piece-of-shit submarine?" Lieutenant Lucifer chafed.

"Maybe my CSEL's not working," Brandon said. "Activate yours, Lucifer."

They turned on strobe lights so the boat could see them in the dark when it rose. Mad Dog attempted to make an emergency contact with a Motorola hand-held radio, but picked up only static.

"Abso-fucking-lutely wonderful," Lucifer exploded. "Fuckers have left us out here with our balls hanging out."

Then the sharks came.

CHAPTER 20

In addition to its ability to smell blood from a quarter-mile away, a shark has excellent hearing. It can hear a struggling fish or a human swimmer at a considerable distance, up to one thousand yards. A long blasting flicker of lightning revealed the first telltale dorsal fin slicing the crest of a comber that rose black and fearsome above the floating human raft of Detachment 2-Bravo. The fin looked easily two feet in height. It lifted with the heavy inhalation of the sea and then fell toward them on the exhale. It sank, disappearing into black depths.

Deltas and SEALs alike were almost without exception combat veterans. Disciplined, hardened soldiers who laughed in the face of danger. Yet, they fell party to all-too-human fears as they imagined the giant predator warily circling them to make its selection.

"Eenie meenie minie moe," T-Bone Jones recited deadpan when the shark failed to reappear.

"Thumbs, are alligators and sharks kinfolks?" Mad Dog wanted to know. "If that shark gets Thumbs, he won't get a complete nigger. Not with that thumb gone."

"You are one sick puppy, Dog," Thumbs replied, unoffended.

Sardonic conversations out of blackness. The dark humor of men facing death, whose only authority over it rested in their capacity to defy it.

"I understand parts of a shark are edible, Ice," Mad Dog said, selecting another victim. "Tastes like scallops."

"You catch that motherfucker, Dog, and I'll cook it."

They all bobbed, tethered together, the taste of brine and fear in their mouths. Gloomy Davis said he finally understood how a worm on a hook felt. Lucifer cursed the submarine for not being on time.

Lightning danced on the sea across the horizon, backlighting the reappearance of the shark's awful dorsal as it cleaved the black water, circling, probing. A little way behind it followed a second fin, small only in comparison to the exceptional size of the first.

"I feel like an Early Bird Special buffet on South Miami Beach on Sunday afternoon before the line opens," T-Bone Jones murmured.

He and J.D. hadn't barked once since Chief Gorrell reminded them that a shark's favorite food was sea lions. And SEALs, Mad Dog added. There was no accounting for a fish's bad taste.

Clouds snuffed out the lightning, plunging the world back into darkness. Sharks made no noise when they stalked or when they attacked. The men fell into an expectant hush.

Ice Man Thompson broke it and his customary laconism. He cried out in surprise, a single guttural whoop, when the big fish brushed against his legs like a Volkswagen covered with sandpaper. The force of the shark's passage lifted him out of the water, the horror on his face recorded in a crack of lightning that left his open mouth and wide eyes seared to the backs of everyone's eyes. Lines secured to T-Bone on one side and Thumbs Jones on the other jerked him back into the water.

The shark missed its first attack. Men began shouting and kicking and splashing to drive it off.

"Belay it, you fucking landlubbers!" Lieutenant Lucifer bellowed. "In its fucking shit-for-brains it sees us as a school of bait fish trying to get away. Damn you all, be still."

Brandon recognized it as good advice. He added his voice to Lucifer's. Shouting and splashing ceased.

"Turn off your strobes," Brandon ordered. "Light attracts fish."

The winking strobes provided no real light anyhow. In between lightning, earth dissolved into a black hole out of which, unseen, the monster might return at any moment.

Lucifer's voice sounded strained, his breathing rapid and hoarse. "Listen up, turds," he said. "You're all panting like a bunch of cunts in heat. Control yourselves. Put your legs together and your arms alongside your worthless fucking sides. Pretend you're driftwood."

They were quiet then. Waiting. Dreading. There were no more wisecracks. They felt the sharks circling. It reminded Brandon of the USS *Indianapolis*.

During World War II, the battle-scarred heavy cruiser *Indianapolis* was torpedoed and sunk in the Pacific by a Japanese submarine. Three hundred men went down with the ship in twelve minutes. More than 900 others went into the drink where for four horrific days and five nights they were savaged by a pitiless sun and schools of blood-frenzied sharks. Sharks ate almost 600 of them, pulling them down one or two at a time.

"Everyone unsnap your lines to each other and hold them in your hands," Brandon ordered.

They understood. No sense in the shark dragging them all under when it made its selection.

Doc TB disconnected himself from the unconscious Winnie Brown. He and Cassidy struggled to keep the ops sergeant's nose and mouth above water. Winnie already looked dead. Intermittent shimmers of sky electricity revealed a face soapy pale and slack in the wash of salt water over it.

Cassidy fumbled with the snap link that connected him to the injured man, his hands stiff from the cold water. Suddenly, before he could unsnap, something happened to Winnie. A glimmer of awareness seemed to penetrate his brain. His muscles tensed like a drawn bow. Maybe it was a nightmare, a hellish premonition. He flailed the water furiously.

That was what it took to help the shark select from the menu. There was a violent surge of water, an unseen presence as the excited beast closed in. It grabbed Winnie's legs like a trout taking a fly and tugged him under. He was gone, stripping Doc TB's line from his hands.

Cassidy, however, remained attached. He bobbed as the line to Winnie tightened. Then he was gone too, pulled under with Winnie, his line in turn plucked from Mad Dog's grip.

Rucks secured to both men skipped across the water, like bobbers on a farm pond pulled by pesky perch. Lightning illuminated a white wake created by the dragged flotation. Fortunately, the floating rucks hampered the great fish's dive.

Acting more from instinct than hope, Brandon released his ruck and life vest and dived deep into the black water after the shark and his disappearing brother. He dived blind, pulling the ocean around him with strong strokes. He drew his Ka-Bar. Intent on hand-to-hand with the predator if that was what it took.

How would he explain his brother's death to the General? And to Gloria?

The fish rolled with Winnie in its jaws as sharks will with a kill, boiling the underwater into a tornadic vortex. Brandon tasted blood in the water. The shark's wide tail slapped him across the head and sent him reeling in the swirling water. He collided with someone else. It wasn't Cassidy. A second swimmer? Who else could be foolhardy enough to dive after a feeding shark?

This someone else had obviously latched onto Cassidy and was being dragged with him. With his free hand, the other swimmer grabbed Brandon's battle harness, a handhold for a drowning man, and pulled Brandon with him.

Darkness. Churning violence. Brandon's lungs burned. He was burning air. If he didn't surface soon he would be forced to gulp death into his lungs.

Thanks to the unknown swimmer, the additional weight of two men curbed the shark's deep progress and speed. With a final desperate effort, Brandon clawed his way past the unknown rescuer and felt Cassidy's ankle held in the man's grip. The man released Brandon as though discerning Brandon's intention. The shark had almost stopped in the water, though it had not relaxed tension on its prey and the line that led from Winnie to Cassidy.

Brandon worked his way hand over hand along Cassidy's struggling body until, still blind in the water, he felt the vibrating rope that linked Cassidy to Winnie and the shark. There was nothing that could be done for Winnie now. A flick of Brandon's razor-sharp Ka-Bar cut the line, permitting the shark to continue its depth-searching dive with its original victim.

Flotation immediately popped the ordeal's three survivors to the surface. Lightning flickered above the turbulent water, revealing to both Brandon and Cassidy the face of Cassidy's other savior. The dark face, black hair, and Satanic eyebrows of Lieutenant Lucifer.

CHAPTER 21

FORMER PRESIDENT KIDNAPPED IN CUBA

Havana (CPI)—Former President John Stanton was kidnapped this morning from Havana's José Martí Airport during farewell ceremonies with Cuban dictator Fidel Castro. Stanton was completing a five-day "goodwill" tour in Cuba when gunfire and explosions suddenly erupted from near a Lear Jet hangared at the airport.

Witnesses say that as many as ten men armed with machine guns and rocket launchers poured from the unidentified aircraft, catching security forces by complete surprise. There has been no explanation as to whom the Lear Jet belonged, where it came from, or what it was doing at the airport.

The assault and kidnapping covered a time span of less than five minutes.

"There was shooting everywhere," said Autberto Palma, a member of Cuba's national assembly. "I got down on the ground. When I looked up, five or six of the *terroristas* were rushing President Stanton to the airplane. He was crying and shouting for help. They threw him into the jet—and it took off very quickly."

The aircraft escaped while the Cuban Air Force was being scrambled. Radar at Homestead Air Force Base in Miami, Florida, picked up the jet briefly, then lost it when it dropped underneath radar coverage.

Three security officers were killed and eight wounded in the fierce exchange of gunfire. One kidnapper was slain and left behind. He has been tentatively identified as Ferdinand Salapuddin, 26, a member of the Filipino Islamic separatist group Abu Sayyaf.

The kidnapping took place as Stanton prepared to return to the United States. It occurred just as Castro proclaimed that, "Friends can be found even among my country's worst enemies, and I consider President Stanton one of these friends . . ."

Stanton's abduction further tests U.S.-Cuban relations, already strained over accusations that Castro may be supporting terrorist acts against the United States. Stanton opposes the U.S. embargo on communist Cuba and is campaigning for its repeal.

U.S. Secret Service agents are not permitted entry to Cuba. The U.S. State Department warns all Americans, including former Presidents, that it cannot protect them while they are on the island and that they travel there at their own risk.

Reactions inside the U.S. was immediate shock. Senate Majority Leader Jake Thierry, one of President Stanton's close associates, demanded immediate negotiations to free Stanton, whom he termed a "national treasure . . ."

CHAPTER 22

MacDill Air Force Base, Tampa, Florida

The War on Terror was a war of many fronts, unlike anything America had ever confronted. Brush fires constantly broke out at unexpected points around the globe. A suicide bombing in Tel Aviv, a hijacked aircraft in Frankfurt, another kidnapping in Colombia, Chechen rebels seizing a theater full of hostages in Moscow, assassination of American missionaries in South Africa . . . Sometimes it seemed to General Darren Kragle that Gloria might be right. "Lawdy, the worl' be going to hell in a handbasket."

The abduction of former president John Stanton was merely another of these brush fires as far as General Kragle was concerned. And not even a major one. News of it reached CENTCOM right after it occurred, but the major commanders of U.S. Special Operations—CENTCOM, USSOCOM, JSOC, NAVSPECWARCOM, Delta—were preoccupied with the Philippine operation of Deep Steel. It seemed none of them had moved from in front of the satellite monitors within the last two hours except to drain coffee cups and burn up cigarettes, even though the monitors were black from loss of satellite feed. The air in the room felt stale, the atmosphere one of sitting up with the dead.

It was nightfall in the Philippines and the fate of the men

of Deep Steel remained up in the air. They were in the drink at last report, the helicopter that dropped them there unable to pick them up again. The submarine *Sam Houston* had repaired its mechanical problems and was en route to their location.

General Kragle ran big hands through his short-cropped hair. He felt uncomfortable with the idea of video-game warfare where commanders directed things from the safety of home plate. A leader should be out there in the mud and the blood with his men, sharing the hardships and the fuckups caused by the brass.

"Unexpected SNAFUs are part of the fog of war," General Etheridge tried to reassure him. "There was nothing that could be done."

"Unexpected SNAFUs are unacceptable, sir," General Kragle shot back. "*We* fucked up. We planned and executed this thing so quickly that we neglected contingencies."

Flexibility and mobility were essential characteristics of Special Warfare, but sometimes you could move so fast you cut yourself off from support. Deep Steel had been conceived, planned, organized, and launched all in a matter of slightly more than forty-eight hours. You had to move like that to stomp out brush fires. Moving like that built in errors.

Colonel Buck called Fort Bragg and alerted Troop Three, designated as backup unit for Deep Steel 2-Bravo. He advised Major Keith Laub to have a detachment ready to move on an hour's notice—in the event Major Kragle's detachment found itself unable to continue. Admiral Nimitz already had SEAL replacements on a navy aircraft bound for Pope Air Force Base to link up with Laub.

General Kragle at the same time forewarned the Special Operations commanders of the Air Force, Navy, and Marine Corps of the Stanton situation and ordered them to stand by for further instructions should anything break loose. It was mostly a waiting game for the time being.

General Kragle paced the room, stopping occasionally to listen to the banks of radios. The USS *Sam Houston* reported it had reached its rendezvous point with the men of Deep Steel; it heard CSEL signals, but so far had seen nothing of the men, who might have turned off their strobes because of a shark threat. The seas were heavy, the sub skipper advised, and he was afraid the small Delta unit might have been scattered in the dark.

General Kragle stopped in front of the cable TVs to give himself something to do. Senator Jake "Douche Bag" Thierry was already on CNN ranting about lack of U.S. reaction to the abduction of the former President. What did the asshole expect the U.S. to do at this juncture when nobody could be sure who was behind the action? There were so many terrorist groups these weird days. Besides, Stanton had been warned to stay away from Cuba. The General even derived a sort of perverse pleasure in the man's misfortune. After having evaded the draft during Vietnam, Stanton had the gall to insult the country's veterans on the day he left for Cuba by announcing that, "I'd personally get in the trenches and fight and die with the Israelis if Iraq attacks them."

Yeah, right. Well, the sonofabitch had his chance now. He had been thrown in the trenches. The bastard was probably shitting his pants about now from terror.

Colonel Buck stopped next to the General to watch TV's live coverage at the site of the abduction.

"Forget I said this," General Kragle commented bitterly, "but the best thing that can happen to this nation is for the tangos to chop off his head and mail it to the American Civil Liberties Union. It'd save our losing *good* men trying to rescue him."

Excitement broke out around the radios. "They've got a visual on them," someone called out.

Minutes passed as *Sam Houston* in the distant Pacific reported on the recovery of the Deep Steel detachment. Colonel Elton Rogers, communications section chief, rushed into the war room with news too good to keep to himself.

"The *Sam Houston* picked up 2-Bravo and has them on board," he announced. "It has temporarily lost *Ibn Haldoon*, but is on-course to intercept it."

He stopped, hesitated. His demeanor changed. "One man is missing. Apparently, a shark—"

General Kragle held up a hand to stop him. They had all heard. No use reiterating the gory details. It was a kick in the head when you lost a good man. The General suffered a pang of guilt for feeling relieved that, if someone had to get it, it wasn't either of his sons.

CHAPTER 23

Cuyo Islands

Lee Soon and her baby brother Gil Su came down seasick as the *Ibn Haldoon* negotiated the storm-tossed waters of the Mindoro Strait. The freighter steamed on through and entered an area of hundreds of small wild islands in the northern Sulu Sea. Here the water was calmer, if only marginally, and with the resilience of youth the Korean children promptly rebounded.

Summer, also known as Ismael, sneaked food out of the galley for them. In between her visits, the little stowaways huddled together hiding in the dingy rope locker while Jang gave his siblings English lessons, whispering, or sketched scenes they all wanted to see when they reached America—

the Statue of Liberty, the White House, Disney World . . .
Cimatu and his men had completed renovations to the cell
next door, such as they were, and seemed to pose no further
threat to the children. At least for the time being.

"My sister and my brother must learn to speak the language of our new home so that they will be Americans too
when we arrive in United States," Jang explained.

The three of them with their stoic acceptance of their hardships and their good-natured optimism that everything was
going to turn out all right wriggled themselves inextricably
into Summer's heart. These kids, she thought, were the kind
of immigrants America needed. They, like refugees who
sought American shores in simpler times, believed that becoming American citizens required them to speak the language, respect the country's traditions, and know and
understand her history.

In "multicultural" America, it was fashionable for immigrants not to have to bother to learn English or to study the
history and culture of their new home. Immigrants, even
those of four, five, and six generations or more, became hyphenated citizens—African-Americans, Hispanic-Americans,
Asian-Americans—and continued to bear allegiance to other
nations, cultures, and causes. No wonder terrorists so easily
hid within the borders of the United States and multiplied
with near immunity. A land divided culturally became a land
divided.

"You will make good Americans," Summer approved. "All
three of you."

Jang gently prompted Lee Soon. "Thank you, Ismael," she
said in passable English.

Troubled, Summer watched the children eating. They
complicated matters, all the more so because of her inability
to establish communications with her control to warn of their
presence. She could neither take them overboard with her
when the expected raid on the SCUD missiles came nor

could she leave them there to go down with the ship. She wasn't sure when or how the raid would go down, but she *was* sure it would be violent, swift, and final. With her and the children in the crossfire.

Satellite communications were often difficult in these latitudes, a difficulty compounded by the approaching storm. Still, you would think that with today's computers and high-speed technology she could make one lousy damned telephone call.

She kept her SATCOM radio and cellphone concealed in a ventilation shaft near her bunk in the crew's bay. Because of the pervert Cimatu and his hungry eyes, she had to be exceptionally careful not to be caught with the commo or spotted coming below to the rope locker with pilfered food. She constantly invented new ploys to divert Cimatu's attention, such as going to chow early and leaving again as soon as possible or putting herself on one of the watches and bargaining with someone else to take her place or exchange with her. In case everything else failed and she had to defend herself, she stole a table knife from the kitchen, sharpened it, and concealed it in the waistband of her pantaloons.

She tried at every opportunity to get a message out. Nothing ever came over the tiny transmitter/receiver except static. She continued to punch in her scrambler code nonetheless in hopes that it would be received even though she received no acknowledgment of it in return. Thinking she might have better luck topside without the interference of so much surrounding steel, she had secreted her cell phone in her pantaloons before visiting the stowaways.

After cautioning the children once again to keep quiet and stay hidden, she left them and made her way toward the main deck. She stopped by a hatch leading outside to draw on a foul-weather slicker. The night before there had been lightning, wind, and rain. There was a lull in the weather the next day, not much of one, for there was still a stinging mist of rain. Salt spray swept the pitching deck.

She made her way to the relative shelter of the craft's superstructure amidships. She looked around to make sure no one was about and that she couldn't be seen from the bridge before she took out the phone. It still didn't work. The batteries must be getting weak.

Frustrated and feeling alone, she remained on deck underneath the angry gray of the low skies. She made it a point never to think of home or her personal life whenever she undertook a mission. In spite of the vow, however, she found her thoughts drifting toward her Delta major and the two glorious weeks they had had together following Operation Iron Weed.

General Kragle, Brandon's father, had flown up to Bragg to have dinner with them one evening. He was a charming man, if opinionated and a bit outspoken, and she very much liked and trusted him. Brandon said he was a much better father to grown sons than he had been to kids. Summer thought the General liked her too, but she was discovering that it took Kragle men a long time to open up and let you see their feelings.

There was no doubt, however, about how Gloria felt. The fat black woman with the red hair, whom everyone called Brown Sugar Doll or Brown Sugar Mama met Brandon and her at the Farm in Tennessee for a weekend holiday. Gloria took a look at Summer, put her hands on her ample hips, and walked completely around the girl, scrutinizing her with a critical scowl.

"Why, Lawdy. This poor underfed little thing don't have hardly enough butt to last till sundown," she finally declared.

Then she grabbed Summer in a great motherly bear hug. "She be so pretty. Looky them eyes!" she said to Brandon while he laughed and Summer blushed. "If my Brandon be loving you—and I sees in his eyes he do—then I be loving you too, chile. Loving you just like my own chil'ren—Brandon, Cameron, and Cassidy. They white boys, but they got black in them 'cause I raised 'em with soul. Honey, welcome to the fambly. Do I see a double wedding? You and Brandon and me and Raymond?"

Later, when Gloria and Summer had a few minutes alone together, Gloria said, "You does love him back, don't you, honey?"

Summer hesitated. "Yes," she whispered.

Gloria beamed. Then she looked serious again. "Just 'cause my boys be big and tough don't mean they don't have hearts," she warned. "They all real sensitive inside, they just keeps it there. Same as they father do."

Summer thought about it. "I understand."

"Does you? Them boys, all three of 'em, again like they father, done already lost once what they love most than anything else."

Summer looked down at her hands. "Gloria, can you tell me about Gypsy?"

"You have to ask Brandon about that, honey."

"He won't talk about it. All he'll say is that she was going to marry Cameron."

"It take the Kragle men some while to open up. But they comes around if you loves 'em enough."

Did Summer love him enough? Was she capable of loving any man enough after having been the Ice Maiden? Even going so far as to sleep with terrorist leaders in Israel in order to lure them to their deaths. The anger inside her, the sense of revenge she harbored against the ilk who had murdered her sisters, made Cassidy's fury seem tame by comparison.

Brandon and she had had two weeks of making love and laughing together. Then one morning the call came.

"I have to go," she said.

"When?"

"Today. This afternoon."

He didn't say anything. She knew he wouldn't. He understood duty.

The last she heard, Brandon was in the Philippines on a CT mission involving American missionaries. He might even now be on one of these islands nearby.

Summer disguised as Ismael stood on the unsteady deck of the *Ibn Haldoon* and gazed out at the gray restless sea spitting back at the rain. She tried to feel Brandon with her soul and her heart. She wiped away spontaneous tears and blamed them on the rain stinging her eyes.

CHAPTER 24

STANTON HOSTAGE TAPES RECEIVED

Washington (CPI)—Two video tapes, one showing former President John Stanton bound and gagged, were delivered hours after the kidnapping by anonymous messenger to the Washington offices of Consolidated Press International. Duplicate tapes were hand carried to FOX TV News in New York. Identical notes attached to each set of tapes bore the message: IN THE NAME OF HOLY JIHAD, WE CAN GET TO YOU AT ANY TIME WE DESIRE. IMPORTANT PEOPLE ARE NOT SAFE FROM US.

In the footage, Stanton appears to be on the floor of an aircraft where he is bound head and foot with a strip of tape over his mouth. In a scene grimly reminiscent of the kidnapping and murder of journalist Daniel Pearl in Pakistan a year before, his masked captors pose with an automatic pistol pressed to the President's temple and a knife at his throat.

Daniel Pearl's body was found beheaded.

Senate Majority Leader Jake Thierry, who has indicated ambition to run for the presidency, accused the White House of dragging its feet in negotiating for Stanton's safe release. No group has yet claimed credit for the abduction.

"How safe is America if during this administration's ill-conceived War on Terror, it cannot even protect prominent people like President Stanton?" Thierry demanded . . .

CHAPTER 25

Cuyo Islands

After retrieving Deep Steel's Detachment 2-B from the ocean, nuclear submarine USS *Sam Houston* achieved neutral buoyancy at one hundred feet depth and continued its pursuit of the Saudi freighter *Ibn Haldoon*. The DDS (dry deck shelter) looked like a giant parasitic barnacle attached to the upper deck of the submarine aft of the sail. A DDS was essentially a huge metal watertight cylinder that could be bolted to the sub and connected to its interior by a watertight hatch. It was approximately nine feet wide and divided into three pressurized sections—a hangar area, in which the ASDV (Advance SEAL Delivery Vehicle), a twenty-foot "minisubmarine," and other systems equipment could be stored; a transfer chamber to allow passage between the module and the host ship; and a hyperbaric, or decompression, chamber, for decompressing and recompressing divers. The DDS was large enough to accommodate an entire SEAL platoon, along with its gear. It provided a dry environment for the transportation of SpecOps people and their equipment; the hangar compartment served as sort of a lounge and was flooded only to launch the SDV while submerged.

Major Brandon assembled the detachment in the DDS as soon as the men ate and changed into dry clothing provided by the boat's quartermaster; their tiger-stripe cammies would be cleaned, dried, and returned to them. They had nearly twenty-four hours to recover from the combined trauma of rough seas, delayed submarine, sharks, and the savage death of one of their teammates.

Master Sergeant Winfield Brown's strange wake beneath the seas that claimed him was appropriately solemn but without the customary tears of such occasions. SpecOps men were tough and nondemonstrative. They concealed their sorrow behind hardened faces.

"Boss?" Gloomy Davis prompted after the detachment assembled. As next-highest-ranking enlisted man behind Winnie, Gloomy filled in the detachment's chain of command by taking Winnie's place as ops sergeant, the top NCO.

Brandon took the cue. "I'm certain that since my brother is a chaplain, he would have far more appropriate words," he admitted. "But I would like for us to pray."

The men gathered shoulder-to-shoulder in the cramped steel compartment and bowed their heads while air hissed through the pressure ducts. The torpedo-shaped SDV on its chocks formed a backdrop in the wan light.

"If I may respectfully say so, Father," Brandon began haltingly, gradually warming to the task, "You are a strange God. It seems You may have special predilection for men who can stand alone, who face impossible odds, who are willing, even eager, to challenge every bully and every tyrant. Possibly it is because You recognize Your only Son in them. We come to Your HQ now because You saw the need to take one of us for that Last Great Ops in the sky. God, I ask in Your name that You receive Master Sergeant Winfield Cornelius Brown as the brave warrior he was. Winnie is our brother and we love him like a brother. I also must respectfully warn you, Father, that the men of Delta and the Navy SEALs know how to celebrate. So if You would, sir, please be ready for Winnie and for the rest of us when You see us at the Pearly Gates."

SEALs J.D. and T-Bone barked. Lieutenant Lucifer said "Amen" with such unexpected reverence that Mad Dog Carson shot him a look.

"Contrary to popular opinion," Lucifer said, "I have no pact with the devil. In fact, my nickname is intended to poke fun at Satan."

"I hear Satan laughing, sir."

They told stories about Winnie and his pretentious Harvard accent, and about his courage under fire when the detachment was in Afghanistan on Operation Iron Weed. They laughed some and remembered and Ice Man broke out a bottle of Scotch he had secreted inside his ruck. The bottle made its rounds.

"Winnie left three thousand bucks for Delta to throw him a party in case he didn't make it back," Thumbs Jones reminded the detachment. "I'm adding five hundred to that. Good ole Winnie's gonna have a party the MPs at Fort Bragg will talk about for the next two generations."

"Put the SEALs in for another thousand," Chief Gorrell offered.

"I'll add five hundred if the Ice Man will gourmet grill a fucking shark," Mad Dog said. His voice broke and he quickly covered it with a gibe at Thumbs. "I always thought sharks liked dark meat."

The black demo man lay a gentle hand on the Dog's broad

shoulder. Mad Dog's head dropped. He jabbed Thumbs affectionately with his fist.

"Fu-uck," he murmured.

At last, Brandon interrupted the memorial before it turned maudlin. "All right. Winnie would know we got a job to do—and we do." He hesitated and looked at Lucifer. "Just one other thing: I'm recommending Lieutenant Lucifer for a medal. We'd have lost another man if it hadn't been for him."

He let that hang for a brief moment, then said, "Thumbs, you and T-Bone—"

"—the Jones brothers—" Ice Man said with rare levity.

"—and Cassidy check out the demolitions. See if we have everything and if it's still in good order. The SEALs will take care of the SDV and the Draegers. Ice Man, inventory the weapons. Mad Dog, I noticed one of the radios sustained some damage . . ."

Mission came first. Always.

Lucifer caught Brandon aside afterward. "Thanks, Major," he said with an attempt at reconciliation.

"This changes nothing, Lucifer."

CHAPTER 26

Cuyo Islands, *Ibn Haldoon*

Ibn Haldoon reduced power after the noon meal and began zigzagging among a series of tiny green islands and coral-rock atolls. Discouraged by her repeated failures to make commo, desperately seeking a solution to her conundrum,

Summer idly thumbed through a magazine in the galley mess hall that served as a crew lounge between meals. She tossed the magazine aside when the freighter cut engines to an idle. The ship retained only enough power to maintain position against the rolling seas.

Curious about why they were stopping, she climbed topside and drew on foul-weather gear against a fine stinging rain before venturing onto the main deck. The ship wallowed in troughs, making it difficult and even hazardous for a team of sailors to prepare to winch a motor skiff over the side. The smaller boat kept banging against the ship's gunnels.

The ship was riding off the lee side of a long, flat island. Through the rain and the dull half-light of the approaching storm, Summer saw an open grassy meadow on the island. Her first frenzied thought was that the SCUDs were about to be offloaded. She scanned the turbulent sea for the approach of a receiving vessel, seeing nothing except the swirl of mist and a streak of white-and-gray as the wind blew an albatross past like a shredded rag.

Still, it was obvious that they were waiting for *something*. Sailors secured the skiff hanging over the side. It could be unhitched with one pull and immediately lowered to the water below. Other ghostly forms in foul-weather gear gathered forward, waiting for an order. They hunched their shoulders and bowed their heads against the rain and held on to the bow railing against the rocking of the deck.

Summer stole away to a sheltered place aft, crawled underneath the tarp that covered a secured lifeboat, and attempted once again to make a radio contact. She soon gave up. Damned technology wasn't always what it was purported to be.

After an hour or so of waiting, nothing happening, the captain ordered the lowering of anchors. Clearly the ship intended to spend the night there. It was extremely dangerous navigating those island-studded waters in the dark. Especially with a storm brewing.

It was coming. Whatever it was. An air of excitement seemed to suddenly infect the ship, pegging out Summer's agitation factor. How was she going to notify Control? Her only hope was that the spy satellites were up and working, even though she doubted even they could see what was going on through *that* cloud cover.

Cimatu, his WWF crony, and the ninja came out on deck in yellow foul-weather slickers and hoods, looking like giant canaries. Captain Darth Vader in his ominous beard and helmet and a couple of the ship's company accompanied them. Cimatu spotted Summer and went out of his way to pass by her. Summer tried to evade, but he cut her off and patted her on the butt. He winked, a gesture that, combined with the scar on his face, made his head appear even more lopsided and corrupt.

"You will yet suck my dick, Ismael," he promised.

The depraved sonofabitch.

The group gathered around the motor skiff and peered anxiously into the overcast. They didn't have to wait long this time. Instead of a boat or ship engine, which Summer expected, she heard the drone of an airplane. The sound surged and throbbed with the rise and fall of the wind. Flying in this weather required a daredevil pilot of extraordinary instrument skills—or a suicidal one with contempt for a long life.

The plane soon materialized as a fast-moving shadow in the clouds. It dropped below the low ceiling. A single-engine, island-hopping Caribou with a low-slung passenger belly and capabilities for STAL, short takeoff and landing. Gusty winds waggled its wings and bounced it in the air. It veered out over the freighter, passing low enough that Summer clearly saw the pilot's face looking down. Bona fides exchanged, the aircraft circled and lined up on the island. The meadow appeared long enough and flat enough for a landing. The plane missed its first approach due to a stiff quartering wind and skittering rain that hampered visibility. It started around again.

Summer wondered what it was all about. Clearly, a Caribou wasn't enough plane to carry a SCUD, even if the ship's sailors could load one aboard the skiff and transport it ashore, which they couldn't.

The airplane landed on the second attempt, splashing up sheets of water from the meadow. It rolled out, taxied back, and stopped out of sight behind some trees. Cimatu and his men lowered the skiff and made a wild ride with the surf to the rocky beach. Darth Vader stood on the deck at the bow and watched the proceedings through a pair of binoculars. Summer had to settle for the naked eye.

She distinguished the men only as a group of tiny figures scurrying about on the beach. One of their number stayed with the boat while the rest charged up to the meadow and disappeared into the trees. The aircraft pilot was obviously in a hurry to take off again before the weather got any worse. He didn't stay around to visit. The Caribou leaped into the air again by the time Cimatu's men reappeared, dragging among them a man who appeared to have his hands tied and was having a rough time negotiating down the bank.

The unfortunate individual was tossed into the boat and made the wild ride back out of the surf. Line and tackle were thrown overboard from the ship to the bobbing boat and it was winched aboard, crew and all. Laughing, Cimatu and his wrestler hoisted the prisoner from the bottom of the skiff and threw him unceremoniously out onto the *Ibn Haldoon*. He slid across the wet deck, screaming with terror, and curled himself into a fetal position. He was muddy and soaked and his hands were tightly bound behind his back. What had been a five thousand dollar blue business suit with a red power tie now looked as though some homeless bum had slept in it underneath a bridge for the past week.

It took Summer a minute to recognize the famous figure. She understood now why a cell had been prepared below decks. The former President of the United States lay in the rain whimpering and pleading like a terrified child.

"Please, please, please?" John Stanton blubbered. "Don't hurt me. I have money I can give. I do understand your pain and anger, and I can help. Just please don't hurt me."

CHAPTER 27

Georgia

Senior FBI agent Claude Thornton had grown up in Mississippi on Stephen Foster's "Old Folks At Home," the Uncle Remus stories of Joel Chandler Harris, and the novels of Mississippi's poet laureate William Faulkner. Hardly materials today's socially aware and sensitive African-American would appreciate. It wasn't until later in college that he discovered the racial consciousness of *Black Like Me* and James Baldwin. It was even later that he became disillusioned with Jesse Jackson, Al Sharpton, and others who made millions being professional blacks trading upon the guilt of White America. Thornton knew as many bigoted black people as bigoted whites. Dr. Martin Luther King Jr. was right. It really was the content of a man's character and not the color of his skin that should matter.

It was, therefore, with bitter-wry amusement that he confronted charges of "racial profiling" by lawyers of the three Yemenis Agent Fred Whiteman arrested at the St. Marys airport on the Georgia seacoast. Claims that the Yemenis were singled out because of their race and religion made all the newscasts. Because JTTF (Joint Terrorism Task Force) fell under the jurisdiction of Thornton's National Domestic Preparedness Office, he was personally attacked as a racist, with no intent at irony. The situation exacerbated when Thornton refused to divulge details of the seizure of the suspects and their ancient C-47 aircraft.

"They are being detained as enemy combatants under the Homeland Security Act," he informed the media. "That's all the information we can provide at this time."

In Thornton's opinion, Americans did not need to know that the airplane might have contained a missile. It would create panic. Mud and grass on the aircraft's landing gear indicated that it had recently landed on an unpaved strip where whatever cargo it contained was likely unloaded onto a vehicle. The plane was leaving the U.S. again, flying nap of the earth under covering darkness, when an engine quit and forced the C-47 to make an emergency landing at St. Marys untowered municipal airport. The aircraft contained various arming devices for missile payloads, fuses, and operating manuals for SCUD and other missiles.

"In the name of Allah, al-Qaeda will triumph and blow up the Great Satan!" one of the three prisoners shouted when Thornton arrived in Georgia and accompanied Whiteman to a cell at the county jail where the trio was being held for U.S. military authorities. "*Allah akbar walillahi'l-hamd!*"

"It ain't Jews or Colombians or Liberians blowing up Americans and poisoning us with anthrax," Whiteman said. "It's little pissants like these. That makes it *racism* to throw their asses in jail?"

Whiteman was a big Texan with a contentious nature and gray-brown hair growing in isolated sprigs on the top of his pink head. He and Thornton, longtime friends, had attended the FBI Academy together years before when they were rookies.

"Who was it dancing on the streets after three thousand Americans were blown up at the World Trade Center?" he demanded rhetorically. "Palestinians and Egyptians and Jordanians. Arabs. I'll begin profiling priests and bishops as soon as Catholics start strapping on dynamite, walking into mosques and crying out, 'In the name of Jesus Christ and the Church of Rome, I now blow ya'all up.'"

The captives refused to answer questions. All they did was spout diatribes against Americans and the United States, wave their fists, and shout, "Praise Allah!"

Thornton and Whiteman spread agents thinly all over southern Georgia and northern Florida to background the detainees and try to find out what had been in the airplane and where it was delivered. Materials in possession of the prisoners led to an apartment above an Arabian food store in an Arab community in Jacksonville. A neighbor told agents she was suspicious of some of the activity that went on at the apartment and in the neighborhood.

"There was constant traffic," she said. "Minivans, SUVs, and all types of brand-new vehicles. New York and New Jersey tags. A couple of Louisiana and Georgia cars. There was honking until all hours, sometimes until four in the morning. But nobody would ever get out of the cars. They'd keep honking until someone came out. Then they'd speed away."

The apartment seemed to have been occupied by people other than, or in addition to, the three captured at St. Marys. It also appeared to have been hastily evacuated as word spread of the arrests and FBI interest. Thornton expressed no surprise at the usual bomb-making literature and other revolutionary and terrorist matter left behind. After all, terrorist sleeper cells in America felt so secure in their persons and possessions, as protected by the U.S. Constitution, that they plotted and schemed and collected contraband virtually in full view of their neighbors and the police.

Some of the stuff was in other languages, which Thornton translated; he had spent most of the past decade as senior resident FBI agent in Cairo and spoke a number of Middle Eastern dialects. It didn't take a genius or code breaker to understand most of it, however. Several maps of the southeastern United States had locations circled in red ink, among them Marathon in Florida, Edith in Georgia, New Orleans, Jacksonville, and Atlanta. Notes and names were scribbled next to cities or towns or in the map margins. Taher and Galab appeared next to Marathon; Goba and Alwan at Edith; Ramzi at New Orleans; Shafal in Atlanta. Terrorists had sketched little missiles in the margins, as though to stress their intentions.

"The scrotes, whoever they are, are blatant about it," Whiteman commented.

"Why shouldn't they be?" Thornton said. "Law enforcement has had its hands strapped by civil libertarians for the past decade when it came to terrorism."

One of the most surprising finds was a detailed map of the José Martí Airport in Havana, Cuba, with the name STANTEN inscribed on it. Obviously, considering what had happened, it was a misspelling of *Stanton*. Just as obviously, it pertained to the former President's abduction. The kidnapping and the smuggling of missiles and nuclear materials into the United States had to be connected.

Thornton phoned a report to his boss, Director Thornbrew of the Homeland Security Agency. Thornbrew recommended he pass the information along to USSOCOM since SpecOps was, "as we speak," involved in a missile interception in the Philippines.

"Give Darren heads up," Director Thornbrew said. "There's a 'Big Picture' to consider in this thing. We just can't see it yet."

Thornton cell-phoned General Kragle on his private number.

"This is not a secure line," the General immediately answered.

"General, this is Thornton. Can you call me back on this number? It's scrambled."

"Hold on."

The General called right back. He seemed please to hear from his friend. "Claude, where are you?"

"In the Land of Sunshine."

"Great. Can you get a chance to run down to Tampa? We're up to our asses in alligators, but I think I can get off to buy dinner. How about tomorrow? Gloria would love to introduce you to her fiancé."

"You say *you're* buying?"

The General chuckled. "Don't let it get around."

"I need to run something by you, Darren. We have a situation up here that may be related to yours in the Philippines."

"Shoot."

"Maybe we oughtn't use that particular word, know what I mean? Briefly, let me tell you what we have. The day before Stanton got himself snatched in Havana, the Coast Guard and the DEA trailed a C-47 out of Colombia that supposedly contained either a missile or stuff with which to make a WMD. As usual, the plane disappeared into Cuban airspace and was picked up again on the way out. That's where things begin to get fouled up. To make a long story short—I'll give you the annotated version later—the plane that came *out* of Cuba wasn't the same one our bubbas saw go *in* to Cuba. The one we got was full of cocaine. Either that was incredibly bad luck for the dope runners, or—"

"—it was used as a decoy."

"Exactly. That's what I thought too. Anyhow, Act one, Scene two: we've seized a C-47 forced to land in Georgia with engine problems. I think it's the genuine original article

we were trying to catch to begin with. Whatever it was hauling was already gone—but there was evidence that it might
have contained a missile."

The General went silent for a minute, as though mentally
connecting the dots. "You think the plutonium from Mindanao has found its way through Colombia and Cuba to
Georgia?"

"I don't know, Darren. There was no indication of radioactive materials. But if we got a missile here, and we have missiles out of North Korea trying to get here, and we have
plutonium disappearing in the Philippines . . ."

"I see. The hip bone is connected to the thigh bone, the
thigh bone connected to the knee bone . . ."

"Something is about to happen, General. We ain't gonna
like it when it does. But, wait. There's more. It looks like
these are all the same people—and that they're the ones who
snatched Stanton."

The General inhaled a deep breath. "You're right, Claude,
we do need to get together and hash this thing out. Take me
up on that dinner?"

"Steak, you say? Not *Burger King*."

The JTTF, a new outfit, found itself short of manpower. The
name of one of the towns marked on the terrorist map—
Edith, Georgia—lay close to Thornton's route to Tampa if he
drove. He volunteered to check it out on his way while Agent
Whiteman used his men in tracking down suspect names in
the larger cities. He rented a blue Buick in Jacksonville the
next morning after a good night's sleep and looked forward
to the drive and the time alone to think.

The sun was an hour's high when he left Jacksonville. It
was a good, fast, leisurely drive on U.S. 10 from Jacksonville
to where he turned north on 441 to Edith on the edge of the
Okefenokee Swamp. Getting drowsy in the morning sun, he
stopped at a roadside gas station and convenience store to fill

up on caffeine. He had changed into jeans and a green short-sleeved sports shirt. When he started up again, the President of the United States was on the radio being asked questions about the incident in St. Marys.

"Although critics charge that the arrests may be unconstitutional," the announcer narrated in grilling the President, "Mr. Thornbrew said they underscore the broad reach of al-Qaeda even in America."

"Then maybe we should listen to Mr. Thornbrew," the President responded. "One by one we're hunting the terrorists down. We are relentless. We are strong. And we're not going to stop. The future will be better tomorrow."

"Mr. President, is there any truth to the rumor that the captured airplane may have contained an atomic bomb?"

"Why on earth would you start a rumor like that?" the President asked.

Thornton sighed. Before 9/11, he had been considering taking his FBI retirement and going back to a little farm he had bought in Mississippi near the old home place. Operation Enduring Freedom, his wife Edith's running off with the Cairo press attaché and divorcing him, and his appointment as director of the Domestic Preparedness Office put a stop to those considerations. He was in the war now for the long haul.

He reached Edith shortly before lunch, shaking his head a little morosely that the town and his ex-wife shared the same name. He slowed the Buick to avoid awaking the sleepy little Southern hamlet. Giant live oaks weeping gray Spanish moss outnumbered residents. Four two-lane "red roads" on the map and a "gray road" intersected either at Edith or a couple of miles north at a wide spot in the road called Fargo. The Okefenokee Swamp began just outside town with cypress giants growing out of hot, stagnant water.

He drove through town twice. The only clue he possessed as to "Goba" or "Alwan," the names associated on the terrorist map with Edith, was a gas card receipt found in the Jacksonville apartment. Three days ago, a man identified as "Sahim Goba" purchased gasoline at a Texaco in Edith. These guys were making little effort to cover their tracks. For potential suicide bombers, that could mean they didn't care whether they were found out or not—*after* the fact.

The Texaco wasn't hard to find. There were only three stations in town. One was British, one had been turned into a cottage rocking-chair factory, and the last was the Texaco. The station attendant was an emaciated cracker with thinning gray hair and oily hands and jeans. He eyed Thornton's credentials suspiciously.

"They really got ya'all Negroes in the FB and I now?" he asked, more surprised than intentionally insulting. His accent reflected corn pone 100 percent.

"A *Negro* is now secretary of state," Thornton replied, smiling.

"Well, now, hot doggie. I be swan, don't that just beat all? What state is he secretary of? Georgia?"

"The United States." Thornton showed him the gas receipt. "Do you know this man?"

Everybody in a town this small would notice a stranger, especially a foreign-looking stranger if he bought gas from you and lived in the vicinity. The pump jockey frowned and squinted over the name, as though mentally sounding out the name letter by letter. He grinned apologetically, revealing two missing front teeth, and took out an ancient pair of horn-rimmed reading glasses. He sounded out the name again.

"Oh! The camel jockey," he recalled. "Furriners, both of them. But friendly like. I don't trust them though, not after what happen in New York or wherever that was."

"New York. Two of them, you say? Do you know where I can find them?"

The guy cackled. "He ain't gonna bomb Edith, is he?"

"I just need to talk to them."

"Well, I don't know perzackly where they living. He said him and this other fella is students from the university. They supposed to be studying swamp critters and writing something about them. They living somewheres out in the swamp in an old cabin, what I understands."

"Thanks for the information."

"You gonna buy something, are you?"

"Fill it with regular test."

The old man grinned. "I ain't heard nobody say 'regular' in a long time, but I know what you mean."

Thornton thought he might like it.

Apparently nothing much, law enforcement-wise, happened around here. The city police were busy somewhere else—a donut shop, Thornton wondered? The sheriff's department was over in the next town. Thornton decided to go out into the swamp to take a look himself. He took the gray road north. Swamp closed in on both sides. He stopped twice to ask about "Goba" and "Alwan." Once at a roadside stand selling cypress knee lamps, and again at a Ranger station.

"These Arabs or whatever claim to be students," the ranger said. He lifted one eyebrow. "Unless the FBI knows something we don't."

"Routine," Thornton said with a dismissive gesture. No use getting people worked up prematurely.

The ranger provided directions to a plot of private ground upon which an old swamp rat constructed a cabin thirty or forty years ago. "He vanished some time back. We figure the 'gators got him."

Thornton soon located the footpath leading off the blacktop like the ranger described. A tan Ford SUV was parked at a turnout area in the grass next to the road. The doors were locked, the engine cold. It was the only car other than the ranger's that he had seen since Edith. Apparently not many people got out this way.

He started to call Whiteman to fill him in, but then thought he'd take a look first. He shoved his Glock 9mm into the back waistband of his jeans, underneath the sports shirt, and slipped his cell phone into its holder on his belt. A bull alligator bellowed from the sloughs to his right as he followed the winding footpath for over a half-mile into the swamp.

The trail abruptly ended at a wooden footbridge sagging above a narrow, brackish trickle of stale water. On the other side sat a cypress-log cabin with a rusted tin roof. Cypress grew straight and red-tinted out of the surrounding bogs. Spanish moss hung like ancient beards from a live oak in front of the cabin.

The agent studied the hut. No one appeared to be around, although the parked SUV at the head of the trail said *somebody* was likely here. No use disturbing things unnecessarily. Whiteman would probably want to obtain a search warrant or, if there was time, place surveillance on it for a day or so to see who came and went.

Thornton backed away until he was out of sight of the cabin. He turned to follow the trail back to his car. A heavily accented voice suddenly barked from the bushes.

"Do not move—or I will kill you in the name of Allah."

CHAPTER 28

New Orleans

Chaplain Cameron Kragle attended the first morning session of the Hands of God Conference at the Convention Center and was not disappointed. The first day was to be devoted entirely to Muslims. Speakers were moderates and either naturalized U.S. citizens or legal immigrants seeking citizenship. In sticking to the theme of the conference—better understanding and communications among Christians, Muslims, and Jews—they condemned the Islamic violence of 9/11. Rather mildly, however, from Cameron's viewpoint. They were more forceful in condemning what they called "human rights offenses" by the American government and its people in singling out Muslims for suspicion.

To Cameron's way of thinking, Muslims lent fuel to American distrust by their generally weak rejection of Islamic terrorism, especially that committed by the Palestinians in Israel. Americans *hanged* John Brown the abolitionist when he carried his faith to unreasonable lengths and began resorting to terrorism.

As a military representative to the Hands of God, Cameron was required to attend in uniform, even though it made him stand out and feel rather conspicuous. Even more so since many of the Muslims wore beards, long robes, turbans, and kaffiyehs. Orthodox Jews from New York also came in beards—with braids and dressed in black. During lunch break, Cameron noticed a young Muslim with a dark, thin face underneath a red-and-white checked kaffiyeh. He made a production of appearing to look for an empty chair at the tables. Finally, as though giving up, he slipped onto the chair next to Cameron.

Cameron gave him a friendly smile and introduced himself.

"I am Yasein Riefenstahl," the Muslim said.

He spoke at length with Cameron while at the same time, oddly enough, he tried to give the impression that he wasn't particularly interested in the army chaplain but was merely responding to Cameron's overtures. He spoke perfect English except for a slightly stilted turn of phrase as he explained how he fled Iraq as a young teenager during the Gulf

War of 1991 and escaped through Kuwait. The United States gave him asylum as a refugee and he became a naturalized U.S. citizen.

"For which I am most grateful," he said. "So you see, I am a good American."

As if it was important that Cameron understood that.

They made more small talk. Yasein seemed uncomfortable and in a hurry. Cameron thought the young man was checking him out, testing him. But for what purpose he had no idea.

"There is not much time," Yasein blurted out finally. "You represent the U.S. Government. You are a man of God and I trust the honesty of your face. I and my friend will be executed if we speak to someone about this matter who we cannot trust."

"What are you talking about, Yasein? You need to go to the police if you're in trouble."

"No! No police." He looked furtively about. "I mustn't be seen talking to you any longer. Will you meet me at the main door after the last session of the day?"

He got up quickly and left. Cameron puzzled over the exchange the rest of the afternoon. Yasein sat on the other side of the convention center and declined to look in his direction.

The remaining sessions of the day turned into a diatribe against Christians and the West. The most virulent of the speakers introduced himself as Professor Ramzi al-Rehman from a south Florida university that had become known as Jihad U because a number of its professors, instructors, and students supported radical Islam. *The O'Reilly Factor*, Cameron recalled, had aired a TV piece about the school's terrorist funding organizations.

Al-Rehman was a medium-sized man, rather light complexioned with a bald head, a neatly trimmed graying beard, rimless eyeglasses, and a thin, critical mouth that gave him the look of an old-time prophet sent to root out heresy. The gist of his jeremiad was that 9/11 was America's fault because America was rich, powerful, and arrogant and because its foreign policy favored Israel. Besides, he ranted, everyone knew Jews controlled the American government and that Jews hated Arabs. America was racist. Everyone knew that.

Cameron bowed his head. The bitterness in the professor's verbal assault stunned him. Tense silence dominated the great hall. Those who were not Muslims kept their thoughts to themselves, knowing they would be publicly castigated should they dare express them. If a Christian minister or a rabbi dared to speak out against Islam the way al-Rehman scolded Christians and Jews, he would be promptly kicked from the conference and exposed as a racist and bigot in the evening media. It was not politically correct to speak openly about how many mainstream Muslim individuals and institutions in America and throughout the world gave moral and financial support to fellow Muslims waging war against the West.

Granted, Christians in history had been responsible for their own atrocities in the name of God—the Inquisition and the Crusades came to mind—but never, at least in modern times, to the point of declaring war against men, women, and children worldwide. Shortly after 9/11, Cameron began reading the Koran and other books on Muslim teachings. His was a constant struggle to comprehend God, man, and their respective relationships. He needed to understand radical Islam and what it was in the nature of the religion that drove young men to blow themselves up in the name of Allah in order to annihilate school kids, old people on buses, and planeloads of travelers.

Try as he might, understanding eluded him. How could God, he wondered, condone suicide bombings against children? How could God defend the practice of stoning women to death for adultery or even for showing their faces in public?

At the end of the day, a long day for Cameron, his curiosity revived when he spotted Yasein angling toward the door in a casual but deliberate manner. Yasein fell into step next to him while pretending disinterest.

From the corner of his mouth, the Iraqi refugee gave hurried instructions: "Meet me in Jackson Square in the French Quarter at eight tonight. It is vital. You must drive, as I do not have a vehicle. Do not come in uniform."

Cameron deliberated over whether he should go or not, but curiosity finally won out over caution.

"You have not seen anything yet if you think this afternoon was bad," Yasein said when Cameron picked him up at Jackson Square. The thin little man literally sprang into the Chrysler's passenger seat and made frantic motions that they should hurry.

He spoke after that primarily to give directions to the al-Farooq Mosque, where he said an alternative to the Hands of God Conference was being presented by the Alkhifa Refugee Center.

"My friend will see us there," Yasein said. "He asks that I arrange for him to speak to someone. It is necessary that you see for yourself first that Islamics are serious about the war."

He had brought along a spare kaffiyeh and a turban to conceal Cameron's blond hair and disguise his square American features. Muslims in the United States often wore slacks, jeans, and sports shirts with Arabic headgear, he said. Cameron shouldn't stand out too much in a crowd except for his exceptional height. Yasein would do all the talking; they shouldn't have any trouble.

City lights twinkled deep and mysterious in reflection against the inky width of the Mississippi River below the Greater New Orleans Bridge as Cameron and Yasein crossed into Gretna on the east bank. Yasein gripped his hands tightly in his lap, the tension almost palpable. The lights of oncom-

ing traffic flashed across his thin dark face beneath the turban. He seemed to have second thoughts.

"If it is dangerous . . ." Cameron offered gently, seeing
how nervous he was.

"This must be done," Yasein said.

Gretna on the east bank was a dingy smugglers town of old
narrow streets. A shabbier extension of the French Quarter.
Yasein directed Cameron past city hall to Lafayette Street.
Vehicles and pedestrians garbed in Arabic costumes crowded
a short block in front of a mosque with probing minarets.
Cameron parked and endured only a few curious glances in
his disguise as he accompanied his host inside. Two cautious
door guards in robes, headdresses, and beards looked him
over, but Yasein got them past with a few words in Arabic.

Cameron was not quite prepared for what he encountered.
The radical world of Islam, he discovered, was complex and
shadowy, full of unfamiliar names and half-known or hidden
activities. Walls were covered with posters and recruiting literature showing masked gunmen brandishing automatic
weapons. Daggers plunged into Jewish hearts wrapped in
American flags. A bazaar of vendors hawked all kinds of fanatical materials—books preaching Islamic Jihad; handouts
calling for the extermination of Jews and Christians; color-
ing books instructing children on such topics as "How To
Kill The Infidel." A tape playing on a TV set showed the torture and forced "confessions" of Palestinian "collaborators"
moments before they were executed. Another TV screened
paramilitary training videos.

Several organizations manned booths: Palestinian Islamic
Jihad; the Occupied Land Fund; Holy Warriors of the Philippines; Hamas; al-Qaeda. It seemed international terrorist organizations of all sorts had set up shop in America to take
advantage of religious, civic, and charitable organizations to
provide cover for recruiting and fund-raising. Apparently,
the cover was more than sufficient to fool the public, the po-

lice, and especially the naïve leaders of U.S. religious and educational institutions willing to encourage and sponsor such groups in the name of "multiculturalism" and "diversity." Even after passage of the Patriot Act, it was difficult to stop anyone from preaching violence short of the "clear and present danger" standard under the First Amendment. Which, Cameron thought, was as it should be. Still . . .

Cameron felt as though he were seeing novelist John Irving's "Undertoad," a foreboding, formless monster poised to drag everyone out of the sunlight and into the dark depths.

A small man in a white robe and a wrapped turban bumped into Yasein as the crowd poured into the seating rotunda. He kept going without so much as an apology.

"That is the signal that he will meet us afterward," Yasein said.

It was a surprise to Cameron, but nonetheless no great shock, when Ramzi al-Rehman took the podium. The professor's performance at the Hands of God Conference compared to that night's performance was constrained. He pulled out all the stops. Looking heated and outraged, he marched back and forth across the stage thrusting his arms about in a manner that reminded Cameron of Hitler. He spoke primarily in Arabic. Cameron felt as though he had entered a chamber in hell.

At one point, the entire assemblage sprang to its feet and began spontaneously chanting with the professor in English: "Death to Israel! Kill the Jews! Destroy the West!"

Yasein translated Ramzi's speech and explained in a low voice as they went along.

"They are Salafists who consider themselves engaged in a global jihad to build an Islamic world which they call *Khilafah*," he said. "Until they come to the United States with its freedom and civil rights, the groups are unable to coordinate their efforts all over the world. Now, they operate here to direct activities in the Middle East and to target America. They love death like Americans love life."

Scary stuff. Cameron sweated profusely in stale air smelling of other sweaty human beings. By the time al-Rehman concluded, the chaplain felt as though he had just fought a twelve-round championship bout with Satan—and lost. The Lord, he thought, had many ways to humble you.

Crowds leaving the mosque seemed pumped up and ready to go out and kill something for Allah.

"I needed you to see this so you will believe what we must tell you," Yasein said.

He hurried Cameron out of sight and down dark and deserted side streets. He stopped and looked around to make sure they were alone, then pulled Cameron into an alleyway that stank of garbage and stagnant water. A dog barked in somebody's backyard near the waterfront, then turned over and went back to sleep.

A slight figure stepped hesitatingly out of the shadows and hissed a challenge. Yasein responded. The mystery friend came near. The alley was dark and Cameron could not see his face.

"He does not speak English well. Therefore, I will translate," Yasein offered. With only a tiny hesitation, he continued. "The terrorists are many and they have bombs and missiles. My friend is a member of a sleeper cell that has been commissioned to explode nuclear bombs in America. He does not think there is time that we can stop all of them."

CHAPTER 29

The little man from al-Farooq Mosque said to call him Abdul, a generic name like John or Bob. Cameron was horrified at the implication of what he revealed and immediately suggested they go to the authorities. Abdul blanched and looked sick.

"He cannot do that," Yasein objected. "That is why we come to you, an official of the government as well as a man of the church. He will tell you all on the one condition that you never reveal his identity, a thing you must promise. If it were known, he would be deported or put in jail. Either way, his comrades would know his name and they would issue a *fatwa* on him so that any Muslim in the world is obligated to kill him in the name of Allah. Sooner or later they would kill him."

"What does he expect me to do?" Cameron asked.

Yasein and Abdul conversed in Arabic. The dog started barking again. A breeze rustled down the dark alley.

"You will know what is happening because he will show," Yasein translated. "You can lead the police to stop it. Abdul is prepared to go into hiding. In order for him to be safe, it must seem that he has nothing to do with the discovery of the plot."

"And if I can't do this?"

"Then the missiles cannot be stopped."

"He doesn't leave me much choice."

"You will promise then?"

Cameron was curious. "Why is he doing this?"

"Abdul has met an American woman, who he wishes to marry. He no longer wants to be a martyr."

Cameron wryly recalled a piece of satire written by political observer P. J. O'Rourke. Although tongue-in-cheek, it seemed to apply to Abdul.

What he wanted to see, the satirist wrote, was a world in which Osama bin Laden calls up a member of one of his sleeper cells. Someone who has been living his cover as an ordinary person in the United States for a number of years. So the sleeper answers his phone.

"Osama? Oh, good to hear from you. Blow up Washington on Thursday? Gee, Osama, I'd love to, but Thursday the kid has got her ballet recital. If you're late for something like that, they never forgive you. Friday? Friday is no good. I've got to see my mom off on her Bermuda cruise in the morning. It's Fatima's yoga day. I've got a big golf match at the club. And Saturday is out; we're driving out to the Hamptons for the weekend . . ."

Abdul was proof that conversions occurred. Apparently, however, they were rare. It stymied the imagination to think that there were people who would plot to detonate nuclear devices in order to wipe out thousands, hundreds of thousands, of innocent people. Nonetheless, the rhetoric, the hate literature and terrorist training tapes, the impassioned chanting of the multitudes at the mosque, all convinced the chaplain that that kind of hate existed in the world. Madmen who truly believed God wanted them to slaughter "nonbelievers" of other religions. As if he hadn't already been convinced by the crashing of air carriers into the World Trade Center and the deliberate spreading of anthrax that took, among others, the life of his younger brother's wife.

Cameron studied Abdul's features, what he could see of them in the darkened alley. The guy wasn't bluffing. After another moment's hesitation, Cameron nodded, acquiescing. In for a penny, in for a pound. He had to get to the bottom of this as quickly as he could. For all he knew, the nukes might be ready to go off at dawn.

Abdul insisted they go somewhere away from the neighborhood of the mosque, somewhere outside New Orleans where there was no chance of his being seen and recognized. Cameron walked back to where he parked the Chrysler, got in and drove it up the block and around to the other end of the alley and stopped. Yasein and Abdul ran out and got in.

They took Highway 10 across the tip of Lake Pontchartrain to Slidell in order to soothe the nerves of the man from al-Farooq. He cowered in the front seat, ducking his head and hiding his face every time they met oncoming headlights. Yasein leaned from the backseat to reassure him, but it didn't seem to help much. There was little conversation until Cameron pulled into an all-night truck stop.

Only two or three withdrawn truckers occupied the restaurant at that time of night. Cameron selected a booth in the far corner away from the window. The bleach-blond waitress brought coffee and suspiciously eyed the Arab headdresses of the two Middle Easterners. Brandon had shed his garb and left it in the car. He paid the waitress his most engaging smile and deliberately let it slip that he was a minister. That reassured her.

"Okay, hon," she said, relaxing. "If ya'all want anything else, just whistle."

Arabs were great tellers of tales. It was in their desert genes, reaching back to nomad days when stories were the chief form of entertainment around lonely wilderness fires. Abdul obviously decided he had to explain everything in order for his audience to understand and believe. Yasein carefully translated. Abdul apologized through him for his poor command of the American language.

Abdul said he, like Osama bin Laden, was from Saudi Arabia. He left Riyadh when he was eighteen to study at a Taliban madrigal in Kabul. He was such a good student and so devoted to Islam that the mullahs recommended he attend one of al-Qaeda's training camps hidden in the Hindu Kush.

Again, he was praised for his devotion to Allah and sent to Baghdad for further training. There, alongside other gifted students, he worked under some of Saddam Hussein's best scientists in the development of bio, chemical, and nuclear weapons. In addition to learning how to construct and use all types of explosives, he became familiar with physics and the principles of nuclear energy. Instructors from Saddam's army taught him to prepare and fire tactical battlefield missiles such as the SCUD, the Sandal, and the smaller Iraqi Al-Samoud.

For more than a year after that, he hid out in Palestine with Hamas. He built explosives for suicide bombers to blow up buses and restaurants full of Jews. He was never asked to do a martyr mission himself. Martyrdom was bestowed upon the young and eager who possessed no special talents.

In 1999, Abdul and other Islam warriors were ordered to enter the United States posing as students. They were to insinuate themselves into American life until at such time as they were called upon to serve Allah. Abdul continued his studies in nuclear physics, paid for by al-Qaeda through various American Muslim cover associations.

Abdul was not selected for the 9/11 mission. His talents were still being saved. He was relieved that he wasn't. He had already met the American woman with whom he fell in love, an unforeseen circumstance that the crusaders for jihad failed to anticipate.

He waited, growing more uncertain over time. Then, two months earlier, he'd been contacted and ordered to meet with Professor Ramzi al-Rehman, a sleeper cell leader who had been teaching at a Florida college for nearly six years. Ramzi was assembling Salafists like Abdul who were proficient in missiles and nuclear explosives.

"Professor Ramzi," Abdul said through Yasein, "is a true believer. We are ordered to prepare to receive a missile and nuclear materials. Our job is to assemble the warhead onto the missile when it comes. Yesterday, we receive a message that the missile is here and that the nuclear components will arrive shortly. We are ordered to be taken to our stations by our team leaders."

"Taken where?" Cameron asked, leaning across the table and gripping his cup. The coffee in it had gone cold.

"No one is trusted completely," Abdul said, "and each of us has contact with a limited number of others."

Cameron's hand trembled. Good God, how could this be happening? "How did the missile get into the U.S. and where is it being delivered?"

Abdul shrugged after Yasein translated the question. Sweat oozed out from underneath his kaffiyeh.

"I am not told. I overhear things."

"And you overheard . . . ?" Cameron prompted.

"Professor Ramzi is on the telephone today with a team. I think it was in Georgia. One missile has already come, but there is to be more. There is a problem of some sort, I think. I do not know. I overhear him say something about a hostage. I think maybe it is President Stanton—"

"Stanton!" Cameron exclaimed.

"He is seized in Cuba?"

"I know that. But what does he have to do with this?"

Abdul licked his lips and looked blank. After a moment, he shrugged again. "I think we have taken him, but for what purpose—? I can only guess."

"Let's try some more guesses then. Which city is the target?"

"I think it must be New Orleans. That is one."

"One?"

"There are others as well. This I am sure of. I overhear that we will soon have three more missiles and the explosives are in Manila or on the way here. That is all I know."

Cameron silently muttered a prayer. *I will undo all that afflict thee . . .* Jesus said.

"Who would know all the cities?" Cameron demanded.

"None would know all, I think. Each must fire one missile. I am escorted to my site where I must remain under guard until after the deed is accomplished. You must follow when they come for me."

Cameron hesitated. This was getting over his head. He wasn't equipped to undertake such a venture alone. He told Abdul as much.

"I have your word not to betray me, else I cannot cooperate," Abdul argued through Yasein. "*You* must be the one to follow. *You* will arrange for the authorities to come. *You* will see that I escape and am not pursue or identify. Perhaps you will declare me dead so there will never be a *fatwa* on me. *You* must do this in exchange for rescuing one city."

Cameron drew in a deep breath. What other choice did he have?

"How much time do we have?" he asked.

"You agree to the terms?" Abdul asked.

"I won't notify anyone until I follow you and locate the site."

"Good." Abdul consulted his watch. "They come for me before daylight. You must be ready."

CHAPTER 30

MacDill Air Force Base, Tampa, Florida

The satellite feed that provided a visual link to the *Ibn Haldoon* in the South Pacific remained down. Puzzle Palace techs advised it wasn't likely to come back on-line until after the typhoon reached the Philippines and swept on through. Nuclear submarine *Sam Houston*, with Deep Steel 2-B aboard, maintained the single communications thread that kept the freighter on the hook and accessible to a take-down action. It had trailed the rogue freighter by sonar throughout the day, weaving in and out among islands of the Cuyo chain, until the ship inexplicably dropped anchor off one of them. Immediately, there was speculation all the way to the White House that the vessel must be preparing to deliver its cargo.

As late afternoon in the Philippines wore on—early morning in Florida and Washington—CENTCOM, CIA headquarters, the Office of the National Homeland Security Agency, and the secretary of defense, Donald Keating, kept open a continuous conference call in an attempt to keep track of the rapidly evolving situation. CENTCOM was Washington's communications line to the submarine.

"So far, gentlemen," General Paul Etheridge reported, "there is no indication of a freight transfer. There's no harbor on the island and no other vessel has approached it."

"Then why has it put down anchor?" NHSA's director,

MacArthur Thornbrew asked through the four-way phone link.

"It's guesswork on our part," General Darren Kragle admitted. "It may intend to ride out the typhoon in the lee of the island. That storm has picked up speed and is moving a lot faster than first predicted."

"How much more time before it hits in force?" That from deputy CIA director Thomas Hinds's gravelly voice.

"Meteorology is saying about twenty-four hours at this point," General Kragle said. "It's not a powerful storm as typhoons go, but there's wind and the entire front is moving fast."

"The *Abe Lincoln* has reduced speed because of seas and won't be reaching the Luzon area until tomorrow," the SecDef said, considering. "Are the waters still navigable?"

General Etheridge received a nod from the meteorology officer hovering nearby. "At this point, yes."

"Then why," Keating mused from Washington, "has the *Ibn Haldoon* gone dead in the water? Could the smugglers be suspicious and are they waiting for the cover of nightfall to sneak out?"

General Etheridge doubted that. "I think it'll overnight there now. These are dangerous waters to negotiate in the dark, in a storm."

The JCS chief, General Abraham Morrison, was eavesdropping from the SecDef's office. "Destruction of the missiles is Deep Steel's most vital objective," he put in. "We cannot permit the freighter to slip away from us and put those missiles in terrorist hands. Getting rid of them is of more concern at this juncture than catching the terrorists they're being delivered to."

"We agree," said General Etheridge. "Tom, are you there?"

The CIA deputy responded immediately. "Right here."

"It'd help a lot," Etheridge said, "if you made commo with

your man on the *Ibn Haldoon* so we'd know what's going on."

"We have a situation there," Hinds admitted. "The last word we had was something about Koreans. Commo was broken and we couldn't understand anything else. There's been nothing but silence ever since."

The four-way, long-distance conversation continued for another twenty minutes, touching speculatively upon different facets of the mission and bringing up for consideration various options. The forest was full of gorillas. The subject of kidnapped former-president John Stanton was even brought up, especially in light of the fact that JTTF had uncovered evidence indicating that the three terrorist airmen nabbed at St. Marys were somehow connected both with missiles and with Stanton's abduction.

"Anything else on Stanton yet?" JSOC's Carl Spencer inquired.

"Not a peep," the CIA man said. "We have feelers out sniffing. We'll have to stand by until something breaks loose. Senator Thierry keeps raising hell about it, but . . ."

As things wound down, the SecDef asked General Kragle, "General, how soon can Deep Steel put a plan into action?"

"I can send the activation code immediately, Mr. Secretary. Now would be the optimum time while the target is stationary."

The operation would be a simple one at this point: 2-Bravo operatives would swim underneath the ship, attach limpet mines, and blow it out of the water with its spine broken. It was a little more complicated once the ship got under way again.

"What's your recommendation, General Kragle?" SecDef Keating asked.

The General didn't have to think about it. "Do it now while we have the opportunity. The situation is only going to get more complex because of the storm. We know Abu

Sayyaf is undoubtedly set to receive the missiles; we can deal with that bunch later."

It would have been nice to uncover the underground railroad that bootlegged contraband weapons into the U.S.—but not if it meant taking a chance on losing the missiles and their showing up again, with nuclear warheads, in Los Angeles or Baltimore.

"Stand by down there in CENTCOM," Donald Keating said, finally breaking up the conference. "I'm meeting with the President to get his input. But if I were you, USSOCOM, I'd get Deep Steel ready to go."

"Yes, sir."

Lines would be held open between participating agencies until the operation ended. General Kragle had a light lunch at his desk, realizing that he wouldn't be able to leave his post for dinner with Claude Thornton after all. He attempted to cell-phone the Domestic Preparedness director, but got only the agent's voice mail. It wasn't like Claude to be out of pocket; he always made a point of being accessible at all times, twenty-four hours a day.

The General left a message that something had come up and Claude should come directly to the Air Force base, where a CENTCOM pass would be waiting for him at the gate. Then he called home to see if Claude might have phoned Gloria.

"I can't keep up with my own man, much less other mans too," she scolded. "General, I wants you to tell me right this here minute: Where am my sons? I ain't been able to get aholt of none of them."

The General could almost see her deadly finger berating the telephone receiver.

"Don't worry, Brown Sugar. We'll all be at your shivaree."

"I done tol' you I got a bad feeling something is gonna happen."

"Let me know immediately if Claude calls, Sugar Mama," the General said and quickly escaped.

He then telephoned agent Fred Whiteman, Claude's old friend.

"He said he was going by Edith, Georgia, to check on a matter," Whiteman said, "then drive on to MacDill to chow down with you. He said *you* were buying. That's the last we've heard."

"If he checks in, Fred, have him call me."

"I'll try to locate him."

The hours dragged by. It was the middle of the night in the Philippines. The *Ibn Haldoon* remained at anchor while the U.S. submarine hung underwater vigil nearby.

The four-way conference call resumed at approximately 1500 hours. It was brief and to the point.

"The President wants the target nullified now instead of waiting for it to make delivery to the terrorists," ordered the secretary of defense. "Mr. Hinds, you want to tell them about your agent?"

Hinds's rough voice sounded reluctant, but it was something that had to be done.

"We've radioed her in the blind to prepare to abandon the ship and link up with U.S. raiders," the CIA spook said. "We can't be sure she received the message. That makes it necessary for a party to board the ship to recover her."

"Her?" General Kragle snapped, surprised and irritated. Everyone knew his opinion that women didn't belong in these situations. "You've put a female aboard ship with a bunch of male terrorists? What were you thinking, man?"

"She's one of our best," Hinds defended. "She won't look like a woman. Her recognition challenge is *Ismael.* She'll be calling it out as soon as she knows Americans have boarded. *Tora* is the correct response to let her know they understand."

The name Ismael ran a familiar trace through the General's mind. Then he remembered from where: Operation

Iron Weed and the female, Summer, who posed as Ismael in Afghanistan. Brandon wouldn't know about the agent being Ismael because it hadn't come up during the mission briefing. An icy chill ran down the General's spine; he had liked Summer and suspected his son might even be in love with her.

Too late to do anything about it at that point. The conference closed. General Kragle ordered CENTCOM's communications section leader to send out the code to initiate the final phase of Operation Deep Steel. From now on, everything was up to Major Brandon Kragle and his detachment of Deltas and SEALs. The brass had little further to do except drink cups of stale coffee and wait until it was over. General Kragle stared at the giant satellite monitor screen in front of him. It remained mockingly blank.

CHAPTER 31

Cuyo Islands

Life, Brandon reflected, was a gambler who dealt unexpected hands. It took all the wind out of him when he learned that the recognition code for the CIA aboard the *Ibn Haldoon* was *Ismael*. The picture was complete when he also learned that Ismael was a *she* disguised as a man. Who else could it be except Summer? In the War on Terror, the SpecOps, law enforcement, and intelligence communities were relatively small and interactive. That wry bastard life had dealt him aces and eights with this mission. He had already lost one good man. Now, Summer was aboard a rogue ship filled with pirates, terrorists, and cutthroats. Information from CENT-COM said radio contact had been lost with her—and it couldn't be certain whether she was still alive, alive and compromised, or dead.

A woman should not be placed in that position. He mustn't think about her.

The detachment had a mission to destroy the ship at dawn. Although they didn't necessarily need daylight for the job, it was only a couple of hours from sunrise when orders came to accelerate the mission. So dawn it was. Get it over with.

The *Ibn Haldoon* still had not stirred from anchor and showed no indication of immediately doing so. Brandon made mission assignments. He personally, along with Ice Man Thompson, would board the ship to recover Ismael before the ship went up. That was a job he wouldn't, *couldn't,* leave to someone else. If she were alive, Brandon was going to bring her off that ship. If she were dead . . . His gray eyes narrowed. He would deal with that when the time came.

Lieutenant Lucifer's black eyebrows V'd malevolently. "Fuck a duck," he blustered. "You're the detachment commander. You can't fucking command from there. I'll go instead."

Brandon held his temper. "Chief Gorrell and you will man the SDV. It may be necessary for a swimmer to be in the water to help recover the teams or the agent. That's you. The chief will have to stay with the SDV."

Brandon had not divulged the true suspected identity of Ismael nor their personal relationship. He told himself it didn't matter. He knew it did, but an operator must not let his emotions influence his job.

Lucifer sulked. "Bosnia was a long time ago."

"Not *that* long ago."

Lucifer should have been convicted at his court-martial.

"You have to let it go, Kragle. I'm a different man."

Brandon thought of how bravely Lucifer handled the incident with the shark.

"Maybe," he said, then hardened again. "Maybe not."

Cassidy wanted to be included on the demolitions team. Instead, Brandon selected Delta's Thumbs Jones and SEAL T-Bone Jones to rig explosives to the freighter's hull. "The Jones brothers," as Mad Dog referred to them.

"I'm good with explosives," Cassidy protested mildly. "I don't need protection just because I'm your brother."

"You won't get it. They have the experience. Your time will come, kid."

It was part of the SpecOps personality profile that no man wanted to be left behind when it came to a job. As a commander, Brandon had come to expect it. He would have been disappointed in any man who didn't protest just a little. Even Gloomy Davis had his moment.

"Boss, the Hooker Hogettes found out they couldn't do without me."

"Neither can I, Gloomy. You're acting team sergeant. I need you to stay on the sub to make decisions in case something should happen while we're out there."

"Boss, what could happen? *You'll* be there."

"Thanks, Gloomy."

Seawater flooded the SDV bay of the dry deck shelter. At a depth of one hundred feet, USS *Sam Houston* maintained neutral buoyancy while it launched the miniaturized version of itself into the black undersea, like a whale giving birth. Those members of Deep Steel left behind viewed the departure through a porthole from the still-pressurized section of the DDS. The twenty-foot SEAL Delivery Vehicle Mark VIII slid like a silent shadow from the DDS.

It was a "wet" boat, not a true submarine, which meant the

interior was flooded. Watery red night-vision illumination cast an eerie glow over the six SCUBA-wearing occupants sitting cramped two by two facing forward. Windowless, the SDV emitted no light that could be seen from the surface. It was as blind as a cave shrimp except for its Doppler computerized navigation system and obstacle-avoidance and side-scanning radar.

Chief Petty Officer Gorrell handled the controls. Lieutenant Lucifer rode shotgun. Behind them sat the demo men, the black Jones and the white Jones, each clutching a satchel containing a pair of limpet mines and the tools of their explosive trade. Brandon and Ice Man Thompson took up the back seat. Ice Man carried a canvas bag containing a grapnel mortar by which the two of them intended boarding the *Ibn Haldoon* while the Joneses planted their mines to crack the freighter like an egg. Brandon carried a frameless canvas pack into which he had stuffed a wet suit, Draeger UBA (underwater breathing apparatus), mask, and flippers for Ismael to use. She could breathe off his tanks. He had also included a spare rappelling rope.

He hoped she knew how to use diving gear. There wouldn't be time for lessons.

An onboard breathing system with full-face masks provided air and a communications system until the swimmers went on individual Draeger closed-circuit SCUBA. There was little need for talking. Encased in the steel underwater coffin with its liquid red light, Brandon heard himself sucking air through the face mask. He heard the hum of the vehicle's electric engines. The submersible pulsated with the sweeping motion of the restless and disturbed sea, challenging Chief Gorrell to keep it on course.

"Ten minutes!" came the chief's voice through the echoing commo system.

Brandon checked his diving gear. At the belt of his black

wetsuit he wore a holstered ZUB underwater pistol along with the WWII Ka-Bar Grandfather Jordan gave him.

"We're approaching," Chief Gorrell warned, his eyes intent on the instrument dash and its radar and sonar screens.

Lieutenant Lucifer turned and looked back through the red-tinted water. He held up a thumb in question: *A-Okay?* Both passenger teams returned his thumbs-up: *Ready.* He turned forward again without a word, apparently still sulking.

The SDV eased off forward motion, but continued to rock with the sea movement. The side door slid up, diffusing the calm interior water with the outer sea.

"The target is fifty yards on an azimuth of one-five-zero," the chief supplied.

The swimmers synchronized their watches and exchanged the boat's breathing apparatus for that attached to their twin tanks. Thumbs reached back and squeezed Brandon's arm—*Good luck*—and then he and the other Jones, the SEAL, doubled themselves out the door, fins swishing, and melted into the black water like fish.

Brandon nodded at Ice Man. The weapons sergeant led the way, setting the azimuth on his luminous compass board. The SDV door closed behind them, slicing off the red glow from the interior. The closed-circuit Draegers emitted no telltale bubbles.

They angled toward the surface and swam directly upon the ship before they saw it, a gray barnacle-encrusted underwater hull riding a dangerous sea. Brandon shot up into the dull half-light of dawn. A breaking curl slammed him into the side of the ship with an impact that ripped the mouthpiece from his teeth. Ice Man grabbed him. Together, coughing and sputtering, they rode the high retreating wave and dropped into the following trough.

After a moment, they stabilized as best they could by using their buoyancy compensators as flotation. The freighter yawed and heaved, threatening to crush them or suck them under. The dock railing seemed an impossibly elusive target high above their heads. Boarding the vessel was going to be much more difficult than Brandon anticipated.

How were they going to locate Ismael once they succeeded in getting aboard? Providing the gale winds kept most of the crew off-deck so they wouldn't be spotted, providing they weren't seen from the bridge. A message had been sent to her in the blind alerting her to the boarding—but there was no assurance she received it.

Brandon had to proceed on the assumption that she was waiting. But first they had to climb the tub's water-slick hull.

It took both men in the churning water to prepare the grapnel for firing. The device resembled a short-barreled 60mm mortar tube, only smaller. One end of a coil of nylon rope was attached to the mortar, the other end to the shank of the grapnel. Its hooks were compressed so that it slid into the mortar's barrel. Ice Man finally managed to charge the gun and drop the grapnel hook down the tube.

Together, holding onto each other and the grapnel, the Deltas fought the sea for position. From behind, Brandon reached around Ice Man with both arms and helped secure the base plate against his sergeant's muscled stomach. Ice Man lay back in the water. As they rode the crest of a wave to its breaking point, Ice Man thrust the coil of rope high above his head, loosening it in his hand.

"Now!" Brandon said.

Ice Man triggered the gun. It coughed a pneumatic sound immediately swallowed by the storm. Rope hissed from the coil. The hooks automatically opened in flight as the grapnel rocketed up toward the deck railing. The rope slackened. Ice Man yanked to set the hooks into the railing.

The rope went limp. Brandon shouted a warning.

The grapnel bounced from the ship and into the ocean. As Ice Man reeled in the line, a wave tugged violently on the hook, then released it like a stone thrown from a slingshot. It whipped through the air and caught Ice Man a glancing blow on the same cheek that had been scarred from a gunshot wound in Afghanistan. Blood squirted.

"Ice?"

"Okay." Ice Man was always a man of few words.

They recharged the mortar. Brandon wrapped his fists in the mortar end of the line. They mustn't lose it. Ice Man fired again. Wind howled as the hook opened and hummed up into the light stinging rain.

This time the hooks caught on the railing just as the ship heeled in the opposite direction, as though recoiling from a shot. Brandon and his sergeant were yanked out of the water like a pair of perch hooked on the same line. They pitched through the air and smashed into the ship's steel hull.

The impact loosened Ice Man. He dropped into the water. Brandon had the breath knocked out of his body, but he held onto the rope while he recovered. The freighter heeled back toward him, wallowing and dunking him into the drink. Ice Man swam to steady him.

Brandon had to shout in order to be heard above the keening of the wind and rain and the slop of seas against the ship. "I'm going up. I'll signal when it's all-clear."

He removed his fins and stuffed them into the pack containing Ismael's gear. With the pack slung from his shoulder, he started climbing the rope hand over hand, pulling up slack and doubling it into his hands to form ladder steps for his feet. Deltas practiced the maneuver on the towers at Wally World. They should have trained under fire hoses while a bulldozer crashed into the sides of the tower.

The going was easier the higher he climbed; the boat hull flared out to meet him. He inched his head up until his eyes were even with the top of the deck. Rain hissed and skittered along the broad surface. No one seemed out and about. Maybe the crew was sleeping in.

Forward, red-and-white superstructure rose to the captain's bridge. The bridge's aft windows were not equipped with rain wipers. Fortunately, they were rain-streaked and fogged over from inside, making it difficult for anyone to see out.

Brandon pulled himself up and rolled onto the deck, a difficult enough procedure while still in full SCUBA and carrying the pack. He held on to the railing and rewarded himself with a moment to catch his breath. He glanced at his watch and calculated that the Joneses should be attaching limpets to the ship's spine about now. He had to hurry to keep up with the Joneses. There was going to be one hell of an explosion in about an hour.

Off the bow to his left lay a green island, hazy and indistinct from the lash of wind and rain in the dawn light. There were no signs of activity either on the island or anywhere else around. So far, so good. But now how did he find Ismael? He didn't know where to start.

He was about to signal Ice Man to come on up when a watertight door opened in the nearest bulkhead of the aft superstructure. Someone must have been watching. Brandon's hand snaked for the ZUB. The weapon was lethal to about thirty yards out of water. Better yet, it was almost noiseless.

Before he could fire, a frantic voice called out, thin and strident in the wind. *"Ismael!"*

She must have received the message after all. Brandon shouted back the response code. *"Tora!"* He leaped to his feet and dashed toward the voice. His mind raced ahead. He recognized the slight figure in the dirty yellow oilskins even before he reached her.

She failed to recognize him until he got near enough to sweep the hood and ball cap off her head. He crushed the precious body against his, but couldn't reach her lips because of the dive mask pushed up on his forehead and the breathing mouthpiece hanging on hoses around his neck.

"Kragle!" she cried, ecstatic with joy and relief. "We're going to have to stop meeting like this."

It was an old joke between them from the Tora Bora.

She ran a small tender hand over his lips and mustache. That was as far as the reunion got. Two things happened simultaneously, both unexpected.

First, the *Ibn Haldoon* suddenly rumbled to life, shuddering as its engines cranked over and caught. Crews poured out onto the forward decks to retrieve anchors.

Second, someone shouted at them in Arabic. Brandon spun toward the voice. A crewman bulky in black foul weather gear ran toward them with a pistol in his hand, whooping and hollering with sufficient alarm to awaken Davy Jones in his locker.

Just when Brandon thought Murphy might be looking the other way.

CHAPTER 32

Something about the crewman cued Brandon at the last moment that he wasn't actually focused on *them*. Brandon held fire with the ZUB. He shoved Summer against the outer bulkhead of the superstructure and flattened himself next to her underneath the sheltered walkway. Rainwater washing from above formed a gray curtain that helped conceal them.

The intruder had a difficult time maintaining balance as he

caromed across the pitching deck. It was almost comical. For every two steps he took forward, he took one back. Obviously he wasn't a seasoned sailor.

"The wrestler," Summer hissed.

The wrestler focused his suspicion on the railing to which the grapnel hook with its attached rope clung like a burr. Somehow it must have caught his attention. He angled the nearest approach to the railing and then pulled himself along it until he reached the hook.

The freighter's propellers caught the sea and the ship lurched forward with power to loosen tension on the anchor chains and allow them to be winched aboard. The movement caused the ship to heel, throwing the gunman backward. He held onto the railing and jerked himself forward. He leaned out over the cable and pointed the gun downward at Ice Man.

"Asshole!" Brandon yelled, charging forward. It wasn't exactly the most original challenge of his career, as Summer was bound to point out later. But it worked.

The surprised terrorist wheeled. His eyes bulged at the sight of the apparition rushing at him in black fishlike wetsuit and diving gear. *Creature from the Black Lagoon.*

Brandon's ZUB used an electrical charge to fire a finned dart. The first shot had to count since the weapon's rate of fire was only ten rounds per minute and its lethal range limited. Brandon waited until the last second to pull the trigger. His opponent was so shocked by the strangeness of his attacker that his reflexes froze for that crucial extra second Brandon needed.

The weapon coughed, a sound smothered by the elements. The man dropped his pistol and seized his throat where the projectile entered just above the *V* of his breastbone. The movement of the ship threw him headlong into Brandon.

They crashed to the deck in a tangle of arms and legs and skittered across the precipitously slanted deck until they slammed into the bulkhead next to Summer. Brandon extricated himself from the entanglement, Ka-Bar in hand to finish the job.

The bulky Filipino lay twitching. One leg kicked spasmodically. He was dying. The dart must have angled downward into his lungs and heart. Brandon's first concern was that the encounter, brief as it had been, might be witnessed. When he looked, however, the sailors at the bow with the anchors, hunched deep into their rain gear, seemed oblivious of everything except the weather and their own misery. Brandon holstered the ZUB and the Ka-Bar, a renewed sense of urgency impressed upon him by the incident. The SDV would be waiting to pick them up. He opened the pack.

"Fins, mask, and wetsuit," he explained tersely. "Strip and get 'em on. You can breathe off my tank."

"I can't go," she replied. "I received commo that you were coming—but I couldn't get out a response."

He grabbed her shoulders with both hands. "What the hell are you talking about? In less than an hour this ship is going to be hurtling through the air at about Mach 1."

She pulled away. "There are three little Korean stowaways aboard," she explained, the words tumbling out. "I promised I wouldn't abandon them."

"Let's get them then. Now."

"There's more."

"I don't know if I want more."

"John Stanton is on board."

"Who?"

"Your old friend, the former president of the U.S. It looks like he's been kidnapped."

"Well, I'll be damned." He found that hard to digest.

"None other."

The freighter inched forward in the water, starting to move.

"Screw him," Brandon said, making up his mind. "He's a scumbag. Let's get the kids."

"Didn't I tell you there was more?"

"I thought Stanton was the *more.*"

"Only part of it. The kids are hiding in a rope locker next to where they're keeping Stanton—and they have Stanton heavily guarded."

Brandon stared at her. Rain streamed down his face. "Was there something you didn't hear, Summer? There are mines attached to the hull of this ship, and they're timed to go off."

"You have to defuse them, Brandon."

"This ship is under way. There's no way to take them off while it's moving."

She looked at him with rain on her lashes and her unblinking eyes the color of an emerald sea.

"Save yourself, Brandon. I'm not going without those kids."

He turned away in abrupt exasperation, eyes darting as he desperately tried to think of something. He considered snatching her up in his arms and leaping overboard with her. Only, she would never forgive him about the kids, for whom she seemed to have developed an attachment. He would never forgive himself for doing it to her.

His eyes settled on the dead man. It might work. He took a step toward Summer and thrust his face down into hers.

"Did you really think I would leave you?"

"No."

"Bitch."

"Yes."

He sprinted to the railing and looked over. Ice Man was on his way up the rope, nearing the railing. Having the gun pointed at him and subsequently seeing nothing else of his commander had aroused his protective instincts; he had started up without waiting for the signal. Deltas never left a man behind. His eyes widened with relief when he saw Brandon. He lifted a hand for Brandon to hoist him aboard.

There wasn't time to explain. "Tell them there are three kids and Stanton on the ship," Brandon blurted out.

Ice Man looked confused. "What—?"

"Three kids. Stanton. Remember that."

Brandon whipped out his Ka-Bar and cut the rope. Ice Man plummeted into the sea. It was the only way. The sergeant would never have deserted Brandon on his own volition, no matter what. The SDV would sonar in on his signal bracelet and pick him up.

Already planning, Brandon hurled the grapnel hook far into the rain to get it out of sight, then hurried back to Summer. He grabbed the dead man by the arms.

"Help me drag him. This guy weighs a ton."

She took an arm. "Into the drink?"

"I have a better use for him. If it doesn't work, we're going to be doing Mach 1 together."

CHAPTER 33

TERRORISTS MAKE DEMANDS REGARDING STANTON

Washington (CPI)—Terrorists claiming responsibility for the abduction of former President John Stanton have sent copies of their demands to three news agencies. FOX News, CNN, and Consolidated Press International received identical copies. The terrorists warn that if their demands are not met, Stanton will be beheaded and his head delivered in a basket to the steps of the U.S. Congress.

The demands:

—All U.S. troops be withdrawn from the Philippines;

—U.S. urges the Filipino government to negotiate a Muslim-controlled state in the southern part of the country;

—U.S. murder indictments against Abu Sayyaf members, including Albaneh Mosed, be retracted;

—Al-Qaeda soldiers detained at Guantánamo, Cuba, be released;

—The President of the United States make a worldwide apology to all Muslims;

—And, finally, that Stanton will be released only in the event a $20 million ransom is paid.

The ransom demands give the President of the United States seventy-two hours in which to respond.

CPI has also learned that Stanton's abduction may be related to an airplane seized at the municipal airport in St. Marys, Georgia. According to unnamed sources, the C-47, registered to a nonexistent company in Florida, is suspected of having delivered a missile into the hands of terrorists hiding somewhere in the southern United States.

The abduction and the mysterious aircraft have triggered a diplomatic crisis between Cuba and the U.S.

"We will not allow any terrorist or tyrant to threaten civilization with weapons of mass murder," said the President of the United States, speaking from Ellis Island with the Statue of Liberty and the forever-altered skyline of New York at his back. "This nation has defeated tyrants, liberated death camps, and raised the lamp of liberty to every captive land. We have no intention of ignoring or appeasing history's latest group of fanatics trying to muscle their way to power."

Senate Majority Leader Jake Thierry urged the President to negotiate with the terrorists for Stanton's safe return.

CHAPTER 34

Okefenokee Swamp

Years ago, Senior Agent Claude Thornton learned a valuable lesson about assumptions while serving a hitch in the army at Fort Polk, Louisiana. He and an army buddy, Romero, another sergeant, were in line at the post package store to pick up a couple of bottles for some Friday night festivities. The buddy was Hispanic. Thornton and he commonly spoke Spanish whenever they wanted to hold private conversations in public.

A black woman who looked to be straight out of some bayou shanty town walked into the liquor store and got in line behind Romero. The woman was so *ugly* that Thornton and Romero couldn't help commenting about her in less than flattering terms. In Spanish.

Who would have thought that the ugliest black woman in the middle of Louisiana would turn out to be a Spanish instructor at the local JC? When she got through blistering their ears in perfect Castilian, their only option was to slink out with their tails between their legs. Thornton never assumed anything on first appearances after that.

Obviously, Sahim Goba and the other one, whom Thornton assumed to be Alwan because those were the two names inscribed next to Edith on the map agents found in the hastily abandoned Jacksonville apartment, had not learned that lesson. Who would think that a big black man with a shaved head in Georgia would speak excellent Arabic? Bound head and foot and tossed into a moldy corner of the swamp cabin, Thornton uttered nothing to clue in his abductors that he spoke anything but English. His only advantage at that moment lay in concealing that fact while he eavesdropped on their conversations.

It became immediately apparent that while the agent's capture caused a share of excitement, he wasn't the only source of it. From the look of things—packed boxes and bags—the terrorists were already preparing to clear out in a hurry. Thornton's entrance complicated matters. The two of them jabbered excitedly over his FBI credentials. Alwan ran down to the road to see if others might be about while Goba kept guard over Thornton. He was gone quite a while. Shadows were lengthening toward nightfall when he returned to briefly explain how he had driven the prisoner's car into a deep bayou where it would not be found.

The pressing question now was what to do with the captive. Thornton's future did not look bright.

"Shoot him in the head and drop him in the swamp," suggested Alwan. He was stocky and cleanshaven, with a broad, rather dull face, thick lips, and a single black brow that made him look even duller. "The crocodiles will eat him."

"They are not crocodiles. They are alligators," Goba corrected. He was so thin he barely cast a shadow. His brown, hungry face reminded Thornton of a rusty knife blade. Like Alwan, he was cleanshaven and short-haired, presumably to better blend into the American population.

"Crocodile or alligator, it does not matter," Alwan said. "Remember how they devoured the lost dog?"

The terrorists regarded Thornton without emotion. He felt like a fish about to become filleted. He kept his head lowered, still pretending not to understand.

At the same time, his eyes darted to take in the single filthy room, looking for some weapon he might reach and employ. There were two sleeping bags rolled up on the floor, ready to be carried out. Also three chairs, one of which had a broken leg; a potbellied wood-burning stove; a battered wooden table; old pizza boxes; open food tins containing spoiled residue; cereal boxes, sour-smelling milk cartons ... A wood mouse sniffed around in the shadows of the far corner. He looked well fed.

Perhaps the broken chair leg would serve as a weapon. If he could get free and reach it.

Undecided about what to do, Goba kept punching in numbers on his cell phone, walking to the open door and looking out nervously while he waited for an answer. Shadows lengthened in the swamp. Goba received no answer. He looked annoyed.

"Where is Ramzi?" he worried rhetorically.

"I should know?" Alwan retorted. "I, stuck in this swamp while Ramzi plays in the city with virgins."

"There are no virgins in America," Goba snapped.

The two men sat down in chairs at the table while they waited to complete Goba's call. Alwan took out a long-bladed pocket knife and peeled a yellow pear, letting the peelings drop to the floor. He then used the knife to cut bites off the fruit, which he munched. From where Thornton lay trussed in the corner, he strained to overhear their conversation. They spoke in low voices, but he understood enough to know they were talking about the missing cargo from the C-47 captured at St. Marys.

From what he gathered, the airplane had carried a *missile*. It had been offloaded at an isolated unpaved airstrip in Georgia, not far from Edith, loaded onto a truck and was now on its way elsewhere. Goba and Alwan acted as intermediaries. They received the missile, sent it on its way, and were waiting on what Thornton deduced to be materials from which to construct a nuclear warhead when FBI raids on safe houses in Jacksonville disrupted plans. This "Ramzi" character, whoever he was, had gotten antsy and ordered the two men to abandon their post. The nuclear materials, along with what Thornton assumed from the overheard conversation to be three more missiles, would be delivered by other routes and alternate means.

That was the situation as best Thornton could determine it before he came along and bungled into the middle of things. It was up to "Ramzi" to make the decision about what to do about him—as soon as Goba got him on the telephone. Thornton watched Alwan's knife as the one-eye-browed man continued to wield it against the pear.

"We will soon have everything we need for our strike against the Great Satan," Goba said. "We are blessed by Allah."

Though restless and anxious about their delayed departure, the terrorists were in a jubilant mood, almost ecstatic over the prospect of striking out against the infidels. They seemed to enjoy talking about it, describing it to each other. Thornton studied them while appearing to show no more than ordinary interest.

Although he had worked with Muslims for a better part of his adulthood and spoke the languages, he still found the depth of fanaticism in the most radical of them a difficult thing to comprehend. To these extremists, martyrdom in the name of Allah was their highest earthly aspiration. One big boom and they were forever in heaven with Mohammed while bevies of virgins administered to their every whim.

He thought of the little missiles sketched onto the margins of the map that had led him to Edith. Al-Qaeda and Taliban prisoners from various levels of the terrorist network had been warning of second and third attacks against America with biological, chemical, or radiological weapons, the objective being to increase casualties, paralyze Americans with fear, and cripple the economy. "Johnny Jihad," an American captured fighting for Osama bin Laden in Afghanistan, confessed to interrogators that he had heard about unconventional weapons being delivered out of Iraq and North Korea. Al-Qaeda, he said, owned a fleet of freighters and aircraft that picked up and transported weapons.

"The next two attacks," Johnny Jihad said, "will be so huge they will make Americans forget about 9/11."

Consolidated Press International obtained an audiotape of Ayman al-Zawahri being interviewed by the As-Sahaab Foundation for Islamic Media. Thornton knew al-Zawahri from when he was stationed in Egypt with the FBI. Knew him as al-Qaeda's primary strategist, an evil, devious man to whom the lives of "infidels" were no more than those of insects.

"The mujahid youth is prepared to send further messages," he declared on the audiotape. "If the first dose is not enough, we are prepared with the help of Allah to inject further doses. We aim to continue, by permission of Allah, the destruction of the United States of America and its infidels. May Allah protect our warriors until they become martyrs."

May Allah, Thornton thought, *ram it up their rosy radical rectums.*

Judging from the talk of Goba and Alwan, sleeper cells of terrorists in the United States already possessed nuclear capabilities. To what extent, Thornton could only guess. But if Operation Deep Steel failed and SCUDs fell into the hands of Islamic radicals in the Philippines and ended up joining the missile that came in via Cuba . . . Jesus to God. Ground zero might be anywhere in the United States. Two, three, four cities. Perhaps more. The casualty rate could be hundreds of thousands, a million or more. Men, women, and children. A death rate to indeed minimize by comparison the toll at the World Trade Center and the Pentagon more than a year ago.

Thornton felt desperation oozing mudlike into his soul. He tried to think. Fred Whiteman knew he was driving to Tampa and stopping by Edith on the way. General Kragle would certainly make inquiries when Claude failed to show up for dinner that evening. The trail Thornton left through Edith in searching for Goba and Alwan wouldn't be that difficult to retrace. Somebody would come looking sooner or later.

But would they get here in time?

Not likely.

Alwan finished his pear and grew more restive. He laid the knife on the edge of the table. He got up and faced Thornton. The sun was down. Goba lit a kerosene lamp on the table, which spread flickering yellow light across the room and revealed that Alwan had drawn his gun.

"There will be other police coming," he said to Goba. "They never come alone, because they are pigs and they are cowards. We must be on our way immediately before we are trapped here."

He pointed the gun at the agent. "I will kill the kafir."

Steeling himself against the expected bullet, Thornton eyed Alwan's knife on the table. Bound as he was hand and foot, it would require superhuman effort and a lot of luck to reach it—and even more effort and luck to use it to cut his bonds and then deploy the knife against two armed thugs. Yet, it was better to go down fighting than to be slaughtered like a caged broiler.

If he could throw himself against the table legs, knocking it over and extinguishing the light, he might stand a chance of getting hold of the knife in the ensuing confusion. He bunched his muscles and casually pulled his tied feet underneath his weight in preparation for the effort. He calculated his chances of success as about the same as a snowflake falling on the Sahara Desert.

His obligation, his duty, was to escape and warn America. He had to try.

Goba's cell phone went off musically. The skinny man jumped to his feet and answered it. Alwan turned away with his gun and picked up the knife, closed it, and stuck it in his pocket. Thornton's last hope went with it.

Goba held his phone conversation while standing in the door where Thornton couldn't hear what was said. It was brief. Goba turned back into the cabin.

"Ramzi says bring him with us."

Alwan frowned. "It is easier to kill him."

Goba shrugged. "He says maybe we can use him to bargain for the release of prisoners the FBI has taken. Ramzi wants to question him. You can always shoot him later."

Alwan looked disappointed, but he stuffed the pistol back underneath his shirt. The terrorists quickly gathered up their few belongings. In English, Goba said to Thornton, "You are going with us. I will free your feet so you can walk. My friend will take great joy in shooting you in the head if you attempt to escape."

It was no more than a temporary reprieve, Thornton realized, but he would take any chance offered him.

They marched him out of the darkening swamp at gunpoint, then re-tied his feet and shoved him into the back of the tan Ford SUV. They covered him with pieces of carpet and piled boxes on top of that to hide his presence from any curious eyes they might encounter during the trip. Thornton lay in total darkness, feeling as though he were about to suffocate. The last thing he heard before the engine kicked over and the vehicle started moving was an alligator honking for a mate—or complaining because it had not been fed.

He wondered how much time he had left. And how much time unknown American cities had left if these terrorists were not stopped?

CHAPTER 35

Cuyo Islands

Stanton and the Korean stowaways aboard the *Ibn Haldoon*, along with Summer's refusal to leave them behind, complicated the hell out of things. It comforted Brandon some to know that Ice Man at least would soon be safely back with the detachment on the *Sam Houston*; no sense in both of them sacrificing their lives in what ultimately had to be an insane and probably futile effort. He hoped Delta understood and that, if he failed, the General would also understand. There was nothing the detachment or anybody else could do at that point to help him. There simply wasn't enough time. Everything was left up to him, the young slip of a girl, and the dead man.

The *Ibn Haldoon* bounced and rocked on the churning sea as it picked up cruise speed and steamed south toward the Sulu Sea that separated the two major Philippine islands of Palawan and Mindanao. Brandon and Summer had difficulty maintaining their balance as they struggled to drag the dead wrestler off the open deck and inside the more secluded companionway. So far they'd been lucky. Neither the anchor crew nor the bridge noticed what went on, else the ship would have been swarming with pissed-off brigands. If they were even luckier, the remaining crew below decks would either be in their quarters sleeping or gambling or in the galley for morning chow. Brandon counted on no one missing the recently deceased for at least a little while longer.

There was no one in the passageways. Brandon closed the hatch behind them and spun the wheel lock, cutting out the thin driving rain and the roar of the angry sea. He stuffed his dive mask into the pack containing the other gear intended for Ismael's rescue and slung the pack over his shoulder. He wore his air tanks, awkard as they were; they wouldn't fit inside the pack. He would need them soon anyhow. His feet in black dive booties left wet tracks on the steel deck. He wiped water out of his eyes and balanced himself against the bulkhead with one hand.

"Can we get down to the engine room without being seen?" he asked Summer.

She looked puzzled.

"We have to stop the ship before I can disarm the mines," he explained, growing impatient. "Now, can we get to the engine room?"

"Maybe. It's below the aft hold. But there's always someone there when under way." She indicated the dead man in storm gear. "What about him?"

"We're taking him with us."

"I thought we were traveling light." Always the wiseass.

"You're the one who booked passage."

The dead man seemed to weigh a ton. Dead weight always did. Together, they pulled him along the narrow dimly lighted passageways and wrestled him down steep steel ladders toward the freighter's bowels. Fortunately, the finned dart from the ZUB opened no gaping wound to leave a blood trail. Their water tracks and drag marks would soon dry.

Their luck held.

Speaking in low, urgent tones, Brandon filled Summer in on his mission to blow up the freighter and its cargo of missiles. Summer in turn briefly explained how she came to be on the *Ibn Haldoon* and about how she found the three Korean kids hiding in the hold. The former president, Stanton, she said, was schlepped aboard the day before and she hadn't seen him since, although she knew where he was being held under guard. She had attempted to relay all this via satellite phone, but nothing seemed to be getting out. It was only serendipity that an encrypted message reached her.

Grunting and straining, they hoisted the heavy corpse's feet free of the last rung of the ladder. Summer pulled on his legs while Brandon from above lowered him to the deck. They paused in the half light to catch their breath.

Summer had left her yellow oilskins topside. Her Arab garb was soaked and clung to her body. She jerked the ball cap more firmly onto her cropped dyed-black hair and, as always, grinned that mocking smile.

"You were really good in bed," she teased.

The unexpected comment flustered him and made him feel guilty because of Brandi. But one-night stands didn't count against you. Did they?

Unable to think of a comeback, he glanced at his watch instead. Twenty-five minutes remaining, more or less. Summer understood and pointed toward a closed hatch. "The engine room's right through there. Do we have time for a quickie?"

"We'd have the world's most explosive climax."

"You do know how to sweet-talk a girl." She sobered. "Brandon, there will be a next time?"

"You bet."

"In that case, it's ladies first."

She started toward the hatch. Brandon stuck out a hand to stop her.

"I'm Ismael, remember? I'm supposed to be on the ship," she said, amused at the big man's protectiveness.

"I forgot."

"I'll check it out and be right back."

"I'll slip into something comfortable."

"I always liked black rubber."

She opened the hatch and disappeared through it. There was nowhere to hide the dead wrestler if someone came along the passageway. Brandon crouched over the body, attempting to merge into the shadows, and kept open a wary eye. Summer soon reappeared and motioned to him, whispering.

"The coast is clear. The engineer's in his office forward of the engine room. Now what about this guy? I'm beginning to feel like Boris Karloff stealing dead bodies for Dr. Frankenstein."

"He's how we're going to stop the engines. Can we reach the propeller shaft?"

"How conspicuous can we be carrying a corpse?" she asked sarcastically.

They lugged the heavy Filipino down the ladder to the engine room. Any noise they made wasn't a factor. Bilge pumps whined in backdrop to the deafening thud of pistons and the roar of the powerful twin diesels. The heat was insufferable; they instantly broke into sweat. Summer stifled a cough from the caustic fumes in her nostrils.

The diesels occupied the entire center of the huge oil-splattered chamber. Summer pointed toward the front, indicating the location of the engineer and his office. The office's one wide window overlooked the engines. The glass was grease-smeared and filthy, but Brandon saw a man inside sitting with his back to them looking at a magazine.

Oil-generator electric lights strung across the high overhead throbbed, brightening and dimming. They chased shadows amid the machinery. Rancid seawater leaked in through the hull's seams and collected along the keel. A slatted wooden walkway paralleled the propeller shaft. The shaft was a threaded steel rod about half the circumference of a fifty-five-gallon oil drum. Whining noisily, driven by the engines, the shaft passed through a series of toothed gears before extending out through the stern to drive the propellers.

Summer's strength for all her small size amazed Brandon. She led the way along the wooden walkway with a dead man's leg under each arm. Brandon took the head and shoulders. Footing was more stable here because of the physics of the ship's long axis.

"This is good enough," Brandon stage-whispered, looking back to make sure the engineer was still reading.

They dropped the body on the walkway next to a set of grinding gears operating against the shaft. The dead man's eyes remained half-open and glazed. Maybe in death he would serve a useful purpose.

"This won't be pretty," Brandon warned. "With luck, they'll think he came below for some reason and fell into the gears. Go on. I'll meet you topside at the hatchway."

"I'm still not going without the kids."

He turned on her. "We don't have time for this," he snapped. "All hell is going to break loose in about two minutes. I won't leave you, Summer. We can come back for the kids after we disarm the mines."

She flatly refused. "At any rate, we have no other choice. I'm not a SCUBA diver and I'm not sure I can learn in rough seas. Besides, how are we going to work on the mines with me sucking on your tanks like a remora stuck on a shark? Now, get the hell on with your business, and I'll get on with mine."

She was one stubborn broad. Why did he always fall for willful women? But she was right. He couldn't disarm the explosives and look out for her at the same time. In less than twenty minutes, if he didn't hurry, they were both going up with the ship. Along with everyone else aboard.

"I'll distract the engineer when the engines stop to give you time to get away," she volunteered. "Good luck, Brandon."

The dead man lay between them. Summer eased around the body without slipping off the walkway. She placed both hands on Brandon's shoulders. She touched his cheek, his mustache.

"I'll be back for you," he promised.

"I know you will." She rose on tiptoes and kissed him on the mouth. "I love you, Brandon."

It just came out. She hurried off without looking back.

Brandon gave her a minute, watching as she strode toward the office. She kept herself between the window and him to block as much of the engineer's view as possible should he turn around prematurely. Then Brandon hoisted the wrestler and draped him over the revolving threads of the screw shaft. He made sure the corpse was on its way toward the toothed gears before he trotted toward the ladder leading topside, carrying the ZUB in one hand and his pack in the other.

He was almost out of sight of the engineering office when flesh, blood, and bone meshed into the gears. The body popped like a watermelon seed, squirting blood against far bulkheads. Smoke issued from the engines as they seized. The *Ibn Haldoon* went dead in the water.

A shout from the engine room. A man's voice, followed by a scream. Summer!

Brandon hesitated at the top of the ladder, stricken by the desperation and fear in her voice. Then he opened the hatch and ran silently down the passageway and took the first ladder that led back to the upper decks. He might save her now, only to lose her forever if he didn't reach the limpet mines in time.

CHAPTER 36

Cuyo Islands, USS *Sam Houston*

By the time Chief Gorrell and Lucifer fished Ice Man Thompson out of the drink and learned of what had transpired with Major Kragle cutting the rope, the *Ibn Haldoon* had picked up speed and the limpet mines stuck like barnacles to her hull were ticking off the minutes to detonation. The two Joneses had already been recovered. Chief Gorrell poured power to the SDV in a futile attempt to overtake the freighter, but the submersible was no match for it. Besides, as Lucifer snappishly pointed out, what the fuck were they going to do even if they caught up with the ship? They couldn't disarm the mines while it was under way. They had no choice except to abandon the chase and return to the parent boat.

Lucifer radioed the bare essentials of the situation to the submarine's skipper, Commander Roger Eales. Mission accomplished. One man lost. Nothing else. The SDV quickly slid into the hangar of the dry deck shelter, which was even more quickly purged of salt water and repressurized. The stay-behind section of the detachment jostled into the hangar as the red night-vision lights illuminated it. The mission crew clambered out of the submersible and somberly stripped off masks, fins, and tanks. Water dripped from the overhead into the tension, sounding like a leaky subway tunnel.

Sergeants Cassidy Kragle and Gloomy Davis were the

first to notice who was missing. They were all over Lucifer, demanding to know where the Major was, what had happened.

"*Why* would he stay on the ship?" Cassidy demanded. "He must have had a reason."

There were no satisfactory answers. Not yet.

"What fucking were his exact words, Thompson?" Lucifer insisted of Ice Man, now that they could talk normally, unencumbered by the SDV's intercom.

Ice Man's face remained under control. That was partly how he acquired his nickname. "Sir, them *were* his exact words. 'Tell them there are three kids and Stanton on the ship.' He repeated it. 'Three kids. Stanton. Remember that.' "

"Didn't you ask him what he meant?"

Ice Man snorted. "There wasn't a lot of time." He turned to Cassidy. "I wouldn't have left him, Cass."

Cassidy clamped a hand on the kickboxer's shoulder. "I know that, Ice. That's why he cut the rope. There has to be a good reason for what he did."

"*Good reason?*" Lucifer exploded. "The sonofabitch is going down with it. What kind of a cocksucker reason is *that*? Who the sweet Jesus is *Stanton*? *President* Stanton? And who are these fucking brats he's talking about? Doesn't the bastard know mission comes first?"

Cassidy's blue eyes gave the SEAL officer a bleak, wintery gaze. "He knows that, Lieutenant. Better than any of us."

Lucifer glared back as though he wished he had let the shark take Cassidy.

The submarine lurched as it prepared to get under way to tail the *Ibn Haldoon* until the explosion. From a safe distance, of course. Commander Eales would be on his way to the DDS to receive the after action report as soon as the boat became steady as she goes. The detachment needed to have everything resolved before then and make its first official report from a unified position. Special Operations was a family. Disputes, dissension, and emotion stayed within the family.

"*President* Stanton?" Gloomy asked, puzzled.

"Who else?" Mad Dog said. "The same bloody Kotex who had us shot out of the air over Afghanistan and killed Rock Taylor."

Chief Gorrell stared. "What's he doing aboard the *Ibn Haldoon*?"

"Pleasure cruise?" Mad Dog said contemptuously and looked away. "All I know is what I heard from one of the boat's commo guys. He said they got a message that a bunch of poor-taste cocksuckers hijacked Stanton in Cuba. Up to me, I'd get the major off the ship and leave that motherfucker there."

That brought them back to the original dilemma. *How* did they get Major Brandon off the moving freighter, along with Stanton, the FBI agent, and, apparently, three children? Or, if unable to do that, *how* did they disarm the limpets?

T-Bone Jones cracked his knuckles and glanced at his watch. Cassidy and Gloomy were staring at theirs, as though trying to make time stop while they wrestled with a solution. Nobody wanted to point out the time, even within that practical, hard-edged band, because to do that reinforced the reality of their plight and their helplessness against it.

Brandon had fifteen minutes left before the *Ibn Haldoon* erupted in the water, whether anyone wanted to say it or not. There was enough C-4 stuck to its spine to break it in half and immediately engulf it in flames, sinking it in some of the deepest waters in the South Pacific. Few aboard the ship were likely to survive, if any. The *Ibn Haldoon* was steaming toward her doom and no force on earth could prevent it.

Cassidy turned away as the others brainstormed the problem and refused to accept the inevitable. He wondered what the General would do under these circumstances. What would Brandon do? Both would go down slugging, he knew that. He also knew they were realists who, if they had to go down, would go under the best circumstances they could engineer for themselves.

For some reason, he recalled an incident when he was about six years old and the General was away fighting an action in Grenada. The Kragle brothers always missed their father, even though they knew him primarily as a big, stern figure who came home periodically, then left again while Gloria continued their parenting. Gloria came into Cassidy's room and found the little boy sobbing into his pillow.

"Oh, honey chile. Whatever be the matter? C'mon and tell ole Sugar all about it."

Snuffling, Cassidy looked up with tear-watery eyes. "I want to talk to my daddy. So bad."

Cassidy wanted to talk to the General now. So bad.

It wasn't going to happen.

He took a deep breath and stepped forward.

"Brandon's my brother," he said in a voice so calm and tight that he immediately commanded full attention. "I know what his decision would be if he were here and any of us was out there. First, there's nothing we can do in the time allowed. I'm sure he's thought of all that, he's aware of the situation and he's working on disarming the mines. That means we have to leave it to him."

Gloomy's head lowered in acknowledgment of the hard facts. "Do we have any other choice?"

"No," Cassidy said, his resolve building. Water dripping from the DDS overhead echoed. They heard Commander Eales outside the pressure locks.

"Second thing," Cassidy said hurriedly. "Lieutenant Lucifer is right: Mission does come first. Our mission was to destroy those missiles to keep them out of terrorist hands. We've done that if the ship goes up. However, if Stanton *is* aboard the ship and we report it now before we blow it up, it's going to cause national and international incidents that we're trying to avoid in the first place."

Lucifer stepped in. He looked at the detachment's youngest member in a new, more respectful light.

"The fucking kid's got it right," he said. "It's up to the major now. If that ship does blow up, it's better that no one knows Stanton was aboard. Not even Eales. It's too late. Stanton and those kids, whoever they are, are collateral damage that no one knows about except us. Agreed?"

There was no dissent.

"Good. So be it."

Commander Eales's footfalls sounded on the steel ladder outside. Cassidy turned away to gather his emotions. He kept his shoulders squared to the others. This was the decision, he knew, that Brandon or the General would have made.

It was a shame though that Brandon had to die with a politician for whom he and the military in general held nothing but contempt.

CHAPTER 37

Cuyo Islands

Normally, a moving object on the water the size of a ship required considerable time and distance to bleed off momentum. Only the skillful use of engine reverse and rudder allowed a vessel to stop and dock without wiping out piers. However, the *Ibn Haldoon*'s heading against oncoming seas on the quarter bow slowed the freighter quickly when the engine quit. It began to wallow from loss of forward thrust. Brandon counted on it.

He reached the main deck without incident. He also counted on the helm watch being too busy with the weather and the sudden expiration of the engines to pay any attention to what went on aft. Hopefully no one else noticed him.

Rain lashed at him as he hugged the superstructure. He cast a painful glance back toward the hatch that led to the engine room. He still heard Summer's rending scream inside his skull. He left her in dire danger, he knew, but he refused to think that he had looked upon her for the last time. He could not let terrorists take from him another woman he loved.

There, he admitted it too. They had an investment in each other.

He hadn't much time left.

He trotted toward the fantail, carrying his pack. He knelt next to the side railing with the wind and rain in his face and emptied his pack on the deck. He knotted the rappelling rope to cleating inboard of the bulwarks, double-roping in a manner that allowed him to retrieve the rope once he hit the water and therefore remove any sign of his having been aboard. He slipped the straps of his fins and dive mask over his arm and up past his elbow so he wouldn't lose them, made sure his tanks and mouthpiece were on and functioning, and lastly inflated his buoyancy vest.

He still hadn't been observed. He tossed the pack and its remaining contents overboard, lay over the side of the bulwark and took the rappelling line between his legs and over his left shoulder to his brake hand in preparation for descending. A carabineer and a rappelling seat would have worked better, but he didn't have time to rig it.

The ship dropped out from underneath him, nearly throwing him into the sea before he was ready. He held on until the freighter lifted again, wallowing toward him. At the precise moment of pause at the top of the wallow, he flung himself over the side and rapidly began walking the rope down the side. Salt spray in the wind stung his face, and rain made footing precarious. When the ship heeled back toward him, swinging him out over the whitecaps, he loosed his brake and burned his way down until the breaker tops grabbed at his legs. He caught himself on the rope and dangled there just above the sea.

He estimated the freighter's forward speed, which continued to abate. Hanging there, he determined he could swim with it. He bit into his mouthpiece and tested the airflow. It took a few precious minutes to pull on his fins and dive mask using only one hand. Ready, he grasped one strand of the doubled rappelling rope and held onto it as he dropped into the water.

He sank rapidly to escape surface churn, holding onto the rope until he felt it come loose from the ship. He released it and swam with the freighter, careful to sink deep enough that its wallow would not crush him.

The ship retained more speed than he thought. He had to swim hard to keep up with it. It gradually slowed, however. He caught up and dived deeper to reach the underwater keel. Wallowing, it battered him ruthlessly about as he worked his way up the spine toward amidships, feeling his way in the murky gray water. The Joneses had placed the explosives halfway between bow and stern in order to open the vessel like an oyster.

Sometimes, like at that moment, Brandon wondered why he didn't accept a staff puke's job as other officers did at this stage in their careers.

He'd be bored to death.

A glance at his dive watch told him he had less than ten minutes remaining. He could almost hear Mad Dog: *Fu-uck*.

There should be four limpets with their timing devices

synchronized to go off simultaneously. Feeling along the hull with hands cut and bleeding from the barnacles—blood in the water, he thought, being a great shark attracter—he was almost to the point of thinking he had gone too far forward when he found the first one. It blended in with the barnacles.

Gray light penetrated water on either side of the ship, but it was so dark underneath that he had to swim directly upon the mines before he saw them. They were stuck to the hull about ten feet apart, two on each side of the spine. Parrot fish with their coral-eating beaks, snapper, and other colorful ocean dwellers swarmed underneath the hull with him.

He treaded water deep to avoid the ship's roll toward him. When the hull above started to rise again, he kicked hard and shot upward with Ka-Bar in hand. These were nonmagnetic explosives that used a tough underwater glue to make them adhere to a surface. He pried on the first one with his knife blade, working his fins to maintain position. He heard air flowing through his hoses.

The glue held as it was intended. The hull rolled back toward him. He retreated, diving deeper in order to escape being mauled.

It took him three attempts before the limpet came loose and immediately sank.

Time was burning. He had to work faster.

He should have grabbed Summer when he had the chance and dived overboard with her. At least she would have lived.

To his surprise and relief, the next two mines popped loose as quickly as buttons. He dived to avoid the freighter's roll, then shot up to the final limpet. He dug at it, prying with his knife, knowing in his desperation that he was taking too long.

The freighter caught him hard on a downward trough, ripping against him with such a vicious blow that it momentarily stunned him. It flattened him against the hull bottom. He felt as if he was in a vise with tons of steel above pressing him against tons of water beneath. He struggled to suck bottled air into his compressed lungs. He felt himself blacking out.

The ship took him deep.

The pressure suddenly relaxed at the moment he felt consciousness leaving. He gratefully drew air into his lungs. He floundered a moment, fighting to regain control. He glimpsed above him the blurring ship as it rose. Just when he thought it was over, that he still had a chance, a few more minutes to finish the job, he heard a sound that sent his blood racing.

The engines kicked over. They caught and began rumbling in that high-pitched ringing-in-the-ears way that machines make underwater. The *Ibn Haldoon* was getting under way. The crew must have removed the cadaver from the gears, or at least the major part of him.

Exhausted, feeling as though he had miraculously survived a bout held inside a giant washing machine, he knew he had one slim chance left. He called upon his last reserves of strength and will and kicked upward. He dared not think of the consequences if he failed.

He caught the mine with one hand. The ship lifted him with it. He felt himself being dragged through the water as the freighter regained power and speed. His first efforts had already released one side of the last limpet. He drove his blade hard between it and the hull and threw all his weight into leverage.

It resisted. He almost heard the countdown, the minutes and now the final seconds ticking off inside his head. The ship was coming back down on him, but he dared not turn loose.

Suddenly, the mine popped free and sank with a swirl into the murky depths. Almost overcome with relief, he dived and swam furiously at an angle to avoid the deadly props about to overtake him. When he reached open sea again where the water was brighter, a dramatic escape from dark-

ness into light, he eased up and let himself drift while he re-
cuperated.

The ship's hull slid by. Deep below, the mines exploded
with a distant rumble that those aboard the ship would never
notice. Minutes later, a mini-tidal-wave swept over him, but
it was much weakened by the depth and caused little discom-
fort.

Summer's scream reverberated in Brandon's conscience
as he waited for the submarine to home in on his bracelet and
pluck him out of the water.

CHAPTER 38

Washington, D.C.

Radio talk show host Rush Limbaugh used the double enten-
dre of the initials *B.S.* when he referred to the famous diva
Barbra Streisand. She *was* a bit of an airhead, Senate Majority Leader Jake Thierry admitted to himself when he returned
to his suite office following an overnight fund-raising gala in
Hollywood. She hadn't even spelled his name correctly—she
spelled it "Therry"—when she fired him a forceful letter urg-
ing him and the party to "have the strength and courage to
stand up for what is right" and resist the War on Terror and its
covert operations that "refuse to give peace a chance." But
what counted was that the star, long known for her support of
progressive causes, understood how to throw an event to
bring out all the fat-cat show people. The previous night's af-
fair raised more than six mil for the cause. Senator Thierry

felt altogether good about himself for having been a part of it, for having been provided a high-profile opportunity to showcase his talents and display his credentials as a potential presidential candidate.

All the beautiful people from the left were there—a star of the successful TV sitcom *West Wing,* known for his sleeping on freezing grates in his championship of the homeless and his highly publicized peace marches in front of the White House; the actor who had just returned from Baghdad where he rambled out near-indecipherable criticism of America that made him sound as if he were high on dope; a fiery former attorney general of the United States who called himself a Marxist and probably always had been one . . .

"It is apparent," said the ex-attorney general when it came his turn to speak, "that the U.S. government around the world is using the War on Terror to erode human rights and stifle political dissent. This administration is literally dismantling justice. This detestable practice of ethnic-profiling Muslims, for example, is no better than crawling in the mud at some right-wing militia training camp in Idaho."

Senator Thierry toned things down somewhat when it came his turn at the podium. After all, he needed to tailor his image for national consumption to reflect himself as a moderate man of the people. In spite of his Al Gore-like upbringing as the son of a wealthy senator, he liked to see himself as Trumanesque and self-made. Also like Al Gore, he had a way of manufacturing homey stories to illustrate his humble roots and his suitability to represent and lead the common people. His anecdote about Anwar Sadat and himself, he thought, really brought the house down, earned him a lot of brownie points, and perhaps an extra half-million for his campaign. He had told the story so many times that even if it weren't true, it *should* have been true.

When he was a young man, he told his glamorous audience, he encountered Anwar on the Egyptian shore of the Mediterranean.

"Son, who are you?" Sadat asked. "What is it you want to do with your life?"

"Sir, my name is Jake Thierry. I'm going to be a member of the United States Congress. I'm going to be President of the United States. I'm going to do good things."

Then he ranged into the meat of his speech, which he devoted to the kidnapped former President. Appeals in Stanton's name still had the ability to squeeze money from the party faithful.

"The spiritual leader of our cause, John Stanton, has been kidnapped," he said, "and our government under this administration is making little effort to find out who did it or why. John and I worked hard and long together on necessary projects when we were in Washington together. We left a legacy because of the mammography centers we created, because children will play in a park that we funded and land that we saved, and because some senior citizens who don't even know my name and nothing about what we're doing today will live at a senior center that we helped to build.

"John and I, we change peoples' lives," he added. "Now John needs our help in return. President Stanton is a man of peace. We must negotiate with these downtrodden peoples who see such acts as their only recourse to gain attention to their plight. I am certain John understands his captors and sympathizes with their pain. Let us urge this administration to have him released by dealing with his captors as needy and rational human beings . . ."

Besides, the cynical side of Senator Thierry thought, *he has to be released alive because I need him and his support in order to win the White House.*

Senator Thierry was still feeling so good about himself as he sashayed into his office that he hummed a little tune from *Miss Saigon*. He sat down with a sigh of pleasure behind his heavy walnut desk and daydreamed for a few minutes about

what it would be like to live at 1600 Pennsylvania Avenue.
Then he got to work.

He made some calls, reviewed a proposed bill from the
Ways and Means Committee for a tax increase on electronic
media that would hit mainly the rich, and reluctantly received a constituency representative from back home who
wanted to talk about public education. This visitor had no
more than departed when his receptionist buzzed in.

"Senator, you have an urgent call on line one."

"Who is it, Delores?"

"He said you'd want to talk to him."

Likely another education complainer or chicken farmer
who thought senators had time for such nonsense. He
smacked his lips with annoyance; he'd have to talk to Delores about screening his calls more carefully. He picked up
the phone, listened, then stiffened with a stricken look on his
pasty face.

"Mr. President! Where are you?"

"I'm on a ship-to-shore relay and—"

Thierry heard what sounded like a slap. Stanton cried out.

"Jake, I can't tell you any more than that. They're going to
kill me!" His voice went thin, almost strident, before it broke
off into a heartfelt sob. "They're going to cut off my head."

"Mr. President, I'm sure that—"

"What do you know about shit?" Stanton snapped, displaying his well-known temper. "We have to do what they
say. Do you hear me, Thierry?"

"John, I'm sure I'll do anything I can—"

"You have to do this for me, Jake. After all I've done for
you. I can make you President. Do you understand that?"

Senator Thierry's eyes narrowed. He had never heard John
Stanton plead like this before. It was not very becoming. In
the situation he recognized a political opportunity. He had
kissed Stanton's ass often enough. Now, here he was with the

perfect opportunity to build up some capital while making Stanton indebted to him.

Butter, as the old saying went, couldn't have melted in his mouth. "Mr. President, you know in what high esteem I hold you and your place in history—"

"Listen," Stanton interrupted. "I'm under a lot of pressure and I don't have much time to explain. Just take my word for it and do what I say."

"Of course, Mr. President."

"Go to Baton Rouge tomorrow morning. There's a restaurant called Slim's on the Mississippi River waterfront. Someone will meet you there."

"Who?"

"It's not important. He'll recognize you. He'll give you a sealed folder and a round-trip plane ticket to Manila. Take the folder with you in a diplomatic pouch and do whatever they tell you to do. You're the only one I can trust, Jake. Nobody's going to question you."

"Mr. President, I know you can't talk now—"

"You're right. I can't talk. My ass is on the block here. Do you understand that?"

"But if this is something that's going to be a national security violation, something illegal . . ." Senator Thierry hedged.

The President came back sharply, sounding desperate. "*You're* talking about illegal, Jake. *You?* Now don't get cold feet on me. You're not to say anything to anybody else about this—or I'm dead. I'm not going to die because you're a chicken shit. So just in case you start having second thoughts, there's one thing you have to remember—Robert Chang."

Thierry blanched. His voice went weak. "What do you mean?"

"You survive in Washington by knowing things," Stanton

said, his voice sounding as if it was about to break from stress. "Let me tell you a few things I know: a wide-screen television set, expensive diamond earrings for your girlfriend *and* your wife, envelopes full of cash delivered to your house late at night . . ."

The senator swallowed. Dryness in the throat arrested his voice. What it came down to, he realized, breaking into a cold sweat, was how badly did he want to become President? And what was he willing to risk to get there and keep Stanton quiet?

Maybe the terrorists would kill Stanton first.

"Don't even think it," Stanton scolded. The sonofabitch could read minds! "If they . . ." His voice cracked. "If they kill me because you fuck up, I've arranged for the Justice Department and every major news media to receive the information about Robert Chang. You couldn't be elected dog catcher after that—especially after you get out of federal prison."

Who was going to keep kissing whose ass?

Senator Thierry surrendered with a small voice. "All right."

"Good. I'm sorry, Jake. Really I am. I didn't want to have to do this. But these people mean business. They want you to tell the President that you heard from me. Tell him that within the next few hours the world will get a little demonstration of their seriousness and their strength. Much more will follow if he plans to reject their demands. Don't tell him anything else—for both our sakes, Jake. Then just go to Baton Rouge and do as you're told."

The line went dead. Senator Thierry stared at the receiver in his hand for a long time. He no longer felt so good about himself.

CHAPTER 39

KIDNAPPED EX-PRESIDENT WARNS OF BOMBINGS

Washington (CPI)—Over 200 people were killed in a terrorist-related bombing after kidnapped former-President John Stanton warned that the attack was coming. Stanton reportedly contacted Senate Majority Leader Jake Thierry through what Stanton described to Thierry as a "ship-to-shore relay."

"The call was apparently initiated by people holding President Stanton to show they mean business in their demands," said a grim Senator Thierry. "The President sounded anxious."

Senator Thierry said he wrote down what Stanton said immediately after the conversation so he wouldn't forget it.

"Tell the President these people mean business," Stanton said, according to Thierry's notes. "Sometime within the next few hours they're going to give the world a demonstration of their might. Much more will follow if we don't concede to their demands. They will kill me."

That, Thierry said, was the beginning and end of the conversation before the line went dead.

Stanton was kidnapped from José Martí Airport in Havana as he was departing Cuba for the United States after his "goodwill tour." The comment by Stanton about a "ship-to-shore relay" has led authorities to speculate that he might be held aboard a ship.

Three hours after the brief phone conversation, a bomb went off outside a night club in Bali, Indonesia, killing over 200 people. The explosion tore through a maze of bars, restaurants, and night clubs at Kuta Beach, a haunt for surfers and young international vacationers. Among those remains identified so far are fifteen Australians, eight Britons, five Singaporeans, six Indonesians, one German, one French person, one Dutch person, one New Zealander, one Ecuadoran, and two Americans.

Traces of the military explosive C-4, a putty-like plastic explosive, were found at the scene. Suspicion has fallen on Jemaah Islamiyah, a group that Singapore says is based in Indonesia with links to Osama bin Laden's al-Qaeda network.

Authorities refuse to speculate on what might have been meant by the warning passed from Stanton to Senator Thierry that "much more will follow . . ."

CHAPTER 40

Louisiana

Unlike his brothers and his father who rarely accepted anyone or anything at face value, Cameron with his religious faith in God sought the good in people. As far as he could tell, Yasein Riefenstahl and his friend Abdul seemed to have no agenda other than the stated one of Abdul's escaping with his fiancée from terrorist clutches. Yasein had an open, honest face; there was no purpose other than good intentions for him to jeopardize his own life in order to expose the terrorists and save his friend. Abdul had motives of the heart, but they seemed likewise sound.

Both young men were obviously scared to death. With good cause, Cameron thought. The "Undertoad" was active in America and around the world. And he was an ugly, bloody beast who sought to subdue his enemies through both intimidation and violence. It took courage these days for anyone, but especially another Muslim, to stand up against the Islamic tide.

Cameron could hardly blame Yasein and Abdul for being frightened. Only that evening, he had personally witnessed the fanaticism of radical Islam at the al-Farooq Mosque. Any reservations he might have once held about the extremists, any lingering inclination he harbored to see good in everything, had been largely dispelled in the chanting of Professor Ramzi al-Rehman's audience: "Death to Israel! Kill the Jews! Destroy the West!" How easy it would be for offended Islamics to slay traitors like Yasein and Abdul, to whom they had ready access. Abdul was convinced they would all be killed if anything went wrong, including Chaplain Kragle. Cameron agreed with him.

The world in recent years was becoming stranger and more volatile. Gloria insisted it was because Jesus was about ready to return. Maybe so, Cameron conceded, but until then it was up to mankind to carry on the struggle between good and evil.

Preparations had to be made before Professor Ramzi and his men came for Abdul at dawn to transport him to the unknown missile site. Cameron argued that they should at least alert the FBI in order to give the agencies time to prepare. Abdul, reared in the Islamic world, did not trust authority. He was afraid the FBI would overreact and not take into account arrangements for his safety and secrecy, thus exposing him to a *fatwa*.

"I trust you, Chaplain Cameron, to do what is right," he said. "I do not trust authorities. You promised not to tell anyone."

"Abdul, I know I promised, but if I'm to get you any kind of immunity and protection, I must notify someone in advance. If they aren't prepared to stop that missile—and if it's fired—no one will be able to do anything for you."

Abdul finally consented to Cameron's notifying the director of the FBI's National Domestic Preparedness Office, no one else. Cameron assured him Claude Thornton was an old friend and as such could be trusted. Cameron cell-phoned the director's number. He didn't look forward to informing the big agent that he should prepare while not telling him what he should prepare *for*. Claude wouldn't be too happy about it. He was a hard-headed man. So hard-headed the General said he might even be a member of the Kragle clan. The General joked that the Thornton family of African-Americans must have had an Irish-American in their woodpile.

Thornton failed to answer his personal twenty-four-hour number. The receptionist at his office informed Cameron that he was not in.

"This is Chaplain Kragle. Did Claude say where he was going?"

"He had a case in Georgia. Then he said he was going to Tampa to have dinner with General Kragle. General Kragle called a couple of times because Mr. Thornton hasn't arrived there. We're beginning to get a little concerned. Are you related to General Kragle? I have his number."

"I have it. Thanks. Let me give you my cell number. Will you have Claude call me as soon as possible?"

Cameron's black Chrysler was too conspicuous to make a good tail car. The best he could acquire for a replacement under such short notice was a cream-colored 1995 Chevrolet from a Rent-A-Wreck out on Canal Street. He accepted the Chevrolet along with a rusted Pontiac Firebird for Yasein. It would be necessary to switch off on the tail to avoid giving themselves away. Cameron had seen enough cop shows to know that.

"You *can* drive?" he asked the skinny Iraqi.

"I have a driver's license from Tennessee."

They stopped at a twenty-four-hour Wal-Mart where Cameron purchased the best pair of walkie-talkies available in the Sight-and-Sound Department. They only had a range of about a half-mile, but that should prove no obstacle to communications between the two vehicles.

After lingering over breakfast and coffee at Denny's, they dropped an anxious Abdul off at his apartment near the French Quarter.

"Please do not let them get away with me," he pleaded.

"I'm praying for us," Cameron promised.

Staked out on the apartment in their separate cars, Cameron and Yasein radio-checked the walkie-talkies.

"Yasein? Yasein, can you read me?"

"This is Yasein. Do you not think we should use secret call signs or something? In the event we are eavesdropped."

"What do you suggest?"

The air went dead while Yasein thought it over. "I will be Hero Two, you will be Hero One."

"Ten-four, good buddy."

The car came for Abdul at dawn—a plain gray four-door Ford sedan occupied by three men, two of whom appeared Middle Eastern but wore nothing more conspicuous than jeans and ball caps. The third man was Professor Ramzi al-

Rehman. Ramzi waited in the back seat while his two companions went into the apartment and escorted Abdul out. Abdul looked small, exceptionally vulnerable and uncomfortable among the larger men. He got in the back seat with Ramzi. The others got in. The Ford pulled away from the curb.

Cameron attempted to alert Yasein over the walkie-talkies. He received no response. He must be asleep. Chafed, Cameron quickly circled the block and found him slumped over the steering wheel. He looked dead. Ice went down Cameron's back. He jumped out of his car and jerked open Yasein's door, almost dumping the little man out in the street. Yasein grabbed for the steering wheel. The chaplain was so relieved that he forgot to scold him.

They experienced an anxious moment when it looked as if they might have lost the Ford. They would never find the terrorist base camp and the missiles without it. Cameron cut back toward the Lake Pontchartrain Causeway on a hunch while Yasein did some fancy driving of his own to keep up. The gray Ford was just turning onto the causeway at Union Station.

Thank You, Lord.

It was easy after that. Apparently, the terrorists were so arrogant they expected nothing to interfere with their plans and therefore took few precautions. Coordinating themselves through the walkie-talkies, Cameron and Yasein switched off as chase car to avoid creating even a slight suspicion. The route led out Airline Highway to Causeway Boulevard and turned north. Traffic across the twenty-nine-mile Lake Pontchartrain Causeway, the world's longest bridge, started to pick up at daybreak, making it easier to tail the suspects without being seen by them. The Ford turned west on U.S. 10 toward Baton Rouge.

At Baton Rouge, Cameron was surprised when the terror-

ist car exited the interstate at the Mississippi River waterfront. He expected the hideout to be in some inaccessible
wilderness. Cameron dropped back to give the Ford some
room. It parked overlooking the river and a barge pier while
Cameron eased his rental Chevy into a warehouse district
and stopped out of sight.

He got out and trotted to the corner in time to see Professor
Ramzi get out and look around, for the first time appearing
cautious. Cameron was glad he had taken the precaution to
hide his car. After a moment, Ramzi started off on foot down
a dingy street lined on one side with seedy bars, pawn shops,
and flophouses. On the other side was the river. The professor carried a brown manila envelope.

Cameron keyed his walkie-talkie. "Yasein?"

Yasein, who seemed to be getting into the spirit of the adventure, came back with, "Hero One, this is Hero Two."

"Do you see the car?"

"It has stopped, Hero One."

"I know. Keep an eye on it, but don't let them see you. I'm
following Ramzi."

"Roger and Wilco and out."

Cameron cut down an alley and came out on the waterfront at a distance from the parked Ford. The professor's red
ball cap was just disappearing into a dingy stevedores' café
called Slim's. Cameron hoped he wasn't overdressed in
faded jeans, soft-soled Dockers, and an old blue T-shirt. He
didn't think Ramzi would recognize him. At the Hands of
God Conference, he was just another face in a crowd of two
thousand. Besides, he had been in dress greens and no one
looked the same out of uniform.

The window of the café was so scummed over and fly-
specked that he couldn't see through it. Acting as though
it were his habit to go there every day for a late breakfast,
he entered and walked directly to an empty stool at the bar

where greasy eggs, grits, and chicory coffee were being served by a Bluto in a pork-blood-spattered filthy apron and a T-shirt to match. Bluto had an anchor tattooed on one hairy forearm and a large machine screw on the other with the inscription SCREW THE WORLD below it. Classy joint.

Cameron ordered coffee before he casually looked around. Whatever Ramzi's purpose for coming here, Cameron thought, it hadn't taken long. He was already getting ready to leave. He stood up from a rear table occupied by a second man and bent over for a final word.

Ramzi's confederate looked vaguely familiar. Cameron committed his face and appearance to memory so he could identify him should it become necessary. The stranger wore a tie but no jacket, which still put him way over-dressed for this place. Skinny arms as pale as a snake's belly stuck out of a short-sleeved, pale-blue, button-down dress shirt. His body looked flaccid, overpuffed and out of proportion to the puny arms. His face was lean and his hair iron-gray and expensively coiffed. He belonged in Slim's about as much as a Boy Scout belonged in a French Quarter crack house.

Cameron thought it would be interesting to know who he was and what that meeting was all about. But Cameron had more vital matters to attend to, matters of life and death for thousands. Ramzi left the café without looking back. The man at the table had the manila envelope now. Cameron stepped outside the café after Ramzi and watched the professor hurrying back toward his car. The man with the over-puffed body and skinny arms pushed out the door and took off in equal haste in the opposite direction, carrying the brown envelope.

The reunited terrorists returned to U.S. 10 and continued heading west, tailed by the cream-colored Chevrolet and the rusted Firebird. Cameron took another try at Director Claude Thornton. Thornton's regular secretary was not as obliging as the previous night's receptionist. She explained that the director was "indisposed."

CHAPTER 41

West of the town of Ramah, the terrorists turned south onto a little-traveled blacktop that twisted into the heart of the Atchafalaya Swamp, a primitive and savage place full of alligators and poisonous snakes and aswarm with egrets, brown pelicans, and other bird life. Because the Chevrolet would have been the last vehicle the terrorists might have noticed in their rearview mirror on the highway, Cameron pulled over and got into the Firebird with Yasein. He expected they were near the end of the journey. They were on their way again, speeding to catch up with the Ford, when Cameron noticed that he had forgotten his cell phone. He had left it plugged into the Chevrolet, recharging. Too late to go back for it now.

They kept far enough behind the gray Ford not to arouse its occupants' suspicions. They caught glimpses of it on the straightaways between curves. After a number of miles, it slowed and turned west onto a rutted road white-dusted with salt deposits.

"Keep going. Don't slow down," Cameron instructed Yasein.

Now the terrorists were acting hinky, which would mean they were nearing the hideout. Just as Cameron suspected, the Ford had stopped a short distance up the road after it made the turn, apparently so Ramzi could check for anyone that might be following. Cameron felt pleased with his instincts. He and Yasein in the Firebird zipped on past the turnoff and continued another mile down the blacktop. They pulled off and waited for five minutes before they returned to the dirt road junction.

The Ford was gone, having proceeded deeper into the swamp. There was no telling how deeply the road reached, where it stopped, or what awaited at its end. Yasein gripped the wheel with both hands, looking excited and terrified at the same time as he turned the Firebird onto it. Since the road map failed to show unimproved roads, Cameron couldn't be sure of it but he guessed they were heading toward the Atchafalaya River, one of two main branches of the Mississippi River in Louisiana. Yasein drove very slowly, no faster than a man could walk, while Cameron leaned forward over the dash to keep an eye open for danger.

"Perhaps I should change my call sign to Hero Five Hundred," Yasein stammered.

The track twisted through the sloughs on dry ground, *dry ground* being a relative term. Giant dragon flies with iridescent wings buzzed over brackish black water into which dipped the delicate gray fingers of Spanish moss hanging from enormous conifer cypress. A large snake with a half-consumed perch in its jaws inscribed a watery pathway. Bulblike reptilian eyes glared at them.

The road became narrower, harder to negotiate. They crept along at barely a walker's pace. Cameron suspected they must be nearing some destination. It would be safer to continue on foot. Yasein killed the engine and the sudden silence of the swamp pressed down on them.

"Did you bring a weapon?" Yasein asked, whispering, his eyes wide and watchful.

"I don't own a gun."

"Now, I think, might be an excellent time to have a weapon."

The chaplain felt no need to explain that he had made a personal pact with God never to resort to deadly violence again. Violence had claimed so many of his loved ones—Little Nana, Cassidy's wife Kathryn, and Gypsy. A vessel opened in his heart every time he thought of Gypsy.

Even though they walked slowly, like soldiers behind enemy lines, they were soon sweating profusely. The sun felt as hot as it had on Cameron's back in Iraq during the Gulf War of 1991. It burned through their clothing and seemed to suck every drop of moisture from their pores. Cameron wished he had thought to bring along a bottle of water. Heat devils jiggered before his eyes.

They came upon the Ford around a sharp dogleg in the road. At first it appeared to be a mirage. Cameron reactively shoved Yasein into the cover of foliage growing at the edge of the road. They crouched there in a long silence, hearts thudding, while they observed the vehicle for signs of movement.

Long minutes passed, nothing stirring, before Cameron finally concluded the terrorists must have gone forward on foot. The camp couldn't be much farther. Yasein wanted to go back and summon authorities. He sweated profusely from nervousness as well as from heat, humidity, and exertion. The adventure was losing its allure.

"We have to make sure this is it," Cameron reasoned. "We've blown everything if we bring in the cavalry now and this turns out to be a mink ranch or something."

"Cavalry?" Yasein questioned, not understanding.

"Never mind. We need to see the missiles. Come on."

"We should not walk on the road," Yasein whispered.

Cameron gestured at the swamp and marshes on either side. "I'm open to alternative suggestions."

"I do not like it."

"Quiet. Too quiet." A quote he had heard in a few dozen

old John Wayne, Clark Gable, and Jeff Chandler movies on the Turner Classics channel. At least he hadn't lost his sense of humor.

They cautiously approached the abandoned Ford and looked inside. Nothing interesting. Beyond it, the road, although narrowing to the width of an ATV, looked beaten and well traveled as it disappeared into the swamp. Mosquito buzz filled the fetid air with energy.

A deafening bang! So near it seemed like two trash can lids slamming together behind Cameron's head, followed instantly by the meaty impact of a bullet striking flesh.

Yasein screamed. In slow-motion horror, Cameron watched Yasein's arms flailing as though attempting to grab the bloody splotch that appeared in the middle of his back. The bullet slammed him to the ground.

Cameron whirled to face the attacker. Realizing he had been suckered. Of course the terrorists would station a sentry. Horrified, he stared into the deep barrel of an assault rifle pointed directly at his face.

Knowing he was next.

CHAPTER 42

Cuyo Islands

Summer had screamed on impulse when she realized the engineer was going to spot Brandon. He popped out of his cubbyhole office the moment the ship's screws and gears consumed the wrestler's body with a squalling of seized metal. From the corner of her eye she saw Brandon's black-clad figure racing for the ladder and escape. Scream was the only thing she could think of to distract the engineer. Brandon had to get away or they were all doomed.

She put everything she had into that one ear-piercing, soul-shattering shriek.

It worked. It was obvious Brandon had escaped and that no one knew what was going on by the way Captain Darth Vader rushed down to the engine room, trailed by Cimatu and his skinny ninja sidekick and a handful of crew. They ran over each other in their confusion. Darth Vader seemed dazed and disoriented underneath his helmet. It took several minutes for them to identify the victim, and only then because Summer confirmed that a hand-sized piece of flesh that contained a nose and an eye once belonged to the face of Cimatu's second man-in-waiting, whose name Summer had never known.

Some raw emotion that was not exactly grief but more akin to rage made Cimatu stomp back and forth while he roared curses and his scarred face and bald head got red and more lopsided than ever. The ninja took one look at the bloody mess in the gears, grew gray in the face, turned away quickly, puked in the bilge water, and stumbled for the ladder out of there.

"Pussy!" Cimatu screamed after him. He turned his anger on Summer, whom he immediately blamed before knowing any of the details.

"Ismael screamed like a woman," the engineer kept saying. "A *woman,* I tell you."

Cimatu grabbed her by the arm and jerked her aside while Darth Vader got a crew working to clean the mess out of the gears and get the big diesels chugging again. Summer's nerves felt raw and vibrating as the remaining minutes of her life ticked away. What difference did anything matter anyhow if Brandon failed to reach the mines in time to disarm them? Knowing the perverted Cimatu would go up with her in the expected explosion provided her a modicum of raw comfort.

She couldn't resist taunting him when he persisted in questioning her about what happened. "We came down here and he slipped on the walkway and fell into the gears."

"Why were you in the engine room in the first place?" Cimatu probed.

"Things," she replied, slyly evasive.

"Things?" Cimatu challenged. "You were doing *things* to him?"

Summer's eyes mocked him. "He said he had a tool for me."

Cimatu's scar turned into a blood-gorged leech. She thought she might have gone too far. He pulled her roughly up the ladder and to the next deck. His rage left a wake of obscenities trailing them. He was too strong to resist. She thought of going for the table knife concealed in the waistband of her pantaloons, but killing him, if she were lucky enough to do so, only complicated matters while doing nothing toward solving the problem of the missiles, the Korean stowaways, and President Stanton.

They all might be dead anyhow within the next few minutes. But if by chance Brandon succeeded in his task underneath the ship, she still had to survive. Kill Cimatu and Darth Vader would cut her throat. Jang and his siblings would never reach America.

Cimatu found an empty locker and bodily flung her into it. She bounced off the steel bulkhead and fell across a coil of hawser. She bounced to her feet, defiant and prepared to ward him off. He sneered a harsh laugh and caught her on the chin with a brutal jab. She slumped unconscious to the deck.

The bald Filipino was bending over her, shaking her, when she revived. The stench of fish from his stomach and his fetid breath cleared her head like ammonia. His dark little-pig eyes said he had forgotten all about his dead comrade. He had other things in mind. Faint light sifting in through the open hatch sought out the coals of lust in his eyes. Summer almost wished the mines *had* gone off. She realized, however, that if they hadn't exploded by this time, they weren't likely to do so.

At least Brandon was safe.

She unleashed a weak kick at Cimatu's groin. He deflected it easily with the side of his thigh. He slapped her. Cruel laughter mingled with the ringing in her ears.

"Now, my pretty little boy," he taunted, "you and I will play with *my* tool. I will slip my tool into your mouth."

Slowly, reveling in the act, watching his victim's reaction with sadistic pleasure, he untied the sash that held up his loose pantaloons and let them drop to the floor around his ankles. His legs were as stubby as tree stumps and as smooth as a woman's—a very heavy, homely woman's. The only hair on his lower body grew wiry and black at his crotch.

The ship bounced on the sea as it once more got under way. The sudden movement threw Cimatu off balance. He staggered, recovered, and grabbed Summer's head with one hand.

"Take it," he ordered. "Put it in your mouth."

She had used sex before to accomplish a mission, but never this crudely. The thought of doing it now, with this disgusting piece of dung, or with anyone else for that matter now that she had declared her love for Brandon, left her nauseated. She gagged. She couldn't do it. Not willingly.

The other option was to resist and take a chance on Cimatu's killing her.

"I'll do it," she said. She gnashed her teeth to make sure he understood. "But they'll be calling you 'Stubby' from now on."

He laughed back at her. From somewhere within his upper clothing he drew a small revolver. He cocked it and pressed the muzzle hard against her temple. He rubbed her cheek with the palm of his hand.

"A boy's face that has never shaved," he commented approvingly.

He inserted his forefinger deep into her mouth. She let him, afraid to pull back with the pistol at her temple. She retched deeply inside her belly. He took his finger out and brushed the broad head of his erection across her lips. She clenched her jaws.

"Take it," he insisted. "The gun goes bang if you bite."

His hand traveled caressingly down her neck. He bent over slightly, exploring with his hand. It traced the length of her torso, across her belly. Her heart pounded as he neared her secret. He massaged between her legs, obviously expecting to find a handful of young male plumbing. All he got was padding.

Surprise, followed by confusion, erased the carnal hunger on his brutish face. He crushed the padding in his fist and looked even more perplexed, as though his brain was having a tough time processing the discovery. He jerked her to her feet and ripped off her pantaloons. He tore off her underwear to reveal the secret she had hidden under the name Ismael— along with her SAT cell phone. It skittered across the deck, even more damaging to her than the fact that she had hidden her femaleness. Cimatu looked as though his circuits were about to overload in trying to digest so much new data all at once.

His brain seemed incapable of exploring two avenues of thought at the same time. He stepped back, blinking. She thought he was going to shoot her on the spot.

He responded the only way he understood. With alternate violence. He whacked her across the cheek with the gun barrel, opening a bloody gash. She fell back onto the hawser coil.

"What . . . ? What—?" he stammered.

His eyes settled on the cell phone, finally recognizing in it something far more exceptional than Ismael's cross-dressing. Lust suddenly turned to suspicion.

He quickly pulled up his trousers and lashed them. He collected the sophisticated little cell phone, holstered his gun, yanked Summer to her feet, and hustled her half-naked out into the passageway.

The next thing she knew she found herself flung into the makeshift cell next to the rope locker where Jang and his little brother and sister hid. She sprawled on the deck. Just before the hatch clanged shut to plummet the room back into darkness, she caught a glimpse of the former President of the United States. He cringed in one corner of the room, his knees drawn up underneath his chin.

Then, total darkness, out of which came John Stanton's terrified voice: "Who are you? What's going on? Please don't hurt me."

Summer gingerly sat up. Blood on her cheek felt warm as it trickled down her jaw. Disgusted, she spat out the taste of Cimatu's horrendous penis that he had rubbed across her lips. She listened to his footfalls pounding rapidly away down the passageway, obviously on his way to Captain Darth Vader with the news. She knew they'd be back. Soon. An old line from a movie flashed through her thoughts: *Ve have vays of making you talk.*

"What are you doing?" Stanton shrilled.

She had never felt so defenseless, so helpless in her life. Half-naked, the only weapon she possessed left behind with the remnants of her trousers, locked up in the dark with a man who had once been the leader of the free world, now reduced to cowering in a corner.

She had to work at it to maintain Ismael's customary wiseass optimism. "Mr. President," she said, "I'm from the government and I'm here to help you."

Chapter 43

MacDill Air Force Base, Tampa, Florida

Too much black coffee and too little sleep since the launching of Operation Deep Steel left General Darren Kragle red-eyed and sluggish. He refused to leave the command center at U.S. Central Command headquarters, as did many of the other officers involved with directing and supporting the operation. Remnants of stale sandwiches remained strewn on tables and desk tops, along with Styrofoam coffee cups and cigarette butts. The big room paneled in computers, monitor screens, and communications equipment smelled smoky and stagnant.

Compared to the War on Terror, Vietnam was simple and uncomplicated and Desert Storm a mere straightforward action. This was truly a *world war* in which brush fires kept popping out at various and unforeseen locations around the globe. Hardly was one extinguished when another flared up.

How could America have been so unprepared? For years now, America's enemies had infiltrated the country and planned for the conflict. Counterfeiting tens of thousands of dollars; amassing explosives; reconfiguring passports to enable radical Islamics to enter the United States where lax INS enforcement overlooked them; enlisting and training recruits for the coming Holy War . . . You had to be blind not to have seen it coming as far back as the bombing of the U.S. Marine barracks in Beirut two decades ago.

"While they planned war on American citizens, we played 'multiculturalism' and did little to monitor these groups," Claude Thornton often complained. "Weak-kneed administrations like President Stanton's opened the doors and overlooked all signs. Now, it's catch-up time—and we're way behind."

Things, as Gloria put it, kept getting "complicateder and complicateder."

She telephoned the General several times a day to scold him about his rest and eating habits and bring him up to date on wedding preparations. "Lawdy," she said, "if I had knew getting hitched to Raymond would be this much trouble, why, bless my poor soul, I would have gone and got a puppy instead. Things keep getting complicateder and complicateder."

She didn't know the half of it—and the General certainly wasn't going to explain it to her, especially since two of the sons were directly in the middle of the complications. She would be on him with that wagging finger of hers like "stink on a hog pen," as she put it.

CENTCOM and General Kragle were busy juggling situations that kept blindsiding them.

One "complicateder" came from Deep Steel. While the various generals and a variety of other support brass huddled at CENTCOM awaiting word that *Ibn Haldoon* and her missiles were on their way to the bottom of the sea, what came instead was a report that Major Brandon Kragle had been successfully recovered from the sea after deactivating explosives already attached to the freighter's hull. Command still didn't know the whole story, wouldn't know until the after action reports and debriefings. All that was known so far was that the mission was scrubbed at the last minute because three Korean stowaway children and former president John Stanton somehow ended up aboard the freighter with the CIA agent.

These revelations about Stanton prompted rounds of high-level meetings in Washington between the President and his advisors and cabinet. At CENTCOM, the brass war-gamed possible scenarios until the chairman of the Joint Chiefs of Staff, General Abraham Morrison, telephoned with the President's decision. The command element in Florida gathered around speakers to listen in on the conference call.

"The matter of Stanton complicates matters," the JCS chairman began in an understatement. *No shit,* General Kragle thought. The chairman sounded weary and beleaguered. "However, we must not lose these missiles under any circumstances. The USS *Sam Houston* will continue to follow the *Ibn Haldoon*. Is it possible, General Etheridge and General Kragle, to conduct a swift and secret boarding of the freighter without risking the lives of Stanton and the other friendlies on the ship?"

General Etheridge, CENTCOM, voiced the consensual opinion of his entire staff. They had already hashed over that scenario. "Impossible for the time being," he said, "and I'll tell you why. First, the ship is under way and we don't have vessels in the AO capable of bringing boarding teams alongside. The *Abe Lincoln* is closing in and has helicopters, but we can't fly choppers in this weather. Second, the CIA has no contact with its agent on the ship. We have no idea where everybody is. Terrorists are notorious for executing hostages when they feel threatened."

"I understand," the JCS chairman said. "What's the weather forecast in the Philippines?"

"The typhoon could hit the Sulu Sea area by as early as tomorrow afternoon," General Etheridge said. "We've already lost satellite feed because of the weather. We can't get an

AWAC in because of it—and the submarine stands a chance of losing contact."

There was a long silence while Chairman Morrison digested the bad news.

"And the *Ibn Haldoon*?" he finally asked.

"She appears headed for Mindanao. *Sam Houston* reports she's maintaining an SSE heading with high quartering-aft seas. No problems so far. This is a stiff typhoon, but not nearly as bad as the ones that come later in the season."

"Gentlemen," the JCS chief concluded, "I don't have to remind you about the concern in Washington over this matter. For the moment, continue to follow and monitor the target until contingencies present themselves. Unless any of you has a better plan?"

No one did.

It occurred to General Kragle that the actions of the *Ibn Haldoon* indicated it was bound for a deep harbor with shelter from the winds, somewhere its captain knew about. Otherwise, it would surely have harbored at one of the known ports along the way. This was no aimless journey. The *Ibn Haldoon* knew exactly where it was going.

"Let's have the people over in Area Studies check the coastlines," he suggested. "Have them look over both southern Mindanao and Palawan and any of the other islands in the vicinity. We're looking for a deep natural harbor with protection from westerly winds."

"It's a long shot, Darren," General Etheridge said.

"Do we have any other shot?"

God, the General hated the waiting. Always had. His sons had inherited the same trait.

Chaplain Cameron Kragle was attending the Hands of God Conference in New Orleans. General Kragle dialed his cell number, but there was no response. He called Gloria and talked for a few minutes, assuaging her fears that the wed-

ding cake might not be ready on time. He hung up and rang
Fred Whiteman, Thornton's FBI agent handling the JTTF investigation of the C-47 in Georgia.

"Have you found out anything about Claude?" he asked.

"We traced him to a swamp cabin near Edith, Georgia.
Crime Scene Investigation found one of his credit cards
stuffed down in a crack of the floor. We know he was there
and in some kind of trouble. All we have so far is a descrip-
tion of an SUV and the names and descriptions of two ragheads."

"Terrorists?"

"What else could it be?"

"WMDs?"

"That too."

"Will you keep me informed?"

"You know I will. We'll find him, General."

The General's brother, CPI correspondent Mike Kragle, telephoned. He got directly to the point the Kragle way. "Darren,
I just picked up something interesting."

"I'm already up to my ass in alligators, Mike."

"One more or less won't fill up the pond then, will it? It's
about the Philippines."

"I'm listening."

"Senator Thierry has been courting hell out of the press
lately," the journalist said. "Fluttering around like a butterfly.
Hollywood fund-raisers with the pretty folk. Stumping in
New Hampshire, pressing a lot of flesh and kissing a bunch
of ugly babies. The guy's running for President."

"What's your point, Mike. That's old news."

"Thierry was the one who got the call from Stanton warning about the bombing in Bali. If Stanton had only one phone
call, why would he waste it on Thierry?"

"They're old asshole buddies?"

"Huh-uh. Try that again, Darren. Could it be because Stanton, or the people holding Stanton, wanted Thierry to do something without telling anybody else? A couple of hours after that mysterious phone call, the good senator takes time off from kissing babies and catches the night flight to Louisiana. There's more. I just found out he's booked for a round-trip flight to Manila. Right in, right back out. All quite a coincidence, wouldn't you think?"

The General didn't believe in coincidences. Everything had a cause and effect. Chains of events, each event of which was precipitated by the one preceding it. It did seem curious that Thierry would suddenly have business in the Philippines—when that was where Stanton happened to be.

"I can hear you thinking, Darren," Mike Kragle said. "I know my nephews are out on one of your operations in the Philippines. Don't deny it. I have my sources, and damned good ones. What I want to know is, does it have anything to do with Stanton's kidnapping?"

"What are you doing following politicians around?" General Kragle evaded.

"A tip about corruption," Mike replied mysteriously. He had been in the news business for a long time, having won a Pulitzer from the Vietnam War. He had a nose for a good story and wouldn't let go until he'd wrung every last nuance out of it.

"Mike, I can't tell you anything yet."

"I figured. I also figured you might need to know about Thierry. If anything comes out of all this from your angle, I want the first dime dropped on me."

"You're getting old, Mike. Ma Bell charges a quarter these days."

"Aren't we all getting old?"

The General hung up, deep in thought. He thought about it a few more minutes, then dialed a number and asked to speak to the director of the National Homeland Security Agency.

Complicateder and complicateder.

CHAPTER 44

Sulu Sea

Detachment 2-Bravo's orders were to stand by on the *Sam Houston* until "contingencies" presented themselves or until it received further instructions. Major Brandon felt in limbo while the submarine continued clandestinely on the *Ibn Haldoon*'s trail. He kept hearing the way Summer screamed when he abandoned her in the freighter's engine room. He suffered nightmares about terrorists shooting the missionaries whenever he napped. The missionaries turned into Summer.

He divided his time between the DDS or the mess hall where the men hung out drinking coffee and scuttlebutting and the communications section in the control room. The message from CENTCOM never changed: Continue surveillance on the freighter; no word from the CIA contact aboard the freighter. Nothing but silence.

"You'll notify me if you hear anything?" Brandon requested of Commander Eales.

The submarine commander smiled and said in his Deep South drawl, "Ya'all can count on it, heah?"

The fracture existing between the detachment and the sub skipper had almost healed after Brandon came back aboard. Lieutenant Lucifer, typically undiplomatic and abrasive had refused to tell the commander anything about why Brandon was trying to disarm the mines once they had already been set.

"You have no need to know, sir," was the way Lucifer put it when Commander Eales cornered him. The evil grin and the Satan-like eyebrows were usually sufficient to put off most challengers, superior to him in rank or not.

"Mister," Eales shot back, "anything that happens on this boat or concerns this boat is my need to know. Where are you from, mister?"

"You can bet I'm not from Alabama or Georgia, sir."

"What's your rank?"

"So fucking sorry. I can't tell you that."

"What's your unit?"

"I can't tell you that either."

"Ya'all are getting yourself into trouble, mister."

"Trouble is my middle name."

If things had gone wrong and the *Ibn Haldoon* blew up anyhow, details about Stanton and the Korean children were sufficient to cause both an international and a domestic crisis had they leaked out. The President's political enemies would have used the fact that U.S. forces sabotaged a ship upon which a former President was held hostage to crucify him and perhaps bring down his administration. That in turn might well have precipitated a confrontation with North Korea, not to mention Saudi Arabia and perhaps China. As it stood, however, no one outside the team would have known who was aboard the freighter if Brandon failed to make it back.

"You did good," Brandon reluctantly complimented Lucifer. "But you could use some tact if you ever expect to make admiral."

To Cassidy, Brandon said, "You'll be an operator yet. With proper guidance from your big brother."

Cassidy sobered. "I'm glad you're back, Brandon. You had me scared."

Summer hadn't made it back. Neither had Gypsy from that time long ago in Afghanistan. Brandon remembered how Gypsy died in the powered parachute while he was flying her out of Afghanistan. He remembered how the Abu Sayyaf troops executed their political captives on Mindanao, which brought him back around to Summer. It didn't matter that he had had no other choice but to leave her on the ship, the guilt and the pain remained.

There was no need to maintain secrecy about the *Ibn Haldoon* once Brandon was extracted from the sea. The information on Stanton and the children had to be communicated to CENTCOM and USSOCOM anyhow. Brandon smoothed things over with Commander Eales by telling him the truth. Everything except that the CIA agent was a woman who said she loved him.

Commander Eales, a tall blond man who, except for the Southern accent, reminded Brandon of his brother Cameron. He was more than proud to command a submarine and wanted to show it off as a gesture that he held no hard feelings against the Delta detachment. Modern nuclear submarines with their sophisticated sonar, he pointed out, were perfectly capable of tracking a surface vessel in any kind of weather. They could stay underwater for months at a time while traveling at thirty knots and manufacturing their own air and drinking water directly out of the sea. Captain Nemo stuff. The *Sam Houston*, Commander Eales assured Brandon, was not going to lose the *Ibn Haldoon*, no matter what.

USS *Sam Houston* ran deep to avoid surface churn as the typhoon approached the islands. Nature's frenzy on the surface transformed itself at depth to a general unsteadiness of the submarine's decks. Doc TB distributed pills for motion sickness, a precaution that set the SEALs to guffawing and ribbing the Delta members of the detachment—until Ordnanceman Second Class

T-Bone Jones became the first to suffer seasickness. He got so sick he couldn't even crack his knuckles or bark like a seal. He dived through the hatch leading from the DDS to make a run for the head. He didn't make it.

"How about another salty herring, *sailor boy*?" Mad Dog Carson chided him.

Later, when the motion got to Mad Dog, he vomited but held it all inside his bellowed cheeks and swallowed it again rather than succumb to it.

"Motherfucker, that is *gross,*" Thumbs Jones said.

"Thank you, thank you, Thumbs. It's no worse than eating pussy. You black boys do eat pussy, don't you? How about you candy-ass sailors? You eat pussy? I challenge you SEALs to a puke-swallowing contest."

No one was up for the challenge.

Restless, Brandon made his way to the galley. Gloomy Davis and the Indian SEAL, J.D. McHenry, were holding court over coffee with some of the other team members. They had Cassidy in the hot seat.

"Is that a fact, Ice Man?" Gloomy addressed the taciturn weapons specialist, but the twinkle in his eyes indicated his remarks were directed at Cassidy. "So you're telling the ladies and good ole boys on the jury that you seen this young lad with your own eyes playing kissy face with Sergeant Margo Foster outside the NCO Club?"

"That's a fact," Ice Man confirmed.

"All I did was kiss her goodbye," Cassidy defended himself. "We were getting ready to deploy, remember?"

Doc TB, who had married young and already had one son, joined the teasing. "That poor little girl is probably moping around Funny Platoon all by herself pining for her Delta trooper."

Mad Dog sauntered into the galley in time to provide his own unique commentary. "Just a kiss, huh?" he snorted.

"C'mon, Sergeant Kragle. That wasn't all you did. Let me smell your finger."

"That reminds me of Arachna Phoebe," Gloomy said.

Mad Dog snurled a lip. "Let me smell *your* finger—if it ain't rotted off by now."

Gloomy turned to McHenry. "No shit, J.D. Did I ever tell you of the time back in Hooker when Arachna was about to marry this ole boy called Bubba? Bubba comes to me real nervous about it. So this is what he tells me:

" 'My mom and pop,' says he, 'has been arrested for growing and selling marijuana and are dependent on my two sisters, one of who is a prostitute in Jersey City and the other married to a transvestite in Tulsa. I have two brothers. One is serving a no-parole life sentence in McAlester for raping and murdering a teenage boy in 1998. The other is in jail in Oklahoma City on charges of incest with his three children. When I was a sailor, I married a Thai hooker and we opened a brothel in the Bronx. I got rid of her, but I still have the brothel and I'm hoping to get my sisters to manage it. It would get them off the streets and hopefully the heroin.'

" 'Have you told Arachna Phoebe about all this?' I asks him.

" 'Oh, yeah, yeah,' he says. 'She's real understanding. My problem is that I don't want her to think bad of me. I love Arachna and look forward to bringing her into the family. Now, I want to be totally honest with her . . . Should I tell her about my cousin who voted for John Stanton?' "

Mad Dog and J.D. rolled their eyes. A sailor from the con room hurried into the galley.

"Mister . . . uh . . . Brandon?"

No rank was known outside the detachment. Brandon stood up.

"Sir, Commander Eales wants you to come to the control room."

Brandon was already on his way. Commander Eales was waiting for him.

"Ya'all have a message from CENTCOM," he said. "They told me you'd understand. All it says is that they received communications from the *Ibn Haldoon* on the contact's secure radio. The voice was a man's, and it spoke Arabic."

Brandon stood there a long moment, stunned, while he digested the implications. If the terrorists had Summer's cell phone or SATCOM radio, it meant she had been compromised and captured. Or . . .

He didn't want to think about it.

CHAPTER 45

AMERICA LOSING WAR RESOLVE

Washington (CPI)—Americans may be losing their resolve to continue the War on Terror. So says a study conducted by a consortium of independent think tanks.

"Almost all the sentiment has faded by now," said Madge Deaton, author, lecturer and director of the consortium. "It has faded from neglect, because nothing real or serious has been asked of the American people. During World War II, there were rationings of butter and steel and other items. There were clothing drives and metal drives. Old people and young volunteered as coast watchers or air raid wardens

while the young men went off to fight. Rosie the Riveter
took her husband's place at the factory.

"None of that has happened this time. We are told there is
a war, while at the same time we are told we defeat the terrorists if we go about our lives in a normal way. So, we continue normal life and soon grow deaf to the sour comedy of
warnings that we must be on guard against inevitable future terrorist attacks. Few are asked to sacrifice for the war
effort. As a result, few will take it seriously, even after
9/11—until at such time as a nuclear device is exploded in
Hollywood or Palm Beach . . ."

It might be well for Americans to remember, suggested
MacArthur Thornbrew, director of the National Homeland
Security Agency, "that terror is like the theater . . . We are
the actors on the lighted stage. Terrorists sit as spectators
shrouded in darkness while they study our weaknesses.
They rise and strike at the moment the actors are most vulnerable. Then they run away to plan an even bigger and better attack . . ."

CHAPTER 46

Atchafalaya Swamp

Thanks to instincts honed by military training, and mostly
thanks to God, Cameron would reflect later, the terrorist's
second bullet missed a vital area. Even as Yasein slammed to
the salt road with a bullet in his back, even as Cameron
turned and looked into the barrel of the assault rifle, he was

already diving for the fetid swamp water. The crack of the rifle was hard and sharp in the sun. The bullet tugged into his T-shirt with a searing pain across his back like a red hot iron suddenly applied.

Water at the edge of the road was shallow. Cameron combat-rolled, splashing, peripherally aware of a second round popping the water next to his head. He bounced to his feet, desperate but determined, and fled into the swamp. Driven only by his intense desire to survive this moment into the next. Bullets cracked around his head and slapped into trees.

He ran with the same recklessness and disregard for his surroundings as when he fled his Abrams after the Sagger struck it in Iraq. One single, compelling thought in his mind—escape! Like the deer or the antelope pursued. An emotion primitive and raw and instinctive.

He was sure he heard the rifleman splashing in pursuit. That spurred him to even greater fear and effort. He kept running even as the fetid water deepened and the growths of mangrove and vines thickened.

He had no concept of how long or how far he fled. His lungs burned from the effort. He sucked at the hot, moist air with a hoarse sound that seemed to vibrate out of his lungs and through his larynx. He glanced back and, although he saw no one, he *knew* the hunter was back there. Coming after him. To kill him as he had already killed Yasein.

He plunged into water that came up to his waist. Primordial muck at the bottom sucked his sneakers off his feet. He threw himself forward into the greenish scum and swam desperately. A snake as thick as his arm glided out of his way. It turned back and paused with its body forming liquid S curves on the surface and its black split tongue flickering.

Cameron ignored it. It was only a second-rate threat at the moment.

The flight impulse gradually wore off, replaced by exhaustion. Still sucking air with the hoarse-frog sound, the last of his strength expended in swimming, Cameron dragged himself out of the water onto a hummock of relatively dry land. He clawed his way toward the bole of a giant live oak and rolled behind it. Had he the energy left, he thought, he would have clawed a hole in the ground and then pulled it in on top of him.

He lay there with his face buried in his arms until he mastered his breathing and stopped making the sound that would attract the predator to his prey. Reason returned with the end of the immediate crisis. He peered around the tree trunk, looking for movement, listening for the splashing of pursuing feet.

All around, on every front, stretched a thick live green curtain of vegetation circular and growing from the top down rather than the bottom up. Great vines, some two or three inches thick, intertwined with one another and anchored themselves to roots crawling across the above-water hummocks. Spanish moss clung parasitically to virtually every tree. Bamboo-like plants five or six feet tall shot up out of black oily scum and formed impenetrable barriers. Everything stank of mildew and decay and stagnation. A peculiar greenish half-light prevented entry of most of the sun's rays, except for a weak shaft of pale yellow here and there. He heard the lone, squawking cry of a bird somewhere, the startling splash of a fish surface-feeding, the buzz of mosquitoes in his ears and a strange low drone in the background, a combination of all this that gave the swamp a voice.

But no one was coming after him. Not yet.

He inhaled deeply to settle his adrenaline. He was calm again. Thinking, not simply reacting. He thought about Yasein. Cameron had seen men die before. They were almost always done for when they fell without making a sound. The little man had died for his friend Abdul.

There was only one reason for an ambush such as the one that took Yasein—the missile site must be nearby. That also meant the terrorists couldn't afford to let him get away and spread the alarm. Even if they mistakenly assumed Yasein and he were tourists—bird watchers, biology students or something—and even if Ramzi or none of the others recognized Yasein from al-Farooq, they would still have to kill Cameron to protect their secret. That they would shoot first said everything that needed to be said about their contempt for human life.

Cameron looked around for something to use as a weapon. A thick club. A heavy stone.

My God!

Was the veneer of civilization and Godliness so thin on his soul that he so easily discarded the vow he made to God and to himself—that he would not kill again, no matter the provocation? Were such vows made only when they appeared effortless to keep and then abandoned at the first challenge?

Thou shalt not kill; and whosoever shall kill shall be in danger of the judgment . . .

He dropped his head onto his arms. Ironic, he thought, how only last Sunday his sermon at Fort Bragg addressed the dual question of whether a Christian should fight for his country and of whether the commandment against killing applied to soldiers at war. His conclusion: A Christian *could* fight and kill if the cause was just and the necessity great to prevent an even more horrendous evil.

But not him. He had made a *vow*. A vow was not subject to situational ethics. Vows must not be broken.

He thought when he left Fort Bragg to attend the Hands of God Conference that God would test his faith in intellectual confrontation with other faiths. He never suspected that God would cast him into the wilderness, as Jesus himself had gone out to confront Satan.

Everything depended on his getting away to alert the authorities now that he was all but certain that he had found, or was at least in the vicinity of, the terrorist base camp where plans were under way to shoot a nuclear missile at New Orleans. He berated himself for having left his cell phone charging in the Chevrolet. That meant his next best chance was to return to the blacktop and seek help.

He wouldn't be fooled this time into underestimating the terrorists. They would likely patrol the roads searching for him. He needed to be exceptionally cautious and avoid roads.

He stood up. The movement increased the burning across his back and reminded him that he had been shot. He twisted his arm to feel for the wound. He flinched at the touch of his fingers, the six-inch furrow gouged across his back being exceptionally tender. Luckily, there wasn't much bleeding and the injury seemed relatively minor. There wasn't anything he could do about it at the moment anyhow. He had more pressing problems.

A short prayer made him feel better. *Deliver me from evil, O Lord.*

He looked around. *Which way, O Lord?*

Which way *was* the blacktop? Was it from *that* direction that he fled? He couldn't be sure. His path while in flight mode undoubtedly curved and twisted. He had paid no attention to where he was going or in which direction, only in getting out of the area of operation as rapidly as possible. But if he *had* come from that direction, which he thought likely, then the blacktop lay to his left. Perhaps two miles?

If he could only detect the sound of traffic . . . He held his breath and closed his eyes to better concentrate. He opened his eyes. The blacktop was too far away. Besides, he recalled learning in army survival training that swamps trapped sound and prevented its transmission as effectively as a sponge soaked up water. There wouldn't be much traffic on the road anyhow.

Undecided, he watched the raised eyes and snout of a

small alligator dimple the green pond scum as it surfaced and dispassionately surveyed him. He shivered with dread at the thought of proceeding through *that*. He had read that alligators up to fourteen feet long had been captured in Louisiana. One pulled a small but full-grown cow into the water and presumably devoured her.

He couldn't stay there. His throat was already dry and parched from thirst. All this water and not a cupful to drink. He picked up a stick and flung it at the alligator. It sank. After looking about for others, and for snakes, he gingerly entered the water on his bare feet and struck out on what he hoped was a straight line toward the blacktop. The first thing he intended to do when he reached civilization, after notifying the FBI, was down an ice-cold *liter* of *Mountain Dew*.

He traveled steadily and exhaustingly for the next two hours, attempting to negotiate a path from hummock to hummock. In between were scummy bodies of water, some pools of which were over his head. He would be wading through when suddenly the bottom dropped out from underneath his feet.

He sighted another alligator, this one quite large. It sank silently into the depths. His heart hammered against his ribs as he imagined it swimming toward him under the opaque surface, getting nearer and nearer, its great toothed jaws opening . . .

He scrambled onto a hummock and threw himself onto the ground, panting from exertion and horror, making that hoarse sound in his throat again. Moss and other algae, fungi, and green scum adhered to his hair and clothing. He resembled the Swamp Thing, something inhuman risen from the grave.

Heat and humidity sucked the moisture from his body and forced him to search for potable water. He thought of drinking the swamp but realized it could make him deathly ill within a matter of hours. He thought he would reach the blacktop before then. But what if he didn't?

He finally located a small reservoir of brackish water trapped in the bottom of a hollow tree stump. He could reach it only with the tips of his fingers. He tore a piece off his T-shirt, washed it as clean as he could in the swamp, then dangled it into the tree stump to soak up the water. He squeezed the life-giving liquid into his mouth. It tasted like urine. He wiped his face with the cloth and stuck it into his back pocket for later use.

Occasionally he stopped to listen and look for sounds or signs of pursuit. He heard only the absorbed silence of the swamp. He scared up a white cloud of egrets from their fishing. Ravenous mosquitoes fed on his exposed face, neck, and arms. Once, he almost stepped on a cottonmouth coiled behind a log. He jumped back in alarm. Nothing moved of the snake except its tongue.

The atmosphere grew even more gloomy and oppressive with the lowering of the sun into afternoon. He tried to judge direction by the sun, but rarely even saw it through the tangle of forest canopy. Surely he must be getting near the blacktop. He could imagine nothing more uncomfortable and foreboding than spending a night in the swamp.

Something blue ahead caught his eye, the only color he had seen in hours that was not indigenous to the swamp. His hopes rose as he hurried toward it, almost trotting in his eagerness. Perhaps it was a scrap of litter tossed from a nearby road.

He stopped as though he had run into a pane of clear glass, his heart sinking as he reached for the piece of T-shirt he had used to soak up water from the stump and then stuffed into his back jeans pocket. It was gone. But there it was now, dangling on a briar that had plucked it out of his pocket. He saw his footprints where he had passed through before.

My God. He was traveling in circles.

He sank to his knees, knowing and accepting that he was hopelessly lost. The terrorists didn't have to find him and kill him. The swamp would do the job for them.

CHAPTER 47

New Orleans

Senate Majority Leader Jake Thierry by his own admission was not a particularly daring or dashing individual. Like his mentor and patron, former president John Stanton, he had evaded the draft to avoid going to Vietnam. While his more audacious confederates took to the streets to march and man the barricades in the antiwar movement, he worked behind the scenes. Then, as now, he avoided direct confrontation whenever possible, preferring to use intelligence and guile in the background to wield power and get his way. Now, at the prospect of encountering resistance or suspicion as he passed through airport security in New Orleans, he was so nervous his hands trembled and his tongue felt like a dry sponge. Damn Stanton for putting him through this.

Uniformed security, recently federalized, checked his ticket and his identification. "Senator Thierry," the guard said.

"That's right."

"You're going to Manila, sir? Business or for pleasure?"

"Business."

"Do you have papers for the attaché case so we don't have to search it?"

"It's a diplomatic pouch," Thierry corrected him.

"Yes, sir."

The senator handed over the proper papers. The man he met at Slim's in Baton Rouge had thought of everything. The papers even bore the White House seal, impressing security no end. The guard looked at them and entered something in his log.

"What are you doing?" Senator Thierry demanded, alarmed.

"We're required to log all official carry-ons that we don't search. Routine. It's something new started since 9/11."

Thierry hadn't counted on leaving a paper trail.

"Have a good flight, Senator Thierry. My wife wants to vote for you in the next presidential election."

What about you? Always the politician, he thought it but refrained from asking. Instead, he opted to get through the baggage line and on the air bus as quietly as he could and with as little fanfare as possible. The fewer the people who recognized him, the better it was.

He relaxed some when he took his window seat in first-class without further questions or challenges. He placed the attaché case—locked and sealed diplomatic pouch—underneath the seat in front of him and sat stiffly waiting for the plane to fill up with passengers and take off. The next twenty-four to thirty-six hours, he expected, were going to be strained and arduous. The ticket he found waiting for him at the counter, under his own name, included an immediate return booking from Manila to New Orleans.

The only thing the diplomatic pouch contained was the sealed brown envelope the strange man slipped across the table to him in the waterfront café. His eyes studied the pouch at his feet. What was so important in the envelope that John Stanton's abductors would take such a chance that he would deliver it as instructed? Why was Stanton so sure he would do it?

They blew up the nightclub in Bali, didn't they? That was serious stuff. It made a believer out of you.

"Get 'em by the balls," he recalled Stanton saying once, "and they're *happy* to do what you want."

John Stanton had him by the balls.

"Who am I to give it to?" the senator asked the Middle Easterner with the trimmed gray beard who came into the café, recognized him sitting at a table, and sat down.

"Don't concern yourself with it," the man responded cryptically. "You will be met. You do understand the consequences if this fails to reach Manila?"

"Yes."

"Not only consequences for Mr. Stanton, who will not look good without his head, but also the consequences for yourself?"

Thierry nodded, his throat so thick he couldn't speak.

"Very good, *Mr. President.*" The man chuckled sardonically, more of a smirk, then got up and quickly left.

Burning with curiosity, Thierry considered opening the envelope. Each time he got close to satisfying his impulse, however, he backed off, rationalizing that as long as he didn't know what was inside he wasn't *really* cooperating with terrorists. In fact, he consoled himself, what he was really doing was for the good of the country. A heroic effort to rescue a "national treasure" abducted in Cuba and now facing execution by his kidnappers.

He was no fool. He knew better. He was doing this, consenting to be a messenger boy for the terrorists, because Stanton wanted it done to save his own miserable hide, no matter the repercussion on the nation or the rest of the world—and he was doing this because Stanton had the dirt on him.

How had Stanton found out about Robert Chang? How much did he really know? What he knew might not be much and it might not be provable, but Senator Thierry couldn't take the chance. There went his bid for the presidency if one word got out to the press. Hell, there went his career, his life. He might even end up in prison sharing a cell with Congressman James "Beam Me Up, Scotty" Trafficante from Ohio.

Every sonofabitch in Washington had a skeleton or two in his closet. Nobody knew how to rattle those old bones better than John Stanton.

Thierry eyed every new passenger that walked on, especially if the passenger wore a suit and looked as if he might be government. A tall man in his fifties stopped in the aisle and prepared to take the seat next to the senator. Thierry's heart pounded with apprehension. The man nodded politely and placed a briefcase in the overhead. He sat down, buckled in, leaned back his head and closed his eyes. Thierry continued to watch him from the corner of his eye.

After his breathing returned to normal, he held up a finger and asked a busy Asian-looking flight attendant to bring him a drink. His voice cracked.

"Of course, sir. What would you like?"

He took two attempts to get it out. "Tom Collins. Double gin."

She smiled. "White knuckles?" she asked.

"What?"

"Are you a white-knuckle flyer?"

"No. Well, yes." He was today.

"A lot of passengers are white-knucklers after 9/11. But you can relax, sir. We have fine security."

Not too fine, he hoped.

He watched out the window as a baggage train snaked across the tarmac toward the airplane, pulled up alongside, and began bringing luggage up the roller to the airplane's hold.

Stanton, he thought. *Stanton, the bastard.*

How naïve he had been when he first got into politics years ago. He really believed the Anwar Sadat story about doing "good things." But Washington was not about "good things." Washington was about wielding power. Who had it, who had the most of it, and who could use it more effectively as a weapon.

John Stanton was the king of politics, the king maker. He used people. Used them up and then discarded them when he got through with them, flushed them down the toilet like tissue upon which he had wiped his ass. The sonofabitch had no moral center. He had more skeletons in his closets than any high-rolling politico in D.C. Somebody was always exposing one or another of them—shady loan and land deals, influence peddling, a debauched personal life, lies up the ying-yang—but nobody seemed to give a damn, he was so blasted charismatic. He could charm hair onto a billiard ball, look you in the eye and tell you "I did not have sex with the ambassador's wife in the Lincoln Bedroom" and you believed him. If you didn't, you knew he was going to survive anyhow.

Thierry had thought he was so smart, smarter than the others who schemed to ride Stanton's coattails to power. Smart all right. He ended up making a pact with the devil because he wanted to be President so badly and Stanton the king maker provided the opportunity and the means. So what was he doing as a result? Playing courier for terrorists.

Senator Thierry felt ashamed of himself, but he still wanted to be President.

He cast an anxious glance at his seat partner, almost afraid the man might be reading his thoughts or feeling his fear and anger. The guy appeared to be sleeping. He didn't stir or open his eyes as the big jets opened and the plane left the loading gate to taxi out to the runway.

The sun was sinking red and streaked by the time the plane was out over the Pacific bound for Manila nonstop. Because they were following the sun, the sky was red and streaked for hours, the longest sunset Senator Thierry had ever seen. He remained awake all through it and throughout the early night that followed and remained early night. He tried to sleep to escape his nagging conscience; his eyes stayed wide open. He went through three or four more Tom Collinses, but they didn't help.

The skies over Manila were dark and rainy from the typhoon south of the island of Luzon, but the airport remained open. Most of the weather, the pilot said, was down around Mindanao.

Thierry got off quickly with his diplomatic pouch. He felt grungy, red-eyed, hung over, and irritable. He walked down to the taxi stands and still no one contacted him. He bought a coffee and was leaning against the wall when two tough-looking Filipinos in dark shirts and slacks cornered him from either side. They hustled him outside and into the back seat of a waiting taxi.

The taxi took off immediately and snaked into the nearby slums where the streets were narrow, dark, and filled with people and loud music from boomboxes. Thierry started to protest, even though he was scared to death.

"Shut up," one of the men said.

Both his escorts were young, in their late twenties or early thirties. Thierry didn't dare to try to say anything else to them. The taxi soon stopped on a side street. A second taxi following the first parked behind. The brawnier of the two Filipinos snatched the attaché case from the senator's hand and ordered the driver to turn on the dome light.

"Key," he demanded, extending his hand.

Thierry fished it out of his pocket. "What—?"

"Do not talk. Do as you're told."

The man opened the case, then ripped open the brown envelope. Thierry was curious in spite of his fear. A number of large eight-by-ten color photos spilled out. Thierry blanched. The Filipino chuckled.

"I see you recognize them," he said slyly.

Thierry and Robert Chang were prominently featured in each of the surveillance photos. The senator recognized the occasion for each—in a restaurant, at the base of the Vietnam War Memorial, even in a private residence. One showed him counting money from an envelope. Others showed Chang handing him stuffed envelopes. Still others depicted a grandfather clock, a set of diamond earrings on his mistresses' ears, a new gold BMW. Documents listed a column of items Chang had given Thierry in exchange for the senator's support on issues favorable to the People's Republic of China, along with proof that Chang was the purchaser.

Senator Thierry had been had big time. The envelope and its contents were nothing more than a test. The terrorists knew they could trust him to follow orders if he arrived in Manila with the envelope intact. If he opened it and looked inside and *still* came he could be trusted. If he failed to show up at all, or if he had gone to the authorities, copies of materials inside the envelope would have mysteriously surfaced on news desks across the United States. It was, he realized, what was called a no-win situation.

He started to sweat.

"You did well," the Filipino spokesman said. "Now that we know you can be trusted, we have a second delivery for you. Another diplomatic pouch. You will be met in New Orleans."

Someone from the second taxi came forward with a heavy square case already sealed and, like the original, accompanied by the proper paperwork. It weighed at least twenty pounds, as if it were lined with lead or something, although it was small enough to fit underneath an airliner seat as carry-on baggage. The two Filipinos got out of the taxi and left Thierry alone in the back seat. The spokesman leaned down and looked through the open window.

"Would you like copies of these pictures for your scrapbook?" he asked, grinning without mirth.

Thierry sweated and said nothing.

"Your President's head along with these photographs will appear on the Capitol steps in Washington, D.C., if this package is not delivered tonight in New Orleans."

The two men walked off and got into the second taxi. Senator Thierry trembled uncontrollably as his taxi delivered him to the airport to catch his return flight.

CHAPTER 48

Sulu Sea

Training, along with experience in Israel, Afghanistan, North Korea, and other dangerous places, had taught Summer Marie Rhodeman self-reliance and creativity under pressure. She quickly recovered her composure after being tossed half-naked into the darkness of a belowdecks cell with the former President of the United States. Whereas the rope locker next door where she had concealed the Korean children afforded stormy gray light through a porthole, this compartment offered no such convenience.

She gained her feet and began feeling her way along the bulkheads in the darkness toward the hatch.

"What are you doing?" President Stanton asked. He sounded sick.

"Why haven't you turned on the lights?" she countered.

"They told me not to move."

"Are you still tied up?"

"No."

"You might as well be."

"What?"

"Nothing. Be quiet a minute."

She groped her way to the hatch. She didn't expect to get out, having seen Cimatu and his men previously removing the inner wheel lock when they were preparing the cell. She pressed her ear against the steel door and listened for sounds in the passageway. She wondered how long it would take Cimatu and Darth Vader to connect the dead man in the screws with her SAT cell phone, draw conclusions and return to interrogate her. The only weapon she had, the knife, was still in the waistband of her missing trousers.

She heard only the throbbing of the diesel engines through the ship's structure.

"Please sit down," Stanton urged. "Don't upset them."

"Or they'll do what?" she snapped. "Throw me into a cell with you?"

He shut up. Summer had never been particularly political. She had still been a cheerleader in high school in Texas after moving back from Israel with her father and mother when John Stanton was inaugurated as President. The Stanton scandals had been hard to ignore, even for a teen girl with little interest in politics. He had made an impression. That impression wasn't improved any in her eyes by what he contrived to pull off against Brandon and her and the detachment during Operation Iron Weed in Afghanistan. Nor was he improving it any now by his behavior.

She found the light chain and started to jerk on the light before she realized she remained bare from the waist down. She tore off the tail of her off-white tunic from which to fashion a bikini bottom. She tied off the ends on either hip bone. Not very fashionable, but it would have to do. She pulled the switch to bathe the dreary steel cubicle in even drearier light.

Stanton blinked at her from where he huddled against the opposite bulkhead, his arms wrapped around his legs and his knees drawn up to his chin. He looked ill from the rough seas. He reminded her of a scared rich kid in his soiled five-thousand-dollar blue suit, filthy white shirt, and tie knot hanging down on his chest. He *was* handsome though, even under the present circumstances of being unshaved, disheveled, and scared. If you liked the coiffed, graying, lawyer-politician types with short fuses. The man's legendary bad temper with underlings, whom he frequently berated in public, seemed subdued or missing entirely.

Summer ignored him as she explored the compartment for something to use as a weapon. Even the empty paint can she had seen before was gone. There was nothing except steel bulkheads, a ribbed steel deck, and President Stanton.

She turned and glared directly at him. His eyes dropped and he stared at the deck while she completed her exploration. She listened through the bulkhead, thinking of the children next door. They would be getting hungry and wondering why she hadn't returned. She dared not try to communicate with Jang through the bulkhead. She didn't trust Stanton not to expose them.

"What was that quote from you I recently read in the papers, Mr. President?" she asked to break the uncomfortable silence. She sat down on the deck across the compartment from him. "It went something like this: 'The Muslims have virtually no way to attack us, at least on a repeated basis.' Do you still believe that?"

His chin lifted. For a moment she saw temper sparked in his eyes. She had never been intimidated by important people, and especially not by this one, the contempt for whom she and Brandon shared.

The spark vanished. "What do they want with me?" he moaned.

She felt pity. A mild disdain.

"How did you end up here?" she asked him.

He bit his lower lip the way he always did on TV to prove his sincerity and his compassion for the "little people" and the downtrodden. She looked away. He found his voice after a moment. He was on a goodwill tour of Cuba, he said, when terrorists attacked at the airport. He was whisked away in a Lear Jet. He recalled a long flight, during which he was tied, gagged, and blindfolded. Finally, he was hustled aboard this ship and thrown into the dungeon.

"Do you know where we are?" he asked.

"In the Philippines."

He digested that. She thought he would really pucker up if he knew they were sitting on a load of SCUD missiles and that the ship had almost been blown out of the water. She dared discuss nothing with him, however, that she didn't want Cimatu and his thugs to find out. From what she had seen of him, she figured he'd tell everything all the way back to the first grade, do anything he was ordered to do, if the terrorists so much as threatened to break one of his fingernails.

"Why did they bring me here?" he asked, as though she knew the answer.

"Why don't you ask them?"

"They won't tell me anything."

The movement of the ship rocked them back and forth. Waves sloshed against the hull.

"It's storming," he said.

"Yes."

"I'm not President any longer. I can't help them like this. Why did they do this?"

"Usually it's for the ransom."

"I've done everything they asked me to do. All they have to do is let me go and I'll pay anything they want."

She looked at him. "It doesn't usually work that way. You have to pay *before*—"

"My word is my bond."

She couldn't keep the scorn out of her response. "Yeah. Right."

Also legendary was his political back-stabbing and double-dealing.

"I mean it. I'll pay anything."

"You don't have to convince me. I said, *usually* it's the ransom. When they kidnap somebody of your prominence, it's for other reasons as well as money."

He looked scared all over again. "Like what?"

He couldn't be *this* naïve. "To show they can do it. To win concessions. To strike terror in other prominent people. To demonstrate no one is safe from them. I don't know. Why are you asking me? Terrorists aren't always rational anyhow from our perspective."

How rational could you be to wrap dynamite around your waist and climb onto a bus full of school children to blow it up?

"What are they going to do with me?" he wailed. It was always *me*.

If he was looking for reassurance, she couldn't give it to him. "They could always eat you," she said.

He stiffened. Summer heard footfalls clanging in the passageway. Defiant, she stood up to meet their callers.

CHAPTER 49

The steel hatch swung outward. Cimatu lurched into the compartment on the motion of the ship riding the seas. Behind him entered Captain Darth Vader, the ninja, and a couple of other rough characters who had boarded the ship when they brought Stanton aboard. They seemed to suck all the air out of the cell. Darth Vader's thunderous scowl and bristling black beard conveyed his wrath over the chain of disagreeable events unfolding on his ship. He looked as though he might have executed the prisoners on the spot if it were left up to him. Summer had observed, however, that Cimatu and his band had taken over the *Ibn Haldoon* when they came aboard in Nampo. They were in charge.

Cimatu carried Summer's cell phone. Lucky for her, they apparently hadn't found the SATCOM radio she kept concealed in an air duct. Maybe she could still talk her way out of this.

Cimatu's dark pig eyes bore into Summer's. She defiantly returned his stare. Stanton jumped into the deadlock.

"I have to go to the bathroom," he pleaded.

"Go in your pants," Cimatu snorted in passable English.

"Why are you treating me this way," the former President wheedled. "Haven't I done everything you asked me to do?"

Cimatu looked at him for the first time. "So far, your man, he has done well," he conceded. "Fortunate for you, John—

May I call you John?—your senator has arrive in Manila and is now go back to the United States. If he keep do as he told . . . Well—" He grinned, a simple twisting of the lips that pulled the scar down toward them. "Well, you keep your head a little bit longer, I think."

"He'll do it," Stanton eagerly reassured him. "I know Jake. He won't let me down."

Puzzled, Summer looked back and forth between the two men. What was this all about? Cimatu gave her no time to dwell on it. He held up the cell phone and switched back into Arabic.

"Captain Khalid is very concerned. A woman on a ship is bad luck. A woman with a telephone is even worse luck. Who are you and who were you calling?"

"My name is Ismael. I promised my mother I'd call."

Cimatu took a threatening step toward her. The scar transformed itself into a leech again. He caught himself and examined the phone without much interest. To Summer's surprise, he seemed willing to explain away the telephone and the death of the man in the engine room as both the byproduct of her sex. After all, a woman could be expected to have a telephone. A woman might well have also sneaked away for a tryst with a man in the engine room, resulting in an accident, just as she said.

Seeing this in the way he began questioning her, Summer changed her defiance to become more conciliatory.

"My real name is Raisa," she told him. "My family has no sons and we needed money because my father is very ill. I pretended to be a man in order to get a job because a Saudi seaman earns fair wages and a woman cannot work. I have the telephone because I promised my mother I would call her to let her know I'm all right."

Cimatu's eyes bore into hers. She couldn't tell if he believed her or not. He gave her cold goose flesh.

"The phone seems to be broken," he observed as he thought things over. He keyed the transmitter. "Hello, hello. Allah is great, Allah is powerful . . ."

Obviously he had been toying with it before. No response came from the phone, not even static.

"It hasn't worked since we left Nampo," Summer said, hoping he believed her. It was almost true anyhow.

"Nevertheless," he finally decided, "Captain Khalid has determined that we must keep you confined for your own safety, now that the crew knows you are a woman. Also, there must be a hearing and perhaps a trial on the death of Boutros."

So that was the wrestler's name?

"I'm a prisoner then?" Summer asked.

"Of course you are a prisoner. You are *my* prisoner, and I will do with you whatever I please. It is not nice to trick Cimatu. I liked you much better as a boy." He chuckled, a sound like a lawn mower. "Perhaps I will feed you to them."

He gestured toward the ninja and the two tough-looking pirates who had accompanied Stanton aboard the ship. Their heated eyes traveled the length of Summer's body, lingering at the V of her legs covered by the thin muslin of her makeshift bikini.

The generator-fed overhead lights dimmed, then caught again. Cimatu sneered another lawn mower sound meant to be laughter. He handed the cell phone to his mean-looking ninja partner.

"Wait outside in the passageway," he said. "The rest of you return to your work."

"What about him?" Darth Vader wanted to know, indicating Stanton.

"He is too frightened to do other than piss his pants. Now, get out of here."

"If you touch me . . ." Summer threatened, knowing the threat to be hollow.

"Allah himself said a woman must be beaten," Cimatu growled. "Especially if the female is a liar."

Terror and loathing chilled Summer's blood as Darth Vader and Cimatu's men left, sniggering among themselves. The watertight door closed with a nerve-shattering clang. Although President Stanton had not understood the Arabic exchange, he watched with horrified fascination.

Summer unleashed a savage preemptive kick at Cimatu's groin. What did she have to lose? Sooner or later, he would kill her anyhow, whether she fought back or not. She might as well get in her licks. It wasn't her nature to passively accept anything.

Cimatu saw the kick coming and deflected her sneaker. She eluded his charges twice, ducking underneath his flailing arms to the other side of the room. He proved surprisingly quick and agile for so large a man and soon had her cornered.

"Get up and help me, Stanton!" she cried out in English.

On his side of the compartment, the former President seemed to have balled himself even tighter inside his arms. He watched with his mouth slightly open and his eyes watery, taking it all in.

Cimatu caught her on the jaw with a hamlike fist that knocked her to the deck. He pounced on her before she could recover and get away, raining short hard punches directly into her face. Blood splattered.

"It is not nice to fool Cimatu . . ." the monster muttered. "If you had been a boy I would take care of you . . ."

Her eyes pleaded with Stanton to help her. He remained frozen in place, as though mesmerized, even excited.

Cimatu punched her hard in the face one last time. She lost consciousness.

When she regained awareness, the Filipino had finished

his beating and left. She was alone with Stanton in the dim overhead light. He continued to stare at her. Her face felt bruised and shredded and bloody and her body ached all over. She lay on the deck for long minutes, mentally checking herself for broken bones. There didn't seem to be any.

She fixed Stanton with a look of pure loathing. Through swollen, bloody lips she mumbled, "You cowardly prick. You watched and did nothing."

"What could I do?" he protested. "He would have killed both of us."

She could barely speak. "I . . . I will kill him. If it's the last thing I do on earth, I will kill him . . . *I will kill him!*"

CHAPTER 50

Mindanao

The western portion of Mindanao, the largest and southernmost island of the Philippine chain, extended into the Sulu Sea in an irregular configuration roughly in the shape of a turkey's head. The end of the beak curved from west toward the south, forming a large southern-exposure basin between the beak and the waddles. *Ibn Haldoon* trailed by submarine USS *Sam Houston* reached this relatively protected piece of geography about midnight. At shortly before 2:00 a.m., the freighter dropped anchor. Commander Eales ordered the *Sam Houston* to neutral buoyancy a short distance seaward and summoned the leadership of Detachment 2-Bravo—Brandon and Lucifer—to the con room. Deep Steel's orders were to monitor the Saudi vessel "until contingencies presented themselves." This was possibly that contingency.

"All the islands of the Philippines are the tops of old volcanic mountains," Commander Eales said in his down-home Southern drawl. "The Philippine Trench northeast of Mindanao is one of the deepest spots in the Pacific. What this means is that the water is deep enough in many places that large ships can pull next to shore in narrow harbors. Sonar tells me that's the case here. The ship is inside a deep, narrow cove where there'll be little wind or sea movement, especially if it's further protected by cliffs."

"So what the fuck are you saying—?" Lucifer responded impatiently.

Brandon had already caught on. He slapped his fist into the palm of his other hand. "It's where the freighter's been heading all along," he said, excited that something was about to break loose. "The *Ibn Haldoon* wasn't *caught* by the storm. It deliberately sailed into the storm to hide its passage. Damned smart. It's offloading the missiles now."

Brandon quickly formed a recon to swim ashore and take a look. Lucifer insisted he lead it—"We SEALs are goddamned fucking trained for this kind of clusterfuck operation"—but Brandon overruled him. To begin with, a leader needed to have a foot on the ground to see what was going on. Brandon was also honest enough to admit, at least to himself, that he had a selfish reason. Summer. CENTCOM overheard a man speaking Arabic over Summer's cell phone, which meant she was possibly a prisoner or a hostage. If she were still alive, he was going to get as near her as quickly as he could. Part of Deep Steel's mission, after all, was to recover the CIA contact from the *Ibn Haldoon*.

"*Your* job when the time comes, Lucifer," Brandon reasoned, "is to take down the freighter and rescue the hostages aboard. DevGroup SEALs *are* trained for that?"

Lucifer acquiesced, although obviously not liking the idea

of staying behind. Anyhow, both detachment officers couldn't be placed on the same element when the team split up. Brandon selected Gloomy Davis, Cassidy, and SEAL T-Bone Jones to accompany him on the recon. Cassidy seemed delighted to have been chosen.

"We'll communicate with the small Motorolas through the sub's commo and firm up an op order when we see what's up," Brandon said in last-minute instructions.

The recon element would have to travel light. It wasn't a combat patrol. Besides, no one could be certain how rough the seas were, even in the cove. That meant handguns and almost nothing else. The follow-up element would be tasked with bringing in weapons and explosives, perhaps even using the Zodiac inflatable boats to do so.

Each swimmer quickly prepared by donning a rubber wet suit and a Draeger closed-circuit breathing rig and stuffing his tiger-stripe fatigues, boots, headgear, radio, and pistol of choice inside a small waterproof bag. T-Bone took along a "Hush Puppy," a 9mm Mark 22 semiauto pistol equipped with a noise suppressor. Its use could be foreseen on any type of clandestine operation within enemy lines. Brandon took his Glock 9mm and Cassidy his Walther PPK. Gloomy muttered in disgruntlement at having to leave Mr. Blunderbuss behind in exchange for a puny Glock that hadn't nearly the range, accuracy, or authority of his sniper rifle.

Commander Eales jockeyed the submarine closer to the cove outlet. The seas were markedly calmer here than they were out in the open Pacific.

"It's raining hard," he joked before the recon team entered the lockout chamber. "Ya'all are going to get wet."

The lockout chamber was a small escape trunk located forward of the sail, as the submarine superstructure was called. It was a spherical space about six feet across, large enough to accommodate up to five swimmers at a time. Mouthpieces and air hoses inside the chamber allowed the recon team to use the sub's air supply system while the chamber was sealed and flooded with seawater. The four men stood doubled over, tanks on their backs, equipment in their arms, all jammed together until the process was complete and the trunk full of water. The outer lock opened for them to swim into the open sea.

The movement of the sea outside sucked them out of the chamber, as though the sub exhaled them. The water felt fairly warm, but it was still rough as it undulated them through the sea. Visibility was virtually zero in the liquid blackness. Each man wore fluorescent strips of tape at various points on his wetsuit. They showed up in the dark like glowing fish, reminding Cassidy that Philippine waters were noted for sharks. They had already discovered that with the loss of poor Winnie Brown.

Brandon led the way with the compass board, following an azimuth on the luminous hands toward an arbitrary point inside the entrance to the cove where the outer breakers wouldn't dash them against the shoals too forcefully. The tape and the compass face were the only illumination in the vast black ocean.

They started out at a depth of fifty feet, gradually rising toward the surface as wave action settled into swells within the protection of the cove. Brandon broke out into air first. Three other heads popped up around him, identified only by the glowing tape on their hoods. Hard rain battered down and churned the black surface. It was so dark it was difficult to tell where sea broke off and atmosphere began. Swells lifted them high, pushing them toward shore, then dropped them into the dizzying blackness of the following troughs. Everyone continued tank breathing.

From the tops of swells, the team saw the *Ibn Haldoon*, ablaze with lights, riding at gentle anchor in the rain next to a kind of natural rock pier. As best Brandon could determine in the greatly reduced visibility, the cove appeared some two hundred meters across at the mouth and enclosed in craggy bluffs half as tall as the bay was wide. Lightning skittering across the upturned black bowl of the sky, webbing and crackling electricity, provided the light to confirm his initial observations. The cove was very well protected. Sounds of operating machinery carried across the water to their ears.

Summer was there, Brandon thought. He *hoped* Summer was there. His jaw tightened around his mouthpiece and he thrust more power into his swim fins.

Surface swimming, using only their fins as propulsion, they made toward a landing some one hundred meters to the freighter's stern. As they drew near they heard the crash and roar of the ocean beating its head against the rocky shore. Beach action caught them. The next thing they knew they were being sucked tumbling and dragging toward land.

Pressed to the bottom, somersaulting in the water, shot to the surface, battered against boulders. It was a wild and savage ride, brine in their mouths, the lightning splintering across the black heavens. At the same time it was magnificent and strangely exhilarating. They didn't so much land as they were evicted, cast high into rocks which combed them out of the retreating breakers.

Coughing and sputtering, on a high from the experience, the recon team pulled itself away from the sea's reach and collapsed from exhaustion. Brandon took out his radio and reported a single phrase to the *Sam Houston*: "Deep Steel has landed."

After changing into combat tiger-stripes and caching their dive gear, the Deltas and their SEAL climbed the rock face that led up and away from the ocean. The driving rain and the dark made footing precarious. They approached the docking area cautiously through a jungle thicket and squirmed the rest of the way through the mud on their bellies until they reached an observation point. Light supplied by the freighter and intermittently by the heavens provided them a clear view of the activities.

The rock pier appeared to have been modified to accept freight. It was about thirty feet wide and some ninety to one hundred feet long, cleared of rock slides and scraped level to accommodate wheeled vehicles. So many men wearing slickers and carrying weapons overran the dock that Brandon knew this had to be part of the guerrilla receiving party. They seemed to be directing the operation, shouting and waving at each other and running about.

No time was being wasted unloading the missiles. A muddy jungle road led down from the top of the island and around the forward edge of the nearest cliff to the dock. One truck had apparently already loaded and was growling and rumbling unseen back up through the forest, sounding heavily loaded and having a tough go climbing out and away from the bay in granny gear. A second flatbed backed out onto the pier. A third waited. Summer had told him when he was on the freighter that there were three missiles.

They had to get closer in order to get an idea where the rockets were being taken. Drumming rain and the night covered their approach. They froze when lightning flashed. Gloomy Davis on point actually stepped out onto the road before he realized it. He jumped back into the jungle and warned the others. They were out of sight of the dock, but they could still hear voices, ship winches, and truck motors.

Nearby voices warned them that someone was coming. They dived for cover. Soon they heard boots squishing on the wet road. A burst of lightning, long-lasting and crackling across the sky, revealed four men, all wearing green military-style ponchos going slickety-slick in the rain. Brandon got a good look at one of them because he wasn't wearing a rain hood or any other headgear. He was a squat, stout man built like an underweight sumo wrestler. He had a shaved head and a hideous scar across his left cheek and jaw line.

The other three men were bearded. Two wore hoods that made them look like Grim Reapers. The third affected an old British World War I helmet crammed down on his head. All had their heads lowered into the rain and shouted at each other in order to be heard above the sound of its rattling in the foliage.

They came from uphill and continued slogging along the road toward the dock, passing within a few feet of Brandon and his men hiding alongside. The guerrilla base camp would seem to be nearby, uphill where the road went.

As soon as the terrorists were out of earshot, the recons followed them, keeping in the brush next to the road. Their assignment was to look for where the missiles were being taken; the best way was to follow the next truck. In the meantime, Brandon wanted to get near enough to see if the prisoners were being brought ashore. He doubted they would be left on the *Ibn Haldoon* as the freighter continued its voyage and pretended to be an ordinary transport vessel.

The scarfaced man and his companions stopped on the rock pier, huddling together to watch the extraction of a long wooden crate from the *Ibn Haldoon*'s hold. The ship's cargo crane swung the crate out over the pier where workers guided it to rest on the flatbed truck. The truck cranked open its engines and growled off the pier and up the road past Brandon and his hiding warriors. Its headlights made the rain look like a solid gray curtain slanting toward the east.

The third truck backed onto the pier to take the other one's place. Soon, an identical wooden crate was extracted from the ship and deposited onto its bed. It pulled off the pier. It stopped where the road began and seemed to be waiting on something. Its headlights blazed angrily in the rain.

It wasn't long before Brandon saw why it was waiting.

There was a commotion on the gangplank as some more people came ashore. The scarface waded into the little crowd of people and soon got it straightened out and in some kind of order behind the truck, which would be used to light the way. The ridiculous-looking man in the British helmet returned to the ship.

The truck led the way with its headlights, engine revving, while the large formation of terrorists and guerrilla soldiers trudged along in its wake. The vehicle slowly rumbled past the hiding Delta recon team. As the hikers crawled past, a flash of lightning revealed the cause of the little disturbance at the gangplank. Recognition more than the lightning sent a jolt of electricity surging through Brandon's body. All the way to his soul.

Neither of the two prisoners wore storm gear. Both were bound with their hands behind their backs and had rope leashes tied around their necks. President Stanton stumbled along with his head bowed, looking defeated, following his master. The scarface Brandon had seen earlier led Summer like a leashed dog. She wore only a ragged blouse of some sort and a makeshift bikini bottom, like a diaper. Her face looked swollen and discolored almost beyond recognition. Yet, unlike Stanton, Summer held her chin high and appeared defiant and undaunted. All this Brandon saw in the lightning. Then it was dark again and he couldn't distinguish her from the mass.

His heart went out to her. Although relieved beyond words to see that she was alive, he also felt rage welling inside his breast. He couldn't help thinking of the missionary's wife, Grace Hoffman, lying in the rain of Zamboango del Norte province while a terrorist pumped bullets into her, her husband, and their nurse in order to prevent their rescue.

Brandon had not identified the CIA contact aboard the Saudi freighter to the rest of the detachment. Therefore, see-

ing Summer prisoner among the guerrillas gave Cassidy a
jolt of surprise. He knew now why his older brother had
seemed distracted and anxious since his return from having
boarded the *Ibn Haldoon*. He reached out through the rain
and darkness to lay a hand on his brother's shoulder.

CHAPTER 51

Shrouded in the forest, Brandon and the three other members of his small recon team waited as at least thirty guerrillas armed with AK-47s and M-16s, knee mortars and light
machine guns slogged past in a loose cavalcade behind terrorists leading the two captives by their necks. Flashes of
lightning lent them a dark and sinister appearance that was
almost otherworldly. They disappeared into the black curtain of rain; it gradually absorbed the sound of tramping
boots. Brandon was reminded of an old song—"Riders of
the Storm."

Gloomy edged next to his commander for a private conversation as soon as it was safe to speak.

"Boss, why didn't you tell us Summer was the contact on
the ship?"

"I didn't think it pertinent to the mission."

"Pardon me for saying so, Boss, but folks back in Hooker
know what bullshit is. We been in a lot of stuff together, you
and me, and I know how you feel. Boss, listen to this ole
Okie cowboy. This ain't Afghanistan and she ain't Gypsy. So
get that out of your mind."

"I didn't know they had therapists in Oklahoma."

"Horses and prairie dogs need loving care too. Remember what I said, Boss. Get everything out of your mind except mission—and getting Summer back is part of the mission. All of us who went on Iron Weed love that girl like she was our sister."

Gloomy had earned the right to talk to his commander like that by virtue of mutual trust and their long association. The sniper started to move away.

"Gloomy?"

"Yeah, Boss."

"Thanks."

Brandon drew the team close around him. "We'll stand by here for a half-hour, then trail them," he said. A half-hour should give things time to settle down. Brandon didn't figure they'd move the missiles far under the present weather conditions.

They waited with the rain beating on them, chilling them to the bone. Cassidy lay next to his brother with a hand resting on his back, a Kragle sign that he understood Brandon's distress over Summer. Kragle men kept emotion to themselves. Cassidy had sat by his wife's bedside watching her die from anthrax poisoning and shed not a tear to relieve his deep hurt.

While they waited, Brandon took the time to assess the situation and attempt to plan in his mind all the angles and contingencies. It was a good sign for both the mission and for Summer that the guerrillas were slack and hadn't put out extra security. They hadn't even posted sentries while they offloaded the freighter. Obviously that meant they didn't suspect Summer of being an undercover American agent planted to direct a strike against the bootlegged missiles. She was probably taken prisoner because of the dead man in the engine room.

He wondered what she had told them about her possession of the cell phone and her being a female. The bikini she wore attested to the fact that they knew she wasn't an Ismael. Someone had beaten her badly, likely during interrogation. Brandon would take care of whoever hurt her when the opportunity arose.

The Korean kids, he noticed, weren't a part of the procession that went by. They must still be hiding aboard the *Ibn Haldoon*. Another complication. When Murphy's Law took over, Murphy sank his claws into everything.

All the lights suddenly went out aboard the freighter, even those on the bridge, plunging the ship and surrounding vicinity into a total blackout except for the lightning. Brandon thought he could depend on the *Ibn Haldoon* remaining where it was, safe from both the storm and unwelcome observation, until at least sometime the next day. Actually, that day. Dawn would soon arrive.

That gave him some time to work with.

Rain drummed on the forest canopy. Higher up the hill, out of the protected cove and lowland, winds howled and occasionally there was a crash as a rotted jungle giant toppled. According to weather reports received before the team locked out of the submarine, the worst burst of the typhoon should reach Mindanao sometime before dawn and pass over during the morning. Weather might even start to clear a little by late afternoon.

That consideration led his thoughts to the missiles. The Philippines most certainly weren't their final destination. These SCUDs were on their way to the United States. Two ways they could get there—by sea or by air. Obviously, they weren't going by sea or they wouldn't have offloaded into the jungle in the middle of nowhere.

That meant air. As a former commercial pilot himself, in his pre-Special Forces college days, Brandon realized that few airplanes could fly in a typhoon and even fewer pilots would attempt it. On the other hand, if the weather started to clear . . . The missiles would be out of here and on their way before attack aircraft from the distant USS *Abe Lincoln* could be directed over target.

That was it then! There was an airstrip up there somewhere with cargo planes waiting. The only thing that stood between the missiles and an unsuspecting America were a few good men of Delta Force Operation Deep Steel.

Neither Stanton nor Summer were likely to survive the day unless Deep Steel worked fast.

Brandon alerted his recon. "We move out in ten minutes."

He raised the submarine on his brick-sized PRC-126 Motorola. Special receptors built into the sub's sophisticated communications gear permitted the exchange and automatically encoded voice into unbreakable code. He quickly explained the situation.

"We're tracking the missiles to see where they're going. Have Lucifer prepare to take down the freighter and get the Korean kids off."

Lucifer himself came on the air. "Shouldn't we bring the detachment ashore while it's still fucking dark?" he demanded.

"Nothing until you get the word from me," Brandon snapped.

Lucifer was right and Brandon knew he was. Lucifer had a way of bringing out the worst and most illogical in others.

"Fucking-A roger that," Lucifer snapped back and the air went dead.

The four men of the recon huddled miserably in a tight circle in the rain.

"Sir, I know Lieutenant Lucifer is a little hard to take," T-Bone Jones said in mild rebuke. In Special Ops, enlisted men enjoyed that privilege. "He was awfully young and impetuous back then."

"You were there?" Brandon exclaimed, surprised.

"Chief Gorrell was."

"He doesn't seem to have changed," Brandon growled. Nonetheless, he raised Lucifer again and granted him permission to bring the detachment ashore in Zodiacs, along with weapons for the recon team.

"Keep the freighter under surveillance," he instructed. "Don't do anything until you get the word from me."

"Fucking-A, sir." Lucifer sounded better.

"What's between Lieutenant Lucifer and you?" Cassidy asked.

A commander never discussed personnel with his subordinates, not even with his brother. Brandon had already said too much.

"Does it have to do with Bosnia when you were working with the SEALs chasing PIFWCs?" Cassidy inquired. PIFWCs—persons indicted for war crimes. "I was just a kid then, but I remember the General and Uncle Mike talking about it."

"It was a long time ago," Brandon said and left it at that.

A waterlogged tree fell nearby with a crash through the undergrowth, making everyone jump. Brandon glanced at the illuminated dial of his dive watch.

"Move out," he said.

If you were good at tracking men, as Brandon was, you derived a lot of intelligence from it. You could tell how many men made up an element and what their morale was like. Did they drag their feet or did they pick 'em up and set 'em down? Did they leave trash and equipment strewn about? You could tell the types of weapons they possessed by imprints in the ground where they rested. Were they well fed, as indicated by their throwing away half-eaten food? If branches were broken at shoulder height along a track, it meant they carried their weapons at port arms and were alert and cautious. If branches were not broken, their weapons were slung and they were lax and felt secure.

Not that tracking this bunch of terrorists required much skill. They were loose and most were not professional soldiers. The trucks with their heavy cargo of crated missiles left deep ruts in the water-saturated road. The following mob also tracked up the mud pretty good. Mostly, tracking them was a mere matter of following the road, but following it cautiously and keeping an eye peeled for pickets.

Cassidy took point; Gloomy brought up rear security. Each man in the patrol guided on the strip of luminous Ranger tape attached to the back of the man's cap ahead. Point man guided on the ruts, supplemented by flashes of lightning that helped him orientate. The lightning could be as much enemy as friend in exposing *them* to the enemy as well as revealing the enemy to them. Rain slashed into their faces, half-blinding them.

As they neared the top of the cliff, emerging from its protection, the rain went from near-vertical to horizontal. Wind howled and whipped their clothing. Each forward step had to be made against its force. The air filled dangerously with ripped-off limbs and forest debris, grass and leaves and sand and occasional hailstones. Brandon felt as if he were running a gauntlet of enemy soldiers all beating him with clubs and rifle butts.

The road curved and all but vanished in forest. The going became even slower. Brandon was about to suggest they sit down where they were and wait for dawn. Cassidy hissed a warning. He turned, grabbed Brandon's arm, and pulled him forward. They were standing next to something large.

A burst of lightning revealed what it was—one of the missile trucks parked underneath the trees. Lightning continued to dance across the sky, unmasking a number of crude shelters and tents tied down against large trees and staked into the ground in a near-futile attempt to keep the storm from blowing them away.

The recon team had blundered directly into the enemy's camp. T-Bone seal-barked in a whisper.

CHAPTER 52

MacDill AFB, Tampa, Florida

Satellite screens at CENTCOM remained either black or static busy. The typhoon approaching Mindanao caused satellite visual and communications problems, leaving relay stations in Manila with the responsibility of keeping an open line between CENTCOM and the Deep Steel submarine *Sam Houston.* The last information from Deep Steel reported that the *Ibn Haldoon* had sought refuge in a protected harbor on the southwestern tip of Mindanao. It was still unclear whether the ship had merely sought shelter from the storm or whether it was offloading missiles.

In another time, years earlier, General Kragle would have been the one out there in the arena instead of a mere spectator in a steel-and-glass observation post thousands of miles away from the action. Now, he simply ordered pieces around on a world globe game board. He ordered the remainder of Brandon's Delta Troop One still at Fort Bragg to prepare to deploy to Manila. He jerked out Major Dare Russell's Troop Two from Qatar; it was now en route to the Philippines. Possible reinforcements should they be needed. The nuclear carrier *Abe Lincoln* with its contingent of Marines and its fighter bombers was steaming at full speed toward Mindanao, battling the typhoon.

The General stood up, restless. All he could do now was wait.

The major in charge of Logistics stuck his head through the door of the command center.

"General Kragle, telephone. Line three."

The General glared at a half-eaten tuna fish sandwich. He *hated* tuna. "Who is it?"

A snigger in the major's voice. "*Brown Sugar Mama.*"

General Etheridge ducked his head and grinned. General Kragle tossed the sandwich into the waste basket and ran big hands irritably through the bristling stubble of his salt-and-pepper crewcut. *Brown Sugar Mama.* Why did she *do* this to him. It had to be because of the wedding; it had had her in a tizzy for weeks now. It wasn't like her to announce herself to strangers in that manner unless she was distraught and not thinking.

"Tell her I'll call back."

He didn't have patience right now for wedding cake woes or the *right* dress dilemma.

"Yes, sir. I'll tell *Brown Sugar Mama* you'll call her back." The major suppressed a grin and ducked out quickly ahead of any incoming.

A minute later he popped back in. "General Kragle. She says it's urgent."

Gloria wouldn't have insisted unless it really *was* important. The General took the call.

"Darren, I done been trying to get a'holt of Cameron all day. Has you heard from him?"

The General had left two or three paging messages on Cameron's cell phone.

"Have you tried the Hands of God Conference?" he asked the black woman.

"Lawdy, yes. New Orleans done tell me Chaplain

Cameron ain't signed in for the conference today. Then I calls the Blakes out at the Farm where they is getting ready for Raymond and me. I even calls Fort Bragg. Ain't none of them heard from him all day neither. I even tried to get a'holt of Brandon or Cassidy. But they ain't there neither. Darren, it be like them boys done disappear."

CHAPTER 53

100 ATTACKS FOILED

Washington, D.C. (CPI)—Over 100 terrorist attacks, some planned to take place on U.S. soil, have been thwarted since 9/11, said MacArthur Thornbrew, director of the National Homeland Security Agency. "We have prevented a number of attacks, both large and small," he said.

Thornbrew cited the arrests of members of an alleged al-Qaeda cell in Lackawanna, New York, and apprehension of individuals in Portland, Seattle, St. Marys, Georgia, and elsewhere.

"It illustrates the fact that we have a large Fifth Column plotting to conduct war and bring it to the shores of the United States," he said. "Some are U.S. citizens, some are immigrants, and many are illegally residing within our borders for the sole purpose of planning attacks against us."

He said he believes there are hundreds, maybe even thousands, of people inside the U.S. who are either potential terrorists or part of their financial and support network. He said they are our neighbors. They teach our children, serve us at restaurants, manufacture our vehicles. Some even serve in the U.S. military or in our police forces. It may take years, he said, to root them out and destroy al-Qaeda and other terrorist groups.

"We will be at war until we make certain every member of the al-Qaeda network is incapacitated in his ability to harm the United States. I think we're well on our way to winning that war, but it is still a war. Al-Qaeda still has the capability of striking us . . ."

CHAPTER 54

Atchafalaya Swamp

The wound across Chaplain Cameron's back burned like a fresh cattle brand, already becoming infected from exposure to filthy swamp water. His bare feet were cut and bleeding, so sore he could hardly walk. He felt feverish and nauseated from dehydration. He admonished himself to keep moving. He had to keep going. Abdul said the terrorists were waiting on final materials—he didn't know what—in order to complete construction of their nuclear or "dirty" warhead, which they would then fire on New Orleans. Did that mean that night? The next day?

Keep moving.

Desperation made his stomach roil with dread. Other than the terrorists, only Yasein Riefenstahl and he knew about the base camp in the swamp and the missile being prepared to destroy an American city. The Iraqi refugee was dead and Cameron was lost in the swamp. Apparently, the terrorists weren't even searching for him anymore. That meant they thought him wounded and dying—or that he wouldn't find his way out in time to stop them from accomplishing their mission anyhow.

Keep going.

Hundreds of thousands of people were going to die in the very near future. Their lives depended on his passing his test in the wilderness and escaping to warn America. If he failed . . . ? He shuddered to think of the consequences to little children and school kids, old people, pregnant women, the hospitalized . . . all going up in a blinding flash of light or initially surviving to slowly succumb in the aftermath to radiation sickness.

He thought of Brandon and Cassidy and the Hebrews passage about "wax valiant in fight, turn to flight the armies of the aliens." As chaplain, he was supposed to stay out of the fray and pray for peace. He wasn't supposed to "wax valiant" on the battlefield.

He struggled on, staggering, feverish.

God, You can't let this happen.

And God replied, *You are my instrument.*

God, I'm weak and I'm lost and I'm not up to the challenge.

Your faith must be strong. You are my instrument.

Cameron often had conversations with God in his head. He could never be sure if they were conversations with God or with himself. He had his doubts. When his doubts were strongest, he even questioned the existence of God. Even if God did exist, perhaps He simply tossed Adam and Eve onto earth and left them there to fend for themselves. Perhaps God had washed his hands of the entire human race. Who could blame Him?

Mosquitoes clouded around his head like vapor. They were vicious enough earlier, but suddenly they were positively ravenous as the sun slowly sank toward the coming purple and black of nightfall. Only a few minutes earlier he had been able to make out the details of cypress boles twenty or thirty feet away. Now the lighter-colored boles resembled eyes staring at him through the gathering dusk. For all he knew he was still walking in circles.

The swamp turned even creepier in the greenish half-light. A bull alligator honked somewhere in the gloom off to his left. The splashing of a fish rising to mayflies made him flinch. What seemed like moss-laden trees in daylight turned to zombies cloaked in the shrouds of their graves. He nearly leaped out of his skin at the warning buzz of an unseen rattler.

Shaken, he stopped to rest on a downed log and use his shirt rag to soak up more rainwater caught inside its hollow. He had ceased sweating hours ago. His skin felt as if a fire burned inside.

While he rested, he tore up the remainder of his T-shirt and wrapped and tied the pieces around his feet like crude shoes. He knew it wouldn't be long before the unforgiving mud left him barefoot again.

He clambered to his feet and set out again. Hopefully in a direction that would take him out of that savage wilderness. Nothing but sheer willpower kept him from succumbing to hopelessness.

Staggering and limping, he detoured around a pond of deep black water and struggled up a bank covered in thick growth. Suddenly he emerged through a copse of trees at the top of the bank into a dry clearing. The sky had turned almost purple, but retained enough light that, to his overjoyed surprise, he saw a huge steel barn in the wiregrass meadow and a small shack of sorts beyond it. Better yet, light shone weakly through a window in the house. A window in the barn also glowed with light.

Hope returned in his feverish state. He waved his arms and started running across the meadow, like a thirst-crazed man coming out of the desert.

He caught himself. What was he doing? He darted back and ducked into the shadows of the trees. He would have to be careful until he could ascertain exactly what that place harbored, whether it was the home of some swamp hermit or even, as was more likely, the terrorist base camp.

He scanned the meadow for signs of life other than the lighted windows. The light was too dim for electricity; that probably meant they were oil lamps. Two four-wheeled motorcycle-like ATVs sat parked by the house. There were no other vehicles in sight. The terrorists had left their gray Ford parked somewhere on the road that led into the swamp, as the terrain this deep in the swamp was likely too rough for conventional transportation.

His eyes settled on a barrel left underneath the eves at the back of the barn to catch rainwater from the roof. The sauna heat of the day had dehydrated him and he was experiencing trembling and fever, both signs of hyperthermia. It was all he could do to restrain himself from running directly to it.

Instead, he limped along in the edge of the forest and kept out of sight below a knoll that dropped the meadow down to the deep black pool. When he found himself on the shortest direct line to the barrel, he looked around for movement and, seeing none, limped quickly across the clearing in the gathering darkness.

The barrel was nearly full of relatively clean water. He immersed his face in it and drank deeply. It tasted brackish from the wooden barrel. He figured he sucked in a bait of mosquito larvae, but never in his life had he enjoyed anything quite so delicious and life affirming.

It was only after he drank his fill and ducked his entire

head into the water to cool his fever that he detected voices. Alarmed, he flattened himself against the side of the barn to listen, holding his breath. The voices came from inside. He eased his way along the outer wall to the window. A screen covered it. Pale yellow light left a square on the grass outside.

Cameron peeked through the window at its lower corner. He first noticed the flatbed farm truck upon which was mounted an erector-launcher containing a missile. This was no nightmare; it was *real*.

Cameron had seen Iraqi missiles before during Desert Storm. This one was a smaller variety of the SCUD, probably a short-range missile of the type Saddam Hussein developed for use in the Gulf War. Maybe an Ababil 100. If Cameron remembered his Delta "know your enemy's weapons" orientation correctly, the Ababil was capable of delivering a nuclear warhead at ranges up to one hundred miles, well within striking distance of New Orleans.

The warhead had been removed. Abdul was working at a long table to the far side, along with the two larger Middle Eastern types who had been with Professor Ramzi in New Orleans the previous morning. Cameron couldn't tell what they were doing, but undoubtedly their labors had something to do with the warhead. Getting the missile ready for firing? One of the two men, Cameron thought, although he had not gotten a good look at the killer, was the one who killed Yasein.

There was no conversation among the three men at the table. The voices Cameron overheard came from an angle not observable from the chaplain's current vantage point. He ducked underneath the lighted window and peered in from the opposite side, stifling a cry of astonishment and dismay at what he saw.

FBI agent Claude Thornton sat tied in a chair, his arms and

hands bound to the chair arms and the rest of him, including his feet, secured so that his head was the only thing that could move. Blood oozed from his nostrils and one eye was swollen shut. He glared at his tormentors out of the good eye.

Three young thugs crowded around his chair, two of whom wore traditional red-and-white checked *kaffiyehs* on their heads. Professor Ramzi himself stood nonchalantly in the background observing the torture through his rimless eyeglasses. Kerosene lanterns burning on Abdul's work table and on the bed of the truck reflected yellow light from the sweat and blood on Claude's dark face and made tiny flames in Ramzi's lenses. The two big men with Abdul turned from the table to watch the entertainment; Abdul kept his back to the scene.

No wonder Cameron hadn't been able to raise the agent on the phone.

One of the terrorists, a stocky individual with a broad, dull face and a single black eyebrow across his forehead, walked over to the truck and returned with a cordless drill. He tested it a couple of times, making it sing. He held the whirring bit in front of Thornton's face. Claude stared defiantly through it. Shrugging, the tango let off on the trigger in order to position the bit on the back of the agent's bound right hand. He paused a minute, looking at Thornton as though in invitation for the prisoner to say something. Claude remained grimly mute.

"All we want to know," Professor Ramzi said from behind him, "is the names of the FBI agents who are working undercover to infiltrate Islamic organizations. That is a simple, reasonable request."

From Claude's looks, it appeared the interrogation had been going on for some time and had now degenerated to the point where the sadist with the drill continued the torture only because he enjoyed it. Obviously, Claude was not going to talk.

The terrorist slowly drilled through Claude's right hand and into the wooden arm of the chair. Blood spurted, bone chips flew. Muscles and sinews stood out like cords in the agent's neck and forehead. Although his black face grew hideous from pain, he uttered not a sound.

Cameron was afraid he was going to be sick. If he only had a gun—

He couldn't use a gun. Hadn't he foresworn violence, made a promise to God? He suppressed a cry of rage and anguish.

Professor Ramzi stepped forward and said something in Arabic. The terrorist extracted the drill bit, jerking it out of mangled flesh. The professor stood with spread legs in front of Claude's chair, hands on his hips, and lectured him in English. Self-righteous, arrogant, as only one can who *knows* he has all the answers to the universe and is Allah's anointed.

"What does it matter now, Agent Thornton?" he said through an oily smile that failed to reach his eyes. "I have kept you because you are a stubborn, foolish man and I want you alive to see what our missile can do to one of your cities. This is only the beginning, Agent Thornton. There will be many more attacks, again and again, until your country *begs* to sue for peace in the name of Allah, the one and only."

He laughed a harsh, unforgiving sound.

"The rest of our materials will be delivered tonight. You will be permitted to watch the firing of the missile when morning comes. I want you to see how futile it is for your immoral nation to resist. Then you will die, of course. As many more infidels like you will die in the Holy War to rid the world of unbelievers who have fouled the Islamic world for generations."

Claude groaned involuntarily in pain. Cameron's heart went out to him. The big agent stared directly into Ramzi's eyes. "You are a mad man," he said, his voice still hard and resolute.

Ramzi chuckled. "Is that your final word, Agent Thornton?"

"No. This is my final word: Screw you and the mangy camel you rode in on."

Still smiling, Ramzi reached down with the butt of his pistol and whacked Claude across the cheek, busting the skin and spattering blood. He handed the pistol to the stocky man with the single eyebrow.

"If he moves at all, Alwan," he said in English for Thornton's benefit, "shoot him."

Alwan pulled up a chair and sat in it facing the captive, pointing the pistol. Ramzi summoned the other men, including Abdul. As they filed out of the barn, he turned back. He had had a change of mind. "On second thought, Alwan, kill him anytime you want. If you have the courage."

CHAPTER 55

New Orleans

Senate Majority Leader Jake Thierry felt sweat trickling from his armpits as the airliner came in low on final approach to New Orleans International. From his window in first-class, with the heavy sealed case underneath the seat in front of him, he looked out upon the glitter and shimmer of the city in the crook of the river, like a giant's handful of stars cast against the darkness.

Damn him. Damn Stanton to hell.

He was still more than a little frightened by his continuing experience, apprehensive about who would meet him and what happened when he landed. Although he was a self-absorbed man, as were many politicians, he retained the capacity to recognize irony when it bit him in the butt. Again and again in speeches and in sound bites to the media he had referred to terrorists as "needy and rational human beings . . . downtrodden people with only one recourse to attract attention to their plight . . ." Well, these needy and rational human beings might well cut off his head.

An old Washington rib came to mind: *How do you describe a conservative? That's a liberal who's been mugged.*

He broke into a cold sweat as the airliner turned onto final. He would make sure to stay in the light and in crowded places where there were witnesses. After all, what *did* prevent the terrorists from killing him once he accomplished what they—and Stanton—demanded of him?

The frigging terrorists better not kill him. He had kissed a lot of fat ass to get in a position where Stanton and the party would support him as a presidential candidate. Stanton owed him after this. Stanton *owed* big time.

Let's just get this over with as soon as possible. Get it over with and I'll go home and forget it happened.

As the plane landed and taxied up to the gate, it occurred to him that blackmail rarely stopped after the first payment. He broke into a cold sweat all over again.

First-class unloaded. In the gateway among waiting relatives and friends stood two white men in dark suits. Obviously they were looking for someone. They weren't terrorists. Not these two slices of American white bread. Senator Thierry's heart jumped into trip-hammer mode. He ignored them and made to quickly walk past.

To his chagrin, they pushed through the small crowd to intercept him. The senator sped up, not looking at either one. The men split up and came up on either side. The taller of the two flashed credentials.

"Senator Thierry? We're with the FBI. We need a moment of your time."

Thierry stopped in the corridor. The twenty-pound case seemed to suddenly weigh a ton or more. He felt as if he were standing there holding an elephant on a leash.

"What about?" he demanded, fighting to keep his composure. What were they going to find in the box? He had purposely avoided that question since the case was passed to him in Manila. He didn't *want* to know what was in it. After all, if he didn't *know,* how could he be responsible— *guilty?*—for anything other than trying to save President Stanton's life?

"You were in Manila?" the shorter agent said. He looked older, more worldly-wise than his partner. Harder to fool or to bluff.

Senator Thierry thought fast. He saw two options. One, he lied or tried to sham his way through. He didn't think that would work, not by the expressions on these agents' faces.

Two, he handed the case over and pretended to have been working undercover all along. Say the terrorists were trying to blackmail him and he simply went along for the good of the country to see what they wanted. He didn't think that would work either. How did he explain it when Stanton's head and the incriminating photos and documents about Robert Chang and him ended up on the steps of the Capitol Building?

There was a third option—run for it. He dismissed that one immediately. These guys obviously knew who he was. They were in better shape than he was. And where would he run?

That put him full circle back to option one. His heart pounded and his mouth turned so dry he could hardly speak. Nonetheless, his back to the wall, he drew himself into a pose of indignity and insult.

"Yes?" he said, laying on the scorn. "So what concern is that to the FBI?"

"What was the purpose of your visit, Senator?"

"Why are you interrogating me? You realize I'm a U.S. Senator on a special mission?"

"Yes, sir." The agents remained soft-spoken, respectful, but nevertheless insistent. "Why were you in Manila?"

"I was there on a fact-finding tour, if you must know."

"I see. Did you accomplish your mission?"

How much did they know? He had to think fast. "I accomplished what I needed."

"At the airport, sir?"

Thierry's mind went blank. "What?"

"Sir, you landed in Manila, then caught a return flight one hour later. Did you forget something at home and come back for it?"

They were toying with him. They already knew why he went to the Philippines.

"What are you carrying in the case, sir?"

Some of his fellow passengers looked curiously at him as they walked by.

"It's a diplomatic pouch," Senator Thierry corrected.

"May we look inside?"

"Certainly not!" His voice rose into a squeak that he hoped sounded outraged rather than frightened.

"I see. Sir, we need to ask you to come with us. It won't take long."

He was fresh out of options. The agents took him by the elbows and began escorting him along the corridor to the escalator that led down to PICKUP, PARKING, TAXIS, BUSES, BAGGAGE. He objected loudly, kept on berating his escorts. He wanted the terrorists to know if they were watching that he was being taken against his will. That he was not cooperating, had not betrayed them. He saw his life, his whole career, flushing down the drain into the sewer.

The airport this time of night was almost deserted. The FBI agents squired him onto the walkway outside where a third agent got out of a blue sedan and opened the back door for him to get in.

"Watch your head, sir."

"My attorneys will hear about this. This is becoming a police state and an outrage against human rights."

"Yes, sir. Please get in, sir."

A black Buick pulled up out of nowhere, its brakes squalling. Doors flew open. Submachine guns opened fire, sounding like cloth ripping, except greatly amplified. Glass shattered. A man screamed. Bullets spanged into metal, thucked into flesh. The agents didn't stand a chance against the surprise attack.

Thierry fell to the pavement, screaming hysterically. Someone wrested the case from his hand. Good thing it wasn't handcuffed to his wrist. A face in a black ski mask bent over him.

"Keep your mouth shut," the shooter growled, "or death will happen to you next time. You'll be contacted if we need you again."

CHAPTER 56

FBI AGENTS KILLED IN ABDUCTION ATTEMPT

New Orleans (CPI)—Three FBI agents of the Joint Terrorism Task Force (JTTF) were gunned down in a blaze of submachine-gun fire at the New Orleans International Airport at approximately two a.m. today. Assistant JTTF Director Fred Whiteman said the agents were on assignment. All three were pronounced dead at the scene, their bodies riddled with bullets.

The shooting occurred when masked gunmen apparently attempted to kidnap U.S. Senate Majority Leader Jake Thierry, who was returning on an international flight from Manila. According to Thierry, he went outside to the parking area to summon a taxi when an unknown number of men in dark ski masks drove up in a black car. They grabbed him and attempted to force him into the back seat. The shooting occurred when FBI agents in a separate car witnessed the incident and attempted to intervene.

Thierry dropped to the pavement during the shooting and was not injured.

"It's apparently terrorist-related," Thierry said at the scene. "They abducted President Stanton—and now they attempt to kidnap me. I think it imperative that we provide personal security for all high-ranking members of our government . . ."

CHAPTER 57

Mindanao

Having stumbled into the middle of the guerrilla encampment, Major Brandon's four-man reconnaissance team began backing out again, rapidly but cautiously. While tents and other shelters were pitched at random in the forest, the team could not be certain whether the guerrillas were actually *camping* or were out and about. The growl of a truck engine laboring above the howl and slash of the storm came to them from farther up. The typhoon might not have driven the terrorists to their holes.

"*Wa'af? Meen?*" inquired a disembodied voice.

It could have come from any direction, whipped about as it was by the crash of rain in the wind-ravaged trees. Brandon and his men crouched in the darkness. All they needed now was a flash of ill-timed lightning to reveal them. Next thing they knew a half-hundred pissed-off suicidal terrorists would be jumping down their throats.

"*Meen?*"

The challenge promised to be louder next time unless it was satisfied. But the Deltas couldn't do anything to silence the guy until they *located* him. At that moment, it was a matter of blind man's bluff, pin the tail on the donkey. The guy sounded nervous. In another second or two, especially if a bolt of lightning exposed them, he was going to cause a ruckus loud enough to raise dead martyrs all the way to Mecca.

Cassidy called out softly, "*Inta moghray.*"

Fast thinking.

"*Aandee inta goyt,*" came the response, closer now, almost directly on top of them.

Now the lightning came. Revealing the challenger only two or three steps away. The flash froze him peering suspiciously into the darkness, a rifle at port arms. He wore rain pants and a top, which explained why the team hadn't heard the whip and pop of a poncho.

Brandon sprang from a crouch, like a big cat, his grandfather's Ka-Bar clutched in his fist. He brought the man to the soaked earth. The man grunted and attempted to cry out in alarm. Brandon's free hand clamped over his mouth. The big knife bit into his chest.

Brandon stabbed him again in the neck to make sure. Pushing the blade all the way through and twisting it to destroy the jugulars. It was messy business, sloppy work, killing close up like that. The major hated it, hated killing. It was sometimes necessary, but it made him feel unclean for days afterward.

On hands and knees across the still body, Brandon dropped his head to catch his breath and let adrenaline drain back to normal, more or less.

"Boss?" Gloomy probed.

"Yeah. Help me with this guy." He held out his knife and hand to let rain wash away the blood.

Gloomy appropriated the guerrilla's rifle, a Swedish K. Together, the four troopers carried the corpse into the trees and deposited it in undergrowth. For all they could tell in the darkness, they might have dumped him at somebody's campsite. But at least he was out of the way for the time being. They huddled together, waiting for another flicker of lightning to help them orient to their surroundings.

"That was fast thinking, Sergeant," Brandon congratulated his brother. "I didn't know you spoke Arabic." Cassidy was proving quite a cool operator under pressure, not at all the revenge-seeking hot head the General feared he might become.

"What did you say to him?" T-Bone wanted to know.

Cassidy hesitated. He chuckled. "I told him he was sexy."

"And what did *he* say?" Gloomy asked.

"How should I know? 'You are sexy' is the only phrase I ever learned."

"You army boys are crazier than SEALs," T-Bone decided.

The parked truck they had previously stumbled upon suddenly cranked over. Lightning revealed it pulling away, gears grinding, the crated missile still riding the flatbed. That settled the question of what next?

"Come on," Brandon said. "Lets see where they're taking these things."

"What about Summer and Stanton?" Cassidy asked. "They must be in the camp here somewhere."

Brandon stared into the black rain. It seemed to him the hostages would accompany the missiles wherever they went. As kind of last-ditch pawns for negotiations in case something happened. Or for ransom. It was just a hunch based on his experience and instinctual knowledge of terrorists. If he was wrong . . .

Either way, mission always came first. It had to be that way. The missiles had to be stopped.

"We'll follow the missile," he said, his voice taut and strained.

They sound-followed the truck at a distance, slogging along a road of sorts cut through the jungle. Brandon counted on the guerrillas not paying attention to them in the hard rainfall and the darkness. Sometimes the best way to hide was in the open. It made more sense than stumbling around blind.

They traveled Ranger file in one of the ruts to avoid becoming separated. Gloomy brought up the rear with his newly acquired Swedish K. They hadn't gone far before the sniper worked his way up to Brandon.

"Boss, we're being shadowed."

Brandon became aware of it too. People walking in their rear. He alerted Cassidy on point. They sped up and whoever was back there increased his pace. Brandon slowed the team; the others slowed. The guerrillas behind were guiding on *them,* depending on *them* to lead the way to wherever the truck was going.

What if somebody moved up and tried to start a conversation? Asked a question or gave an order? Their shit was about to get awfully weak.

Brandon looked back during a long spider-webbing series

of vein lightning. He spotted a file of shadows all trudging along with their heads down against the rain and wind and their rifles slung muzzles down. He passed the word to Cassidy in front and to Gloomy and T-Bone following. "Get ready, follow me."

They couldn't just *disappear* into the jungle. That was bound to arouse suspicion and perhaps attract a search party. Instead, abruptly, Brandon turned back on himself with the others close behind. They walked directly toward the enemy element following them, not hurrying, merely as though they might have received a new mission or had forgotten something at camp. If Cameron were here, he would surely be praying for continuing darkness without lightning for another few minutes.

Brandon held his Glock close to his leg, finger on the trigger. Just in case.

The guerrillas were also in a Ranger file. The two formations passed each other, one in one rut going one direction, the other in the opposite rut going the other direction. A guerrilla said something in Filipino or Arabic. Questioning. Not a challenge.

Brandon grunted irritably and kept going. So did the guerrillas. He breathed again when they vanished into the storm.

They couldn't keep bumbling around like this. Sooner or later they were going to be discovered—and the proverbial feces would hit the proverbial fan. Not only was he risking his own men and compromising the mission, he was also endangering Summer's life. She was dead if the terrorists discovered *them* before he rescued her.

Overcoming his need for action, for doing *something,* he led the team into jungle off the side of the road and burrowed by feel into the densest thicket he could find. He then radioed the submarine and Lucifer of his decision to hide out until dawn. Lucifer had already infiltrated the remainder of Delta-

2B ashore by Zodiac under cover of darkness and the typhoon. He was also hiding out and awaiting daylight.

"Are you with the ship?" Brandon asked.

"Like stink on shit."

"I'll settle for a 'roger.'"

"Fucking-A roger that."

Asshole.

"Any other movement at the ship?" Brandon asked.

"It's like a black hole."

"Keep me advised."

"You fucking keep *me* advised too, Major."

The three Deltas and the SEAL coveyed like quail in the thicket in order to share body warmth. The forest whipped violently around them as the brunt of the typhoon arrived. Trees cracked with thunder-like explosions and fell to the ground. Branches and other forest debris banged around in the air and smashed into things. Even though the recons were marginally sheltered, the wind almost sucked away their breath. Rain stung exposed skin; it felt like gravel flung at them. The typhoon howled like a giant wind tunnel used to test fighter aircraft. Gusts reached nearly one hundred miles per hour. Brandon held onto a thick vine.

"We had this tornado one time in Hooker that blew off Arachna Phoebe's underwear," Gloomy began, then left it at that, too miserable to continue.

Water poured down the back of Brandon's collar. He hunched his shoulders against it and tried not to think about Summer. And about Gypsy.

CHAPTER 58

Daylight never really arrived. The eastern sky lost a few layers of black. Darkness merely softened to the color of the storm that slammed Mindanao with winds and undulating drenches of rain. Wet and stiff, Brandon roused the others as soon as he could discern shapes at a distance of at least ten feet. Gloomy Davis, sleeping fitfully, looked more lugubrious than ever. T-Bone Jones appeared withdrawn and grim, weary lines webbing his eyes. Cassidy seemed eager to get on with it.

They set out to find the trucks. After a surprisingly short hump through jungle, they came upon thinned trees that soon opened onto the edges of a large natural meadow. Rolling waves of rainfall blowing almost horizontally washed across it. T-Bone pointed toward two indistinct shapes at the downwind end of the field. Brandon glassed them with his small binocs, quickly determining that they were C-130 Hercules aircraft covered with camouflage nets. They were anchored at all points to prevent the storm from wrecking them.

Brandon had flown check rides in 130s, had logged a few command pilot hours in them. They were rugged airplanes able to take off and land in amazingly short distances, fly in severe weather conditions, and carry a payload of 45,000 pounds. This field was certainly long enough for an airstrip. With a relatively light load such as one or two missiles and added fuel tanks, they could extend their ranges up to 7,000 miles while flying at a cruising airspeed in excess of 350 mph. All they required in order to easily reach the United States or Mexico was a single refueling stop on some remote Pacific island.

It always amazed Brandon at the resources available to al-Qaeda and its associated terrorist networks.

The three flatbed trucks were parked nearby, still loaded with the crated missiles from the *Ibn Haldoon.* They were not camouflaged. Brandon glassed the area for movement, for some evidence of Summer. No one stirred. Evidently, the terrorists were under shelter waiting out the storm before they loaded the missiles onto the C-130s.

Whether Summer was there, as he hoped, or back at the main camp, Brandon knew they had to work fast if he ever expected to see her alive again. He understood the terrorist mentality well enough, especially after the missionaries, to know that any captives they seized were unlikely to be released alive.

As soon as Stanton became more of a liability than an asset to generate political capital, chances were good his head ended up in a basket. Imagine how demoralizing it would be to an American public already feeling besieged if the head of a former American President ended up at the gates of the White House or at the Pentagon.

As for Summer, it seemed to Brandon that her life depended upon how much information her interrogators obtained from her about who she *really* was and what she was doing aboard the *Ibn Haldoon.* From the glimpse Brandon got of her in the rain, she had obviously been beaten and perhaps tortured. That she had divulged nothing so far was probably the only thing that kept her alive. Cold fury welled in Brandon's heart at the thought that she was of far less value to her captors than was a former President.

He scanned the tethered aircraft across the rain- and wind-swept distance. He saw nothing to indicate the presence of the hostages. He shoved that concern to the back of his mind. He was already thinking mission, planning.

"Gloomy, what's the range?" he asked.

Gloomy Davis peered at the birds. "I'd say seven-fifty, eight hundred meters."

Brandon indicated the Swedish K slung over the little sergeant's shoulder. "How well can you handle that?"

"Not as well as Mr. Blunderbuss."

No one in Delta shot a rifle like Sergeant Gloomy Davis.

"What's up, Boss?" Gloomy asked, suddenly interested.

"I don't know yet. Hold on."

He squatted in what shelter a large tree trunk offered and raised Lieutenant Lucifer on the Motorola, asking him for a sitrep on the *Ibn Haldoon*.

"It's awfully quiet," the SEAL lieutenant said. "There's been no movement at all since daylight."

"What's the minimum number of men you need to take it down?"

"Either a battalion of UN troops or—" He paused. "—three or four SEALs. It looks like you took the asswipe puke maggot ragheads with you. Nobody's left except the ship's crew. I don't think these goofy fucks are armed with anything except peashooters. I could *walk* aboard it right now and take over."

"Good. But not yet. Don't board it until you hear gunfire. Get the Korean kids off and on the submarine. Then stand by for us. Don't fuck it up, Lucifer."

"You worry about your end of it, mister."

Brandon swallowed a retort. He took a deep breath to calm down and then filled Lucifer in on the situation with the airplanes.

"How are you going to stop them?" Lucifer asked.

Brandon still didn't know, although an idea was beginning to germinate. "Send me Ice Man, Mad Dog, and Thumbs

Jones with all the explosives you can spare. Also our weapons."

That left Lucifer with Doc TB and the two SEALs—Chief Gorrell and J.D. McHenry. Cutting the lieutenant short of talent, but he *said* he could do it. On the other hand, Brandon really could have used a battalion.

Ice Man came on the radio and Brandon gave the weapons specialist instructions on how to circumnavigate the guerrilla camp and reach the airstrip clearing on top.

"The storm's keeping most of the tangos under shelter," he concluded. "You shouldn't have much problem. We'll keep a light out for you. Stay in contact via the miracle of Motorola. And, Ice, we need you fast."

Brandon clicked the radio off and stood up to glass the aircraft some more. Thunder rumbled in long, booming rolls across the meadow, accompanied by the near-constant flickering of lightning. Typhoons always bred smaller storms and tornadoes. There was still no movement around the C-130s or the trucks.

"I have a hunch," he said to the others, "that Stanton and Summer—"

"Summer?" T-Bone asked, puzzled. "The woman?"

"The CIA agent. I'll explain later. Anyhow, it makes sense for the prisoners to be held near the airplanes. I'm thinking the tangos will fly them out with the missiles. That gives them bargaining power in case they're intercepted. Cassidy and I are going to have a look—"

He held up a hand to stop Gloomy Davis's protest. Gloomy had long ago taken it upon himself to function as his commander's personal bodyguard.

"If things go the way I expect, Gloomy, I'll need you and your expert shooting here. That's why I asked if you could handle that K. You and T-Bone keep on the radio with Ice and direct them to you. If we don't get the captives out before things start, well . . . You do remember Reverend Martin Hoffman and his wife?"

Gloomy nodded somberly. He remembered the missionaries all too well. They had also been executed in the rain.

"Boss, the two of you alone can't get them out," he objected.

"All we're going to do right now is look things over. But if you do hear shooting before Ice and the others get here with the C-4 . . . Whatever else happens, Gloomy, remember that mission comes first. You'll be in charge. Those missiles cannot be allowed to get away from us."

Gloomy stuck out his hand and shook the major's, then Cassidy's. "Good luck. Both of you. Bring Summer back if you can. That girl has balls," he added admiringly.

Before the two brothers departed in the rain, Brandon exchanged his Glock for T-Bone's silenced Hush Puppy. Cassidy grinned at Gloomy. "I didn't want to tell you this before, Gloomy," he said, "but Arachna Phoebe sounds like a real slut. It doesn't take a tornado to get her pants off."

CHAPTER 59

Louisiana

Louisiana state trooper Lance Bagger had had another big fight with his wife Juanita. Their quarrels were always about the same thing. He had a bachelor's degree in education and a master's in business administration. According to Juanita, he was wasting his life for a paltry policeman's salary when he could use his education and be *somebody*.

"I'm doing an important job in law enforcement," he argued.

"What?" she scoffed. "Being a traffic cop? Giving out tickets to old ladies who don't come to a complete stop at an intersection?"

"It's more than that."

"Oh, yes. I forgot. There's also the donuts."

She especially resented the graveyard shifts when he was away from home until after dawn patrolling that stretch of U.S. 10 and its side roads between Baton Rouge and Lafayette. He really ought to dump the bitch, he thought. His dad always said she had a sharp tongue and a sharp-tongued woman was a blessing to no one. Trouble was, he *loved* the bitch. Go figure.

He wrote a speeding ticket outside Grosse Tete and assisted a grandmother with a flat tire near Ramah. Neither helped his bad mood from the fight with Juanita. He sought out *his* blacktop road that crossed south through the Atchafalaya Swamp. There was hardly ever any traffic on it, especially at night. It always lightened his mood and put him in a better frame of mind to get on that road and blow the cobwebs out of his marked Ford. He exhilarated in speed, had ever since he was a kid building hot rods with his dad. Go figure that too— a kid with a potful of speeding tickets becoming a cop.

Dispatch issued a BOLO—Be On Look Out—for a black car, maybe a Buick or a Chrysler, occupied by three or four Middle Eastern males. Suspects were wanted for shooting FBI agents at the airport in New Orleans. The crime had just occurred. No further details.

Trooper Bagger dutifully jotted down the info on the notebook clipped to the center console. Nothing big ever happened out here. He caught some hijackers once, a couple of kids who held up a 7-Eleven in Baton Rouge. Every once in a while he got a hot car. But something like this, the killing of FBI agents . . . The "big boys" took care of those things.

He pegged his speedometer at about ninety, skillfully maneuvering the Ford around the curves and into the long straightaways. One night along here, he outran his headlights and almost hit a deer. Sometimes alligators crawled up on the road. That didn't happen often though.

He eased into a curve and accelerated coming out. Up ahead, his headlights reflected red off the taillights of a car parked alongside the road. Maybe it was the black car from the airport. Naw. It hadn't had time to get this far.

What was anyone doing out here on this road at night anyhow? There wasn't a house or anything around here for miles if you didn't count the old abandoned Mutter place about fifteen miles down the road. The trooper let off power and pulled in behind the cream-colored Chevrolet with its New Orleans license plate. Maybe the driver had had car trouble and was out on foot going for help.

The trooper ran a radio make-and-wanted on the tag through dispatch. While he waited on the return, he sped south to see if he came upon the stranded driver. He turned around at the dirt road that led back into the swamp toward the Mutter place. He didn't think the driver would have walked up *that* spooky road. Just to be sure, he got out to look for footprints in the salty sand.

What he found instead were fresh car tracks. A number of them. Probably made sometime during the day. Why would anybody be going back in *there*? You couldn't get a car all the way up the road to the Mutter place anyhow.

The radio calling his unit number interrupted his pondering. He walked back through his headlights and sat behind the wheel, one foot outside on the road. He picked up the mike. "Go ahead."

"Vehicle checks to Rent-A-Wreck, 2408 Canal Street, New Orleans," the dispatcher informed him. "It's a 1995

Chevrolet four-door. No wanteds. It was rented by a
Cameron Kragle. Be advised that Cameron Kragle also
rented a second car at the same time, a 1993 Pontiac Firebird."

"Ten-four, thanks," Bagger said.

Why would anyone rent two vehicles at the same time? He
sat there a minute studying the question and the car tracks in
the road illuminated by his headlights.

Finally he decided it had to be fishermen going back in
there. A bunch of swamp Cajuns in old pickup trucks hooking brim for their suppers. Well, he wasn't going to take a
chance getting his car stuck on account of a bunch of Cajuns.
He backed out and floored the Ford back in the direction
from which he had come.

"Send me a wrecker," he advised dispatch. "I need to tow
an abandoned vehicle."

He wondered if Juanita was still up watching television
and waiting on him to come home so she could take up the
quarrel where they left off.

CHAPTER 60

Atchafalaya Swamp

Alwan sat alone in a chair in front of FBI agent Claude
Thornton after his comrades filed out of the barn. He toyed
with the pistol. Thinking about shooting the agent. His single
black brow wrinkled down to touch the top of his nose. His
thick lips thinned.

Cameron watched from the window, his nerves stretched as taut as parachute shroud lines. Sweat broke out on his brow even though the night was cool and he was bare-chested, having used his T-shirt for makeshift shoes in the swamp. He felt helpless.

The barn was equipped with two windows, both covered with screens, a wide double door for vehicle access, and a pedestrian door. There was no way to approach the gunman without being seen and heard. Alwan would get off at least one shot. Even if he missed, the others in the shack would hear it and come running. There were at least five of them.

How did he save his friend's life and stop the missile from being fired?

You are my instrument, God had said to him.

The chaplain prayed silently, selecting a verse from Matthew: *Verily I say unto you, If ye have faith and doubt not . . . ye shall say unto this mountain, Be thou removed, and be thou cast into the sea; it shall be done.*

Alwan stood up and walked around behind the helplessly bound agent. He looked very alien and threatening in his red-and-white checked *kaffiyeh.* He pressed the pistol muzzle against the black man's temple. Claude stared stoically straight ahead out of his one unswollen eye. Blood trickled down the side of his face where Professor Ramzi had hit him. Cameron's estimation and appreciation of Claude's courage and character jumped up the ladder another dozen rungs.

Desperate thoughts raced through Cameron's head. He was at the point of recklessly hurling himself through the screened window—he had to do *something*—when the scene began subtly changing.

Alwan started sweating in the orange lantern light, as though he had just run a three hundred meter dash in sun-shine. He licked his thick lips. His gunhand began trembling, the pistol muzzle tapping against Claude's shaved head. He emitted a little strained laugh to cover his nervousness, then jumped back as though he had touched a hot electrical wire. Some men required an audience to support their back bones, the encouragement and comfort of the pack.

The terrorist collected himself with a physical effort. With forced nonchalance, he reoccupied his chair in front of the bound agent.

"Ramzi is correct," he said. "First, I will let you see the missile fired and on its way. Then I will kill you."

Relieved, Cameron slumped against the side of the barn, feeling even more weakened and ill. He was afraid Alwan would hear his bones rattling, he shook so violently from fever. His stomach revolted against all the water he had sucked out of the rain barrel. Dry-retching, he sank to the ground and crawled away from the barn on all fours to keep Alwan inside from hearing him.

He vomited painfully between his hands into the grass, continued to retch even after his stomach was empty and his contracted muscles drew him in on himself. Further weakened, he rolled over onto his back away from the vomit and looked up at the stars dizzy-swimming over his head.

The sound of a four-wheeler ATV starting up aroused him. Trembling, he rolled over onto his belly and pushed himself up on his elbows. Up by the shack, one of the two ATVs switched on its headlights and roared off down the narrow track through the swamp toward the blacktop road. Two people were on it. Cameron recognized Ramzi's voice coming back through the night air before the noise of the engine faded from hearing.

Earlier when he was eavesdropping through the barn window, he had overheard the professor say something to the effect that "the rest of the materials" for the missile shot would be delivered that night. He wondered if Ramzi and the other terrorist were going to pick up the delivery now. Their departure left at least two armed terrorists and Abdul inside the shack.

The remaining ATV gave him an idea. There was no way he could walk out of here in his present exhausted state of physical deterioration. Surely the terrorists had already disposed of the Firebird. That left the rented Chevrolet up on the blacktop. If he could reach the little off-road ATV, get it started and find the Chevy, he could bring back help in time to rescue Claude and prevent the firing of the missile.

Light still glowed through the window of the shack. The door opened, emitting a rectangle of light across the rickety porch. A silhouette stepped outside. Cameron heard the terrorist urinating off the porch. He finished and went back inside, closing the door.

Cameron decided to let things settle down and the terrorists go to bed before he made his first attempt at vehicular grand theft. Even the minimal effort of rising on his elbows left him trembling and nauseous. Sour bile burned in his throat. His head felt like somebody was pounding it with a hammer. The gunshot wound across his back felt infected. If he could just lie down and rest a few minutes . . .

His stomach suddenly revolted and spewed bitter bile. Earth and stars and night whirled around and around. He collapsed face down into the expelled contents of his stomach and lost consciousness.

The light in the hut was off when he revived. He glanced at the illuminated dial of his wristwatch and was aghast to find that it was after 4:00 a.m. He had been lying there for hours, since before midnight. His head felt clogged and dusty with webs. He stank from lying in his own vomit. But he seemed to feel better and was more aware.

He had to work fast. He clambered to his feet and, staggering, made his way across the meadow toward the dark outline of the terrorist shack. The second ATV was still gone. He felt around for the ignition on the one remaining, disappointed

when he found the key missing. He understood finally why
Brandon always talked about Murphy's Law.

He glanced anxiously toward the east. The sky seemed to
be getting lighter. Dawn was coming. This would be the last
dawn a large portion of New Orleans would ever see unless
he got this thing started and got out of here to bring help.

He had learned to hot-wire vehicles during Delta training,
but that had been a long time ago. He remembered the basics,
however. Bypass the ignition with a hot wire from the battery
directly to the starter.

He felt around until he located the battery compartment.
Two wing nuts held on its protective plating. With hands still
shaking from fever, he traced wires that led from the battery
and were routed underneath the gas tank cowling toward the
handlebars. Other wires spliced off toward the motor. Darkness and lack of tools handicapped his mechanical efforts.

It wasn't his imagination. The sky *was* getting light.

He jerked one of the wires loose and felt around until he
located the starter. He used his teeth to bite off insulation,
then touched the naked end of the lone wire from the battery
to the bare starter wire. The ATV should kick off. He counted
on the terrorists inside the shack being asleep and not hearing
it; the barn and Alwan were a good distance away.

There was a pathetic whir—and then nothing. He pressed
his forehead against the seat with disappointment. The battery was dead. He would have to push it to get it started. If he
had the strength.

He struggled with the heavy machine to get it turned
around in the high grass and pointed toward the swamp road.
So involved was he in the task that the returning ATV was almost upon him before he heard the revving growl of its engine. He looked up in alarm as headlights flickered through
the trees and rounded the little bend that curved up out of the
swamp onto the meadow. He blinked like a deer caught in

headlights, which was exactly what he would be in another few seconds.

He scrambled lurching and staggering toward the cover of the barn while the return of Professor Ramzi and the other man awoke Abdul and the others inside the shack and produced immediate excitement at the terrorist hideout. Apparently, Ramzi had brought back "the rest of the materials." The entire cell converged on the barn where more lanterns were lit and the men, laughing and shouting "*Allah akbar walillahi-l-hamd*," got back to work on the missile and its warhead.

Lord, You're going to have to do Your part, Cameron prayed, *or poor Saint Peter is going to be mighty busy in a few hours with a bunch of people knocking on the Pearly Gates.*

CHAPTER 61

Daylight would arrive in another hour. From his old observation post outside the barn window, Cameron saw that Abdul wore a worried expression on his thin brown face. He and two of the terrorists were working on the warhead, obviously equipping it with nuclear explosives Ramzi had obtained and brought back from somewhere. The doomsday weapon was almost ready. It would likely be fired within a matter of hours at most. Cameron felt helpless to stop it, having already fouled up his best shot at escaping.

His last chance at finding help, he decided, was to make a run for it down the road to the blacktop and hope a car came along to take him to the rented Chevrolet he had left parked alongside the road. In it was his cell phone. At least the terrorists wouldn't be chasing him this time, having apparently assumed him to be wounded and either dead or lost in the swamp.

He felt stronger after another drink from the water barrel. At least he held the liquid down. He stopped to take another look at Claude Thornton before he took off. He couldn't help thinking this might be the last time he saw the agent alive.

God help him, please, and have mercy on a good and brave man.

Something seemed to be breaking loose inside. Alwan, who couldn't shoot Claude during the night when he had no audience, now swaggered about with the gun, pointing it at the fed and laughing. Professor Ramzi, looking totally out of place in this environment with his rimless eyeglasses and carefully groomed beard, jumped down off the bed of the truck where he was directing labor on the missile system.

Although the language exchange in Arabic between Alwan and Ramzi went unregistered with Cameron, the body language and the berating tone of the professor's voice suggested he was unhappy that Thornton was still alive. He pointed at Claude and made motions toward the swamp. Alwan paled and balked, but quickly seemed more than anxious to escape Ramzi's blistering tongue.

He untied the agent from the chair while Ramzi held the gun. Claude's bindings had cut off circulation to his limbs. He tottered and could hardly stand when Alwan jerked him to his feet. Ramzi stood in front of Claude and smiled while Alwan twisted the agent's arms behind his back and roped his hands tightly.

"I really must apologize for taking your seat before the show begins, Agent Thornton," Ramzi said in English. "The truth is, we have no further need for your services. I truly expected Alwan to end your wretched life during the night, but you really can't get good help anymore. Quite obviously, you showed up at the wrong place at the wrong time. That was your misfortune. Now you are, quite bluntly, simply in the way. Be assured, however, that your journey to the hell of the infidels will not be made unaccompanied."

He laughed a little madly. "Many others will join you presently," he said. "Get him out of here, Alwan. Shoot him like the other one and feed him to our hungry friends in the swamp."

Overcompensating for his cowardice, Alwan grabbed Claude's bound hands roughly, lifting the agent up on his tip-toes, and escorted him out of the barn. Abdul watched them go from his workbench, his face carefully neutral but his eyes revealing his hopelessness and despair. His American fiancée lived in New Orleans at ground zero.

Cameron flattened himself in the darker shadows against the barn. Alwan steered Claude past and across the meadow, their outlines moving against the dawning sky. Cameron ducked low to cut down on his silhouette and followed, trotting silently if painfully on his bare wrecked feet while his heart pounded from exertion and dread. Why did God continue to place him in such impossible situations?

The two silhouettes merged into the line of cypress near the deep black pool next to which Cameron had emerged from the swamp the evening before. Alwan's voice guided Cameron when they disappeared over the crest of the knoll. The terrorist commanded Claude to get down on his knees near the water. Claude told him to go fornicate himself. There were sounds of scuffling in the grass.

The chaplain dropped to his hands and knees and crawled to the edge of the knoll. There was enough light now that he made out shadows. Alwan had forced Claude to a kneeling position next to the alligator pool and stuck his gun to the back of Claude's head. Something splashed in the dark ink of the pool.

Alwan was obviously experiencing his old queasiness. He hesitated in squeezing the trigger. His equivocation provided Cameron enough time to crawl within attack distance. Although still rocky from fever and heat dehydration, the chaplain sprang to his feet and flung himself at the terrorist.

Alwan sensed his attacker at the last instant. Started to turn. Cameron caught him hard in a tackle. They went down together, arms and legs enmeshed, grappling. Rolling down the grassy slope toward the water. Cameron trying to tear the gun from Alwan's fist. Alwan surprisingly strong. It was all Cameron could do to hold onto the gunhand with both his hands while the terrorist rained blows into his face with his free fist.

Cameron sank his teeth into the gunman's wrist. Tried to tear out flesh and skin like from a chicken drumstick. Alwan grunted and cried out in pain, wounded. He relaxed his hold on the pistol. Cameron took advantage. He used both hands to rip the pistol from Alwan's hand. It flew through the air and landed in the grass.

Both men scrambled to where they heard it hit. Cameron found it. He rolled and came up with it pointed directly at Alwan. Alwan hesitated, crouching in the still-darkness like a ghoul just risen from the grave.

"Shoot him!" Claude hissed. "Shoot the bastard!"

Cameron froze, finding he couldn't go against his vow. Alwan sensed the hesitation and made a dash toward the barn.

Even though his hands were tied behind his back, Thornton hurled himself against the fleeing shadow. Both crashed into the grass. Cameron watched the two shadows battling on the ground, still pointing the gun, but frozen into momentary inaction at the war going on inside himself over the prospect of taking another man's life.

Claude's tied hands put him at a severe disadvantage. But desperation lent him strength and determination. The two men tumbled head over heels down the slope toward the

black water. The terrorist pounded Claude's face, butted him,
bit him. He broke free and scrambled to his feet. Claude
tripped him before he could get away. His legs, conditioned
to a five-mile run nearly every morning, were his best
weapon. He twisted like a cat, bringing one leg over and behind the struggling man, and locked his ankles around Alwan's waist and twisted the other way. Piling Alwan onto his
head with a splash at the edge of the water.

Alwan came up from the water, screaming and clawing.
Breaking free of the leg hold, he lost his footing and stumbled backward, falling into the pool.

Higher up on the slope, looking down toward the black
water, Cameron glimpsed only vague moving shapes. He
charged downhill to help the FBI agent. A scream of utter
horror stopped him short. The water roiled and churned. A
mighty tail slapped the surface. Then there was eerie silence.

An alligator slew its prey by locking it inside its powerful
toothed jaws and dragging it twisting around and around to
the bottom until it drowned.

Which of the two men had it been?

Cameron heard one of them staggering up the slope. He
pointed the gun with both hands out in front, crouching in a
combat stance. There was no question of whether he *could*
kill; like his grandfather and father, uncle and brothers, he
had gone through the SF and Delta courses and been trained
to kill. He had even killed before. The question was much
larger than that, at least for a man who now dedicated himself
to God. The question was: *Should* he kill? *Would* he kill even
if it meant saving hundreds of thousands of innocent lives?

A shadow materialized in front of him. The larger shadow
of the FBI agent.

Thank You, God.

Cameron fell to his knees and bowed his head, feeling sick
all over again. Claude Thornton dropped down next to him.
"I don't know who the hell you are," he said, not recognizing

his rescuer in the darkness, "but you saved this Mississippi nigger from getting tossed to the alligators. Now untie me. Quick."

"Claude. It's me. Cameron."

"Chaplain! What the hell! What are you doing here?"

"I should be asking you the same question. Claude, I'm sorry. I just couldn't shoot him."

Claude inhaled deeply, still catching his breath. He turned his head toward the pool. It remained silent.

"I understand, Chaplain. I think God took care of it for you."

He turned his back to Cameron. "Untie me, Chaplain, and do it quick. I don't know how much they might have heard of this up at the barn."

While Cameron fumbled with the knots, Claude briefly explained how he had been taken captive in Georgia and brought here. The day before, he said, the terrorists shot and killed some poor dumbass who wandered into the wrong place. They tossed his body into the black pool for the alligators to get rid of, which only attracted more alligators, including the giant that got Alwan.

"I can't say I'm sorry about this perp," he said. "Seeing you here now, I figure you must have been with that dead guy from yesterday. Is that right?"

"His name was Yasein."

"You can tell me about it later."

Claude flexed his good hand to restore circulation as soon as he felt his bonds slipped. He took the pistol from Cameron with his injured right hand and almost dropped it. He groaned from the pain of the drill bit wound. He transferred the gun to his left hand and fired a shot into the air.

"They were expecting a shot," he said. "Chaplain, they're getting ready to fire that thing in there—and there ain't nobody else to stop them except you and me."

CHAPTER 62

AL-QAEDA THREATENS NUCLEAR ATTACK

Qatar (CPI)—Terrorists have placed nuclear missiles in position to strike U.S. cities, warns a top al-Qaeda operative in an interview with al-Jazeera television in Qatar. The threat was made by Saddam al-Usuquf, al-Qaeda's Number Three operative. Consolidated Press International obtained a copy of the interview and had it translated into English.

AL-JAZEERA: What is the objective of the al-Qaeda network?

AL-USUQUF: To destroy the Great Satan. That is, the United States and Israel.

AL-JAZEERA: Does the al-Qaeda network have the military capacity to make war on the United States?

AL-USUQUF: Yes. All of them are ready to die. Long live September 11. It was just a beginning. A way of calling the world's attention to what is still to come.

AL-JAZEERA: How will this be done?

AL-USUQUF: With the destruction of large American cities, along with other measures.

AL-JAZEERA: By what means will this be done?

AL-USUQUF: Using atomic bombs.

AL-JAZEERA: How is that possible?

AL-USUQUF: Millions of cargo containers arrive in seaports

each day, and no matter how efficient security is, it's impossible to check, search through, and examine each container. Airplanes also bring in millions of pounds of cocaine every week. It is not difficult to do.

AL-JAZEERA: So what is the plan?

AL-USUQUF: The beginning will be the detonation of a nuclear device through a missile, which will cause the death of between eight hundred thousand and one million people and create chaos on a scale never seen before.

AL-JAZEERA: Which will be the first city?

AL-USUQUF: The first city will be that in which optimal conditions present themselves. For example, clear skies, and winds of eight miles per hour or less in the direction of the country center so that radioactive dust can contaminate the maximum possible area. The process will have begun. It will be simply a question of time before the entire economic structure collapses and turns to dust. If our objectives are reached with one missile and the smallpox, probably we'll save the lives of others. However, that's unlikely, and it's probable that three more missile bombs will be detonated. One per week, and other attacks with chemical weapons and smallpox will be carried out.

AL-JAZEERA: Aren't you fearful that al-Qaeda's plan will be discovered?

AL-USUQUF: The plan is already in its countdown, and nothing can stop it . . .

CHAPTER 63

Mindanao

The typhoon was at its most ferocious. Lightning streaked and webbed across the low sky, cracking like doom, and thunder rumbled continuously from a giant's throat. Rain fell like "a cow pissing on a flat rock," as Gloomy put it. But the weather, for all its fury, posed less concern for Major Brandon Kragle than the enemy. In fact, the weather could be an asset in that it camouflaged movement and kept the guerrillas under shelter.

A KISS plan slowly formed in Brandon's mind. KISS—Keep It Simple, Stupid. He had to find out where the prisoners were held in order for them to be snatched at the beginning of any action. Once the captives were located and reinforcements arrived to link up with Ice Man and Gloomy, the real business would begin. Detachment demolitionists covered by an assault and security element would rush the missiles to blow them in place. At the same time, Summer and Stanton would be grabbed and ushered to safety. After that, it was a matter of disappearing into the jungle and making their way to a join up with Lucifer's element, which should by then have rescued the Korean kids from the *Ibn Haldoon* and sent the freighter to the bottom of the bay.

They would then get aboard the *Sam Houston* and get the hell out of Dodge. Strike aircraft from the *Abe Lincoln* thundered in when the weather cleared, maybe this afternoon, and bombed hell out of the guerrillas. Filipino Scout Rangers operating somewhere in the area could do the mop-up.

Simple enough. Except, Brandon thought, you always had to factor in Murphy's Law.

Brandon and his brother Cassidy cautiously fought their way through thick jungle toward the guerrilla bivouac area at the other end of the field. Hopefully, they would have located Summer and Stanton by the time Ice showed up with Mad Dog, Thumbs Jones, and the C-4. It was exhausting traveling. Everything was drenched, making footing slippery. They were constantly tripping and falling. Even with the forest acting as a windbreak, stinging rain in horizontal sheets worked them over good.

As they neared the objective, the two Deltas fell out for a rest break underneath a freshly toppled jungle giant whose roots and soil mass formed a sort of cave. No rainwater had yet settled in the excavation. They squatted in the dimly illuminated shelter where the howl of the storm was muted and the wind and rain did not reach them. Their saturated tiger-stripes dripped water. Brandon searched his cargo pockets and came up with a John Wayne chocolate bar from a MERC ration. He split it with Cassidy. Cassidy nibbled on his, making it last, and gradually stopped shivering. Brandon devoured his in one bite to infuse his body with a dose of sugar energy.

"Gloria will give the old man hell if we don't make it back in time for the wedding," Cassidy said, looking a bit homesick. "Nobody can raise hell like Brown Sugar Doll."

Brandon was looking out into the storm.

After a moment's silence, Cassidy said, "Gloomy told me about Bosnia."

Brandon looked at him.

"Colonel Buck Thompson was Troop One commander then," he went on, feeling his brother out. "You were a butter bar lieutenant and Gloomy was a corporal. A detachment of Deltas and some SEALs were secreted into Tuzla in eight-foot-high metal containers to search for war criminals. Like modern-day Trojan horses. Is that right so far?"

"You're telling it."

"Lucifer was an ensign right out of the Academy. You and Gloomy and another Delta along with Lucifer and two SEALs were dispersed to safe houses in the countryside around Tuzla to detect and apprehend PIFWCs—war criminals. You located one of them and radioed for Lucifer to link up. He never came."

The old memory welled up in Brandon's throat as bitter as bile. "The bastard caused one of my guys to get killed," he snapped. "If he had showed up like he was supposed to, we would have had the advantage of surprise and it would have gone down without a problem."

"Instead," Cassidy said softly, "he was chasing two other PIFWCs. Gloomy said he caught them. That was the only thing that saved him at the court-martial."

"There is no place in SpecOps for cowboys."

"Brandon, you once called me a hothead."

"What's your point, little brother?" Brandon sounded irritable.

"You gave me a chance," Cassidy said. "Don't you think you owe him one?"

"He's getting it now. Rest break's over. Let's move."

They approached the trucks and airplanes from the south, through the trees drumming with rain and thrashed by the wind. They crawled on their bellies the last few yards to the edge of the clearing, squirming in the mud like salamanders in a pond. Brandon nudged his brother and indicated at least two men who had sought shelter underneath the nearest flatbed. Others seeking shelter beneath trucks and the two airplanes were almost invisible through the dark gray curtain of the downpour. Trucks and airplanes alike rocked back and forth in the tempest. Aircraft camouflage covers popped and cracked.

"Maybe she's in one of the planes or in the truck cabs?" Cassidy suggested.

That was something Brandon hadn't counted on. He pondered it. The guerrilla and terrorist leadership probably used the dry airplanes as their command posts and left the truck cabs to the various small unit leaders. That left *underneath* the trucks for the troops. Terrorists were never particularly considerate of the comfort and safety of their captives; Stanton and Summer might well be tied to a tree somewhere.

Unless . . . A dark thought occurred to him. Unless the bastards were using Summer in the airplanes for their pleasure.

Controlling his temper, thinking *mission*, Brandon committed to memory the lay of the land for future reference. The three trucks containing the missile crates were parked in no particular order nearest where the road came out of the jungle into the clearing. A small stream or drainage twisted between the trucks and the two airplanes. The stream ran full of water, riveleting across rocks and entering the forest where it spread into fingers and soaked into deep humus.

From the looks of things, it occurred to Brandon that most of the troops, and perhaps even the prisoners, may have remained in the main camp below, to be moved up only when the weather cleared to help transfer the missiles to the aircraft for takeoff. Still, there would have to be a second camp somewhere in the vicinity. Cooking and other necessary troop duties couldn't be conducted inside the airplanes and trucks. Tapping Cassidy on the shoulder, Brandon pulled them back into the forest and circled to the right.

Sure enough. They heard the camp before they saw it—tent canvas popping in the storm, almost like rifle shots. Brandon got low and led the way, guiding on the sound, T-Bone's Hush

Puppy in his fist and ready to use. They crossed the road, two deep ruts cut through walls of green foliage. They came upon the first tent about twenty yards on the other side of the road. It was made of heavy OD-green canvas, what American troops called a GP-Large. Smoke huffed out a rear opening and instantly diluted into the driving rain. Brandon suspected it must be the mess tent. He smelled something cooking. Spicy and—

"Smells like shit," Cassidy murmured, making a face.

Beyond were a half-dozen other tents. Another GP-Large and the rest were smaller four-man shelters. One of them ripped up its windward stakes and began bellowing like a loose sail. A guerrilla shot out through the flaps, only half-dressed, and began lashing it down again, anchoring it more securely. He yelled and blackguarded Allah and in general bitched his displeasure like soldiers in any man's army.

He finished and quickly dashed back inside and tied the flaps behind him.

Brandon and Cassidy circled the campsite, but detected no other movement. Brandon couldn't help feeling that Summer was being held in one of these tents. It was almost like a psychic experience, as though their minds were touching. He concealed himself with Cassidy on the perimeter and pondered the challenge of determining exactly which of them she might be in.

He was at the point of crawling up to the tents one at a time and peeking inside when loud voices attracted his attention. A man's voice and a *woman*'s. Shortly, a man shouting angrily emerged into the rain, jerking on a rope that led back through the flaps of the tent. He gave a final vicious tug and Summer Marie Rhodeman, hands tied in front, popped out on the other end of the line. It was still tied around her neck. The terrorist berated her for bumping into him; she shouted back just as fiercely.

Brandon's heart leaped. She was still alive, *alive*. Although she was clad in the drenched rags of her makeshift bikini bottom, top, and sneakers, looking battered and worn—eyes swollen, cuts and bruises on her cheeks, lovely legs scratched and scabbed—Brandon thought her the most beautiful sight he had ever beheld. Water matting her bobbed black hair made her look like a woodland nymph.

Apparently, the dispute was over her need to use the bathroom. The cammie-clad guerrilla pointed furiously to the leeward side of the tent with his rifle barrel. Summer argued back, blistering him in Arabic, and gestured with her head toward the bushes. She jerked back on the lead around her neck.

Brandon gripped his pistol. He had an *investment* in this girl. Given the opportunity, he was going to collect on it.

The guard finally relented and followed her, grumbling underneath his breath, his head lowered against the slashing storm. Summer kept her head up, looking around, as though she too had had a psychic event and fully *expected* Brandon to be coming for her. She was one self-willed lady, Brandon thought with an amount of pride in her, for whom no terrorist would ever be a match.

Taking a chance, he stood up quickly when she looked in his direction. She spotted him immediately. If she was surprised, she concealed it. He ducked back down. Summer changed direction and led her reluctant keeper directly toward the shrubbery where Brandon and Cassidy hid. She stopped just before she got there. Keeping her body between the guerrilla and the bushes, she turned and tongue-lashed him until he turned his back to give her privacy. He held onto his end of the rope.

Unable to know her rescuers' strategy or capabilities, Summer devised her own. After glancing around to make sure no one else was out and watching, she suddenly lunged back against her neck rope, pulling the astonished guard off-balance. The move also caught Brandon by surprise. He sprang erect with the Hush Puppy. The guerrilla, recovering, sidestepped and swung his rifle around.

Brandon shot him in the chest. The coughing *Pfft* of the silenced pistol blended virtually unheard with the boom of electrical bolts and the popping of tent canvas. The guard dropped face-up in the rain, dying nerves causing his arms and legs to twitch.

Brandon lost no time. In two strides he swooped Summer into his arms and carried her at a trot away from the camp. Cassidy covered the withdrawal with his Walther. They stopped long enough once they were out of sight for Brandon to slice through the ropes that held Summer's hands. Her wrists were inflamed and bleeding and her fingers swollen like sausages. She winced with pain but nonetheless retained her wry sense of humor.

"We're *really* going to have to stop meeting like this."

She kissed Brandon quickly on the lips, then kissed Cassidy. Tears filled her eyes. Brandon had never seen her cry, not even during the worst days in the White Mountains of Operation Iron Weed. She really must have been through an ordeal. She batted her eyes until the tears dried.

"You'll never know how glad I am to see the Kragles," she said.

They were crossing the road again when the hullabaloo flared up in their wake. Someone had discovered the guard with a bullet through his heart.

"May we live in interesting times," Brandon said.

"But not *too* interesting," Summer quipped back.

CHAPTER 64

MacDill Air Force Base, Tampa, Florida

General Darren Kragle settled into the CENTCOM's large swivel chair and looked across the desk. FBI agent Fred Whiteman of the Joint Terrorist Task Force took one of the armchairs. Whiteman was a large square man in his late forties whose genial face veiled a shrewd intelligence stocked with information about organized terrorism in the United States. That early morning before breakfast, he wore jeans, a sports shirt, and a short green windbreaker to conceal the semiauto pistol holstered at his ample girth. Usually a jolly man, he was that day as serious as the pope delivering a speech on abortion or the Priest Scandal. He was on his way to New Orleans by FBI jet, but had detoured via Tampa to provide USSOCOM a courtesy briefing since he feared the General's son, Cameron, might somehow be involved in Claude Thornton's disappearance and the mystery missile delivery in Georgia.

"I'm on standby until we come up with something," he informed the General. "Maybe we'll find something now that it's daylight."

"What *do* you expect to find?" General Kragle asked. "Missiles?"

Whiteman took out a stick of gum, slowly unwrapped it,

and stuffed it into his mouth. He always chose the most inopportune time to quit smoking. He looked up, his face grim.

"We think New Orleans is the target of the next al-Qaeda strike," he said, inhaling deeply.

"When?" Cameron was in New Orleans—or at least he was the last time anyone heard from him.

"Today. We think today."

"How sure are you about it?"

"If we'd had this kind of intel before 9/11, circumstantial as it is, there might not have been a 9/11. Here's what we know: The airplane we intercepted at St. Marys airport had a missile aboard, which it had already delivered to homegrown terrorists. We've verified that from a number of sources. As for Claude . . ."

Whiteman briefly explained the circumstances of Agent Thornton's abduction in Edith, Georgia, and how JTTF had tracked the abductors through gasoline credit receipts to Baton Rouge.

"We can hope they've kept Claude alive for some reason," he said.

"Terrorists have sometimes hung on to their captives for years, for no apparent reason," the General said. "What has this to do with my son?"

"I'm getting to it," the JTTF agent said in his crisp law-enforcement style. "Yesterday morning, we got a call from the New Orleans police, who were questioning the fiancée of an immigrant Saudi named Abdul Atef, a student in physics."

The American woman told police about how Abdul left home in a gray car with three Middle Eastern–looking men, destination unknown. All she knew was that he was scared and that he told her he had met an army chaplain at the Hands of God Conference, who had promised to help him stop something bad from happening. She didn't know what it was.

Whiteman paused to collect his thoughts. "About four o'clock this morning," he continued, "a Louisiana trooper found a rental car abandoned alongside a blacktop that cuts off U.S. 10 down into the Atchafalaya Swamp west of Baton Rouge."

The car had been rented by Chaplain Cameron Kragle. So far, there had been no sign of the chaplain.

The General stood up and paced around the room and back. His and Gloria's telephone calls to Cameron's cell phone had gone unanswered. He sat back down and raked big hands through his short-cropped hair.

"At two o'clock this morning," Whiteman went on, "three of my agents were gunned down at the airport in New Orleans after Mr. Thornbrew suggested I send them there to stop and question Senator Jake Thierry."

General Kragle looked up through his brows, but said nothing about the information on Thierry that his CPI brother Mike had passed on to him and that he in turn relayed to Director Thornbrew.

"Thierry claimed the attackers were attempting to kidnap him and the agents tried to intervene," Whiteman said. "He's lying. What they wanted was the large diplomatic pouch—box actually—that Thierry picked up in Manila. At first, Thierry claimed he didn't have the box. He changed his story when we confronted him with the facts. What was in the box? We don't know. Thierry said it was full of reports analyzing the terrorist situation in the Philippines."

"You don't believe him?"

"It seems to me that the men who gunned down my agents weren't there to kidnap the senator. They were there to *meet* him and pick up the box. My agents just happened to get in the way. It also seems to me that a diplomatic pouch is a sure way of smuggling something into the country if you need it fast."

"Thierry's a douche bag," the General said. "Still, he's also a U.S. senator . . ."

"They may be blackmailing him," Whiteman said. "You know how the saying goes—When you got 'em by the balls, their hearts and minds will follow."

The agent paused to stuff another stick of gum into his mouth before he grimly resumed. About an hour earlier, he said, police located the black car used by the shooters abandoned in Baton Rouge. It had been reported previously stolen.

"The bad guys wanted that box bad enough to kill three feds for it," Whiteman pointed out. "Suddenly, right on cue this morning, the al-Jazeera story on that nut Saddam al-Usuquf hit the media and it all started to make sense. It's a common terrorist ploy. You strike without warning the first time to show it can be done, then you build up suspense and create anticipatory terror before you hit with the next big one. This time, I think we've got the real thing coming down. I think the plutonium your son Brandon missed in the Philippines the first time he was there was in Senator Thierry's Pandora's box. I believe al-Usuquf when he said the plan was on countdown. The shithead specifically stated that in the beginning will be one missile, with probably three more to follow. They're counting on those three SCUDs from North Korea getting through to be used in follow-up strikes."

General Kragle gave a sober nod.

"Everything indicates the first missile is hidden in the Atchafalaya Swamp and that it's aimed toward New Orleans," Whiteman concluded. "We have aircraft, boats, and vehicles beating the bogs for it. When we find it, I think we'll also find Claude and your son. Hopefully they'll still be alive."

He stood up.

"Hopefully," he said, "we'll get there before they fire the missile."

CHAPTER 65

Atchafalaya Swamp

Agent Claude Thornton and Chaplain Cameron Kragle sprawled on their bellies on the rise away from the alligator pool and peered across the wiregrass meadow. The tin roof of the corrugated barn reflected first light as the eastern sky turned quickly from orange to pink to even paler rose. Light seemed to seep out of the sky and from out of the terrible black pool to drive the darkness back across the meadow almost as fast as a man could walk.

Cameron turned his head toward the pool. A thin red stain that had nothing to do with sunrise spread across the surface of the pond. Neither the big reptile nor Alwan's body had reappeared. The water was deep enough that there were no swirls or other activity. The chaplain's breath sounded like it was being sucked through a corroded brass pipe. He was still shaky. Sweat on his brow resembled droplets of water on pale soap.

"You all right, Chaplain?" Claude asked. "You want my shirt?"

"I'll be a lot better, God willing, when this is over. I saw what they did to your hand, Claude. I was watching through the barn window."

Thornton held out his right hand. Where the drill bit had gone through resembled a bloated sausage with five appendages. The rest of him didn't look, or undoubtedly *feel,* a whole lot better. One eye was swollen shut; gashes on his cheeks and head oozed a corruption of blood and pus that dried into putrid scabs; his feet were twice their normal size from his being tied so long and could hardly be contained inside his sensible FBI shoes. He gave a low, sardonic chuckle. He didn't know if he could *walk* from there to the barn, much less fight when he got there.

"They'll be missing this one soon enough when he doesn't come back," he said, indicating Alwan who had most recently reverted to alligator cuisine.

The agent slipped the clip from Alwan's pistol and counted the bullets. Four rounds left. He uttered a curse. "The Glock they took from me was fully loaded," he complained.

The two worn-out men lay in the coming of the new day, watching the barn, trying to recuperate while they debated options back and forth for handling the situation. They didn't have many. Attempting to escape to bring back help was clearly out of the question. Cameron looked too weak and sick to walk much farther than from there to the barn himself. Plus, there simply wasn't time. The missile was almost ready to be fired. From what the agent had overheard, it *was* going to be fired. Soon.

"They don't know I speak Arabic," Claude explained, "so the ragheads spoke freely in front of me. They didn't have the right stuff until this morning. I heard them talking about a shootout at the New Orleans airport. Some lowlife piece of diplomatic shit apparently brought the radium through in a protected pouch. The brainy little raghead is putting it together for them now—"

"Abdul. That one's Abdul," Cameron interjected.

The chaplain explained about how Yasein and he tailed Abdul to the swamp after Professor Ramzi and the others picked him up in New Orleans. "Abdul's with us," he concluded.

"That's good," the agent noted sarcastically. "That cuts the odds down, know what I'm saying? We are one sorry beat-up pair to take on a band of cutthroats."

Storming the barn, getting the drop on the terrorists and capturing the lot of them might work in a Tom Clancy novel—but it didn't work when the good guys had a force of two men, one of whom was an unarmed half-naked chaplain too weak to much more than stand on his own sore, bare feet and who refused to kill, and the other of whom was a beat-up, middle-aged black dude with one useful hand and a gun loaded with only *four* bullets. There were at least five potential martyrs inside the barn, not counting Abdul. All were as heavily armed with handguns and assault rifles as any rifle squad. And, of course, they had one nuclear missile.

What options were left? No one on the outside had any idea where they were. It sounded a little melodramatic, but what it boiled down to was that it was up to the two of them, ready or not, to save New Orleans. Somehow.

A single-engine Cessna buzzed over just above treetop level, flying from east to west. It passed over the barn and kept going.

"Are you sure no one's looking for you out here?" Claude asked.

Cameron shook his head. Abdul had insisted he tell no one.

"Fred and the others probably think I'm still in Georgia somewhere," the agent said.

One of the terrorists popped out of the barn, looking up at the sky. The knife-faced one called Goba who, along with Al-wan, had taken Thornton prisoner. He watched the departing aircraft until it disappeared from view. Satisfied, he turned toward the black pool and took a few questioning steps in the direction of where Cameron and Thornton hid in the grass. He shaded his eyes against the rising sun and called out, "Al-wan? Alwan?"

Cameron tensed. Thornton gripped the pistol, a Beretta, with his left hand.

"Alwan?"

The scraping sound of the barn doors opening distracted him. He stepped out of the way as a truck engine started and the flatbed slowly pulled out into the now-sunlit meadow. Sunshine glinted in sinister rays off the mounted erector-launcher and sleek, deadly looking rocket. Cold, knotted lumps of fear and dread formed in Cameron's stomach as he saw that the warhead had been reattached.

Professor Ramzi stood to one side adjusting his rimless glasses and displaying a thin determined smile. A terrorist with a compass took azimuths to New Orleans and directed the truck into position, waving his hands and pointing and shouting. The other terrorists gathered around, all armed as though to repel any last-minute opposition. They wore red headbands in an apparent tribute to the 9/11 martyrs, who had also donned headbands before crashing airliners into the World Trade Center and the Pentagon.

Goba replaced his *kaffiyeh* with one of the red bands, picked up a stubby Uzi submachine gun from the bed of the truck and started walking across the meadow toward Cameron and Thornton, calling out, *"Alwan?"*

CHAPTER 66

Mindanao

Terrain, howling wind, the cracking of lightning, rain coming down so hard it penetrated even triple forest canopy to pound the earth and reduce visibility; it all combined to work in favor of the Kragle brothers as they withdrew from the terrorist camp with Summer.

They stopped long enough for Brandon to strip off his heavy uniform blouse and offer it to Summer. She initially refused, protesting that he needed it. Brandon impatiently shoved her arms into its sleeves and buttoned it for her. He still had his OD-green T-shirt. The blouse hung nearly to Summer's knees and her hands disappeared inside the sleeves, but it provided more protection than the expedient diaper-bikini thing. He almost laughed at the picture she made, standing there in the rain looking like a tiny WWII orphan garbed in a too-big castoff GI uniform. Instead, he crushed her to his chest out of pity and thankfulness and . . .

"I *would* give you my pants," he murmured.

"I figure you need to wear the pants in the family."

"Is that a proposal?"

"Proposal is a man's job, wouldn't you say?"

Even after what she had endured, she retained the wiseass banter that had so exasperated Brandon when he first knew her as Ismael in Afghanistan but that later endeared her to him when he came to know her as Summer.

"If you two can break this up a minute," Cassidy interrupted. "I might point out that—"

"Yeah, yeah," Brandon and Summer responded in unison.

Navigating on foot through tropical rain forest was an arduous process under even the best conditions. Roots twisted and gnarled and protruded from every angle and at heights from toe-stubbing level to head-knocking reaches. There was no level ground. Everywhere were lumpy hummocks and gashes in the earth, all of which were matted and entangled with growths of various sorts ranging from jungle vines and lianas dangling from the tops of arboreal giants to thickets of thorned palms and impenetrable canebrakes. They had to stop frequently to let Summer rest. Oddly enough, they neither saw nor heard signs of pursuit.

Brandon noticed there was something different about Summer other than the physical signs of the beating she took and her weakness from lack of sleep and food. It dwelt in the emerald eyes, which looked painfully sharper now, somehow predatory and haunting. He had seen eyes like that on prisoners of war who had been abused and savaged. He didn't want to know what happened to her, not yet. It was all he could do to contain his fury, even *not* knowing what happened.

She tried to hide it from him, knowing how he was, but it still came through. What happened was something they would both have to work through. Later. Right now they had a mission to accomplish.

"Was Stanton being held with you?" Brandon asked her.

"Not in my tent. He was poor company anyhow."

"Do you know where he is?"

"We were led up together, but then they took him somewhere else. I think he might have made some kind of deal with them. I overheard them talking. With Cimatu and the one they call Albaneh—"

"Albaneh Mosed?"

"Everybody who's anybody has showed up for the party. Stanton told me he was negotiating with them for our release."

"Sure he was," Brandon sneered. "If that sonofabitch could save his own ass by giving them somebody else—"

He dropped it. The terrorists would probably shoot Stanton now anyhow, as they had executed the missionaries when pushed too hard. Brandon felt no remorse at the thought.

"We'll try to pick him up later," he said. Rescuing Stanton was part of the mission requirement.

In addition to Albaneh Mosed, the leader of Abu Sayyaf, Summer had also recognized Abdurajak Janjalani, the founder of Abu Sayyaf, and Jamel Khalifa, a Saudi businessman with financial connections to all Islamic extremists in the Middle East. Osama bin Laden was his brother-in-law. Khalifa was an extremely dangerous man and one of the most fanatical of the Islamics. It was he who issued the public statement: "We shall leave a million heads of Americans and Jews on their doorsteps."

Organizing a Muslim separatist/terrorist movement required leadership, important and influential connections to sympathetic foreign groups, and funding to procure weapons and more troops and equipment. Janjalani and Khalifa helped supply all this. The presence of such high-level leadership demonstrated the importance being placed on the delivery and acceptance of the missiles.

The element consisting of Mad Dog Carson, Thumbs Jones, and Ice Man Thompson successfully negotiated the main terrorist camp below and made its way at a forced pace toward Gloomy Davis and T-Bone Jones. Since, oddly enough, the guerrillas still seemed not to be in pursuit, Brandon got on the Motorola and ordered the two elements to link up on him instead. That would put the detachment within striking distance of the terrorists and the missiles. They had to move even faster than intended now that the bad guys knew hostiles walked among them.

Gloomy and T-Bone arrived first, using directions Cassidy supplied on the encrypted radio. T-Bone took over the Motorola to guide in Mad Dog's group while Brandon, Cassidy, and Gloomy, after his reunion with Summer, slipped out to the edge of the forest to place surveillance on the target. The missiles were only about five hundred meters away. The rain seemed to have let up, providing better visibility. Instead of whooping horizontally across the meadow, it arrived at more of a slant, indicating a decrease in wind velocity.

As might have been expected, discovery of the dead guard and the disappearance of the prisoner stirred up the guerrillas like poking a stick in an ant mound. They swarmed all over the trucks and aircraft, although they appeared more occupied with protecting the missiles and preparing them for offloading than searching for whoever might have slain one of their number. An ancient crane rumbled out from somewhere and positioned itself at the rear of the nearest C-130, ready to hook up to the first missile crate.

Two patrols of four or five men each set out to work opposite side of the field. They were in no particular hurry, merely slogging along the edges of the clearing with their heads bowed in the rain and rifles slung. The weather caused them to bunch up in their bulky rain gear. Brandon couldn't figure it. Why were they taking the presence of an intruder so cavalierly? Was it because they thought Summer might have somehow obtained a gun, escaped on her own, and wasn't worth the time to pursue?

The patrol on the near side of the field consisted of four soldiers in wind-whipped ponchos and bush hats. Fifteen or twenty minutes and the enemy would be upon them. Gloomy twitched the bill of his patrol cap low to shelter his eyes and checked the "borrowed" Swedish K. "I could pick 'em all off, Boss, like a bunch of prairie dogs."

"Hold off, Sergeant."

Mad Dog's element was coming in. The Dog, a little way out, got on the radio with T-Bone.

"Fu-uck," he said by way of introduction, an unmistakable call sign. "I think I got you in sight, but it's dark and wet as hell in these woods. Blink me a red light so we can be sure it's you—else we are going to fuck over somebody . . . Okay, T-Bone. I got you. We're coming in. I don't want to hear any sea lions barking."

The team reunited, bringing with it extra weapons, Thumbs's ruck full of explosives, and a surprise for Gloomy—Mr. Blunderbuss, his .300 Winchester sniper rifle. Gloomy fell all over Mad Dog in gratitude.

"I could almost kiss that ugly mug of yours," he threatened.

"Let me drop my drawers and you can kiss my hairy airborne ass."

The burly commo man did a double take over Summer. He looked at long bare legs coming out from the uniform top and growled. "They didn't use to issue soldiers like this. You know, Ice Man, parts of them are edible."

He grinned his best leer. "Hey, little girl," he greeted. "Want a candy bar?"

"Disgusting as always, Carson," Summer taunted him in return. She hugged him hard and kissed him on his unshaven cheek. He blushed royally. In spite of the man's rough nature, everyone knew he would willingly lay down his life for any of them. "But I would love that candy bar."

She hadn't eaten in two days, making Brandon and Cassidy feel guilty for the chocolate they ate before they rescued her. Mad Dog tossed her a John Wayne bar.

"It's a good thing the major got you back," he said, "or I'd have kicked *his* ass."

Dog's element rearmed the detachment, including Brandon's MP-5 submachine gun and M4A1 5.56 carbines for T-Bone and Cassidy. Cassidy, who had kept watch on the terrorists from the wood line, crabbed back to report that the enemy patrol was getting near. Brandon concealed the detachment along the trees in a hasty ambush formation. Summer plugged herself into the line with the Swedish K.

"Let them pass if they will," Brandon ordered.

The enemy patrol disappeared behind the roll of the land as it approached, but then reappeared minutes later at the top of the knoll. Heads bowed into the rain, splashing miserably onward. It occurred to Brandon that this was no search party looking for the escaped prisoner and her allies. This was merely security for the airfield—and it obviously expected no trouble.

The four terrorists trudged past within ten meters of the Deep Steel detachment enshrouded in the jungle. They stayed in the grass clearing where the walking was easier, casting only an occasional cursory glance at the forest, unaware of how near death waited should they change directions or grow suspicious. Soon, the last shabby one went out of sight, bending against rain that was still hard but nowhere near what it had been even ten minutes previously.

The guerrillas' behavior puzzled Brandon. Life was cheap in the terrorist world, but this bunch should still be jumping through their asses trying to find whoever killed their man. Instead, it was as if they thought whoever did it wasn't here in force, else there would already have been an attack. Like the guerrillas had more important matters to which to attend.

Security around the aircraft and trucks had in fact been strengthened. Everyone else jumped frantically about removing camouflage nets from the airplanes, revealing two dull green Hercules workhorses from the Vietnam era. The wind caught one of the nets and sailed it into the treetops, where it got snagged in branches and remained there flapping wildly. No one attempted to retrieve it.

Both C-130 tail ramps lowered to the ground. The trucks roared and gear-scraped their way across the drainage ditch stream, the guerrillas pushing when they almost got stuck, and backed up near the open cargo bays. Gangs of workers using the crane began transferring the huge crates from the flatbeds to the bellies of the airplanes.

It appeared they were preparing to take off with the missiles. The Hercules was one tough airplane that could actually navigate turbulent weather—they were sometimes used as hurricane hunters—but there was no way they could take off from a flooded grass strip in high winds.

What the hell were they doing?

Brandon caught himself when it suddenly dawned on him that the rain beat almost straight down onto the bill of his patrol cap instead of being blown into his face. The winds were actually abating. The aircraft no longer rocked and bounced on their tethers in the blast of the typhoon. Some soldiers were loosening the aircraft tie downs.

He understood what was happening with a jolt of foreboding. It wasn't that the terrorists were unconcerned about intruders; instead, they were concentrating their energies on their priority, which was getting the missiles safely off the ground and on the way to their destination.

Brandon had never experienced the eye of a hurricane or typhoon, but he had read how there was a dead space in the center that sometimes lasted for ten or fifteen minutes, sometimes more than a half-hour. The terrorists *were* alarmed at the possibility of exposure. That was why they weren't waiting for the tail of the storm. They were going to attempt a takeoff through the typhoon's eye. The C-130s had an excellent chance of making it through the rest of the storm once they became airborne—and a better chance than that of avoiding U.S. satellites and radar. Within a few hours they would be approaching the coastline of the western United States where low-flying aircraft might enter with slim chance of detection at any number of places along the rugged shores of northern California or Oregon.

CHAPTER 67

Had the Deltas possessed M72 LAWs (light antitank weapons) with ranges in excess of two thousand meters and the capability to penetrate 400mm of rolled homogenous armor, they could have sat back at a very comfortable distance and blown engines and wings off the C-130s, leaving them and the missiles sitting ducks for carrier warplanes after the storm. But you couldn't work an operation on *if*. What mattered was the reality of Deep Steel's capacity at this precise moment. There was no way to plan for all contingencies in such a rapid-changing scenario.

Seven men and Summer. A full Delta detachment except for Doc TB and Winnie Brown. Brandon had left the young bear of a Doc with Lucifer because the SEAL lieutenant needed at least four men to knock down the *Ibn Haldoon* and T-Bone Jones was already in the field with the recon patrol. Besides, Doc TB's medical expertise might be better utilized toward the rear, where he was safer. Any wounded—and Brandon feared there *would* be casualties—could be littered back to him when the withdrawal began.

Gloomy complained because somehow a bandoleer of ammunition for his .300 had been mistakenly left aboard the submarine. The rifle had a total of eight rounds in its magazine.

"Fu-uck," Mad Dog hedged, shifting his shortened M-870 twelve-gauge shotgun to his other hand. "You'd bitch, Gloomy, if we buried you using a new shovel."

Brandon called the detachment together for a team planning meeting under cover of the forest; rain no longer slashed through the green canopies. Any Delta officer who neglected to solicit and accept input from his men in the field was a fool. Special Forces troopers were selected and trained to be independent, strong-minded, capable men whether they operated alone or in elements.

Summer knelt next to Brandon, his shirt she wore pulled down around to cover her legs. A stillness even more alarming than the fury of the storm settled over the jungle. Somewhere water dripped on rock. Time for options was running out.

Brandon first explained his expectation that the C-130s were going to take off through the typhoon's eye, then opened the meeting to ideas on how best to prevent it.

Gloomy suggested he pick off the pilots with Mr. Blunderbuss. Brandon had already thought of that. He handed his binocs to the little sniper so Gloomy could go see for himself why this would not work. Gloomy returned shortly while the serious discussion forged ahead within the tight little circle of determined men and Summer.

"The aircraft are at the wrong angle," Gloomy reported. "I can't get shots into the cockpits unless I make it to the opposite side of the clearing."

"We haven't the time," Brandon pointed out.

"There might be a moment there when they start to turn back on runup—"

"Not good enough, Gloomy. The angle is wrong too. You'll be shooting *upward* into the cockpit, which leaves you virtually no target at all."

Gloomy agreed. "Those tires are puncture proof," he brooded. "With only eight cartridges—" He glared at Mad Dog—"maybe I can disable *one* of the planes . . . I know, Boss. Not good enough . . ."

"Thumbs?" Ice Man interjected, speaking for the first time since the linkup. He had a way of communicating with a minimum number of words.

"Few of the world's problems can't be solved by a few sticks of TNT," the black demo man said.

Brandon looked from face to strained face in the circle. He had already worked out his KISS plan, but wanted to see if any of his teammates might have a better one.

"Everyone agreed?" he asked.

"I don't see another way, Major," Ice Man said.

"Then Thumbs and his demo it is," Brandon said.

He nodded solemnly through the water dripping off the bill of his cap. He brushed jungle debris off the ground in the middle of the circle to clear a sand table. He used a stick to carve out features in the spongy soil.

"Here are the airplanes and the trucks. A little stream, a water drainage, runs across the end of the clearing between the woods and the aircraft. It'll provide some cover for the demolition element. Thumbs, that's you and me. I'll keep them off you while you plant demo. They almost have the missiles loaded. If we can put C-4 inside the bays of both birds, those missiles are headed directly for the junkyard. If not, we'll go for blowing the landing gear . . ."

"Roger that, sir." Thumbs delved into his ruck and began rigging fuses and det cord to blocks of C-4 plastique.

"T-Bone, Mad Dog, and Cassidy—you're the assault-security team," Brandon detailed. "Your job is to fight them off us until we plant the explosives. Cassidy, you remember where that drainage ditch flattens out into the woods? We saw it earlier."

Cassidy nodded.

"The five of us will start from that end and use the ditch as cover. T-Bone and Cassidy are also demo men. Be ready to take over for Thumbs if . . . T-Bone, you'll be next in line if Thumbs goes down."

"Hoo-ya!" T-Bone concurred, taking a look at Thumbs.

"Boss . . . ?" Gloomy questioned.

"Gloomy and Ice Man are our best shooters," Brandon said. "You will dig in right here. When the shooting starts down there, I want the two of you picking off anybody that tries to keep us away from the airplanes. We'll leave the K with you for when you run out of ammo for your Blunderbuss."

"Piece of cake," Gloomy said.

Summer was looking at Brandon, waiting.

"Summer will stay here as spotter for the snipers. Anybody have any questions?"

A few comments and suggestions about positions and timing helped firm up the plan.

"What about Stanton?" Cassidy asked.

"First we disable the aircraft," Brandon said. "We think Stanton will be in or near one of the planes. Thumbs and I'll snatch him if he is. If not, the security team will check for him in the camp once we scatter the G's. Clear?"

"Leave the cocksucker with 'em," grumbled Mad Dog.

His friend Rock Taylor had died when the C-141 was shot down over Afghanistan in Operation Punitive Strike. Brandon let it ride. The Dog would do his duty, no matter how he felt about it. As would they all.

"Any other questions? Good. We move out in five."

Summer knew enough not to confront a commander in front of his troops. She took Brandon aside.

"I'm going with you," she declared.

"You're staying here," he shot back. "You're not in good shape. That makes you a liability."

Her good emerald eye narrowed to match the swollen slit of the other. This was a hill on which she was willing to die. "What are you going to do—arrest me and tie me up like *they* did? That's the only way I'm staying behind."

Angry, he pulled her farther out of earshot of the other troops who were readying weapons and stripping off nonessential gear.

"For one goddamned time, Gypsy, why won't you listen to me?"

Gypsy? He tasted the slip like a bitter taste even as it rolled off his tongue. Summer's face froze and the full lips thinned. A heartbeat of cold silence inserted itself between them.

"Look at me, Brandon. *Look at me.* It's me—*Summer.* What happened to Gypsy *happened.* We can never have an *investment* in each other until you give up your investment in a woman that's been dead two years. And I have to do this something now before I can have an investment in myself again."

He glowered at her.

"You are one stubborn man," she said. Tears flooded her eyes. She batted them back. "Brandon, that sonofabitch beat me. And he kept beating me like I was a slave. I'm going to kill him for that, Brandon, like he was going to kill me. With you or without you, I'm going to kill him."

"Which one?" he asked.

"It doesn't matter. It's my problem."

"It matters to me. Now, goddamnit, which one?"

Her lips quivered. "Cimatu. The one with the scar."

"I'll take care of him," he promised in a thin, deadly voice.

"Don't you see, Brandon? This is something I need to do for myself."

He dropped his gaze from hers and twisted his head away, feeling her anger and sense of outrage. There were things in life, he knew, that you had to do for yourself or you never got over them. Cassidy had had to take personal action for the anthrax death of his bride, else his revenge would have continued to burn until it burned out his soul.

"I'll never be whole again," Summer said in a small, determined voice, "until I do this thing."

He looked at her again. The wind had died even further and the rain pattered on jungle canopy and dripped down like veils. "The odds are against us," he pointed out.

He didn't know if he meant the odds were against the mission or against them. She said nothing.

"Tell Ice Man to give you his pistol," he said.

CHAPTER 68

Atchafalaya Swamp

Although the wiregrass meadow glowed almost turquoise in the fresh sunlight, the rows of cypress along the alligator pond threw shadows across FBI agent Claude Thornton and Chaplain Cameron Kragle. The risen sun beamed red light directly into Goba's eyes. He shaded them with his palm, holding the Uzi lightly with the other hand, and peered to where his friend Alwan had taken the fed to kill him. Alwan should have been back by now.

Claude watched him while he also studied the others still working with the truck and the missile. Professor Ramzi looked smallish and rather scholarly even with the revolutionary's red band around his head. He glanced toward Goba, then back to the missile and truck that were apparently rolling into place for the shot. The truck engine went dead.

Abdul and a terrorist in a clean white robe—Worn in reverence to this holy event of jihad?—hit a lever. The missile's sleek, sharp nose slowly lifted to point toward the south, toward New Orleans.

"Can you trust that one, that Abdul, to stay neutral?" Claude asked, whispering directly into Cameron's ear.

"I think he will."

Claude's right hand was swollen to the size of a balloon. He tried to force his finger into the trigger guard of Alwan's pistol; it wouldn't fit. He grimaced in pain and switched the weapon back to his left.

"I'm a lousy shot with my left hand," he complained. "Come on, raghead," he whispered, his good eye narrow and fixed on Goba. "Come on, a little closer, asshole."

Goba was looking all around. He charged a round into the Uzi's chamber and held it low in both hands across his front.

"If I can get my hands on that Uzi," Claude whispered, "we'll bring down some shit on these camel jocks. While I keep them busy, you make a run for the truck. Drive it off into the swamp, wreck it in the trees. Anything. Just don't let them fire the missile."

"God be with you, Claude."

"And with you, Chaplain."

Goba took a few more cautious steps toward them. The sun shone directly onto the knife edge of his lean brown face, thinning his mouth into a cruel slash. The tails of the red headband hung down the back of his neck, fluttering in the morning breeze like dying butterflies. Professor Ramzi's eyeglasses glinted back the sun as he turned toward Goba and called out something in Arabic.

Lying concealed in the grass, Claude took aim with the semiauto in his left fist. The barrel wavered. He pressed his sausage-like right hand on top of his left to steady it.

"C'mon, c'mon," he urged underneath his breath. "Your virgins are waiting, cocksucker."

Goba approached cautiously, his head ratcheting back and forth. He paused almost at the crest of the little decline that sloped down to the alligator pond. His dark eyes looked directly into Cameron's. The realization of what he had done, walked into a bushwhacking, widened his eyes with such a jolt that even Cameron felt it.

Claude pulled the trigger. The pistol barked deafeningly in Cameron's ear. Goba's skinny body leaped into the air from the impact. He emitted a yelp of surprise. He slammed to the ground screaming with an otherworldly mixture of pain, fear, and rage. Claude *was*, in fact, a lousy shot left-handed. The slug only winged the terrorist.

Goba rolled over and over in the grass, spraying bright blood from his side. Thinking him hit hard enough to be out of the action, the FBI agent scrambled to his feet and rushed to wrench the Uzi from the wounded man's hands. Instead, Goba saw him coming. He triggered a desperate burst in Claude's direction. It sounded like ripping cloth amplified.

Claude fell to the ground hard. Cameron thought he was hit. He bunched his legs to run to him.

"No!" Claude yelled.

The agent clawed his way back over the crest of the pond knoll while Goba jumped up with the Uzi still in hand and fled in the opposite direction toward the barn, dragging his left leg and holding his side with his elbows pressed tight. Pandemonium broke out around the truck.

"Plan two!" Claude snapped. "I'll divert them. You get that truck."

Without waiting for an answer, he got to his feet and sprinted in plain view along the edge of the meadow toward the rear of the barn. Terrorists shouted. A couple of pistol shots. They weren't Claude's. He only had three rounds left and was saving them. He disappeared into the trees at the northern edge of the clearing, pursued by two of the terrorists, one of whom snatched Goba's Uzi as he ran past the barn.

Professor Ramzi shouted threats and encouragement, jumping around in his excitement like a big grasshopper. Goba slumped against the side of the barn, still screaming at the top of his lungs. He was out of the fighting, waiting to see Allah. He didn't seem all that pleased to be going to his virgins.

God have mercy on him, Cameron automatically prayed. *God watch over Claude.*

You are my instrument.

Only partially successful, Claude's hastily conceived plot eliminated Goba as a threat and drew two of the terrorists away from the meadow in pursuit of him. That left Ramzi, Abdul, and the character in the clean white robe. Abdul and the robe were on the back of the truck, straining to see what was going on behind the barn. Apparently, they were the missile's designated firers. Ramzi scurried toward the barn and disappeared inside, either to hide or to retrieve a weapon.

Cameron had only one thought in mind, one objective. Myopic vision focused on the driver's door of the truck. It was partially ajar. The chaplain raced to his left, bent over in low profile to keep below the crest of the meadow and the skyline. When he reached the closest point to the vehicle, he stormed toward it. Across the open in the sunlight, running and staggering, tasting the sourness of his stomach about to turn inside out again. He swallowed his own sickness and lurched on.

He didn't think anyone had noticed him yet. All he had to do, with God's help, was start the truck and drive it and the missile fifty yards or less into the deep alligator pool. Sounded simple enough. If the keys were in the ignition! A picture of himself attempting to start the ATV flashed into mind.

He reached the door. Jerked it wide. From the corner of his eye he glimpsed the robed terrorist on the flatbed reaching down to point a pistol at him. He tightened his muscles to receive the bullet.

A blur of movement. Abdul was no longer a spectator, a puppet. The little Saudi threw himself at the robe. Both went down on the bed of the truck, struggling and wrestling, lodged together in the launcher frame like two tom cats fighting in a sack.

Breathless from the sprint, debilitated from the ordeal of the past day and night, Cameron attempted to heave himself into the truck cab. His foot slipped off the floorboard and he fell to his knees on the meadow, still holding onto the open door, feeling inadequate and foolish. He heard the Uzi ripping cloth out behind the barn. A pistol answered it.

Did that mean Claude had only two rounds left?

Cameron heard an angry and startled shout as Professor Ramzi emerged from the barn and charged like the leader of a banzai attack, firing a handgun as he came. Maddened, enraged, screaming insults that drowned out even poor Goba's unearthly caterwauling. Rushing Cameron as though he intended to trample him underfoot like an enraged bull.

Bullets spanged into the open inside of the truck door, sparking. Cracking past Cameron's head. One bullet seared across his cheek bone. Another bit into the upper part of his shoulder, throwing him against the door.

No bigger than he was, Ramzi hit Cameron like an NFL lineman. Cameron gave to the assault, tumbling backward and grabbing the professor by his shirt front as he fell. Using his knees and feet and Ramzi's own momentum, he catapulted the terrorist chief up and over. Ramzi flew through the air for a good ten feet before he landed and rolled. He bounced back to his feet with the agility of a cat, gun still in hand. Pointed at Cameron's belly.

Cameron jinked to one side and ran at him. Kicking, he

connected just below Ramzi's wrist. The gun flew out of his hand and sailed twenty feet downfield. The fury of the kick jerked Cameron's legs out from underneath him. He landed so hard on his back that it knocked the wind out of him. He gasped painfully for air, his head reeling, looking straight up into an incredibly blue sky.

On the one side of his peripheral vision he saw the robed terrorist doing something with the missile. Cranking it, aligning it. Something. Getting it ready to launch. Where was Abdul?

From the other periphery, he saw Ramzi run and drop down on hands and knees in the grass and start frantically searching for his weapon. At the same time, Ramzi shouted back at the missile man in Arabic: *"Haree'a! Haree'a!"* It took little imagination to translate it: *"Fire! Fire!"*

Cameron headed for the truck. Ramzi came up with the gun. Cameron veered toward Ramzi, half-running, half-crabbing across the thirty feet or so of grass.

Ramzi fired once. Missing.

Cameron tackled the terrorist. They tumbled over and over on the field. Fighting for the single weapon whose possession Ramzi retained. Although he was an academic, Professor Ramzi was strong and wiry, made even more ferocious by his fanaticism. Fighting him was like wrestling a wild coyote. The two men jabbed and punched and clawed and bit. Brawling to take command of the weapon.

For a chaplain and a man born and reared in the spirit, Cameron had nonetheless engaged in his share of schoolyard fights and had trained in Delta hand-to-hand combat. Nothing he had ever experienced in his life, not even Punitive Strike in Afghanistan nor the 100-Hour War in Iraq, compared to this for sheer personal savagery.

Cameron felt his muscles straining, his lungs burning. He was losing strength fast, reaching the limits of his reserves. It was all he could do to hold onto Ramzi's gunhand, straining to prevent the black muzzle from discharging into his face.

They rolled over and over in the grass, getting farther and farther away from the truck and the missile. Ramzi had him by the throat with one hand, squeezing until Cameron's vision filled with flashing lights and his breath rasped. Cameron whipped Ramzi's gun hand back and forth, trying to make him loosen his grip. He was going to black out.

He shifted his grip, catching the barrel of the gun with both hands. Holding on, he flipped himself backward and jerked the weapon out of Ramzi's hand. He rolled, came to his hands and knees. He hadn't the strength left to keep fighting.

Ramzi still came at him. The only way to stop him was to kill him. Cameron pointed the gun. It was the second time within a few minutes that God had put him in this position.

God in heaven—

CHAPTER 69

Mindanao

From five hundred yards away, Sergeant Gloomy Davis settled into what he called his "cocoon," that mental state in which he totally isolated himself emotionally from his surroundings and concentrated on a single objective: one shot-one kill. At least for as long as his eight cartridges lasted. The eye of the typhoon was arriving over the turkey's head of the island. The wind and rain abated, making for flat, easy shooting across the field. He could work around the mirage-creating mist that interfered with his sight picture through the Redfield scope.

Gloomy preferred the tight-legged sitting position, as had the distinguished Marine sniper in the Korean War, Gunnery Sergeant Vernon Mitchell. Ice Man Thompson took up a prone position behind a log he used as a rest for his carbine. For all that Ice Man was a fine shooter, he operated at a disadvantage in that his carbine had open sights and was actually outside the limits of its most effective range. At that distance, he could just as well have been shooting at ants.

The pounding of Gloomy's pulse made the crosshairs rise and fall against the image in his scope. No matter how many times he did it, settled down for a shoot, he still experienced that initial sense of excitement. He swept the picture in the scope slowly across the entire scene unfolding around the terrorist aircraft, making his selection of targets in advance.

Two missiles had already been unloaded from the trucks, one onto each of the aircraft. The crane was working on the third, had it hoisted off the flatbed and was swinging it into the second C-130 to join the previous crate. The first two trucks pulled back across the shallow stream into a sort of enclave formed where the road from below came out of the jungle.

At least a score of armed guerrillas stood or walked security posts while others assisted with the missile loading. Men came and went out the open tail ramps of the C-130s, securing the huge crates inside and making necessary weight-and-balance adjustments. The man who appeared to be the job foreman, a husky individual with an AK rifle slung over one shoulder and a canvas bandoleer of ammo across his chest Pancho Villa–style, invited himself to be the first target. Gloomy peered through the scope into the man's eyes, a picture so clear he could almost count the hairs in the guy's beard. He moved the scope on. There was no advantage in getting to know the enemy personally.

He studied the area where the drainage ditch entered the jungle. It was from there that the Boss intended to launch the assault. He saw no movement, although he knew the Deltas must already be in place and ready.

He lowered the scope from his eye. He pulled the Swedish K closer to his left knee to be ready when he expended the single mag through Mr. Blunderbuss. After inhaling a deep, slow breath to calm his nerves, he went back to the scope. The images in it were as steady now as if he had no pulse. He placed the crosshairs on Pancho Villa's left chest area and was prepared for the fight to begin at the airplanes.

Immediately, what sounded like the distant popping of strings of firecrackers came to Gloomy's ears. Action jumped to fast forward. The foreman looked startled. The surprised look was still on his face when Gloomy drilled him. The rifle report clapped against the wall of forest on the other side of the field.

Gloomy panned his scope until he picked up a guerrilla carrying a bipoded automatic rifle and running for cover behind one of the trucks. He dropped him cleanly.

At the same time, he heard Ice Man fire and say, "Shit!" Ice shot again and winged his target, who fell in the grass, got up and hobbled as fast as he could into the trees.

Gloomy almost laughed at all the confusion suddenly sown in the guerrilla stronghold. One guy popped his head up out of the grass—a prairie dog out of its hole. Gloomy made his head explode like a pumpkin. Seeing it so terrified his comrade that he jumped up and blindly bolted for the forest. He hadn't gone more than a few steps before Gloomy dropped him too.

Within less than a minute after the first shots were fired, six of the enemy lay dead. Four as a result of Gloomy's unerring aim, two ditched by Ice Man. Gloomy had four rounds left. He conserved them for the time being. He panned over the scene until his scope found the major.

Brandon was churning up the middle of the knee-deep stream toward the airplanes, followed by Thumbs Jones and Summer with Ice's pistol in her hand. Her bare legs glistened in a blur, she ran so hard to keep up. Gloomy burnt a fifth round to pick off a terrorist who seemed to be aiming at her. He had been secretly a little in love with Summer ever since Iron Weed. He searched for other enemy who might pose an immediate threat to either her or Brandon, watching over them like a vengeful angel of death.

Mad Dog's three-man security-and-assault element assumed temporary positions in the stream ditch near the woods, from which it lay down blistering grazing fire to cover for the demolitionists. T-Bone Jones burrowed in there while Mad Dog and Cassidy maneuvered farther into the field to offer more authoritative protection for Brandon's group. There was a lot of firing. A *lot* of it. Ebbing and flowing, high-pitched and angry.

A bearded man cut across Brandon's direct front, leaping the ditch as Brandon boiled up the middle of it. Brandon stitched him across the middle with his MP-5. Bullets thucked into flesh and bone with resounding echoes, hanging a pink mist in the air as the terrorist tumbled into the water.

A second man appeared. Gloomy Davis took him out from a distance. His chest literally exploded from the large-caliber, high-velocity round. What was left of his heart and lungs spurted out his back in a red geyser.

Good ole Gloomy, watching over them.

Brandon's tiny group vaulted over the dead men floating in the water, their goal—the first airplane—just ahead. Several riflemen defended the plane either from the weeds at the end of the open tail ramp or from inside the belly of the plane. Brandon, Thumbs, and Summer went to ground and engaged them fiercely, winging at least one. The remainder lost courage and withdrew in a panic toward the second aircraft and the empty flatbed truck still parked next to it.

The element of surprise was wearing off. Heavy rifle fire originated from the vicinity of the two trucks to the right and from the third truck directly ahead. More sporadic fire came from here and there in the tall grass. Mad Dog and Cassidy, not twenty feet behind Brandon, threw out a remarkable velocity of lead attempting to suppress the opposition.

Mad Dog's shotgun boomed in measured intervals as he sprayed the field with double-aught buckshot. Cassidy concentrated on the pair of trucks with his carbine, then paused to hurl a grenade. The little bomb bounced off the hood of the nearest truck. Somebody shrieked as the grenade exploded with a magnified bang, insinuating a cloud of smoke into the saturated air.

"Fu-uck all'a you and the virgins you rode in on!" Mad Dog shouted.

All firing around the first plane had ceased. Brandon lay so near it that he peered directly into its shadowy cargo bay. It looked empty except for the single large missile crate.

Summer rose to her knees to look around. Brandon jerked her down next to him in the water.

"You want to get your pretty ass shot off?" he yelled at her.

"Have you seen Cimatu—the man with the scar?" she demanded.

"Right now, just keep your head down or I swear to God I'll knock you cold."

"You'd do that for *me*?"

"Wiseass bitch."

Gypsy was dead; he had to keep Summer alive in spite of herself. He must have been out of his mind to let her come along, but he knew he couldn't have stopped her short of knocking her out and tying her up. She was probably safer with him than trying something on her own.

Brandon tapped Thumbs. "It looks clear," he said.

"I'm on my way."

"I'll cover. Do the nose wheels. Make it a short fuse."

The black demo man squirmed out of the ditch and started toward the nose gear. Crawling on his belly in the grass, dragging his demolitions ruck behind him.

"Thumbs, watch out for your other thumb!" Mad Dog shouted.

An instant later, the sound of a hammer pounding against a side of raw beef slammed Mad Dog to the ground. He rolled, splashing in the water. His head fell back. Just when Brandon thought he was gone, he shook his massive body. One long gorilla-like arm reached out and retrieved his shotgun. He dragged himself over on his belly, staining the water pink from the wound through his ribs, and let loose a round.

"Fu-uck!" he roared. "I ain't leaving this fight until I kick some serious diaper-head ass!"

Brandon concentrated on the nearest defenders around the second plane to keep them from rushing Thumbs before he got his explosives rigged. Throwing short bursts from his submachine gun. Return fire was rushed and inaccurate. Gloomy and Ice evidently watched the situation unfolding from their vantage point and were applying their skills to it, making the enemy paranoid about showing too much of himself.

Mixed odors of cordite, smoke, wet grass, blood, and fear filled the air.

It didn't take Thumbs long to complete his job. He returned through the grass as swiftly as a snake, his carbine slung over one shoulder, dragging his ruck and paying out detonating cord from a spool. He slithered into the ditch and fished around inside his pack to produce an M-60 fuse lighter. He cut the det cord, crimped the M-60 to its end, then looked at Brandon.

"Let it go," Brandon said.

"Fire in the hole!"

Det cord contained a core of very high explosive PETN powerful enough to cut down small trees by itself. It burned at a rate of *five miles per second*. Thumbs touched off the M-60, producing a linear flash through the grass. A near-instantaneous explosion shook the ground, throwing the nose of the big Hercules into the air on top of a ball of flame and a billowing cloud of smoke.

The blast twisted the plane to one side and sent pieces of it sizzling through the air. Parts of the wheel assembly landed nearly one hundred meters away. The plane settled back to the ground at an odd angle, its entire nose past the cockpit blown off or mangled.

Shooting ceased for several seconds, as though to pay awed homage to the demonstration. Then it resumed, fiercer than ever.

One plane down, one to go. The second, however, promised more of a challenge. Suddenly, unexpectedly, its engines turned over, coughing puffs of exhaust. The four huge propellers caught with a whine-humming roar and began whirring, glistening in that wet light and stinging the air with sheets of blown water.

It was taking off. With two of the missiles securely aboard.

CHAPTER 70

The Hercules took no time for a run-up. Its engines roared and sucked up water off the grass and ground and blew out a cataract in its wake, engulfing the guerrillas around the truck and hampering visibility. The C-130 began to inch forward, its nose pointed upfield into the now-moderate wind for take-off.

The detachment was starting to take a beating as the guerrillas recovered from the surprise attack, laying down withering fire in preparation for a counterattack. Mad Dog was wounded, but remained dangerous and in the fight. Thumbs Jones moaned as a round went through the meaty portion of his left thigh. He, too, stayed in the fight, popping off rounds from his carbine with cool precision. Summer contributed to the overall din of the battle by engaging Ice Man's pistol in a personal duel with a gunman who tried to creep up on them through the grass. She sent him packing with pistol rounds zinging around his ears.

If anything prevented the terrorists from rallying to overrun the attackers, it was T-Bone Jones's carbine chatting angrily from the edge of the woods and the deadly sniping of Gloomy Davis and Ice Man Thompson.

Brandon ignored the lead snapping around his ears. His focus was on the airplane. The missiles were getting away. He saw Operation Deep Steel failing right in front of his eyes. He realized he had one last long shot at saving the mission.

"Thumbs, how bad are you hit?" he called out.

The plucky demo man responded by slinging his ruck and lurching to his feet, bent over but ready for action. He immediately toppled face forward into the ditch with a splash as another round caught him in the chest. He lay still with his dark face underwater. Summer pulled his head to the side so he could breathe—but he had breathed his last.

"He's gone," she said.

"Damn!"

T-Bone was supposed to take Thumbs's place. Cassidy didn't wait. He took Thumbs's place instead, dragging the demo ruck off Thumbs's body and crouching in the ditch alongside Brandon and Summer.

"Let's do it," he said, "before the missiles get away."

Brandon looked at his little brother. He nodded. "All right. I'll cover you. When we get close, pull the pin on a grenade and stuff it in the ruck. Throw the ruck as far as you can through the ramp door. Summer, stay here with the Dog."

They wasted no more time. Brandon led the way in a crouching sprint toward the departing airplane, keeping to the minimal cover of the ditch. Murderous fire filled the air, snapping and cracking in sonic reports all around their heads while they ran like passengers about to miss their flight. It was like what the General said about his Vietnam days—running through raindrops. Only the raindrops were lethal.

They had almost reached the airplane when Cassidy's legs flew out from under him. As if he had hit a trip wire at full speed. He tumbled into the grass, plowing up the soaked earth. Brandon twisted back and hit the ground next to him, horrified at the thought of his brother already dead or, worse yet, horridly maimed and dying.

Instead, Cassidy was very much alive, though in obvious pain. The round had shattered his ankle and filled his boot with blood. Grimacing, clamping down on the pain with his willpower, he thrust the ruck at Brandon.

"Here! Go on. Go for it!" he encouraged. He rolled over in the grass and opened fire on a target. He released the empty mag and reached for a fresh one.

Brandon was already gone with the explosives, running hard for the open ramp on the C-130 as it gradually picked up speed. He wasn't alone in the chase. Three men suddenly appeared in his peripheral vision, on a collision course with him. The man in front he immediately recognized—the sumo with the shaved head and the scar. Cimatu. He also recognized the second enemy, bearded, wearing camouflage fatigues and a bush hat—Albaneh Mosed, the Abu Sayyaf leader with whom he had clashed in Zamboango del Norte province. The third man was skinny, mean-looking, and armed with a pistol.

Apparently the trio overestimated the strength of the attacking force and intended to leave with the missiles anyhow.

So focused were Cimatu and Mosed on catching the plane that they failed to notice Brandon also racing to catch it. The third man ran some distance behind the others. Brandon thought he must be the one Summer referred to as "the ninja." He began shooting at Brandon at almost point-blank range, pistol thrust out in front at arm's reach, muzzle blossoming.

Brandon fired at him one-handed with the submachine gun. A single round before the weapon went dead on an empty chamber. Definitely an *Oh, shit* Murphy moment.

The ninja ran directly at Brandon. Everything went into slow motion, as it did with an overdose of adrenaline. The ninja wouldn't miss the next shot. Not at this range. Brandon discarded the useless MP-5 and went for the Glock holstered on his combat harness. Knowing he was too late. That he would die failing his last mission.

He looked down the barrel of the advancing weapon. It was almost as if he saw the slug with his name on it.

The ninja hit an invisible wall and came to a dead stop, shock written indelibly on his skeletal features. The haft of a SOG SK 2000 combat knife appeared magically in the center of his chest, the blade buried deep into flesh. He toppled backward, kicking and flailing his arms spasmodically. Brandon drew his pistol and shot him in the head, finishing him off. Hey, life wasn't fair.

Brandon glanced back in gratitude to see his brother on his knees after having hurled the knife. Cassidy looked past him, frantically waving his arms. Then he dropped back into the grass and slapped a fresh magazine into his weapon.

The situation had changed completely in that fraction of a minute that Brandon was diverted by the ninja. Summer—

damn her!—had spotted Cimatu and charged out onto the field after him. That was why Cassidy was waving. The tiger-stripe tunic billowed around her tiny frame and her bare legs flashed through the grass. She bore down on her tormentor as though she intended destroying him with her bare hands. She had Ice's pistol shoved out toward him, but she wasn't firing. Brandon assumed she must be out of ammo.

Great props whipped up a rainstorm as the C-130 gathered speed. Cimatu and Mosed scurried up the ramp still dragging through the grass, their heads down against prop wash. They seemed oblivious of everything else around them.

Summer sprinted up the ramp after them and disappeared inside.

Brandon had been one of the fastest tailbacks in the history of Army when he was twenty years old. He needed all that speed now to catch up with the Hercules before it accelerated for takeoff. He gave it everything he had. He was back in the Army/Navy game, pigskin tucked into his elbow, heading for the goal. Running. Running. Hearing the roar of the crowd. *Touchdown! Touchdown!*

As he ran, he tore a frag grenade from his combat harness. He yanked out the pin and held the spoon closed in his fist. The missiles had to be stopped. Lives depended on them not getting off Mindanao. Thousands of lives. Mission came first.

"Summer! Summer!" Running and sobbing now, still chasing the airplane. Doing what had to be done. She was as good as dead anyhow if the airplane got away. Damn her. Damn Murphy's Law.

He let go the spoon. It pinged free, arming the grenade. Four seconds!

He stuffed the live grenade into the ruck containing enough C-4 explosives to blow the C-130 in a fireball completely off the field. He veered to the left of the open ramp as a right-handed athlete would to gain that little extra momentum and distance for a shot put or javelin throw. Knowing he was sacrificing Summer, the woman he loved. He reared back his good right arm that could still snap a pass sixty yards with reasonable accuracy—and he flung the ruck.

"Summer!" An animal sound of raw anguish.

CHAPTER 71

Atchafalaya Swamp

Although Chaplain Cameron Kragle held the gun on him, Professor Ramzi al-Rehman seemed to know the chaplain would not shoot him. Maddened, obsessed with his unholy mission to destroy anything or anyone that got in his way, the professor stalked toward Cameron, who knelt too exhausted to get to his feet. Ramzi had lost his glasses in the struggle, causing a squint that further twisted features already distorted by rage. Cameron froze with his finger on the trigger as the fanatic spat at him, snarling like some infuriated beast.

"You are weak and corrupt," the professor shrieked. "With Allah's help and the courage and the sacrifice of our Holy Warriors, we will destroy the Great Satan and relegate you to the dust bins of history . . . Go on, infidel, shoot me if you have the nerve. Shoot me! Shoot me—or I will take the gun and shoot *you*."

He continued to advance, raving like a man possessed. If ever the chaplain were to believe in demonic possession of a human's soul, it was at that moment. No human had eyes like that—dark and evil, behind which monsters lurked ready to

be unleashed upon the world. There was surely a hell ruled
by Satan; Cameron recognized its presence in Ramzi's eyes.

A phrase from the Bible passed unbidden through
Cameron's mind, a phrase he would remember for the rest of
his life. *O God, be not far from me; O my God, make haste
for my help.* For God answered him and Cameron *believed.*
Totally and completely, he *believed.*

God made haste. Suddenly, helicopters filled the sky. FBI
SWAT teams in black began rappelling into the meadow
while loudspeakers bellowed: *"This is the FBI! Drop your
weapons!"* Vehicles roared up the ATV road through the
swamp. There was some more shooting out behind the barn,
but helicopters disgorged men there too.

Professor Ramzi looked stricken. Cunning replaced rage as
he crouched in the sunlight, his shadow long and sinister
across the wiregrass. Behind him, the missile slowly lowered
to the horizontal position as Abdul cranked it down to prevent
its being fired on New Orleans. The terrorist in the white robe
sprawled unmoving in the grass off the edge of the truck, either dead or knocked unconscious. Abdul had prevailed.

Martyrdom took over Ramzi's eyes.

"Don't do it! Give up!" Cameron implored, still pointing
the pistol.

Ramzi wheeled abruptly away and started to bolt toward
the truck. He obviously thought Cameron wouldn't shoot
him and that he could reach the missile and fire it before the
raiders got to him. Having been facing away from the missile, he didn't know that Abdul had already traversed it off-
target and had leaped down to scramble into the driver's seat.

He froze in his tracks. He looked as though someone had
kicked him in the crotch. He found himself staring directly at
the front of the truck. Abdul sat behind the wheel, peering
down the length of the hood at the professor, his eyes narrowing. The engine rumbled, then roared as Abdul slammed
in the gas feed and the big vehicle lurched forward.

The impact threw Ramzi's red headband high into the air. It came fluttering back down like a wounded bird as first the front wheels and then the dual back tires bounced over the terrorist leader, crushing his life and spirit from his body and sending him to receive his virgins from Allah.

Cameron slowly rose to his feet and stood staring at the bloodied remains still partly underneath the truck's heavy back tires. The pistol fell from his numbed fingers. He dropped to his knees again. He prayed with his eyes closed, thanking God and asking God to have mercy on the souls of his enemies.

SWAT officers swarmed over the clearing, rounding up the surviving terrorists. After a short while, someone knelt next to Cameron.

"It's over, Chaplain," Claude Thornton said. "It's all over."

Chaplain Kragle opened his eyes and in them shone the sadness of once again having witnessed evil in the hearts of men.

"What I'd really like," he rasped hoarsely, "is an ice-cold bottle of *Mountain Dew.*"

CHAPTER 72

Mindanao

Brandon knew he couldn't do it even as the ruck of live explosives left his hand. There was no more time than that to think about it. A finger snagged the ruck, deflecting it to the side. The ruck sailed high into the air. Within the brief sec-

onds before it exploded, he reached deep inside himself for
every ounce of reserve strength and speed he had, sprinting
toward the open rear of the C-130. Its props projected water
stinging into his face as the airplane opened its engines wide
for the takeoff run.

The C-4 in the ruck detonated with a tremendous clap of
thunder, the energy and concussion from which nearly
shoved Brandon off his feet. He stayed upright by wind-
milling his arms. He used the extra boost to throw himself at
the open ramp as the Hercules surged forward.

One hand succeeded in catching part of the locking mech-
anism at the ramp's trailing edge. He held on doggedly as the
plane dragged him bouncing on his belly through the wet
grass, rapidly gaining speed. He held on for his life—and for
Summer's life. He felt himself airborne, still holding on. In-
congruously, he recalled one of Gloomy's Hooker stories
about when the little Okie was rodeo clowning. During a
cowboy wreck with the bull, Gloomy dashed in and caught
the bull by the tail before it dawned on him: What did you *do*
with a 2,000-pound bull once you had it by the tail?

A C-130 Hercules making a short field takeoff used full
power and full flaps, causing it to literally leap off the field
and rise with amazing swiftness into the air, almost like an
elevator. Brandon's feet dangled in the air as the open field
receded below. For a moment he experienced a commander's
view of the action—figures darting about down there, growing smaller and smaller; trucks and crane and *Ibn Haldoon* in
the cove rapidly becoming children's toys; columns of black
smoke boiling up from the disabled aircraft.

The sounds of the firefight down there diminished and
quickly faded into the roar of the aircraft engines as the plane
struck turbulence in the ring of storm surrounding the typhoon's eye. The airplane shook like a wet dog, as though
trying to rattle him loose. Prop wash and crosswinds blew his
legs and lower torso around at precarious angles. He felt his

grip slipping. He dropped the Glock from his free hand and grabbed on with both hands.

Muscles straining, he slowly chinned himself up to the ramp, seeing nothing inside except the two shadowy ends of the missile crates. He heaved a leg onto the ramp and pulled himself up. He lay unarmed on the skid plate, holding on, catching his breath for a moment, studying the situation.

The two missile crates were strapped together in the center belly, leaving a narrow dark walkway on either side. Summer was up there somewhere, along with at least Cimatu and Albaneh Mosed. But he saw nothing moving within the shadows, heard nothing except the aircraft itself. A C-130 was incredibly noisy, especially with the ramp down.

He crawled on up the ramp to get away from the plane's great open anus. It kept trying to buck him out. He clambered to his feet and flattened himself against the ends of the crates. What indeed did he *do* with the bull once he had it by the tail? He possessed a knife against at least two armed and dangerous men. What kinds of odds were those?

Damn you, Murphy!

He inched to the corner of the crate and snapped a quick peep around the edge. Nothing. Where the hell had everyone gone? Including Summer. He made his way to the opposite corner of the other crate, back flattened against the rough wood. There he froze, his finely honed instincts for danger sensing *nearness*.

He turned around in time to see Albaneh Mosed leap out from behind the crate. Beard and bush hat, dark fierce eyes and a pistol aimed directly at him, a hair's breadth away from going off.

The jouncing of the airplane threw Mosed off-balance before he squeezed the trigger. He grabbed for the missile crate to steady himself and his aim. Out of that brief interval erupted such a horrendous scream of terror and despair that it left both men stunned. Before either recovered, former President John Stanton burst out of nowhere.

Brandon would never know if the former President committed a single selfless and courageous act on behalf of someone else—or whether in some disoriented state of mind he thought the airplane was still on the ground and attempted to escape off the open ramp. Whichever, he saved Brandon's life.

Arms tied behind his back, Stanton threw himself directly at the terrorist chief blocking his path to the ramp. Mosed wheeled to meet the threat. His gun barked sharply. The sudden odor of cordite stung Brandon's nostrils.

Stanton's momentum carried him past and out onto the ramp. The plane was still climbing nose up, even though using flaps, and its ramp was down and sloped toward earth. Wounded, Stanton finally fell. He bounced once on the ramp like a rag doll slung across a room and vanished into gray nothingness, plummeting to his certain death.

For an instant, Brandon's thoughts flashed onto the American C-141 then-*President* Stanton had ordered shot down over Afghanistan in order to save his "peace initiative" and his legacy, an act that led to the direct deaths of good American SpecOps and Delta men. Even Gypsy would not have died except for that. Somehow, in the moment Stanton vanished off the ramp, it seemed fitting that he should die in this manner. And that his death should close those unfortunate chapters in Brandon's life.

Recovering and seeing his chance, Brandon sprang upon the terrorist leader. He grabbed him by the back of his tunic and gave him the bum's rush off the tail ramp, casting him out into space after Stanton. Mosed's scream faded immediately. Brandon almost regretted not being able to watch as both men collided with Mama Earth, smashing themselves like bugs on a windshield. He hoped the sonsofbitches had plenty of time to think about hell before they hit.

"Brandon!" Summer's voice. Desperate. Warning.

Instinctively, he flung himself to one side. Too late. The gunshot and the flash of pain in his head coalesced into the same thing. The steel ribbed deck came up and smacked him in the face.

CHAPTER 73

Mindanao, on the Ground

As those who have gone to war understand, life has a way of compressing itself in battle so that past and present and future all seem to coalesce into a single *now*. Even the *now* takes on a certain surreal quality whereas events fail to unfold sequentially. Rather, there are snatches of reality, sound bites, as though the mind and emotions become so overloaded that only the most impactful details imprint themselves.

That was how it was with Sergeant Cassidy Kragle as he lay in the wet grass field with his ankle shattered and in pain so great it brought tears to his eyes. He slapped a fresh magazine into his carbine and waited, bullets grazing above his head, while he watched his brother race to catch up with the departing airplane. It seemed every enemy on the battlefield took pot shots at the running man. Incredibly, Brandon remained on his feet.

Cassidy held his breath as Brandon slung the explosives at the airplane. He was going to blow up Summer with it! He exhaled relief when the detonation occurred to the side and rear of the airplane instead of inside it, then caught his breath again, mesmerized by the impossible spectacle of his older brother dangling by one arm from the tail ramp as the aircraft took off.

He breathed again when Brandon hoisted himself up on the ramp to get inside. By then the aircraft was a thousand feet in the air and almost to the other end of the field.

A tiny figure hurtled out of the Hercules, unidentifiable at this distance. A moment later, a second figure shot out, expelled from the airplane as carelessly as poop from a low-flying seagull. Cassidy winced as each body struck earth, as though he personally felt that final jolt of bones and flesh and blood turning to jelly.

His head dropped onto his arms; his body convulsed in a single dry sob. Brandon and Summer charged onto the airplane as it took off. Two people were thrown from it. They were dead. The mission had failed.

The C-130 with two of the missiles aboard disappeared into the returning storm.

Snatch of reality: Mad Dog yelling at Cassidy from the ditch. "Goddamn you, Kragle. Talk to me if you're still alive!"

Cassidy shook himself. "I hear you, Dog." He fired a couple of rounds at the guerrillas over by the truck and crane.

"Fu-uck, let's get outa here, boy. Party's over. I know when I ain't welcome."

Cassidy crawled through the grass to the cover of the ditch, dragging his wound. It hurt like a motherfucker. He rolled into the water next to Mad Dog, who had slung his shotgun across his back and was using Thumbs Jones's carbine to keep the enemy at bay. Blood from his own wound smeared his hands and face and, darker, the front of his tiger-stripe tunic.

Thumbs still lay in the water with his head resting on the bank. Rushing water moved his floating legs back and forth, like a canoe tied up against the current, pulling out a red stain that turned pink with the flow. Thumbs's eyes were closed and he appeared to be sleeping.

"I shut his eyes for him," Mad Dog volunteered. "Damn. Thumbs and me . . . We was pretty tight."

He jumped up and fired a burst, screaming obscenities to relieve his grief. He dropped back down. Eddies of black smoke from the burning aircraft clung to his patrol cap and blew across the ditch. The eye of the typhoon was passing over and the wind starting to pick up again.

"We gotta get our sorry airborne asses outa here," Mad Dog said. "Can you walk, Kragle?"

A look at Cassidy's ankle answered the question for him.

"Fu-uck. I ain't leaving Thumbs here by himself either."

Gloomy and Ice Man were doing a bloody good job keeping the enemy's heads down with their sniping. It couldn't last. Gloomy was already out of ammo for Mr. Blunderbuss. Fire coming from their position was less accurate with the open-sighted carbine and Swedish K. The guerrillas seemed to be getting bolder too, their fire shifting from point to point as they consolidated for an assault.

What were they waiting on?

Then Cassidy understood. They were waiting on machine guns and reinforcements to come up from the lower camp. Even now, the two security elements patrolling the airfield—eight or nine fighters—were probably maneuvering on their flanks to catch them in a crossfire.

The chatter of T-Bone's carbine near the tree line proclaimed he was still in the fight and doing damage. In addition to him, the detachment consisted of two wounded men, two snipers, and a dead soldier.

"Can you say Alamo, Kragle?" Mad Dog said.

Snatch of reality: A tremendous explosion the size of a bomb rattled the ground and seemed to shake a new downpour of rain from the lowering cloud banks. Black smoke filled with flickers of flame boiled up from the protected bay below. It swelled and formed a mushroom cloud that umbrella'd out over the field and blended with smoke from the flaming and disabled C-130.

Dingy darkness descended, imposing upon the world the hushed atmosphere of primitives watching the moon gobble the sun in an eclipse. Guerrillas stared in awe and confusion, expecting attack from a new quarter or from the air. Fighters around the truck and crane bolted for the protection of the forest and the other trucks to the rear. Mad Dog sprang to his knees and popped caps at them, winging one and causing the remainder to shift into overdrive.

The enemy's abandoning the truck and the distraction caused by Lucifer's sending the *Ibn Haldoon* up in smoke gave Cassidy hope. He grabbed Mad Dog and pointed.

"The truck!"

Mad Dog's face brightened. "It might work. We damned sure ain't walking outa here."

"Get T-Bone. We don't have much time."

Even with a bullet through his ribs, the big commo man took off downstream at a hard pace, bent over and splashing water. Cassidy raised Gloomy on the Motorola.

"Sounds like a hootenanny down there," Gloomy said. *"What's going on? Where's the Boss? We lost the missiles?"*

"No time to explain," Cassidy shot back, rushing into his game plan. "You and Ice make a beeline for the road. We'll pick you up in a truck where we hid out this morning until it got daylight. Remember? Don't waste any time. We're going to be in a hurry."

He then raised Lucifer. The General would have been proud of the way he took charge in the absence of both the detachment commander and operations sergeant.

"Tell the major we got the gook kids off the freighter okay," the SEAL lieutenant said.

Cassidy wasted no words. "Lieutenant, we're coming back on a truck. Roger that?"

"Roger that, kid."

"Tell the submarine to notify USSOCOM that one of the planes and two of the missiles got away."

"Oh, fuck!"

"Roger *that.* Tell them if they got anything in the area that can intercept and shoot it down—"

"Leave it to me, kid. Get your fucking asses back here in one piece. I didn't save your slimy butt from the goddamned shark so you could get it shot off. We've got the Zodiac. You roger that?"

The truck was a deuce-and-a-half, old, beat up, and faded red. Mad Dog carried Thumbs's body across his broad shoulders at a jogging run while Cassidy used T-Bone as a crutch. The crane between the guerrillas and them masked most of the incoming fire, while black smoke in the returning rain and freshening wind further reduced visibility and helped hide them.

Dog heaved Thumbs up to the flatbed, then pushed Cassidy up after him. T-Bone barked like a sea lion, cracked his knuckles, and raced around to get underneath the wheel. Mad Dog clambered into the passenger's side and lay the barrels of his shotgun and Thumbs's carbine out the open window. T-Bone cranked up the truck, floored the gas pedal, and took off even before Cassidy was set.

All six wheels thumped into the air as the truck hit the drainage ditch, sailed through the rain, and landed on the other side with a bone-jarring jolt. Thumbs's body bounced three feet into the air. Cassidy grabbed him and shoved him back into place against the cab.

T-Bone kept the pedal to the metal. Engine wound tight, the truck fishtailing directly toward the main concentration of terrorist guerrillas. Rifle fire crackled from all sides.

Windshield glass shattered. Mad Dog's scattergun inserted its dominant *Boom Boom* into the melee.

"Motherfu-ucking diaper heads!"

T-Bone yelped out sea lion barks from the top of his lungs.

The truck bed wasn't the most stable shooter's platform. Cassidy lay down fire anyhow, picking out running targets. Missing mostly.

Some guy wearing a wet yellow turban and a poncho flapping like wings raced alongside the truck. He leaped onto the running board and clung there, reaching through the open window and clawing at T-Bone and the steering wheel. T-Bone pounded back at him with his fist, nearly losing control of the truck. It swerved and came dangerously close to rolling over.

Cassidy thrust his carbine out from the truck bed with one hand, finger on the trigger, pushed the muzzle into the terrorist's belly, and squeezed the trigger. The guy screamed and fell to the ground. Dual back wheels speed-bumped over his head.

Another guerrilla crouched in front of the truck and fired into the windshield. T-Bone hit him head-on. The truck speed-bumped again.

"Beep-Beep!" Mad Dog whooped. "Fu-ucking Wile E. Coyote never learns."

Then they were through and past the two other trucks. On the road with a howling mob of guerrillas chasing after them, laying down withering fire. Cassidy shot at them from the bed of the truck while Mad Dog got in his licks from the window.

"Kick their asses!" Dog cheered.

Guerrillas pursued in the two other trucks, piling onto the flatbed like a bunch of Saturday night drunks out on a toot in a mining town. It wasn't exactly a high-speed chase. The road, such as it was, cut narrow and muddy and twisting through the jungle, the ruts mined with rocks and roots that kept vehicles dangerously out of control. Wild firing broke out every time pursued and pursuer glimpsed each other on the short straightaways. Cassidy held onto the flatbed with one hand while he operated his carbine with the other. He also had to stay prepared to catch Thumbs's body when it started to vibrate off.

Cassidy pounded on the truck cab when he spotted the telltale fallen tree that marked their rendezvous site with Gloomy and Ice Man. T-Bone applied brakes, sliding nearly sideways on the road. He and Mad Dog jumped out on either side and took a knee, weapons ready.

They all blasted away when the unsuspecting lead truck rounded the curve behind them. Cassidy lifted one guy cleanly off the flatbed with a bullet and deposited him into bushes at the side of the road. The truck skidded to a stop, throwing a couple of men into the road. They jumped up and headed for the jungle. The remainder also abandoned the vehicle while the driver tried to get his vehicle in reverse. Mad Dog's double-aught buck disintegrated the windshield, whereupon the driver himself heard someone urgently calling him from the rain forest.

The abandoned truck sat in the road. The second truck kicked out troops behind the curve. Muzzle flashes winked and blinked in the rain while black smoke from the sinking ship roiled low overhead.

They couldn't have held off the guerrillas much longer. Cassidy and T-Bone each had one frag grenade remaining when Gloomy and Ice Man ran out of the jungle. Gloomy popped away with his pistol, the empty Winchester slung across his back and the Swedish K discarded, its magazine depleted.

"Taxi service!" Mad Dog sang out, relieved to finally see them.

Gloomy looked quickly about. "Where's the Boss?" There was dread in his voice.

"He didn't make it," T-Bone said. "Get in the truck."

Gloomy staggered back as if a mule had kicked him in the belly.

"Summer?" he asked in a thinner voice.

No one answered him.

The explosions, the firefight, and the running gun battle left the lower terrorist camp confused and pulled into a defensive mode. Unaware that one of their trucks had been commandeered, guerrillas ran out to see what was going on when they saw it speeding down the road with a hard rain falling and wind blowing. T-Bone drove right through the mob, scattering men like a flock of chickens on a country highway.

Beyond, the road dropped off steeply toward the cove, winding down against the side of the cliff with thick forest opposite rocky outcroppings. Sheets of rain and more wind accompanied the passing of the typhoon's eye. T-Bone shifted into low gear to prevent sliding off onto the tops of trees in the drop-off to his right. It would have been safer and faster for the detachment to bail out on foot—except someone would have to carry Thumbs's body, Cassidy couldn't walk, and Mad Dog was growing weak from loss of blood. From the sounds of pursuit, the enemy would soon be upon them like a pack of beagles cornering rats in a hay loft.

T-Bone worked the flatbed through a pass between gigantic lava walls. Rear wheels skidded and banged the bed against the lower rampart, nearly dislodging passengers. The truck slid on through.

Lieutenant Lucifer's distinctive figure, carrying a carbine, materialized out of the gloom and rain beyond the pass. Chief Gorrell and J.D. McHenry squatted next to the road with a SAW (squad automatic weapon, 5.56 caliber). J.D. opened up with it, spraying the road through the pass. Lieutenant Lucifer trotted alongside the truck holding onto the door handle with his free hand.

"Where's the major?" he asked.

"This is all that's left," T-Bone said.

"Jesus Christ! All right. Keep going all the way to the bottom, but stop at the curve before you get to the ship. We'll handle these fuckers."

He jumped off to the side. Doc TB came out of the woods and vaulted onto the back of the moving truck with his aid bag. He looked at Thumbs and batted back tears. Then he turned to patch up Cassidy.

"Wait until we get to the sub, Doc," Cassidy advised. "You might want to take a look at the Dog."

Ice Man got off and stayed behind with the SEALs. Cassidy heard the SAW chattering. Minutes later, C-4 planted in the pass detonated with an echoing roar that repeated itself as its thunder rolled out across the restless sea. A cloud of smoke rose and meshed with the rain. The SEALs and Ice Man caught up with the truck, running, before it reached the curve. They had sealed the pass with a few tons of rock and dirt.

"That'll hold the cocksuckers for a while," Lucifer said, grinning his evil grin. Obnoxious though he was, Cassidy thought, he was a true professional in the CT business. An asset to the detachment.

"The Zodiac is directly below," Chief Gorrell said. "We're out of this hell hole."

The *now* of combat, the snatches of reality, gradually merged with the normal pace of life. It was a subdued and battered Operation Deep Steel that piled into the rubber Zodiac with the three Korean children Lucifer's element rescued from the *Ibn Haldoon*. J.D. McHenry coxswain'd the little outboard through the breakers at the mouth of the cove. The motor alternately purred and revved with the rise and fall of the gigantic ocean swells. Wind laden with graveled rain drove them seaward from the land.

No one wanted to look at Thumbs, whose body lay forward at the bottom of the inflatable, nor to think of Major Brandon and Summer who had not made it back. Someone would have to retrieve their bodies from the field. No one was ever left behind. Four KIA on a single mission, counting Winnie Brown—and still Deep Steel had failed.

Next to the stone dock, the *Ibn Haldoon* was sinking, its stern already submerged and its burning prow rising high into the air. It would be gone in another ten minutes. Surviving crewmen, disarmed and cast ashore during Lucifer's raid, huddled on the rocks and watched their ship sink. Beyond, smoke still spiraled up into the clouds from the burning C-130.

Gloomy Davis's mustache drooped in the rain and covered the grimness expressed in his lips. He looked as though he had lost all spirit and would never tell another Arachna Phoebe story. He wore that thousand-yard stare that often followed combat during which friends and comrades were lost. Major Brandon Kragle and he had been together a long time, since the mission in Bosnia.

Cassidy watched the three Koreans huddled together in the bottom of the boat between Mad Dog and Ice Man. Rain and salt spray glistened on their round little faces. Jang, the teenager, clutched the little boy and girl so tightly it looked as though he might suffocate them.

"We are going to America," he cooed to them, soothing their fears.

Cassidy dropped his head into his hands. Rain hissed on the inflated gunnels. The outboard whined. The crash of the seas tossed them about. Lightning cracked and thunder boomed.

He opened his eyes. The world was a dark, wet gray. The sun had been devoured and would never return to warm his frozen bones. Terrorists had taken too many members of the Kragle family.

A gentle hand fell on his shoulder.

"After what happened before in Bosnia," Lieutenant Lucifer said, unusually serious and open, "I wanted a chance to earn back your brother's respect."

Cassidy swallowed the lump in his throat. "I think you have, sir," he said.

Ahead of them, the USS *Sam Houston* surfaced like a huge gray-black whale.

CHAPTER 74

The Philippines

When the shot rang out from further within the aircraft, something inside Brandon's head felt as though it had ruptured, releasing a surge of lava that burned even his eyes. He remained conscious, barely. He knew he had been shot, but not *where* he was shot.

He blinked, but the lava's red glow remained in front of his eyes. Into the glow moved a pair of thick legs wearing dirty cammie trousers dripping water. Someone bent over him, giving him the impression of something huge, even monstrous. Slick brown head with no hair. Hideous scar pulling down one eye almost to the center of his face. Body odor as strong as ammonia, like that of a wet dog with mange and sores.

The monster began dragging him like a bag of trash. Dazed though he was, he knew he had better grow wings quick. He glimpsed eternity in the swirling gray of clouds whipping past the open tail ramp.

He concentrated on clearing his head. Cimatu dropped him at the edge of the ramp, stood up and started to kick him off into space. At that moment, with a final effort born of desperation and survival instinct, Brandon grabbed the man's legs and twisted toward the interior, rolling and pulling the sumo down on top of him. Brandon was also a big man, six-four and a few pounds over two hundred, or he could never have done it.

The two big men, clenched together, rolled around on the open ramp, jostled and bounced about by renewed turbulence as the C-130 departed the typhoon's eye and entered the trailing edge of the storm. They fought to the very edge of the ramp until it seemed both might plunge to their deaths still locked together. Brawling like two drunks, fighting with silent, deadly determination.

This was the man who would have eventually murdered Summer. That knowledge infused Brandon with strength and resolve. There were some men whose only contribution to the betterment of the world was in dying—and it was in killing them that other men contributed.

Somehow, Cimatu had the gun back in his hand. Brandon seized his wrist and slammed it against the steel floor. Again and again until the pistol went flying. It landed near the edge of the ramp, caught in one of the ribbed squares of the flooring.

Cimatu broke free and made a dash for it. It was then that Brandon noticed the tail ramp was closing, slowly narrowing the opening between it and the plane's upper fuselage, steepening its angle. It was that sharper incline and the resulting precarious footing from turbulence that prevented Cimatu reaching the gun.

Ignoring the warm splash of blood in the hairline above his ear where the bullet grazed him, Brandon sprang up the incline. He tackled the Filipino and jerked him down. They slid to the very edge of the ramp where Cimatu arched his thick body and threw Brandon to the side. The big man pinned the American to the ramp as quickly as a cat switching ends.

Looking up, Brandon saw the fuselage of the aircraft closing on his head like a slow-motion guillotine. He struggled savagely to extract himself from the trap, but Cimatu had him pinned good. The Filipino grinned so that the scar gave his eye the appearance of a Cyclops. He pulled his own head to the side out of danger and, holding on, waited for the ramp to sever Brandon's head from his body.

Summer suddenly appeared on the ramp, climbing fast like a monkey on her hands and feet. The terrorist was so engrossed in finishing off his enemy that he failed to notice Summer liberating Brandon's Ka-Bar from his battle harness. The knife blade rose over the Filipino's broad back.

"Cimatu!" Summer shrieked in a voice unearthly and terrible in its passion. "Here's a tool for you, you sonofabitch!"

The blade flashed downward like a striking cobra, biting deep with hate and loathing into the brute who had beat her so badly.

He grunted deep with shock, the way a man did whose vitals had been penetrated. Brandon flipped out from underneath, throwing Cimatu aside. The terrorist's head ended up in the space between the closing ramp and the fuselage. His eyes bulged in that instant before the ramp closed with a final surge to seal the door, neatly severing his head. The head fell to earth; his body flopped about like a chicken with its neck wrung as it tumbled down the incline of the closed ramp.

Brandon rushed Summer down the ramp away from the hideous scene.

"I had to. I had to . . . do it!" she cried. "He was killing you . . . He was . . . I *wanted* to kill him . . . I wanted to . . . *wanted* . . ."

"They didn't see me when I got on the plane," Summer explained as they sat on the floor with their backs against a missile crate, recovering. "There were only two of them except for Stanton and whoever's flying this thing. I'm sorry, Brandon. It was a dumb thing to do, chasing after Cimatu when he got on the plane, but I thought he was getting away."

She clutched his hand; he gripped hers back.

"It was foolish," he agreed. Except for her, the plane would have been blown up by now and it would all be over. He couldn't entirely blame her though. She had seen Cimatu and Mosed escaping while both Cassidy and Brandon went down in the grass.

"I-I thought they shot you," she said, and there were tears in the Ice Maiden's eyes. "After that, I didn't care if they killed me, but I was going to get him first." She looked back to where Cimatu's headless corpse lay dimly outlined at the base of the now-closed tail ramp. "Then I was going to try to crash this plane if I could. My pistol was empty though. I kept the missiles between me and them so they wouldn't see me while I tried to find something to use as a weapon. That was when I ran into Stanton. I told him to hush and keep still. He didn't listen. He looked half-insane with fear. I heard him start to scream and then he was gone."

Brandon told her how he had gone off the tail ramp. She nodded thoughtfully.

"I can't truly say I'm sorry," she said. "Not after what he did to us in Iron Weed."

She paused a minute, then inhaled a deep sigh. "Brandon, I've been thinking about resigning from the . . . from my job."

He nodded, pleased. "Yes. I wouldn't want to lose my investment."

She touched his cheek with her fingertips where the blood was drying. "I almost lost mine."

Brandon retrieved Cimatu's pistol and they crept toward the front of the aircraft and the cockpit. Three steps led up from the cargo bay past the radio/navigator position to the flight deck. Because of the plane's hurried departure, the pilot was the only crew aboard. He was a small, neat Middle Easterner wearing a khaki tunic and a blue aviator's cap with gold braid. In his haste to get off the ground, he had taken off by himself. He was too busy flying the storm to know what was going on in back.

On IFR, full instruments, he was leaning forward with one white-knuckled hand gripping the yoke and the other milking the throttles. One preoccupied terrorist pilot. Visibility in the clouds was almost nil. The instrument panel rattled, the airspeed indicator surged and retreated with alarming suddenness, and the artificial horizon was going wild.

Brandon removed one earpiece of the flyer's headphone and pressed the muzzle of his gun in its place. He grabbed the yoke as the man started to shove it forward to put the C-130 into a suicide dive.

"Tell him not to even think it," Brandon said to Summer, speaking loudly above the noise. She translated quickly.

The pilot held onto the yoke, shouting something back in Arabic.

"He says we'll crash," Summer interpreted.

Evidently, his motivation for martyrdom wasn't too high. He relaxed in his seat.

"Tell him to unbuckle and get up. I'm taking over."

"What?" Either she couldn't hear him or the announcement startled her. He repeated it, louder. Summer stared at him.

"You ever hijack a plane before, Kragle?"

"No, but I know how it's done."

"I take it you *can* fly it?"

"We'll find out."

He had flown a total of six hours in type—three years ago. It would come back to him though. He had flown other multiengine recips.

"In a hurricane?" Summer persisted.

"It's a typhoon."

"Whatever."

"You want me to fly it—or do you trust him?"

"Good point. I'll tell him to get up. I've said it before—you do know how to show a girl a good time."

Brandon handed her the gun as the scared pilot vacated his seat. Brandon took over, holding onto the yoke, and quickly buckled himself in.

"What am I going to do with this guy?" Summer asked.

"Lock him in the john."

The airplane was in the storm big-time when she returned alone, holding onto things to keep from being bounced off her feet. Gray and black shreds of cloud whipped across the windshield, while the wipers worked frantically in a futile attempt to keep up with the wash of rain. Their teeth rattled, the plane shook so violently. Constant lightning inside the storm turned everything into an old black-and-white movie.

Brandon bled off most of the remaining flaps and reduced power, tapping on the throttles to gradually increase rpms on the downwind engines while decreasing power to the upwind pair. The plane was crabbing almost sideways. He focused on his instruments. No use looking out the windows. They were flying blind and entirely dependent upon instruments.

"Have a seat," he invited.

She watched him a minute. He *looked* as if he knew what he was doing. She buckled in and put on the copilot's head-phone, making conversation easier through the flight deck intercom.

"Tune the radio to Flight Service in Manila," he instructed, providing her the international frequency. "The freq knobs are those two on top. Tell them who we are and that we're on our way to Manila. Give them the phone number at CENT-COM and let them know the mission is a success. We don't want to be shot down when we leave the storm."

She did as she was told. After some discussion with Flight Service, followed by a pause and transfer to the tower, an air controller came back with a clearance to approach and land.

"How long until we're out of the typhoon?" she asked, holding onto her rattling seat.

"I think a half-hour, forty-five minutes. We'll head west into the tail of the storm, then cut north to Manila. We could never go back and land in that field now that the eye has passed."

They both thought of the detachment still in combat on the ground. There was nothing they could do to help it now.

"Brandon?" she said after some time, seeming to relax un-der his air of self-confidence. "You called me 'Summer.' "

He shot her a questioning look, then returned his eyes to the instruments.

"That *is* your name."

"Yes, but . . . I mean . . . You know what I mean," she stammered, flustered. "It wasn't 'Gypsy' this time, even when you were under stress."

He said nothing for a few minutes, concentrating on fly-ing.

"It'll always be Summer from now on," he said.

She smiled at him. Then they both lost their stomachs as a

downdraft dropped the Hercules and an adjacent updraft caught it.

"Think you can find Manila in this soup, Kragle?"

"With a partner like you, how can we miss an island as big as Luzon?"

CHAPTER 75

CPI NEWS DIGEST
FORMER U.S. PRESIDENT SLAIN

Manila (CPI)—Former President of the United States John Stanton was slain yesterday on the Philippine island of Mindanao. First reports indicate he may have been executed by guerrillas of the Abu Sayyaf, an Islamic separatist movement with known terrorist ties to al-Qaeda. Stanton was kidnapped in Cuba earlier in the week during his "good will" tour of the communist island nation.

Stanton's body was recovered late today (Philippine time) by a company of Filipino Scout Rangers during clashes with guerrillas on the southwestern tip of Mindanao. At least eighteen Abu Sayyaf fighters are known to have been killed during the day-long fighting. Their leader, Albaneh Mosed, was also reportedly killed . . .

SAUDI SHIP LOST IN STORM

Manila (CPI)—A freighter registered to Saudi Arabia, the *Ibn Haldoon*, was reported to have sunk in storm-tossed seas off Mindanao when a typhoon struck the southern Philippines. Six of the ship's crew, including her captain, survived after swimming ashore on Mindanao. They were rescued by Filipino Scout Rangers, who were fighting separatist guerrillas in the same area.

Also rescued from the sinking ship were three North Korean children, believed to have been stowaways aboard the *Ibn Haldoon*. The children were delivered to the American embassy in Manila, then flown to the United States where the State Department announced it will grant them political asylum.

Ibn Haldoon crew members were initially believed to have ties with Abu Sayyaf. However, they were questioned and released after Saudi Arabia filed a diplomatic protest with the Philippine government. The crew has refused to make any statements to the press, other than to say their ship was "lost at sea . . ."

PRESIDENTIAL CANDIDATE MAY BE CHARGED

Washington (CPI)—Senate Majority Leader Jake Thierry withdrew today as a candidate for President under allegations that he accepted lavish gifts illegally from Robert Chang, a campaign contributor and lobbyist for the Chinese trade delegation. Photographs and other evidence of the charges were released to the news media by a lawyer for deceased former President John Stanton. Attorney Robert Bernhoff said the packet of materials had been anonymously delivered to him with a signed letter from Stanton ordering him to release it in the event of his death.

It has also been learned that Thierry may be charged with criminal offenses involving terrorism. Unnamed sources indicate he was blackmailed into smuggling nuclear materials into the United States under diplomatic immunity. He has been linked to the deaths in New Orleans of three FBI agents of the Joint Terrorism Task Force and to the attempt by al-Qaeda terrorists to fire a nuclear missile at New Orleans.

Thierry, a frequent critic of the War on Terror, is expected to resign from the U.S. Senate today.

"Don't feel badly for me," he said in a statement released through his lawyer. "I've changed people's lives. I'm proud of every day of it. I could not stand the pain if any failing on my part damaged the things and the people I fought for all my life . . ."

HOMELAND SECURITY AGENCY REORGANIZED

Washington (CPI)—The National Homeland Security Agency became the Homeland Security Department in Washington ceremonies early today. MacArthur Thornbrew was sworn in as director and began the daunting job of stitching together tens of thousands of workers who patrol America's borders, secure computer networks, check for contamination of crops, respond to the threat of chemical, biological, or nuclear attacks, safeguard infrastructure, and otherwise help guard against terrorism.

Among the agencies it will take over are the Secret Service, Coast Guard, Immigration and Naturalization Service, Customs, and the Transportation Security Administration. The new Cabinet agency is the largest government reorganization in more than a half-century, a response to the September 11 attack and the threat of further terror.

Thornbrew said he believes America is safe for the time

being following the failed terrorist attempt to fire a missile at New Orleans. No other missiles, WMDs, or nuclear materials are believed to have been smuggled into the U.S.

So far, the government has disrupted terrorist cells in Buffalo, Portland, Jacksonville, Detroit, and other cities. The Department of Justice has won convictions or guilty pleas from about 100 people in terrorism-related crimes. Almost 500 potential terrorists have been deported. The arrest of a former roommate of two 9/11 hijackers led to 40 more arrests in a Visa fraud scheme. Six men have been arrested in St. Marys and Jacksonville for airspace violations related to smuggling in weapons. Three more are dead in the New Orleans missile plot, and two were arrested. Over 200 airport workers in Washington, D.C., New York City, and Dallas have been arrested for document and immigration fraud . . .

"The war isn't over by a long shot," the President said during the brief ceremony at the White House, "and it won't be until all the malarial swamps of terrorism are completely drained. We've learned that vast oceans no longer protect us from the danger of a new era."

CHAPTER 76

Collierville, Tennessee

There was a delay in the wedding. Chaplain Cameron had seen to the final decoration of the living room in the main house at the Farm. He stood pastorally at the front among wreaths of flowers and burning candles, clutching the family Bible passed

down to him through Little Nana. Waiting. Gloria and Raymond were there in all their marital finery, Brown Sugar
Mama blushing and giggling and appearing twenty years
younger, Raymond grinning awkwardly and looking like what
Gloria teasingly called her "big field hand." Waiting.

Enough uniforms, both army and navy dress blues, popu-
lated the room to turn it into what Gloria called a "bell hop
convention." The General wearing all his medals was having
a conversation with Senior Agent Claude Thornton of the
FBI, whose right hand was thickly bandaged, and with Lieutenant Sean L. "Lucifer" Shape. Delta's Colonel Buck
Thompson toasted a glass of punch with Sergeant Cassidy
Kragle, on crutches, and Sergeant Margo Foster, the pretty
brunette from Funny Platoon, who clung to Cassidy's arm
and elicited sly, grinning comments from the other former
members of Operation Deep Steel.

T-Bone Jones and J.D. McHenry seal-barked at each
other and T-Bone cracked his knuckles. Chief Gorrell
seemed embarrassed for them and joined Ice Man and Doc
TB on the other side of the room. Mad Dog and most of the
rest of the detachment looked bleary-eyed and hung-over
from the three-day party at Wally World to commemorate
the passing of Winnie Brown and Thumbs Jones. It had
been, in Mad Dog's immortal final assessment, "a puking,
shit-faced drunken, helluva bash that olc Winnie and
Thumbs woulda liked. Except for the gourmet cooking.
Burnt fish is burnt fish, no matter what you call it. Fu-uck."

"What's the holdup?" Brandon wanted to know.

No one answered him. They continued to wait.

Gloomy Davis told an Arachna Phoebe story, sanitized, to
Raymond's family from North Carolina, then eased over to
join Major Brandon, who was entertaining Summer's mother
and father from Texas. A small bandage covered the wound
above the major's ear. He looked anxiously around the room.
Waiting.

"I talked to her on the telephone," Brandon said, "and offered to pick her up at the hotel. She said she was capable of getting here on her own."

"Don't worry, she's coming," Colonel Buck said, overhearing. He came over as Mr. Holt and his wife, caretakers at the Farm and the day's hosts, distributed more punch. He took a glass and looked around, satisfied.

"I see Lieutenant Lucifer and you have declared a truce of sorts," he said to Brandon. "I've endorsed the recommendation for his decoration and sent it on up."

Brandon nodded. "He deserves it."

"So does your brother. I've released Cassidy from his extended probation. He's a full-fledged Delta trooper."

"Squared away," Brandon said.

Waiting.

Brown Sugar Mama didn't seem to mind, and it was her wedding. In fact, she almost seemed to expect the delay. As though she were keeping a secret. She kept looking in Brandon's direction and laughing. Sometimes, spontaneously, she broke away from Raymond and hugged all three sons, one at a time. That wasn't good enough, so she went around and hugged everybody.

"She promised to tack my hide to the wall if her sons weren't all back home in time to attend her wedding," the General said. "Raymond will learn the same as I did to stay out of her way when she gets like that."

Waiting.

Suddenly, a hush fell over the room. All eyes were riveted on the door as it opened. Brandon slowly turned. There she stood, the sun behind in the doorway haloing the white bridal dress, train, and veil. Her hair, though still short, was back to its original sunburnt color and the big emerald eyes were misty with emotion. Brandon thought her the most lovely creature he had ever seen. He took an uncertain step toward her. Gloria's Aunt Pitty-Patty began playing the piano: *Here comes the bride* . . .

Summer laughed softly and reached out a delicately gloved hand to Brandon. "Well, Kragle. Are you going to marry me or not?"

DET 0104